ROOMS

JAMES L. RUBART

ROOMS

A NOVEL

PUBLISHING GROUP
Nashville, Tennessee

Published by B&H Publishing Group,
Nashville, Tennessee

Dewey Decimal Classification: F
Subject Heading: SPIRITUAL LIFE—FICTION \ SOUL—
FICTION \ MYSTERY FICTION

Scripture quotations or paraphrases are taken from: the
New American Standard Bible®. © Copyright The Lockman
Foundation 1960, 1962, 1963, 1968, 1971, 1972, 1973, 1975,
1977, 1995. Used by permission (www.Lockman.org). Also
quoted are *The Message*, the New Testament in Contemporary
English, © 1993 by Eugene H. Peterson, published by NavPress,
Colorado Springs, Colorado, and the King James Version.

For Darci

What can you ever really know of other people's souls—
of their temptations, their opportunities, their struggles?
One soul in the whole creation you do know:
and it is the only one whose fate is placed in your hands.

—C. S. Lewis

CHAPTER 1

Why would a man he never knew build him a home on one of the most spectacular beaches on the West Coast?

Micah Taylor stared out the windows of his corner office overlooking Puget Sound, rapping his palm with an edge of the cryptic letter. Cannon Beach, Oregon. Right on the ocean and built by his great-uncle Archie, at least that's what the letter claimed. But of all the towns up and down Highway 101, why there? A place that repulsed him. A place he cherished. Both at the same time. Fate wouldn't be that cruel.

Shake it off. There couldn't really be a house in that spot with his name on it. No way. Not there. This was exactly the kind of practical joke his team might try to pull off. No one would ever accuse RimSoft's culture of being stoic. If they only knew how badly they'd misfired this time. Micah sighed.

But if the letter *was* real—

"Time to go, boss."

Shannon stood in the doorway, eyes bright behind her Versace glasses, short-cropped salt-and-pepper hair outlining her face. She'd been Micah's administrative assistant for three years. Smart and not easily intimidated, what churned in her five-foot-eight frame made her one of the strongest links in his company's chain.

"I hate being called boss." Reminded him too much of his dad.

"Yes, I know." She pulled her glasses down and gave him her pirate look—one eye closed, the other squinting.

Micah tried to smile and tossed the letter announcing his inheritance onto his desk. *Shake it off,* he told himself again. It didn't help.

"You all right?"

"Yeah. Great." He grabbed his notebook and wagged his finger at Shannon as they walked out of his office. "You shouldn't call someone boss when you're almost old enough to be their m—"

"—much older sister."

"Right," Micah said as they fell into step and marched down the halls of RimSoft. Normally he loved Fridays. The creativity his team poured out was astounding. If employing people better than yourself were an Olympic event, Micah would be swimming in gold.

But today wasn't a regular Friday. Today a bizarre letter sat on his desk trying to dredge up memories he'd buried forever.

As they turned the final corner on the way to the conference room, Kelli Kay, one of Micah's more talented programmers, approached. "Want to hear something really cool?" Her red curls bounced like a Slinky.

"Absolutely." Micah kept walking—now backward—his Nikes scuffing lightly on the teal carpet.

Single mom until four months ago, Kelli put herself through computer school while working forty hours a week and taking care of her ten-year-old son. Never complained about fifty-hour weeks. Never complained about sixty-hour weeks.

"My kid won that art contest I told you about last week; he's headed to L.A. this summer to compete in the national—"

"You serious? Listen, if he places, let's fly him and you and that new husband of yours to New York to see the MET. I'll bring Julie, and we'll all go check out the art with him and time it so we catch a Mariners-Yankees game."

"Really?" Kelli half-jogged to keep up with him.

"RimSoft's already made $2 million off that little antivirus program you developed last year. You're amazing." Micah turned and picked up his pace.

Shannon picked up hers too, her white Adidas running shoes helping in the effort. He couldn't believe this was the same woman who showed up her first day wearing three-inch heels and a business suit straight out of Uptight Dresses for Corporate America. Micah told her to get rid of the heels and put on whatever she loved wearing and felt comfortable in.

"You could actually stop when you talk to people."

Micah frowned at Shannon. "We have a meeting. You know, the company? Work to do. Software programs to develop. Lots of sales. Happy stockholders. Make money. All that stuff." He brushed past a lush, broad-leafed dracaena plant and walked faster.

"You're not exactly yourself this morning."

"A lot on my mind."

"They just want more time with you, Micah, to know you like them."

"I like everyone. But, to be sure, let's get out an e-mail that says, 'From Micah Taylor. To you. I like you. I really, really like you.'" He pushed open the conference room door and held it for Shannon. He returned her glare with a forced smile.

The conference room was small but comfortable. No vaulted ceiling, no massive table, just two light tan leather couches and six overstuffed espresso brown chairs all circling the center of the room. RimSoft's version of Camelot. The room wasn't designed for ego; it was crafted for efficiency.

The couches held two people each. On one couch sat Micah's head of Legal, with his jet-black hair and John Lennon glasses. Next to him slumped his VP of Mergers and Acquisitions, thirty-one years old but looked fifty with his premature gray hair. On the other couch perched his VP of Marketing, looking more every day like a young Oprah. Next to her sat his chief financial officer. Two of Micah's software development VPs sat in the chairs.

Shannon also sat in a chair; Micah paced in front of his.

On a table in the center of the room sat a steaming pot filling the air with the aroma of Seattle's Best Coffee. Clumped next to it were mugs from Disneyland, the University of Washington Huskies, and cups with RimSoft's logo on them.

Good. All the pieces were in place. Time to check out the condition of the chessboard.

"All right," Micah said, a slice above his normal volume. "Let's roll. Where are we with the i2-Rock alliance?"

"Done," his Mergers VP said.

"We love their hardware; they still love our software, right?"

"Madly."

"Excellent, great work." Micah focused on Oprah's twin. "Is the ad layout done for *Wired*?"

"Yep."

"Last one you did was a home run into the rafters, so let's keep the hits coming." He turned to his right. "Beta testing on version four is done, right?"

"Finished Wednesday."

"Very nice work. I can't believe you already have it almost bug free." Micah looked at the head of his legal team. "You've finished the docs for the Bay-C buyout?"

"Not quite." The man glanced up at Micah. "We're almost there."

Micah stopped pacing. What was this guy's problem? Everyone else knew how to fire on all cylinders. He couldn't afford to have the guy keep playing with his B game.

Micah whipped his pen around on his yellow notepad like a poor man's Picasso, then held it up for everyone to see. "This is a sketch of underwear. But not just ordinary underwear; it's asbestos underwear." He turned to the head of Legal. "You need a pair."

"Why?"

"Well, you said your team would be done on Tuesday. It's now Friday. So since it isn't done, your team falls into the category of 'liar, liar, pants on fire.' I would think the asbestos underwear would help squelch the flames a bit."

The head of Legal squirmed and mumbled, "We'll get it done by the end of the day."

"When?"

"End of the day."

"When?"

"By two o'clock."

"What comes out of a toaster?"

Legal Guy frowned and shifted in his chair. "Toast?"

"You're not sure?"

"Toast."

"Positive?"

"Yes."

"It's nine thirty now. What will you be if your docs aren't finished by noon?"

Legal Guys's face flushed. "Toast."

"A little louder please so the whole class can hear."

"I'll be toast."

One of Micah's team coughed. The rest kept their eyes glued to the agenda.

Micah turned and looked out the conference room windows overlooking Puget Sound. One breath. Two. Wow. Not the way to win friends and influence stock splits. He turned back to his team. "Okay, let's move on."

A half hour later Micah glanced at each member of his team. "Thank you. For two things. First, for being good enough at what you do that this company could no doubt survive without me. Second, for not being so good there's no room left for my input." He grabbed his notebook and strode toward the door.

Too harsh in there on Mr. Always-Late-Legal? Probably. Micah sighed. Definitely. Where did that stuff come from? He rolled his eyes. Micah knew precisely where it came from. Cannon Beach.

Shannon stepped into the hallway just ahead of him and clipped down the hall like a speed walker.

In two bounds Micah caught up to her. "Hey, slow down."

She walked faster and didn't respond.

"You've got that Micah-was-a-jerk look again."

She looked up at him with a thin-lipped smile. "It's only the first time this year. You're improving."

They walked seven paces in silence. "I was trying to make a point with a little humor. That's not who I really am."

"Oh?"

Four more paces.

"You're right; I was a royal, platinum-certified jerk in there," he whispered. His face grew warm as he fingered the scar on his left palm. "It's just . . . some realities about life have stuck with me whether I wanted them to or not."

"So you weren't this way from birth?"

Not always. Only since he was nine.

He looked down as he gave his head a tiny shake.

"Zero! Zilch! Nada! That's what you'll always be, kid!" The rest of the scene—the torn jersey, the humiliation, the message—tried to surface, but Micah slammed the vault to his heart shut and the memory vanished.

By the time he arrived at his office, his breathing steadied and his focus shifted to the letter from his great-uncle that sat on his teak desk. Micah picked it up and flopped into his black leather chair. The yellowed paper was probably white once, though the fluid script looked as crisp as if it had been scrawled yesterday.

The envelope it came in had been sealed with wax, the outline of a lion's head distinct in the dark-blue paraffin. Micah leaned back and stared at the name above the return address. Archie Taylor. Definitely strange.

Archie was his great-uncle whom he knew less than a paragraph about. He'd been dead since the mid-nineties, and Micah had never met him. Archie had made quite a bit of money and hadn't married, but the rest had always been a mystery. Until Micah's late teens, he hadn't known Archie existed. When Micah had asked, his dad only said Archie was odd, a man to stay away from.

Micah opened the letter and wondered once more if it was real.

September 27, 1990

Dear Micah,

You are likely shocked to have received this letter as we never had the opportunity to know each other. The reason for the letter will surprise you more.

I have asked a friend to mail it when you turn thirty-five or when you acquire enough financial resources that you no longer need to labor. Consequently, if you are reading this letter before reaching your thirty-fifth birthday, you have already made a significant amount of money, which is sometimes a beneficial occurrence at a young age but usually is not.

If my instructions have been carried out, a home was built during the past five months on the Oregon Coast, four miles south of Cannon Beach. I designed it for you. I assume by this point you've asked yourself why I would choose to build this house in Cannon Beach of all places.

You likely already know why.

Because it is time to face your past.

It is time to deal with it.

My great desire is that the home brings you resolution and restoration, and if the builder followed my directives, I believe it will. It will certainly—if you'll forgive the cliché—upset your applecart if you allow it. The home is all you.

Your great-uncle,

Archie

P.S. There should be a key enclosed with this letter as well as a card with the address.

Micah reread the last line and frowned. "The home is all *you*"? Typo. Must mean all *yours*. He leaned his head back till it hit the back of his chair. His dad was right. This guy was a whacko.

Face his past? His past was dead. Buried. Forgotten.

And it would stay that way.

‖‖‖‖‖

A noise in the hall made Micah look up. Julie. Good. Back to real life. Julie was the perfect business partner. Tenacious skiing partner. Recent romantic partner.

Her shoulder-length blonde hair bounced as she pranced through the door of his office, her crisp beige suit complementing her gleaming pearly whites.

"Hey!" Micah rose from his desk and opened his arms.

When she reached him, she ruffled his dark brown hair and kissed him softly.

The faint scent of Safari floated up to him. She never wore too much, almost not enough. Julie. Powerful yet tender at times. Driven and radiant. It was nice to have her back.

"How was the trip, Jules?"

"We're richer, but I'm so glad it's over." She slid out of her blazer, flicked a piece of lint off the lapel, laid the coat across the back of Micah's chair, and patted it once. "I did find the perfect SLR digital camera to add to my collection. You'll model for me, please? Your baby-blue eyes are worth taking up two or three hundred megs on my laptop."

When they'd started KimSoft six years ago, he never imagined they'd strike such a rich vein in the software gold rush. Of course, he'd never imagined their long-term platonic relationship would bud into romance, either.

Micah sat down and stared at Archie's letter. He had to get down there. And if the house existed, get rid of it. Now.

"You with me here?" Julie leaned against Micah's desk.

"Huh?"

"I asked about Monday's board meeting, and I think waiting five seconds for a response is long enough." She laughed.

"Sorry, didn't hear you. Brain freeze. I got a bizarre letter from a long-lost relative. In fact, this weekend I might have to go—"

Julie pressed two fingers against his lips. "We cannot allow those thoughts to escape."

"What thoughts?"

"Of nixing our Whistler trip this weekend. You and me and snow and spring skiing and fireplaces and old, old bottles of cabernet. Ring any bells?"

"Hmm." He grinned, raised his eyebrows, and hoped Julie would understand a change in plans.

"If you're canceling, you'd better have a really, really good reason." She straightened the collar of his olive green polo shirt.

"Apparently I've inherited a house right on the ocean, just south of Cannon Beach."

"Cannon Beach?" A scowl flashed across her face. "Didn't you once tell me you hated Cannon Beach?"

"I used to love it."

"What? You did?"

"Forget it." *Sorry, Archie.* The emotions that stupid letter wanted him to face would never see daylight.

Julie stared at him, but he ignored it.

"Let me see something." Julie leaned over him as her red fingernails danced over his keyboard until a sampling of Cannon Beach oceanfront homes for sale flashed on-screen. "Take a look at these prices." She tapped his monitor. "Your little gift could be worth $3 million plus. Throw a sign on it and make some quick cash."

"Exactly. The quicker the better."

"That's why I love you, Micah. *Cha-ching.* Where did this mystery house come from?"

He picked up the letter and drew it across his hand like a blade. "My great-uncle, whom I've never met, had it built for me."

"You never met him and he gives you a house?"

"Weird, huh?" Micah snapped his fingers. "So this weekend, let's head for the sand, see if it's real, and if it is, put a For Sale sign on it and make some money."

"Instead of Whistler?" Her shoulders sagged.

"You're right." He ran his finger over the surface of the letter. "Let's go skiing."

"Wow. You really need to get this taken care of, don't you?"

Julie didn't wait for an answer. A few seconds later, Google Earth splashed onto Micah's monitor. "Address?"

Micah read it to her off the letter. In moments they gazed at a patch of dirt overlooking the ocean.

"Not even a pile of concrete," Julie said.

"Maybe, maybe not." Micah punched a few keys. "Look. That satellite image is seven months old. Archie's letter says the home was built by somebody during the past five months." Micah's gaze stayed riveted on his screen. "There could be—"

"How 'bout I make you a deal so you can go to the beach, Mr. Break-My-Heart."

"Hey, it's not that important for—"

"No, no, stay with me here. I know that look. You have to go. If you switch out our weekend at Whistler for a week in the Alps, we have a deal."

"Then you'll come with me this weekend?"

"No."

"What? I'm not sure I want to do this by myself."

Julie slid her finger across Micah's cheek and turned his head toward her. "Something tells me you need to do this alone."

It would be his first time in Cannon Beach in more than twenty years. And his last. Without question the last.

CHAPTER 2

Too late to head for Cannon Beach to see if the place was real? Probably. Micah walked through his penthouse doorway that evening the moment the numbers on his digital clock snapped from 8:59 to 9:00.

He tapped his phone to get his messages and slumped onto his couch, hoping one would be from his dad—dreading one of them would be from his dad.

"Hello, son," his dad's deep voice trundled out from the machine. "*Received your call today. No need to call back. The only response for anything having to do with Archie Taylor is to run in the opposite direction. I don't need to know what the letter says. Burn it and forget it. That's what I'd do. What I expect you to do.*"

Micah sighed. Joy. That'd be a fun call to return.

He got up to pour himself a glass of Diet Coke and stopped on the way to the kitchen in front of a framed picture of Julie and him on the cover of *Inc.* magazine hanging in the hallway. Their first cover story. A lifetime ago. He kissed his fingers and touched the glass. He'd popped the cork on a bottle of champagne that day. They'd made it.

Too bad the champagne of success seemed to be losing its bubbles.

After getting the Diet Coke, he clicked on his Panasonic big screen and glanced at the wall on either side of it. Blank. Last time Julie was over, they'd had the same conversation they had ten times before about his penthouse's lack of decor.

"Why don't you put some art on the walls, Micah? Some paintings? Or pictures? At least something."

"I don't have any."

"Well, buy some, or put up those drawings and paintings you did back in high school and early college. The ones stacked in the closet. They're pretty decent if you ask me."

"They're horrible." His high school counselor had encouraged him to major in art in college. No way. No money in it. A shot too long to seriously consider. That part of his life was over.

"Then why have you hung on to them for the past twelve years?"

"Yeah, I will. Soon."

"Which? Toss or hang?"

Micah didn't reply. He didn't know the answer.

That was a month ago. He took a sip of his Diet Coke and glanced over at the closet door, cracked open just enough to see the edge of the stack. He still didn't know the answer.

Micah turned back to the TV and watched ESPN with the mute button on and thought about Cannon Beach. He loved the annual sand castle contest. His brother and he came in second place in the seven-to-eleven age group the year they built the dragon. That was their last trip. Two days after the contest . . . He didn't let himself finish the thought.

He looked over at *The Fellowship of the Ring* novel on his end table. He'd been meaning to read it for two years. "I'm taking you with me."

Saturday morning he rolled out of bed at seven, whipped up a bacon-bits-and-kalamata-olive omelet, and called his dad. Talking to him more than twice a year was too often, but if anyone had a clue why Archie had left him a house, it would be his father.

The phone rang three times. "Taylor residence. Daniel speaking."

His dad had answered the phone that way for as long as Micah could remember. Sounded like it was straight out of a 1950s textbook on manners. Probably was.

Micah rubbed his forehead. He had to stay focused. Get the info and get off the phone. And try not to loathe the man more when he hung up than when he started.

"Hey, Dad."

"You're eating while you're talking to me, son."

"Yeah."

"What are you eating?"

Micah pressed his lips together and closed his eyes. As usual his dad was in fine drive-you-crazy form. "Why does it matter?"

"What are you eating?"

"Just my special scrambled eggs and toast, coffee. Nothing fancy."

"Get some fruit in your diet, son."

Micah rubbed the scar on his left hand. "I want to talk to you about Archie's letter."

"I thought I explained my position in my message last night."

"You did." Micah rubbed his neck. "But I hoped I could get you to—"

"Fine. Read me the letter."

Micah read it and waited. Three seconds. Five. His dad broke the silence at seven.

"Stay away from Cannon Beach. Why would you consider going back there even for one second?" Micah knew he'd have a reaction to where the house was located. Just as he knew his dad would fail to address the accident in any direct way. And Archie was a character straight out of Looney Tunes. How do you know the letter is real? It's probably from a competitor trying to distract you." His dad coughed. "You've accomplished a tremendous amount in the business world."

"Thanks," he sputtered. It was the first time his dad had mentioned RimSoft's success. Ever. Micah looked at the *Inc.* picture of Julie and him on his wall. He'd sent a copy to his dad when it came out. His dad never acknowledged it.

"Also, what makes you think a house is really there? If there is, it's probably no bigger than an outhouse and doesn't smell much better. Leave it alone, son."

His dad rarely called him anything but son, and Micah had grown up longing to hear his name spoken every now and then. "Thanks for the thoughts. I'll think about 'em."

"They're not just thoughts; they are facts. What are you going to do?"

"Think about it!" Micah instantly regretted raising his voice. But every conversation with his dad was like talking to Spock. All he wanted was a little emotion from the man.

"I've obviously said too much. I'm not trying to tell you how to run your life. But you asked for my opinion and—"

"I'm sorry. I just want—"

"—I know I'm not good at these . . . um . . . and in the past I've done . . . I'm just not . . . You'll make a good choice, I'm sure."

Micah hung up and looked out the window of his twenty-first-floor penthouse overlooking Seattle's Elliott Bay. It was a radiant spring day, the sun in full bloom, casting long morning shadows on the tiny grass park just north of Pike Place Market. A man lay in the center of the emerald carpet. His arms and legs were spread out, as if he'd stopped in the middle of making a snow angel.

The scene sparked a memory of himself when he was seventeen, eyes closed, lying in the center of a park near home.

"Hey, Micah, what are you doing?" a friend from his basketball team had asked, interrupting his daydream.

"Not thinking." Micah opened his eyes. "Do you ever have so many thoughts of what you have to get done that you want to escape from your own mind?"

"Nuh-uh."

"I do. Never want to be one of those fame or power players so wiped out from racing through life and trying to keep what they have that they never get a chance to enjoy it. I'm going to enjoy being alive every day."

"You're weird, Micah."

A conversation from another lifetime. Micah opened his eyes as the memory faded. He was a pretty naive kid back then. The life he'd created had perks he never dreamed of. But when you get to the top of Everest and it's not all that great, what do you climb next?

The guy sprawled out on the lawn was still there, undoubtedly thinking about nothing. Or more likely stoned out of his mind. Whatever the case, the guy wasn't trying to climb a molehill, let alone a mountain. Micah shook his head and tried to smile.

Resistance is futile. Life changes people. It changed his dad. Turned him into . . . something else.

And it seemed life had turned Micah into Sir Edmund Hillary. Accept it. Twenty minutes later he stood at his front door, black leather Vaqueta briefcase in one hand, a Nike gym bag in the other. Anything else?

Yeah. Grab some sunflower seeds for the trip down to the beach. He set his bags down just inside his front door, then trotted down the hall toward the kitchen. Wait. Something was wrong. Out of place in the hallway. Micah stopped and did a slow spin. Not out of place. Missing.

Where was it? He looked down, expecting to see it lying on the ginger-colored carpet. Nothing.

Waves of heat washed over him. Impossible. He'd glanced at it forty minutes ago while talking to his dad.

The framed *Inc.* magazine cover on his wall had vanished.

CHAPTER 3

Showtime. Time to find out how fully his great-uncle Archie had abandoned his rocker.

Just after three o'clock Saturday afternoon, Micah took the first Cannon Beach exit, lowered his window, and breathed deep. The tang of the ocean air filled him. In it he tasted gut-wrenching memories and, for reasons he didn't understand, hope.

The odds of the house being real were zero, but he had to see the dirt. It was the fastest way to get Archie's letter out of his head. Micah had pulled up the satellite photo once more before leaving Seattle, hoping to answer the question before he left. It still showed the outdated patch of open land where Archie's house now supposedly sat.

If it did exist, the place would be four miles south of Cannon Beach so he didn't need to go through town; but since he hadn't been there in more than twenty years, he wanted to see the changes.

It wasn't the real reason he pulled off Highway 101.

Part of him desperately wanted a house to be standing at the address on the card. He wanted to believe someone was crazy enough—or maybe cared enough about him—to build him a home on the Oregon Coast. But a bigger part didn't believe, and driving through town would delay the inevitable disappointment.

He turned onto Main Street, and a few seconds later Osburn's Ice Creamery filled his vision. Still there! His family used to camp up and down the Oregon Coast every summer. And every trip ended at Osburn's for two scoops of whatever flavor his brother and he wanted. The two scoops were never sweet enough because they meant a summer of adventures had ended, and the bittersweet taste of fall and a new school year would settle on his tongue during the cheerless drive back to Seattle.

But those drives ended when the accident shattered his life.

South of town he took the winding road fifty feet above the beach. Micah slowed his car to a crawl as he watched seagulls pirouette in the cobalt sky above Haystack Rock. A few minutes later he pulled back onto 101 and swallowed hard. Then again. There was no reason to be nervous. The thought didn't help.

His GPS showed the house would be just south of Arcadia Beach State Park. As the park came into view, he slowed to five miles per hour, pulled onto the shoulder, and studied the numbers on little posts till he found 34140. He tapped on his brakes and took furtive glances up and down the highway.

Micah's heart quickened as he turned right and his tires crunched slowly over the gravel driveway. It curved to the right, enough to block a view of where the house might be. A faint briny smell seeped into the car, and as he lowered his window, the roar of a thousand waves filled his ears. He stopped his car before the view in front of him could answer the question pounding through his mind.

"C'mon, God, let something be there. And let it be more than an outhouse."

The words spilled out before he could stop them. Where did *they* come from? Prayer wasn't part of his to-do list. Or at least it hadn't been for eons. Opening his eyes Micah looked up at the sky and let the prayer linger, watching the thought of it float up into nothingness. Then again, maybe God was still up there, even after all these years.

The pace of his breathing increased. Couldn't put it off any longer. A bead of sweat ran down his forehead into his eye. He wiped it away and pressed the gas pedal, as if it were a feather.

His car scrunched forward, and a corner of the house appeared. He let out a long, low whistle as more came into view. First glance said it could compete easily with any of the mansions the Vanderbilts had ever constructed. He leaned forward over his dashboard. Whew. Top of the slate roof had to be twenty-five, maybe thirty feet high.

He got out of his car and walked under the awning that led to the front door, pausing to marvel at the flowering gardens on his right and left. They smelled like sunrise. A reflecting pool to his left showed the image of a stone chimney rising up along the east side of the house. The pool flowed out the far end in a cascade of water that rained down on mossy boulders before it settled into a pond dotted with lily pads. Probably filled with koi. Micah shook his head and chuckled.

Two magnificent stone columns ran up on either side of a solid fir door highlighted by a bronze knob that looked ancient and new at the same time. Two nineteenth-century gas lamps framed the polished limestone entrance.

As he slid the key into the lock, a severe case of déjà vu splashed over him. He'd seen this before. In a dream? A picture of a house just like this? Micah shivered as he turned the key.

The feeling intensified as he walked through the front door. He had been here, hadn't he? No. Not possible. The thing had just been finished. *Get a grip.*

As he wandered forward, a puff of laughter escaped his lips and he grinned. Amazing. Four towering mahogany windows framed a spectacular view of the Pacific Ocean. Huge cedar beams held up a ceiling at least twenty feet high. A fireplace made of river rock dominated the wall to the left. Along the right wall were built-in mahogany bookshelves, ten feet tall.

In front of the windows sat an oversized, overstuffed chair. A lamp next to it would no doubt cast a warm, golden light. An ideal spot to watch the waves.

Archie might have been a loon, but whoever built this place for him nailed it. Micah felt like he'd been coming here his entire life. How did Archie know? He and his great-uncle must have had identical tastes in style.

Micah studied a massive painting of Haystack Rock hanging over the maple fireplace mantle. Influenced by Monet, no question, with maybe a splash of van Gogh. Micah tilted his head back and closed his eyes. Peace seemed to flit about him like a barn swallow. An unexpected emotion. But very welcome.

His cell phone screamed at him, shattering the moment. He grabbed the phone. "What?"

"Wow, excuse me," Julie said. "I just wanted to see if you were there yet. See if the place is real."

"Sorry, deep in thought. You startled me. I got here two minutes ago. You should see it, Jules." Micah spun on his heel. A spiral staircase wound up to what looked like a long upstairs hallway. Of course the staircase would be spiral. He'd always loved them. "It's stunning and bizarre at the same time. It feels . . . familiar."

"How can a place you've never been to before feel familiar?"

"No idea." Micah turned and walked back to the picture windows to watch the surf. Could he kayak in it?

"But you like it."

"Impressive, so far. I'll take some shots, show it to you next week."

"You mean day after tomorrow, right?"

"Yeah." Micah hesitated. "Monday."

After hanging up, he padded past the overstuffed chair that faced the window and thumped the armrest. "I'll be back to you in a moment."

French doors led to a massive deck above the beach. He swung them open, and the pungent ocean air rushed at him. He watched the waves pound out their mesmerizing pattern, and amid the roar of the water he listened to the solitude.

If only the waves could heal instead of stir up the past.

Yin and yang. He loved being here. He hated being here.

He closed his eyes and let the wind—which couldn't figure out which way it wanted to blow—joust his face and hair before he stepped back inside and kept his date with the leather chair.

He propped his feet up on the ottoman and did nothing. Forced himself to think nothing. Looked at nothing but what was straight ahead. When the horizon faded to black, he was still in the same position. He believed people called this relaxing. He used to do it, eons ago, before RimSoft started sucking every minute of his time.

A few more minutes and he'd get up and explore the house, at least find the master bedroom. But that intent sank into the chair along with his last moments of conscious thought.

|||||||

Micah woke the next morning still in the leather chair. Remembering where he was took a few seconds, but the stunning ocean view that greeted his half-open eyes did wonders for his memory. He spent the night in the chair? How could he fall asleep before seeing the rest of the house? Time for a self-guided tour.

The rest of house didn't disappoint with its fully stocked kitchen, complete with an indoor grill and subzero freezer and granite countertops.

Game room with foosball, pool table, and darts.

Colossal media room with maroon movie theater chairs and a screen at least eight feet by five.

A study with dark built-in bookshelves, wireless router, and a teak desk.

The guest bedrooms were themed, one with sports, one for thrill seekers, and one for history buffs. This place just kept getting better. Just like the living room, the home was how Micah would have built it.

He reached the master bedroom, and his palms started sweating. The entire house was *exactly* as he would have done it. It was laid out as if someone had been inside his head and picked his favorite colors and styles and dropped them perfectly into place.

His dream home, straight out of his dreams.

He didn't like the idea of someone he had never met knowing his tastes with this much precision. His mind spun. The construction had to cost millions, let alone the cost of the land. Add the home's contents and it was probably one of the more expensive homes on the Oregon Coast.

Why spend that kind of money? And build it for anyone, let alone him? It didn't compute. Micah returned to the main floor, walked out on the deck, and looked up at the house. Rough guess, it was nine thousand square feet. And it was his. Unbelievable.

That was the problem. The home was not believable. There had to be strings. They had to be attached somewhere.

Good thing he wouldn't be around to find out.

Micah glanced out over the ocean. He was going to sell the place. As soon as possible.

His stomach growled and he glanced at his watch. Ten o'clock. He walked back inside and grabbed his keys off the granite countertop with the intention of heading to town. Just before stepping outside, he stopped himself. A door at the end of one of the ground-floor hallways was slightly open, a shaft of bright light spilling out of the room onto the carpet.

A feeling washed over him. The feeling of a string about to be pulled.

CHAPTER 4

The door hadn't been there the day before. Had it? Micah pushed his front door closed with a soft click, never taking his eyes off the one at the end of the hall.

He'd done a full tour of this part of the home the day before and didn't remember a room even being there, let alone leaving a light on. He hung his leather coat on an oak peg near the staircase, then eased down the hall toward the open door.

He pushed it open the rest of the way with two fingers and peeked inside. It was well lit. Too well lit; so bright he had to squint. At least twenty spotlights drilled down on a variety of magazine covers sitting on glass pedestals. Other pedestals held plaques; still others had laminated newspaper articles on top of them. Even before Micah's eyes adjusted enough to see clearly, he knew what the room was.

How could—? He squeezed his eyes shut. When he opened them, he half expected the room to be gone.

It was a shrine to his meteoric rise in the world of software. Micah and Julie were on the cover of each magazine displayed: *Forbes*, *BusinessWeek*, *Wired*, *Fast Company*, and more, as well as newspaper articles from *The Wall Street Journal*, *USA Today*, and *The New York Times*.

The plaques were awards RimSoft had won, from their first up to an award from last month. Whoever collected them hadn't missed a thing. Micah shook his head.

Wow.

Weird.

He gazed at the walls filled with photos of Julie and himself, pictures from the earliest days of the company up to the present, just the two of them along with movie stars, athletes, and leaders in the world of software.

It must have taken months to dig all this up.

As Micah contemplated how they'd done it, he noticed a small door at the back of the room, only open an inch or two. He walked over to it and pushed, but it scraped to a halt after a foot and a half. He leaned his shoulder into it, and the hinges squealed in protest but opened enough for him to enter. For a new house this door was decidedly out of place.

The room was dim, and Micah couldn't find a light switch, but his eyes slowly adjusted from the glare of the room he'd just left. The only light came from an oil lamp sitting on an oak nightstand in a corner.

More oil lamps circled the room, all sitting on oak stands, all unlit. Their charred wicks were evidence they'd burned once, but all were now out of oil. He turned back to the still-burning lamp. Next to it rested a Bible covered in a fine layer of dust. Beside the Bible were two pictures. Micah was in both of them.

In the first picture five kids and he handed out egg salad sandwiches at Seattle's Union Gospel Mission. In the second his arm was around his best friend from high school youth group. Micah smirked. He was really into religion back then.

Almost against his will, he approached another lamp stand. On it was a sheet of paper. He held it up and squinted at it in the dim light.

Micah gasped. Impossible. Where would Archie have found it? It was a flyer for a concert—*the* concert—the one he'd gone to on a whim. The one where he'd decided to follow God.

Sweat covered his palms. This was beyond strange. It was bizarre.

There's no way Archie's builders could have gotten that flyer.

The pulse in his neck beat double time. He'd never understood people who had panic attacks. How could they go from feeling normal to expecting their body would explode any second? Now he knew.

He slowed his breathing. No help. Goose bumps broke out on his skin.

Archie wanted to highlight his career? Fine. Nice display. But the other room? Why dig so deep into his past? Who cares?

Archie. The words in his letter rang in Micah's head. *"Time to face your past. It is time to deal with it."*

He rubbed the scar on his hand and made himself breathe slower. Pulling up long-dead memories that were none of anyone's business. Why go to this much trouble to weird him out?

His body yelled run, and his mind joined the chorus. But where? Out onto the beach? The highway? Nothing was attacking him. Nothing was after him. So why was he trembling?

Get control!

He ground his teeth as he forced himself out into the hallway. He closed the door, and Micah stared at the knob as if the door might open and suck him back in. Make him face—no!

His breathing calmed but his hands still shook. He shoved them into his pockets. It helped. Slightly.

What was wrong with him?

Micah jogged into his living room and burst through the French doors onto the deck. As the ocean wind whipped through his hair, his dad's comment about the precarious condition of Archie's sanity came back to him. Which meant one of two things to his father—either Archie was consumed with God, or he had never made any money. The building of the house ruled out the latter, so Micah assumed Archie was, in his dad's words, a Jesus-freak.

His dad believed all Christians had a serious crack in their psyche. He wasn't vindictive about it. To Daniel Taylor it was fact. When Micah started following Jesus during his sophomore year of high school, his dad wanted to send him to a psychiatrist. In the end they agreed to make it a taboo subject, which pushed them even further apart if that was possible.

During college the world of software captured him, and the whole God-thing had faded. It wasn't overt, just a slow slide onto the back burner of his life and then off the back of the stove to sit with the dust and grease spots where Micah didn't miss it.

But obviously not missed by everyone. Archie had built two shrines. One to Micah's worldly success, one to his God-stuff past. God was fine at one time. But that time was over. Whoever pulled off this stunt for Archie had stepped over the line. Micah grabbed one of the Adirondack chairs on his deck and tossed it against the railing. The idea of someone digging up his ancient history felt like someone had broken into his mind.

Micah stumbled down his deck stairs till his feet thudded onto the wet sand. He plopped down on a battered rain-soaked log, not caring about the dampness seeping through his pants.

In his mind he slapped a roll of crime-scene tape across the door of the shrine room. He'd slaved to create his software empire. He wasn't going to let some crazy great-uncle slam him for it.

That night he had a double bacon cheeseburger at Bill's Tavern & Brewhouse. Afterward he drove up to Astoria and plunked down money for a raunchy comedy he almost walked out on. Just like he'd done in Seattle the week before.

Why did he watch those things? He always felt like he wanted to take a shower afterward. Simple answer. They were the best way he'd found to keep from thinking—about the past, about the ever-pressurized world of software, and at the moment, the two rooms in Archie's house. Both screaming at him. One screaming louder than the other.

He woke Monday morning as gray gave over to the light of day. Only a few lazy clouds hung over the ocean. Micah walked out to sit on his deck but his feet kept moving, and shortly the waves sent ice pricks into his feet and ankles. He stared at the ocean, and it stared back with no expectations, no pressure, no stress from frantic employees or clients pounding on his brain. Heaven.

So what if Archie was a little eccentric and had given him a blatant message from beyond the grave? He'd junk the stuff in both rooms, keep the door shut, and let the questions they asked die a quick death.

He turned back to Archie's gift. A thread of light pushed over the mountain ridge to the east and lit up the top of his roof like gold. He faced the ocean and drew in its pungent smell. This had been his favorite place in the world before his mom died. Before his sand-castle world was washed away with one massive wave.

Maybe part of him did belong here.

No, it didn't. *Sorry, Archie. The past will stay there.*

No question. He'd sell the place.

He strode through saltwater swirling around his ankles back toward the stunning house.

But maybe not right away.

After breakfast Micah pulled onto Highway 101 and headed for Seattle. Traffic was light and he made good time, even with the rain that pelted down as soon as he hit Olympia. In less than four hours he crossed the Seattle city limits; twenty-two minutes later his tires squealed as he pulled into his parking spot in his condo garage. He'd take a quick shower, then head for the office.

Micah pulled out his cell phone to record his mileage, a habit held over from the early days of RimSoft. Eat Top Ramen six days a week, never turn on a light unless forced to, and record everything possible for write-offs on the ol' tax return.

He squinted at his odometer and looked back at the file on his cell. Strange. Didn't seem right. Micah did a quick calculation in his head. It couldn't be. Again he looked at the odometer and the total on his cell phone. Too weird. One of the two machines was wrong. Had to be.

Or he'd just driven 16,341 miles in the past two days.

CHAPTER 5

Isn't this energizing?" Micah asked Shannon on Tuesday morning. "Seeing all these people streaming through the doors, ready to conquer new worlds?"

She stood next to him in RimSoft's foyer, her ever-present notepad and minicalendar in hand. He'd bought her an iPhone the previous Christmas, but she'd never taken it out of the box. They watched the lobby become a river of workers.

"Energizing? Not really. Does it energize you?"

He hesitated. "Most of the time it still does."

Shannon stared at him. "Most of the time?"

"Life at the speed of light, three thousand miles wide, a millimeter deep."

"You're not getting philosophical on me, are you?"

He ignored the question. Micah spotted Brad, his racquetball partner, across the lobby. Brad's crew cut and horn-rimmed glasses made him look like a blond Buddy Holly, but he played racquetball like the Tasmanian devil.

"Hey, Bradley, get over here."

Brad sauntered over. "You want another beating like last month, huh?"

"What? Can you say delusional? I can, and you should. I took you down three of the four games last *Wednesday*, the fourth game fifteen to zee-row. Memory okay, my friend?"

A few people chuckled as Brad came to a stop in front of Micah. "Nice try, boss man. Maybe in your dreams. It's been a month since we played. I admit, you sliced and diced me the first game but lost the next three straight. Would've been four if we'd played another."

"Ignoring the fact you were beat like a rug won't change history. After that session last week, I even had to go to the bone crusher to straighten my spine. Remember?"

Brad's grin drained from his face. "We didn't play last week." He blinked.

"You okay, buddy? Of course we played."

"No, I was in San Fran last week. The whole week."

"So, your twin stood in?" Micah laughed. "That's your excuse for losing!"

Brad reached into his briefcase and pawed through it. He pulled out a rumpled piece of paper and held it at his side. "Tell me you're kidding, Micah."

"About?"

Brad held up the paper. It was an Alaska Airlines itinerary. "Take a look at my flights. What's the first date?"

"April 6."

"And the second?"

"April 10."

"So blow my brains out and tell me how we played racquetball on Wednesday, April 7, if I was in San Francisco?"

Micah stared at the paper.

"CAT scans are amazing these days. Check it out maybe?" Brad tapped his head. "When you're stressing, the memory always goes first. I'll beat you again Friday morning if you're free."

A shiver sprinted down Micah's spine. He stared at Brad, then Shannon.

"Micah, want to play?"

"Yeah, sorry." Micah turned to Shannon. "Am I open?"

"Let me look . . . yes."

He flashed a thumbs-up as Brad walked away. "Shannon, what did I do last Wednesday?"

She licked her finger and pawed through her calendar. "Conference call at nine, a quick meeting with the bank at ten fifteen, then you got ready for an afternoon board meeting."

"No racquetball?"

She studied her calendar and smirked.

"You find this amusing?"

"Only a little." She spun toward him. "You have to admit, Mr. Never-Miss-A-Beat, Always-In-Control, missing a beat and being out of control is slightly comical."

"Hilarious. But that's the point. I don't ever miss a beat. There's not a sliver of doubt in my mind that Brad and I played racquetball last Wednesday. But apparently my memory is the only one in which it exists. That's more than missing a beat."

"It wouldn't hurt to take a day off." She adjusted her glasses.

"I just *did* take a day off. Last weekend. Cannon Beach?"

"Oh yes, that's right." Shannon grinned. "Did it help?"

Micah glared at her. They walked toward the elevators, their tennis shoes squeaking on the polished faux marble floor.

"So tell me about the place at the beach. Like it? Don't like it? Somewhere in between?"

"I like it slightly more than I hate it." He punched the button for the top floor.

"That makes no sense."

"No question about that."

Shannon tapped her lip with her forefinger. "Julie tells me you're going to sell it."

"Yep."

"You want me to find a real estate ag—?"

"Nope."

"So you really don't want to sell it."

He watched the elevator numbers light up from 16 to 17 to 18. "I do want to sell it. But I need to get a better feel for the area first, get a feel for what it would go for."

"Isn't that what an agent does?"

Of course it was. It wasn't rational, his wanting to go back down. But something about the house felt so . . . He couldn't name the emotion.

"Do me a favor okay? The next four Fridays, can you clear my schedule?"

"Interesting." She raised an eyebrow. "You *do* like this place."

"No." Micah looked at the ceiling. "I'm intrigued."

He walked into his office and pulled up his appointment calendar on his computer. He stared at it for more than a minute as a thin layer of perspiration grew on his forehead. He swallowed twice and kept his eyes riveted on the screen. But it didn't matter how long he stared.

The racquetball games he knew he'd played with Brad had vanished.

|||||||

Two hours later Micah stood at his office windows and studied the ferryboats chugging across Puget Sound's dark green waters. The same ocean lapped at the sand at Cannon Beach. Thoughts filled his mind of snow-white sand dollars, sand squeaking under his shoes, and those massive picture windows perfectly framing the surf.

If only Archie could have built the house in Lincoln City or Newport. Then he'd keep the place forever.

But he didn't need Cannon Beach reminding him of the day that ripped his life apart every time he stepped onto the sand.

Shannon stood in his doorway. "Julie's meeting starts in five minutes."

"What?" Micah blinked and spun toward her.

"Welcome back to Earth." Shannon pointed down the hall. "Julie's meeting."

"Right." He left his office and met Julie at the conference room door. "You ready?"

Julie smiled. "Completely."

For the first few minutes of her marketing presentation to their board of directors, Micah listened intently. But as Julie moved into the breakdown of their ad budget, his mind wandered. Three minutes later a sketch of his house at Cannon Beach and the surrounding mountains appeared under the rapid movement of his mechanical pencil.

". . . and RimSoft's logo will get an overhaul . . ." Julie's voice droned.

Need to put a sand castle in there. A few more turrets on it. Perfect. Maybe a few kites in the sky. That's an idea. He should buy one of those high-tech stunt kites. What a kick to learn to fly—

"Micah?" Julie's voice cut through his moment of admiration. She and the board stared at him. "You with me here, partner?"

The lead at the tip of his pencil snapped off as he looked up. "Yeah. Sorry." He set his pencil down and folded his arms. *Resist. Julie needs the support.* He glanced down at the sketch. It begged for a golden retriever. As Julie turned to her left to answer a question, Micah picked up his pencil and clicked twice. The lead leaped out as if at attention, ready for orders. Micah stopped drawing the instant Julie finished giving her reply.

When the presentation was over, he mouthed, *"Nice job"* to Julie, who shook hands with board members. She frowned at him.

As he strode out the door, his stomach alarm clock went off, and he shut it off with a Diet Coke and a turkey sandwich—extra mayo—from the company deli. When he got back to his office, Julie was leaning against his desk, arms crossed.

"I know you like doodling sketches when you're in meetings, but this time was a little much. I think you caught two minutes of my presentation, max. Was your mental sabbatical to anyplace interesting?"

Micah ripped his drawing from his notepad and held it up. "Hmm?"

In the foreground was the ocean, then the beach with two sand castles, a stunt kite, and a golden retriever leaping for a piece of driftwood spinning through the air. His home was the focal point of the drawing, framed by trees on both sides, the picture windows in perfect proportion. Smoke curled out of the chimney.

"I take it that'll be part of the brochure to get the thing sold?" Julie pulled her arms in tighter and leaned back.

"Hadn't considered that. Yeah, maybe."

"Don't tell me you're starting to like the place."

"No way." He stared at his drawing. He couldn't keep his mind off Archie's house. It drew him like a magnet. Yes, Cannon Beach was laced with razor-sharp pain from his past. But now, in some strange way, it filled him with anticipation. And that weird familiar feeling in the house continued to pull at him.

"I need to ask you something." Micah laid the drawing on his desk and smoothed it out with both hands. "I want to make the next three or four weekends long ones and hang out down there. Be all right with you?"

"Wow." Julie tried to laugh. "I've been ditched for another woman before but never a house."

"Come with me." He kissed her on the cheek.

"Do you want me to?"

"Sure. Yes." Micah turned back to his drawing. "Of course."

She shook her head. "Nope, sorry."

"Why?"

"Because I know you. You want to be there." Julie walked over to Micah's windows and tapped on the glass. "But you don't want me to be there with you."

Micah coughed out a laugh. "I just said come with me."

"'Come with me' is very different from saying 'I want you to come.'"

Micah slumped into his chair. "Do we have to play the semantics game every time we talk? It's exhausting." He leaned forward and waited for her to answer. She didn't.

"Fine. I want you to come."

"Why do you let things come out of your mouth that your eyes tell me are a lie?"

Micah snatched his cedar letter opener off his desk and tore into the pile of envelopes sitting next to his laptop. "I thought you said you didn't like the ocean."

"I don't, but I still wanted to see what you'd say."

Micah slapped the letter opener down on his desk. "Do you think you could serve me up a nice slice of guilt pie with that side of manipulation?"

"You don't get it, do you, Micah?"

He sighed. "What do you want from me?"

"You really want to know?" Julie leaned in till their faces were inches apart.

"Yes."

"A decision. Take your next three or four weekends, fine. But when they're over, you'd better be able to tell me if there's a ring in my near future."

CHAPTER 6

Freedom. Sweet freedom. Micah walked out of his office Thursday evening at six thirty and took a deep breath. Free of having to give Julie an answer he wasn't ready to give, free of the grind. He used to love the rush of RimSoft—seventy-hour workweeks were never a problem. *Were*, past tense. He could get used to a forty-hour workweek.

Plus it would feel good to get away from what had become Seattle's version of Bizarro World. The missing racquetball game and the cross-country trip his car took by itself gnawed at his mind like a gopher on steroids. Not to mention the framed *Inc.* cover that decided to do a Houdini vanishing act. Wait. Houdini was the escape artist. Perfect. That's exactly what Micah would do. In the morning, when he woke up to the roar of the ocean, his escape from the unexplained weirdness in Seattle would be complete.

There was no plan for the weekend. His Seattle life was so scheduled and under such control, having no agenda unsettled him for a moment. But as his car chewed up the miles with Jack Johnson's soothing guitar and vocals purring in the background, he allowed himself not to know what the next three days would bring.

When he reached Astoria, he shot up a quick prayer. Couldn't hurt. The first two times it stuck in his throat. The third he said, "God, I don't know if You hear me anymore. But this house . . . it draws me. It scares me. Both at the same time. Can You explain why Archie built the place there? Plus the strange stuff going on in Seattle . . . I . . ."

He didn't know what else to say. "I hope You know what I'm trying to tell You. Amen."

God was silent, but Micah had expected Him to be, so it was all right.

When Micah arrived, he set down his bags and went straight to the master bedroom and crashed. He didn't move again till just after seven the next morning.

As he sipped a cup of dark roast coffee from his French press, he watched seagulls dive through the air like *Star Wars* TIE fighters. To fly. What a rush that would be. The thought gave him sudden inspiration. Running. Back in high school he'd flown, running the eight hundred meters faster than anyone in his school ever had. His senior season he finished first in state, which the paper deemed extraordinary since it was only his second time to compete in the event.

But it didn't impress his dad. Not even when KING 5 TV did a feature story on Micah. His dad didn't watch when the piece aired.

He hadn't run consistently for years, not from lack of desire but lack of time. Now, at least for two days, he had an abundance.

He threw on a Windbreaker and headed south toward Hug Point. He'd discovered the spot on the Internet the week before. The tide in front of the point never got low enough to allow people to walk around it on the sand. In the late 1800s settlers working their way up the coast solved the problem by blasting out a massive section of the rock that jutted into the ocean. They paved it with concrete, smooth enough for their wagons, and for the first time they could bring supplies as far north as Cannon Beach.

The road was still there and could be walked on. But only at low tide. The rest of the day waves crashed onto the ledge and caught uninformed tourists in a saltwater bath.

Micah wanted to see the pieces of concrete the sea hadn't yet claimed, and according to the Internet, there were caves and a waterfall worth seeing just past the remnants of the old road.

In less than thirty minutes, he reached Hug Point State Park. He imagined kids playing in the waterfall or in the three caves during the summer. Perfect for families. Not today. It was a dreary April morning that had reserved the entire beach for Micah.

Or so he thought.

An unexpected burst from above sent rain pelting down so hard he headed for shelter in the biggest of the Hug Point caves.

The cave softened the crash of the surf, and the rain offered no noise to prove its existence. It felt like someone had muted the world. Micah saw no movement from his vantage point. He could be the only one left on Earth, and he wouldn't know it.

The cave walls were almost black and slick with moisture. A crack ran along the ceiling, widening as it zigzagged toward the back wall. Nothing to worry about. It would take an earthquake to make this thing collapse. Micah took two steps toward the entrance.

Ten seconds later a man in a baseball hat, blue sweatshirt, and black workout shorts half ran, half walked toward him.

"Wow!" The man yanked off his St. Louis Rams cap and threw the rain from it onto the sand. "Makes me think of the ark." He turned to Micah with a huge smile. "Rick." The man extended his hand.

Micah fixed his gaze on Rick's eyes. A shifting shade of sea green, they were intense and gentle at the same time. He was a bit taller than Micah, maybe six foot two, with thick hair the color of sandstone just starting to go gray. Micah liked him immediately.

He introduced himself and shook Rick's hand. After they both commented on the forecast for the next few days, Micah asked Rick if he was a local.

"Lived here for a little over a year."

"What do you do?"

"Oh, take walks on the beach, read good books, love watching old movies on rainy Saturday nights. And I still run or mountain bike three times a week, even at my age." Rick stood up straight and pulled his sweatshirt tight against his stomach and smacked it twice with his palm. "Have to fight to keep this thing under control."

Rick didn't look like he was rolling in cash and couldn't be much past fifty. "You're retired?"

"No, still gotta work for another decade at least. I own the gas station in town. Mostly I bang away on the cars in back while the kids out front pump the gas. We're one of the few stations that still actually work on folks' cars. But I get out front every now and then to squeeze out a gallon or two of the octane. Can't pump your own fuel in Oregon. Gives me a chance to see friends and meet the tourists." He squinted at Micah. "You haven't been gassing up in Seaside, have you?" His eyebrows furrowed in a deep, mock frown.

Micah chuckled. "Not anymore." He glanced at Rick, then turned back to the sheets of rain sweeping over the waves. "Um, when I asked you what you did, I meant . . ." He stopped. It was obvious Rick knew exactly what he'd meant.

Rick dug a trench in the sand with his shoe. "Pretty sad that we define each other by what we do to put bread on the table rather than what makes us come alive."

Come alive? What was that supposed to mean? It sounded like

a line from one of those self-help gurus he was always being sub-
jected to at national software conventions. Micah was silent as the
rain continued to hammer the sand in front of the cave. Good thing
Rick didn't ask what made *him* come alive.

How would he answer the question? No idea. In that moment
he realized something inside was very, very dead.

Rick broke the silence first. "So you here on vacation or a new
resident?"

"Neither. I inherited a house. I'm kinda blown away. Nine
thousand square feet, right on the ocean. I'm here to check it out,
check out the area, then get the thing on the market. Should get
some decent coin for it."

"You don't like it?"

"Love it." Micah coughed. Where did *that* come from? He'd
never even admitted it to himself.

"But you're selling it?"

Micah wiped the combined sweat and rain off his forehead.
"Probably going to. Haven't made the final decision yet."

"Ah." Rick took off his Windbreaker and tied it around his
waist. "It's a wonderful house."

"You've seen it?"

"If I'm thinking of the right one, I watched it being built. Just
a few houses south of Arcadia Beach State Park, right? Finished a
month or so ago?"

"That's the one."

Rick smiled without a hint of jealousy. Intriguing. Micah had
gotten used to those around him smiling on the outside while
the green monster of envy inside them snapped at his money and
fame.

"I've looked forward to meeting the owner." Rick smiled his
massive grin again, his eyes almost disappearing. "Small-town
ocean life agreeing with you so far?"

"It's turned out better than I thought it would." Micah rubbed his cold arms and gazed at the surf. "Even with this kind of weather."

Rick nodded. "There's a saying around here about the beach:

Where ocean breezes storm the soul,
Where love of strife grows quickly old,
Where the touch of God is beheld in power,
Where the spirit finds rest, in its darkest hour."

Micah wasn't into poetry, but that one struck a nerve. Rest. Simple word. So elusive. And his hours? They certainly seemed to be moving his spirit toward darkness, thanks to Uncle A.

Silence.

He looked at Rick out of the corner of his eye. There was an intimidating confidence about him, and Micah was never intimidated. He easily spotted people's insecurities hidden under their posing and posturing. Most of the CEOs he dealt with, no matter their age, were scared little boys inside who covered themselves with a false confidence. Rick? His self-assurance was genuine.

Three minutes later the rain stopped. Rick shook Micah's hand, said good-bye, and ambled down the beach. Micah walked five paces in the opposite direction before he turned back.

"Hey, Rick! I've got a car mystery for you. Mine gained sixteen thousand miles overnight. That possible without someone messing with it manually?"

Rick's eyes shifted from playful to serious. Intense. A moment later they shifted back. "It's rare, but yes, I've seen it happen."

"What's the cause? Bad odometer?"

"A much deeper issue than that." Rick turned to walk away. "Maybe we'll bump into each other again, and I'll have a chance to explain it."

CHAPTER 7

Micah arrived at RimSoft early Monday morning with Rick's enigmatic response still swirling through his mind. Deeper issues? With a car? Explain it when? Maybe next weekend he'd try to find Rick's station and get an answer.

Micah pushed the mystery out of his mind for the moment and booted up his computer. Getting to work at five o'clock meant he could get a majority of his work for the week finished before the inevitable fires started.

By the time Shannon arrived at eight, he'd plowed through all of his work slated for Monday and Tuesday.

He stretched, stood, and strolled over to his window to watch gray clouds roll in, painting a dreary ceiling for the ferryboats chugging across Puget Sound.

He returned to his desk. Next on his to-do list: Call Rafi Cushman about the phone system. After twenty seconds of listening to an instrumental song that should have been shot, Rafi came on the line.

"Hi, Rafi, Micah Taylor. Wanted to follow up on our talk at J. B. Olson's party two weeks back."

"Uh, I remember John having a party, but I don't remember meeting you, Micah. I mean, I know who you are, of course, but—"

"We talked about both graduating from UDub the same year. And we both played Les Paul guitars back in high school." Micah whistled inwardly. Did the guy want RimSoft's business or not? He should have had Shannon call him. This was a waste of time.

"Wow, sorry, it's just not clicking for me. You're sure it was me?"

"You probably met a lot of people. I just wanted to see your proposal for a new phone system."

"Sure, I'd love to develop a plan for you."

Micah wrapped up the conversation and shook his head. Unbelievable. The guy couldn't remember a conversation from two weeks ago that could result in a sizable account. Must have been drunk.

By the time six o'clock rolled around on Wednesday evening, the week was wrapped, delivered, and under control, so he left for the beach a day early.

||||||

Thursday the sound of the surf woke him at seven-thirty. He rolled out of bed, grabbed coffee, and took a long look at the waves as they tossed milk-bubble foam up on the beach.

After firing up his laptop and checking RimSoft's stock price, he pulled up his e-mail and breezed through fifty of them in half an hour. Then he answered Julie's three e-mails. Done in two minutes. He probably should have taken more time, but he signed each one with "I love you." He hoped that would be enough but knew it wasn't.

After checking ESPN for anything interesting, Micah headed into town for groceries. He glanced at his fuel gage. Almost empty. Perfect excuse to stop by Rick's gas station to pick up on last week's conversation.

Rick's Gas & Garage stood out in forest green letters on top of a building that looked its age, even with the fresh coat of paint, which tried in vain to hide decades of soggy Oregon Coast winters.

He got out of his BMW and watched a towheaded kid, who couldn't have been over five foot two, pump his gas.

Micah wandered into the garage and found Rick underneath a late-model Lexus. Before he could say hello, Rick rolled out from under it and announced to the vehicle in his deep baritone, "Done with you forever."

Micah started to reintroduce himself. "Hey, Rick, we met last—"

"Great surprise to see you, Micah!" Rick sat up with a grin. "What are you doing right now?"

"Right now?"

"Yep, right now." Rick yanked a clean rag from his back pocket and wiped the oil from his hands.

"Grocery shopping."

"Starting or finishing?"

"Finished."

"Excellent." Rick waved his thumb at the Lexus. "Now that I've got this emergency handled, I gotta make a quick trip into Seaside. Wanna come?"

"Well, I, uh . . ." Micah almost laughed.

"Sorry, gotta go now. You coming or not?"

Rick's piercing eyes were hard to resist. Plus it was a chance to ask about deep odometer issues. "Why not."

"Terrific." Rick finished cleaning his hands and strode out of the garage, hardly looking as he tossed the rag twenty feet through the air into a large, rusty drum filled with oil-covered cloths. When he reached his '89 Ford, he gestured toward it. "It's not luxury like yours, but I guarantee it won't break down."

As they pulled out, Rick called to the gas-pumping kid. "Devin! You'll let the Petersons know their Lexus is ready? And if Micah's keys are in his ignition, could you move his car away from the pump?"

Devin flashed a grimy, grease-covered thumbs-up.

Micah opened his eyes wide.

Rick winked. "Don't worry; he'll clean up a bit first."

As they pulled onto Highway 101 and headed north, Rick said, "So is romance a part of Micah Taylor's life these days?"

Too big of a part. Too much complication. Too many questions with no answers. Why did Julie have to put the full-court press on him? He loved her. She loved him. Couldn't it stay that simple for a while longer?

"Yeah."

"Care to expand on that?"

"I don't know."

"Sorry if I hit a nerve."

Micah rapped his knuckles on his knee. "Been going out for a year, been business partners for six. Great business partner."

"You see a long-term future together?"

Wow. The guy didn't mind going for the throat à la Barbara Walters. "Not sure. I was handed an ultimatum ten days ago. She wants a ring."

"Do you want to give her one?"

"I love her."

Rick adjusted his Rams hat. "That's not what I asked."

"I'm not sure." Micah shifted in his seat. "That's a lie. I am sure.

I'm positive I'm not even close to ring-ready. I want to be. Part of me, at least." Micah loosened his seat belt. "I should be ready. But the idea of getting engaged makes me . . ."

Micah stared at the yellow lines in the middle of the road as they zipped under Rick's truck. Strange. He barely knew the guy, yet here he was spilling out his Julie problems all over the front seat of Rick's Ford.

"'I feel as if I'm in a room screaming and no one even looks up,'" Rick said.

"What?"

"It's from *Titanic*. Kate Winslet describing her life before Leonardo DiCaprio frees her. You feel like Rose?"

Micah turned toward the passenger-side window. He wasn't ready to spill everything. He turned back to Rick. "Pretty good quote. Where'd you come up with it?"

"I'm a bit of a movie-trivia buff."

"Really. Want to take me on?"

"Absolutely." Rick grinned. "Ready?"

"What decade should we focus on?"

"How 'bout the one you were born in?"

"Fine." Micah nodded.

"Top-grossing movie of '86, and you're only getting one clue."

"I don't need one, *Maverick*."

Rick burst out laughing. "Impressive! All right, name two movies Tom Cruise made before *Top Gun* sent him into the stardom stratosphere."

Micah tapped his forehead in mock concentration. "Wait, wait. How 'bout *The Outsiders* and *All the Right Moves*."

"Not bad."

Micah volleyed back. "Staying on the same path, name at least three actors or actresses in *The Outsiders* who went on to stardom other than Cruise."

Rick turned left into the parking lot of an auto parts store that looked even older than his garage. He hopped out with a quickness belying his age and linebacker-sized body. "I'll just take five minutes to get these parts."

"Whoa. Sorry, Charlie, no tuna for you till you answer the question."

"No time-out to pick up the parts?"

"No way. You might pull up IMDb on the computer in there," Micah said.

"IMDb?"

"The Internet Movie Database. Playing dumb doesn't work with me."

Rick laughed, propped his elbows up on the open window, and stuck his head inside. "Okay. Would you count Diane Lane, Patrick Swayze, Rob Lowe, and Matt Dillon as having had a little time in the sun?"

Rick slid into the parts store and Micah shook his head. He was drawn to the man, as if he were at the end of a bungee cord stretched to its limit. Confident. Well spoken. Intelligent. Why did this guy run a gas station in a tourist town? Every ounce of him spoke of more than oil changes and alternators. Micah suspected his list of accomplishments went beyond working on cars. And yet as much as he searched, he couldn't find an ego hinting at hidden fortune or fame.

As they pulled onto Highway 101 and headed back toward Cannon Beach, Micah said, "You want to tell me about the deeper issues of life surrounding odometers that gain sixteen thousand miles?"

Rick stayed silent for more than a minute before he spoke. "In every moment we make choices. Those choices ripple out and affect every area of our lives. A butterfly flapping its wings can cause a hurricane thousands of miles away."

"I understand the Butterfly Effect, but, uh, what are you talking about? Isn't this about my car?"

"Not really."

"Okay." Micah stared at Rick. "What is it about?"

"Your life."

"What about my life?"

"Choices." Rick kept his eyes on the road. This time the silence was only ten seconds. "More to come later. Give it time, okay?"

It wasn't a question; it was a command.

The guy was magnetic, but Micah couldn't get rid of a wariness that flitted around the corners of his mind. More a feeling than anything concrete. Until now. Talk about cryptic. Something about the man made Micah feel like he was immersed in an episode of *LOST*.

The rest of the way back they talked sports, local politics, and Cannon Beach history. When they shook hands good-bye, Rick said, "Can we connect up again soon?"

"Sure, I'd like that."

"Me, too." Rick clapped Micah on the back and strode into his gas station. "Don't worry." He turned back to Micah. "Answers will come."

|||||||

Back at the house Micah lost himself in *The Fellowship of the Ring* so thoroughly that by the time he stopped reading, the sky had turned from misty gray to the sooty blackness of a foggy April night. He headed toward the master bedroom more relaxed than he'd been in years. Despite the unanswered questions and being within miles of where his heart had shattered, he felt at peace.

He didn't wake on Saturday morning till nine. When was the last time he'd done that? Too long. His RimSoft life never allowed it. But didn't he own the company? He could choose to get off the hamster wheel. Was he running RimSoft, or was RimSoft running him?

||||||

Taking the next three Fridays off turned into taking the next six Fridays off, which followed a consistent routine. He worked ten to twelve hours a day Monday through Thursday, made a late-evening drive down to Cannon Beach that night, then spent the weekend exploring the area, running, and having breakfast on Saturdays with Rick at Morris' Fireside.

Sunday afternoons he filled up at Rick's before heading back to Seattle. His quick stop to refuel always turned into an hour plus of conversation about the ups and downs of RimSoft, his relationship with Julie, and the lure of Cannon Beach. Rick always listened with genuine interest, quick to clarify a comment to make sure he understood the situation, slow to give advice unless Micah pressed him.

After Micah's final, "I gotta go," they each tried to stump the other with a new movie-trivia question. It never worked, but they promised next week they'd find one that would.

Rick had moved into a position in Micah's life that few people occupied: friendship with no strings attached. It felt wonderful. Pursuit not because of his money or fame but simply because Rick enjoyed knowing him.

It only bothered Micah slightly that Rick somehow seemed to know him much more thoroughly than Micah knew Rick.

||||||

During the week at RimSoft, work was packed with meetings on the new beta version of their flagship product. It was a roller-coaster time, not knowing if the testers, and by association the critics, would go into rapture over the new software or try to bury it, and Micah loved every second of the ride. It was RimSoft's Super Bowl, and it never failed to give him a rush.

Julie and he had dinner on Tuesday or Wednesday night each week, but her frustration at his new weekend life grew.

The Wednesday after his sixth weekend in Cannon Beach, they went to Palisade, the lights of West Seattle blinking at them from across Puget Sound. As soon as they were seated, Julie folded her arms and tossed Micah on the grill.

"So what's your answer?" she asked.

"About?"

"Don't insult me." Julie smacked her menu against the table. "You said this dinner was about our future."

"Can't we order first?" Micah studied the restaurant's specials.

"No." She waited till he looked up. "I asked for an answer in four weeks. It's been six. That place has you hook, line, and heart."

"So does Seattle."

"Seattle includes me. Cannon Beach doesn't."

"It could." Micah slid his finger down the side of his water glass, then wiped the moisture on the tablecloth.

"Do you love me, Micah?"

"Yes."

"Do you want to marry me?"

Micah sucked in a deep breath and held it. Five seconds passed. He knew it was far too long. That question required an instantaneous answer. "Yes."

Julie folded her russet cloth napkin into a neat triangle, set it on her plate, and pressed down the crease with two fingers. Then she stood.

"What are you doing?"

"You can't have both."

"Both what?" he said.

"Don't play dumb."

"It's just a beach place." Micah motioned for her to sit back down. "I won't be spending a bunch of time there much longer. Things will get back to normal. I'm going to sell the place like we talked about. Seattle's where I belong."

"You're obsessed with the place. You said you couldn't stand Cannon Beach even though you won't tell me why, but you keep going down there. It makes no sense." She put on her coat and buttoned it all the way to the top. "I need you to decide. Very soon."

A rush of heat filled his face as Julie strode away from the table. Micah wasn't sure if it was from the stares of the people sitting around him or the lie he'd just told her about wanting to get married.

After insisting on giving Palisades money for occupying a table for ten minutes, he got in his car and stared out the window seeing nothing.

Maybe he'd head for the beach a day early.

It was becoming his sanctuary.

As long as he could continue to keep his childhood memories at bay.

And if no new room popped into existence to scramble his brain.

CHAPTER 8

Julie was right. He had to decide if his future had her in it. Soon. For both of them.

Saturday morning Micah sat in his overstuffed leather chair and watched the Pacific's horizon through a pair of Steiner binoculars, wishing the choice were simple.

Part of him wanted to be with her forever, but if the proverbial gun was pressed to his temple, he would probably decide on a life without her.

What a mess.

No question. The house was monkey wrench central. It would be a lot less complicated to dump the thing, marry Julie, and get on with RimSoft's conquest of the world.

Leave this place? It was the logical choice. But the right choice? No clue. It felt like he was playing tug-of-war—RimSoft, Seattle, and Julie on one end; the house, Cannon Beach, and Rick on the other. He was the rope.

A cool May wind swept through the open doors that led to his deck, dousing him in the chilled outside air. He grabbed his empty Tigger coffee cup and shuffled toward the kitchen. As he looked up, his fingers went limp and the mug slipped out of his hand and made a thunking sound onto the carpet. His knees weakened, and he almost joined Tigger on the floor. At the back of the kitchen was a doorway and beyond it a hall.

A hallway that had not been there before.

Micah staggered through the kitchen, through the doorway. At the end of the hall was a door. *Not again.*

Breathe.

He leaned into the wall as his legs bounced like jackhammers. Sliding down the wall to the floor, he squeezed his head with both hands.

Think!

Maybe it had been there. He thought back to his last visit. Was it there? No. Not a chance. He'd either lost his mind or someone had added a sizable addition to his house in four days.

He fought down the impulse to run. He knew he wasn't going crazy, knew the hallway wasn't there before, and knew this addition couldn't have been completed during the week he'd been in Seattle. But there was no fourth answer to defer to. He rubbed his face with both hands, stood, and gripped the dark chocolate brown, semishag carpet with his toes, as if to anchor himself to reality.

The walls of the hallway were painted in a faux gold parchment. They led to a dark, six-panel door with a brass knob. He crept toward the door. When he reached it, he inched his shaking hand up to the knob, then pushed with his pinkie finger.

The door swung open on silky hinges, and Micah let out a low whistle. The ceiling and walls were made of glass giving a 180-degree view up and down the coastline. Two chairs made from Brazilian tauari hardwood faced the front windows, and a bookshelf set along the back held what looked like picture books.

In the middle of the small room an easel held an oversized canvas. Next to it were a myriad of brushes and oil paints along with sketches and photos of ocean landscapes.

Micah stared at the canvas. A stream meandered down an ocean beach through logs rubbed smooth by winter storms, and the artist had started creating jade ocean waves. Mountains shot up in the distance, and the rough outline of trees along the shoreline had been started.

The painting exploded out at him. He could almost hear the gurgle of the stream running over sand and rock and see the wind weaving through the trees. Micah traced the edge of the beach with the tip of his finger, feeling the undulation of oil paint on canvas, imagining the soft, grainy feeling of running his hands through warm sand.

The shadows cast by the mountain felt cool, seagulls crying overhead filled his ears, and the ocean thundered, explaining everything and telling nothing.

This was creation. No photo could ever capture the emotion of a painting like this. This was legacy. It stirred a longing to create more than software. This was art worth devoting a life to. Pinpricks of joy fired off inside as he took it in. The painting wasn't even a third complete, yet it captivated him.

After twenty minutes he left the room, trepidation and pleasure filling him simultaneously. This room? Impossible. Yet it was here. He closed the door, then stood gazing at its surface. This room was a treasure. He placed his fist on the door, then slowly opened his fingers, stretching them to the point of pain, as if he could cover the whole door with his hand. The finish on the wood felt like cool silk.

This house held secrets. He shuddered and eased away from the door without taking his eyes off it. As wonderful as the painting room was, Micah had to get away, try to put the room out of his mind. One strange room he could handle; two was over the edge.

Sending him to the funny farm was apparently Archie's primary objective.

He took a spin through the rest of the house with the hair on his neck at full attention. Nothing different. It didn't help him relax.

A painting room. Okay. Yes, the painting was captivating. But what was next? A torture chamber? Worse, what if he walked into a room that was an in-living-color replay of what happened on this stretch of coast twenty years ago?

The memory flashed into his mind before he could stop it.

"Micah, Dad and Mick will be back from the store in a few, so we've got some time to play a just-you-and-me game." His mom pulled down her pale blue sunglasses and winked at him.

"Beach Ball Bonanza!" Micah said.

"You start, kiddo."

Micah grabbed the rainbow beach ball, set it up on a little mound of sand, and scuffed back ten yards, his brows furled in concentration. Then he sprinted toward the ball and kicked it hard, an *oomph* spurting out of his mouth as his foot connected, sending the ball over his mom's head.

"Mom! Wind's got it! It's going into the ocean!"

"I'll get it."

"But those waves are big monster waves—"

"They're much bigger to you than they are to me."

"But what if—?"

His mom stopped and smiled. "I'll be fine, Micah. Really."

Micah yanked his mind back from the abyss and forced the memory down into the recesses of his heart.

No. He wouldn't go there. Never. *Nice try, Archie.*

He grabbed a Diet Coke and paced through the living room, staring at the fireplace, out the windows at the storm clouds gathering over the ocean, at the hallway leading to the painting room.

Going crazy was not an option. He should get it over with, sell the place. Or simply leave and never come back. Push the house out of his mind. Get things right with Julie and move on with his life. She deserved a ring; he deserved his sanity.

He would do it. Put the house on the market and set a wedding date. Micah picked up his cell to call Julie; a second later he tossed it onto the hunter green couch in front of his fireplace.

Impossible.

Julie was right. In spite of what happened to his mom here, this place had a grip on him, and his heart was changing addresses.

Which would make their meeting on Monday a powder keg.

CHAPTER 9

Monday morning Julie walked into Micah's office, looking like a tiger that hadn't eaten in a week. Her countenance sent a clear message. He was dinner.

"Hey, how are you?"

Julie didn't answer.

Micah pulled away from his computer and leaned back in his leather chair. She stared at him, her lips pressed together so hard they were white.

"I'm sorry." He stood and hopped over to her. "I've blown it. I've been distant. Blah, blah, blah, okay?" He flashed a smile.

"Not funny. This is serious, Micah."

"I know. Really. I've been emotionally absent these past few weeks and I'm sorry." He ran his fingers down her arms and slid them into her palms.

"A few weeks? Try six." Julie yanked her hands out of Micah's grasp. "What is going on with you? You're my business partner.

And my soul mate, I thought. Both of those relationships require spending time together, talking to each other. And I need an answer about our future, one way or another."

"We have been talking." He rubbed the back of his neck and walked toward the wet bar at the back of his office to pour a Diet Coke.

"E-mail is not talking. We haven't had a conversation since our abbreviated dinner last week. Are you going to explain what's been going on with you?"

"I'm . . ."

"I need the answer now. Is our romance on hold? 'Cause that's the message coming across the line clear and sonic-boom loud."

"No. Of course not. I don't want to lose us. I'm just trying to—"

"To what, Micah? Break up gently?"

"It's hard to explain." He walked to his windows, turned, and scuffed back to his desk. "We're not on hold. Really. But things are going on inside me."

"What things? Tell me."

What could he tell her? He hated Cannon Beach because it's where his mom died? Sorry, no one knew that. But that he was also weirdly attracted to Archie's house because it felt so familiar and even peaceful? That part of him would refuse to ever face his past, but maybe a part of him was willing? Tell her the man who was always in control and knew exactly what he wanted didn't know anymore?

"I can't, Julie. Not yet. But I will. Trust me. Please?" He touched the tips of his fingers to the tips of hers, and this time she didn't pull away.

"You have to be done very, very soon, okay?" She nestled into his arms, and he held her tight.

A few minutes later Micah sighed as he watched her walk into the hall. He would be done with Cannon Beach soon. He just needed a little bit longer.

Yeah, as if all he needed was more time.

||||||

He didn't leave for the beach till Thursday night at nine for work-related reasons. But in reality they were flimsy excuses to delay arriving at a house that both drew and repelled him. *No more new rooms, Archie. Please.*

Friday morning he dropped in on Rick. Devin was out front wiping his palms on a rag dirtier than his hands.

"Anyone in the old guy's office?"

"Nah, good timing," Devin said. "Head on back."

Micah opened Rick's door and found him sitting in an ancient leather chair, head down. Indistinct mumbling came from his mouth. The sound was passionate. When Rick looked up, tears were in his eyes.

"Sorry. I didn't mean to interrupt your . . . your, uh—"

"It's called prayer, Micah." A sigh and a laugh slipped from Rick's mouth.

"You're a full-blown Christian? You're kidding me."

The instant the words slipped out he regretted it. He'd known Rick was a Christian from the moment he met him. It burst out of him like a geyser. "What a crock. Of course you are. I see it all over you."

"How are you, pal?" Rick stood, grinned, and smacked his open palm into Micah's. "Feels like it's been a year."

"For me, too."

He'd seen the man five days ago, but it seemed like five weeks. He had a connection with Rick missing from almost all his other relationships. Not true. Missing from *all* his other relationships. His other friendships were roles, acts he and they put on to cover up the truth: That they raced together on a treadmill with no finish line, too busy to really know the person running beside them.

It was that way with his board of directors, his employees, the friends he still saw, even with Julie. Everyone acted out his or her part in the play, recited his required lines, none of them knowing who the other was when the lines were gone. But with Rick there were no lines to recite. No masks to put on. Because Rick never wore one. Or did he?

Something about the man didn't compute. Something was just . . . off. Everyone was flawed—had faults, blind spots, whatever you wanted to call them. But not Rick. No cracks in his veneer. He was kind. Strong. Wise. Had a good sense of humor. It scared Micah. He could always tell the TV evangelists who had the secret perverted life going on underneath because of their perfect hair. Rick's hair wasn't, but everything else about him was. Warning. Warning. Danger, Will Robinson.

Micah forced himself to let it go. The man was one of the greatest friends he'd ever had, and he barely knew him. Innocent till proven guilty.

"You pray a lot?" Micah said.

"Jesus says the Holy Spirit will guide His followers, and His followers will hear His voice. So I'm stocking up on wisdom."

"Uh, yeah. Hope you get a huge store of it."

"What about you?"

"Nah, not me."

"You knew His voice, once. But your ears have filled up with other things. You just need to start listening again."

"Relax, Rick. Maybe my faith's cooled a little over the past few years, but I still believe God exists." Micah flopped down into a wicker chair that screeched in protest. "There's a lot more to life than reading your Bible and going to church. Worlds out there are begging to be conquered. I've just shifted my priorities around a little."

Rick stared at him.

"Hey, if you think life is about other things, I'd love to hear it."

"Really?" The corners of Rick's mouth turned up.

"Really, really."

Rick leaned forward, his eyes bright. "Jesus came to bring life. Full life. Make people whole. To break the chains wrapped around people's hearts and set them free. It's not about rules and regulations. That's religion. It's about freedom and friendship." Rick leaned back in his chair. "How free are you, Micah?"

Micah swallowed. "Life is different now." He sat up and patted his knees. "That was so long ago."

"Oh no, son, it was just a moment ago."

Micah looked out the window and searched for a response. There was none. Break the chains around his heart? He wasn't even sure his heart still existed.

When he got home, he threw on a pair of sweats and went for a long walk on the beach. At the end of the walk, he sat on a log with deep scars caused by long ocean winters and closed his eyes.

"God, what are You doing to me? I thought we understood each other. You keep Your distance; I'll keep mine. Why can't You let the past stay buried fifty feet under where it belongs? You're setting me up. Rick is setting me up. Archie is setting me up. What do You want from me? What does that house want from me? I have a life. One I love."

He stopped. What was the point in lying to God?

"Fine. Maybe Seattle isn't perfect, and maybe I have lost part of my heart, and maybe You've got something going on down here that will help me, but I don't think I want it. I know I don't want it."

Enough introspection. He stood and jogged back to his house. Tomorrow he'd wander into town. Meet a few normal people. Have a few ordinary conversations.

At least that was the plan.

CHAPTER 10

Saturday afternoon Micah strolled into Osburn's Ice Creamery on Main Street to order two scoops of frozen bliss.

The girl behind the counter dug out a double portion of Cookie Dough Hunk for the customer ahead of him as he breathed in the sugar-sweetened air and waited for his turn.

Micah glanced back and forth between the comics on the wall—some new, some faded from years of entertaining tourists with a taste for Rocky Road and Chocolate Chip Mint—and the girl with shoulder-length dark walnut hair. A wayward strand draped across her eye. Tiny dimples set off her genuine smile perfectly. Beautiful.

She was quick with the ice cream and quicker to share a smile with the tourists on their way to a cold sugar high. "Hi. What can I get for you?"

Micah gazed out the window and watched the tourists meander down the sidewalk, thinking about how radically different this world was from the one back in Seattle.

"Ice cream! Anyone up for ice cream today?" The girl pretended to call out to the whole crowd before turning back to Micah. Her smile filled the room.

"Sorry. Yeah, ice cream." He looked into her eyes and saw laughter behind them, then glanced at her left ring finger. No gold.

"What flavor is calling to you today?"

"Pralines and Cream, definitely."

"Ah, he goes for the slightly plain ice cream with just enough flavor to avoid the 'vanilla' label." She brushed the hair away from her face, but it drifted back down.

"Do you always give personality profiles to people based on their ice cream choices?"

"Only when they've just returned from a foreign land in their mind."

He smiled inside. This girl had wit.

She dug out a huge scoop of Pralines and Cream and packed it down tight. "New in town?" She handed Micah his scoop on a waffle cone and winked.

"Aren't all the tourists?" He handed her a five-dollar bill over the top of the Plexiglas ice cream case. She took it, bumped the cash register with her hip, and the drawer opened.

"You're not a tourist." She gazed at him with the hint of a challenge in her double-shot espresso brown eyes. He waited for her to explain how she knew that, but she reached into a register overflowing with Georges and Abes and handed him his change without comment.

"And what, Ms. Sherlock, is your first name?"

"Watson," she said with a twinkle in her eyes but no smile on her lips. "But I only let my friends call me that." She turned to the next person in line and asked for his order.

Micah eased over to the side of the cash register. "So how'd you figure out I'm not a tourist?"

She started working on a triple scoop of Strawberry Cheesecake for the next customer. "Most of the tourists stay the weekend, a week, maybe even two. Then they go home. So since you've been frequenting these parts for six or seven, I figured you were down here for more than a few pictures."

Micah blinked. "And you know I've been here off and on for seven weeks because . . . ?"

She glanced at him, one corner of her mouth turned up, but didn't reply.

"You the owner?" Micah took the first bite of his ice cream.

"No, why do you want to know?" She looked away to make change for a Vanilla Fudge Ripple customer.

"Well, I feel I have an obligation to let him know—"

"Let her know."

"An obligation to let *her* know her employee spies on tourists."

"Wouldn't get you anywhere. She's a spy just like me."

The girl didn't smile but Micah grinned. He toasted her with his cone. "Touché."

He turned and walked out of Osburn's, the smile staying on his face. He put buying another couple of scoops at Osburn's in the near future on his mental to-do list.

||||||||

Micah got back to the house at six-thirty that evening. After a quick run down to Haystack Rock and back, and an even quicker dinner of pot stickers and rice, he strolled toward the library. He never got there. Next to it was another new door.

Great, here we go again.

Micah paused, pushed open the door, and groped for a light switch. As he snapped it on, he eased inside. The room smelled like a winter morning and felt unnaturally still. More than the absence of noise, the silence felt like a panther ready to strike. In his peripheral vision he saw the far wall move. No. Did it?

Fear darted around the room like a bat. Micah walked in farther, refusing to lose his nerve. Against one wall from floor to ceiling were mail slots—the type seen in an old office building. Nothing else was in the room. Each mail slot was six-by-three inches, with off-white paint peeling from the edges. Each held papers. Most were crammed full; others held only one. All were yellowed, some stained with water, some with corners torn off.

The room was wrong.

When he reached the slots, his hand seemed to move in slow motion toward the first paper. Just before he touched it, something inside said stop.

Too late.

The instant his forefinger touched the parchment, his stomach twisted as if he were free-falling from ten thousand feet. He turned and looked at the door. It was shut. He knew he'd left it open, but it hardly mattered. Micah forced himself to stay calm as he opened the parchment. A series of headlines scrawled on the paper described memories of deep pain from his childhood.

His favorite Hot Wheels car getting smashed by his dad at age six.

His fourth-grade teacher joking that he was "Mindless Micah" almost every day during class for the entire year because he couldn't understand the problems.

Headline after headline about what he had missed, lost, failed at, and what had been stolen from him—the sting as fresh as when they'd first happened.

Halfway down the page he pulled away and looked up. It would've been better if he'd kept his eyes on the paper.

The wall in front of him was covered with moving pictures of more disappointments. He spun to his right to avoid them. It was futile. Every wall—even the floor—played grainy, mini-film scenes from his life, as if an old Super 8 camera had recorded every emotional scar from childhood and was replaying them all at once.

A girl promising she'd go with him to the seventh-grade dance then dumping him for his supposed best friend.

Being bullied on and off by Brandon Kopec during his freshman year of high school.

Dropping the game-winning touchdown pass in front of the whole school in tenth grade and getting ridiculed by his teammates for weeks afterward.

He dropped the parchment, tried to steady himself against the wall to his right, and fought the vise grip clenching his stomach. Micah stared in fascination and fear as the images came faster, now covering the ceiling as well.

Cut from the basketball team his sophomore year because one of the coaches' pet players spread the lie that Micah was smoking pot.

Chewed up and spit out by his boss for ruining a stack of wood at the sign company at sixteen. "*You idiot! I should call you Scarecrow. Get a brain!*" His boss swore for thirty seconds straight, jabbing his finger like a metronome into Micah's collarbone.

Micah sank to the floor and gasped for air. He felt as if twenty-foot waves were pounding him into the sand. As the torrent assaulted him, part of his mind shouted, "This isn't real!" But his body wouldn't listen. He struggled to get to his knees. Not possible.

He wanted to strike out. At anything. Everything. Rage and rejection slammed into his mind.

Come on! He had to get control.

He raised his arm, as if he could block the hurricane of emotions.

Clarity. Have to focus. It . . . is . . . not . . . real!

But it was.

The memories jumped back and forth across the years and went faster.

"Leave him alone!" he shouted as he watched his fifth-grade basketball coach scream at his younger self for missing a free throw in the last game of the season.

Tears formed as he watched his three best friends from junior high go to the Alanis Morissette concert without him, laughing about how they'd been able to ditch Micah.

He lashed out with his arms. "Help me."

No answer.

"If You're here, help me!"

All the images vanished.

Silence.

It was over.

Wasn't it?

An instant later a scene filled the entire back wall of the room. A nine-year-old Micah ran along the beach, stumbling, lips trembling, deep lines of worry etched into his face.

"No." A moan escaped his lips and surged into a guttural scream. "Not this."

"Come back, Mom! Come back!"

Micah leaped into the air, straining to see out over the ocean. The boy spun and screamed north up the beach, "Help her! Help my mom!" He turned south and screamed again. He started to run toward the row of houses behind him. Two quick paces before he stopped, turned, and ran back to where he'd started, his bare feet kicking sand onto a Spider-Man beach towel.

Then he froze, not knowing which way to go. What to do.

Micah's mind continued to scream what he was seeing wasn't real; his heart screamed louder it was all too genuine. "This will kill me. I can't do this. Can't see this. I need You, God." The last part was a whisper.

The young Micah leaped into the air, legs shaking, eyes filled with tears. Micah now watched himself scream again and again and again.

He huddled on the carpet on his side, knees held up to his chest.

"God, help me!"

The room shifted. Hope appeared inside like a pinprick of light in a black sky. The pain receded somewhat. Breathing came easier. The tentacles of fear wrapped around his mind loosened. But not enough.

"Please help me." He didn't know if he'd said it out loud or only in his mind.

The struggle raged on.

The younger Micah knelt in the sand now, sobbing. A man sprinted past him into the waves. His father.

"Don't make me face it!" Micah shouted at the scene.

He wasn't going to make it.

Micah slid into darkness.

In that instant it came. A flash of light, then peace, and a sensation he hadn't felt in years—the presence of God.

Silence. This time it remained.

The peace built till he was able to get off the floor and stumble through the door, through the house, into the star-filled night, onto the beach.

He reached the sand, collapsed, and let the tears come.

|||||||

When he awoke, the sun had climbed halfway to noon. He guessed it was as late as nine o'clock. He rubbed his eyes, stumbled to his feet, and eased toward the ocean.

People clad in bright jackets ambled up the beach. Three kids filled the sky with their multicolored kites, laughing as they kicked up little clouds of sand with their dark feet, racing to keep their flying machines aloft.

It made last night seem like a dream.

Maybe it was just a nightmare.

But he knew it wasn't. God had rescued him. Right? Or was He the one who pushed Micah into that room?

But he'd felt God, just like he did back in high school. At least he thought it was God. Maybe it wasn't.

Micah stood in the surf, and his stomach churned—maybe from hunger, possibly from the thought of going back inside. Probably a combination. The thought of facing that room again made hackles dance on his neck. He paced in two inches of water for ten minutes. But there was no way he would let one of Archie's rooms have control over him.

As he trudged toward his house like a climber taking the final steps to the top of K2, strong gusts pushed gray clouds off the ocean, blocking the sun.

He stepped inside, his sight roving from the fireplace to the circular staircase leading upstairs, to the hallway, to the kitchen, back to the fireplace. Looked normal. Even felt normal. After grabbing a bagel and an apple, he stepped back outside onto his deck.

He needed a moment to settle his thoughts.

A gust of wind smacked into him, almost tearing the food out of his hand. Must be blowing thirty or forty knots. Rain swept in a few seconds later, pelting him with fat drops. Families and couples jogged off the beach, hoods pulled over their heads. A storm was brewing. Micah shook his head. Perfect metaphor for what was happening in his brain.

As bizarre as the room was, he wanted to fight. To conquer his fear of the past. He marched inside and headed for the memory room. A cold blanket of sweat broke out across his back.

"Don't . . . back . . . down. You want me to face what happened here all those years ago, Archie? All right. Let's do it."

As he walked down the hallway toward the door, Micah bowed his head and wiped the sweat from his palms on the side of his jeans.

When he reached the door, he wouldn't hesitate; he'd walk right in. But he didn't get the chance. The door was gone. Where it had been was now smooth wall. No evidence it had ever been there.

It wasn't a comfort.

He sucked in two quick breaths.

Micah tramped back down the hall toward the living room. When he reached the fireplace, he slumped to the floor, head in hands. This was not a dream. There would be no waking up. He checked his pulse with clammy fingers. Clammy? They were wet.

Yeah, maybe God had come through. Or Micah might simply be turning into a certifiable whacko.

A peal of thunder rolled over the house just before a flash of lightning filled the room. Micah didn't bother to look up.

But it was over, right? He'd faced his mom's death, and that was enough. Done. He'd never have to go there ever again.

If only more of him believed it.

He fumbled in his pocket. Yes. He pulled out his cell phone and called the one person who might have a clue about what was going on.

CHAPTER 11

"Hello?"

"Rick, it's Micah." He stood with his forehead pressed against one of his picture windows and watched the ocean churn.

"Hey, buddy."

Micah didn't say anything. Telling someone his house was alive wasn't something he'd been trained on in the corporate world.

"You there?"

"Yeah, I . . . need to talk." Micah eased over to his river-rock fireplace and stared at the smooth stones. "About my house. And God."

"Okay."

Where to start? Not with the house or the memory room. He didn't even want to talk to himself about it. Start with the God-stuff. "I think it's time to check Him out again. Maybe. A little bit anyway."

"*Star Wars.*"

"What?"

"Episode V, *The Empire Strikes Back*. Yoda. 'Try not. Do or do not. There is no try.'"

"You're quoting Yoda?"

Rick chuckled. "Truth is truth whether it comes out of the mouth of God or the mouth of Baal."

"Pretty profound."

"That's not mine; it's George MacDonald."

"Who?"

"Not important. Want to tell me what happened?"

"Yeah. But not sure how much I want to tell." Micah glanced at black ashes in the fireplace hearth. Good time for another fire.

"Say as much as you want to. But don't say less than that either," Rick said.

By the time flames dodged around three red cedar logs up the chimney, Micah had told his friend every detail except the scene with his mom. About the shrine room, the painting room, the memory room, his crying out to God and how it ended with God's presence surrounding him.

"What's going on with me?" Micah said.

"You really need me to answer that question?"

"Yeah."

"God is grabbing your heart, drawing you back."

"Not sure I want to be drawn back."

There was only silence on the other end of the phone.

"So, was the memory room my imagination? I went back the next day, and it wasn't there. C'mon. Am I having hallucinations or just losing my mind?" Micah stood and walked back to the place in the hall where the memory room had been. "God might be in this, but I don't want to be in my own house anymore."

"Einstein felt, at most, man had attained 1 percent of the possible knowledge of the universe. Do you think it's possible God

is able to do unexplainable things with the 99 percent we don't
understand?"

Micah sighed. "Maybe."

"Then trust Him." Rick cleared his throat. "But I will admit, if
that room was for real, it sounds like you have a fairly extraordinary
house. And I'd guess this is just the beginning."

"Great."

Micah hung up and threw a few things into his Adidas tote bag.
He wasn't going to spend the night. The house was extraordinary?
Try freak show. It was time to head for Seattle. Get back to a world
of sanity and order. A world he could control.

‖‖‖‖‖

The next week at RimSoft proceeded like clockwork. Every meeting. Every phone call. Every software test.

Late Thursday afternoon he went to his office window and
watched little beads of rain scurry down the pane like ants on their
way to a picnic. His team was working like a Swiss watch—precise
and efficient. It was the best of times. RimSoft had just announced
a 23 percent rise in sales for the quarter. The week before a vendor
handed him a Seattle Seahawks suite. Another gave him an Italian
cruise for eight friends and him aboard the *Wind Surf* anytime he
wanted to go. And market share for each of their products was
climbing.

Micah paced in front of his desk and tried to feel like a little kid
at Christmas again. These were grown-up presents few ever found
under the tree. He should be thrilled. He sat at his computer, and
a few seconds later a satellite image of Cannon Beach filled his
screen. After a few minutes of staring at his house from above, he
shot an e-mail to Shannon giving her the Italian cruise. She would
enjoy it much more than he would.

He scratched the back of his head and stood, then continued pacing. What was wrong with him?

That weekend he stayed in Seattle to break up his routine. That's what he told himself. Reality was the house had spooked him into staying in town. Maybe Rick was right; God was in it. But maybe his dad was right, and Archie had built a haunted mansion that would eventually kill him.

Micah played basketball on Saturday, then took himself to a movie that night. He should have seen it with Julie. Why didn't he ask her? She was smart, beautiful, and perfect at those cocktail parties where she always seemed to meet just the right people to bring them more contracts worth millions. An ideal business partner in the boardroom and on the schmooze circuit. They were perfect for each other. And they looked great together on the cover of *Fast Company*. Perfect couple. Perfect life.

Next month they'd be featured on the cover of *Wired*.

He tried to care about being on top of the world, but the emotion flitted away like a startled hummingbird. His life with RimSoft and Julie was a movie set. Picture-perfect buildings from the front, every blade of grass in place; but when you went around the back, there was nothing but two by fours propping up a facade.

||||||

Monday morning Micah walked through Schmitz Park, a lush green paradise even longtime Seattle residents sometimes weren't aware of. Earmarked in the early 1900s for preservation by the city, it boasted long, winding paths running from the north side of Alki Point almost two miles south into the heart of West Seattle's residential district.

In the center of the park, he sat down and gazed at the massive maple tree above him. A seedling whirled slowly down, back and forth like it was on an invisible string, till it landed on his knee. A feeling of peace flavored with hope and adventure settled on him. An emotion he never felt in Seattle anymore. One he felt almost constantly in Cannon Beach.

After roaming the trails for a few more minutes, he called Shannon.

"You're not at the office," she said.

"I took a walk."

"A what? A walk? You took a walk?"

"Yeah. In a park."

"Instead of coming in to work?"

"Yes." Micah ambled toward his car.

"The temptation to ask why is bubbling out of me."

"Don't."

"Then at least tell me if you came to any great conclusions about life, liberty, and the pursuit of software."

"Actually, I did. And because of those conclusions, I need you to check and see if Julie's free for lunch today. Or for an afternoon meeting. And if that's booked, then dinner or breakfast and so on."

"My internal radar says big change is coming."

"Yeah."

"Should I notify a disaster cleanup crew about the meeting?"

"Not a bad idea."

|||||||

At one o'clock he walked toward Julie's office with his heart ticking at least a few beats faster than normal. It wasn't every day you dropped a nuclear bomb on your partner's desk.

She didn't look up as he walked in.

"We need to talk, Julie."

"Okay." Her eyes stayed riveted on her computer screen. "Are we still on hold? Or are you ready to give me an answer?"

"That's what I came to talk to you about."

"So this is the official breakup?"

"Not exactly."

She stood and walked toward him, drumming her fingers on her arm in a staccato rhythm.

"I'm going to start working from the beach for a while."

"You're what?" Julie's eyes narrowed. "One more time, please?"

"I'm going to split my time between working down there and working up here, mostly down there. Work fewer hours."

"You are not seriously saying this."

He leaned in toward her. "Yeah, I am, Julie. I am seriously saying it."

She stalked to the window, then whirled to face him. "You're insane. Look around you. It's not the time to kick back. You think you're going to telecommute? Yeah, that'll work great. It'll infuse the stockholders with massive confidence. Once the press gets a hold of it, I'm sure our sales will go through the roof. Plus it'll suck the last breath of life out of our relationship." Julie turned back to the window. "All I wanted was a ring."

"I'm not breaking up!" Micah said louder than he intended. He rubbed his hands on his pants and glanced at the ceiling, as if it would give him the right words. "I just need to get away from here, do some thinking down there."

"What will you think about? This company is your life."

She was right. His entire identity was wrapped up in the company, which made his choice both crazy and exhilarating. What did he have in Cannon Beach? Memories he didn't want to face, a seriously bizarre house that nearly killed him, and a friend twenty-three years his senior. Where was the draw in all that? Yet there was a draw. Deeper and more alive than anything he'd felt in years.

Julie lifted her palms. "Let's pretend I agree to something that idiotic and pretend you're not breaking up with me. What would you do with your extra time? Learn to fly a kite? Start painting again? Cook?!"

"Maybe."

"I'm serious."

"So am I."

What *would* he do down there? He could only take beach runs and hang with Rick for so long. Three weeks and he'd go nuts. His life had been so ordered and driven for so many years he wasn't sure what to do next. Free time? What was that? His iPhone was almost grafted onto his body. Between his to-do list and Shannon's reminders, every moment for the past six years had been filled with goals, appointments, setting vision for the company, and worlds to conquer.

Julie sighed, walked over to Micah, and took his hands. "It's just me. Let's talk. No partnership. No RimSoft. No stock options. Just me before we gained the world."

They stared at each other, Micah trying to tell her with his eyes why he needed this. Julie asking with hers how he could put the kingdom they'd sweated blood for on hold.

"I need to be there. Stay a while. Figure some things out."

"Figure what out?"

"I don't know. God maybe."

"God? Are you kidding?" Julie pulled away and scowled. "I thought you gave up the Jesus-freak thing back in college."

"This place, it's . . . I'm drawn to it. I need to . . . I want to, find out . . . Come with me to Cannon Beach." He looked into her eyes. "See what God is up to down there."

"Wow. The 'God told me to go' argument. Insurmountable. And completely whacko."

"Come with me."

Julie closed her eyes. "You know that old Robert Frost poem about two roads diverging in the middle of the woods? You're going down one road; I'm headed down the other."

"Julie, no."

She leaned toward him and kissed him on the cheek. "Goodbye, Micah."

||||||

Micah made it to Cannon Beach by five o'clock, the emotion of his talk with Julie completely faded by the time he arrived. He stopped at Rick's to gas up before heading to the house. As Devin stretched his undersized dough-boy frame over Micah's BMW to clean the windshield, Micah snuck up on Rick who was bent over the engine of a late-model Nissan.

Micah slapped him on his side and kept moving around to his right. "Hey, buddy!"

Rick straightened, almost whacking his head on the car's hood. "What're you doing here this early in the week? RimWare handing out sick days?"

"RimSoft."

"It's not RimWare? That would be a great name for your company. Rim*ware*, soft*ware*. Get it? You're sure it's not RimWare?"

"Pretty sure. Always been, always will be RimSoft."

Rick stared at him for a few seconds. "Right." He motioned up the street, and they walked onto the sidewalk and strolled toward a small park fifty yards north of his garage.

"Made a decision," Micah said once they reached the park and could see the ocean.

"Yeah?"

As Micah explained his plan to work part time from Cannon Beach, a smile formed on Rick's face.

"You're not surprised."

"The draw of this place can be powerful." Rick's grin grew.

"Tell me how you knew. I'm serious."

"So am I. This place can be a magnet for certain kinds of people at certain points in their lives." Rick folded his arms and turned toward the sea.

"There's more to it than that."

"You've got it all—looks, youth, money, fame, career." Rick motioned wide with his arms out toward the water. "But a long time ago you had more. A lot more. You had the Lord. So much of Him in fact, you knew the other things on the list didn't matter. Maybe He's torching the list."

"Maybe I don't want it torched."

"Your choice. Choose wisely."

Micah gave him a crooked smile. "C'mon, Rick. Don't hold back, no time to be shy here. Say what you really think."

Micah laughed, and Rick joined him as they trudged back to Rick's garage.

"Breakfast at the Fireside on Saturday?" Rick asked as Micah got into his car.

"Absolutely."

|||||||

Rick watched Micah's BMW till it crested the hill and vanished from sight. "And so, Mr. Micah's even wilder ride begins."

CHAPTER 12

On Friday, Micah grabbed his mountain bike and rode north toward Cannon Beach. He took the Cannon Beach Loop Road exit and rode past fifty or so gray houses, none with the view their richer brothers west of them had of the ocean. He rode on, past the Tolovana Inn, then past the Ocean Lodge and the Stephanie Inn, luxury hotels just steps from the sand.

The sun poked holes in the fog, warming him inside and out. Perfect day for riding. Perfect day to run into that girl from the ice cream store. He laughed at himself. Couldn't fault a guy for dreaming.

He wound up the hill that overlooked Haystack Rock, where houses were separated by inches, perched on the cliff leading down to the beach like rabid fans looking for a movie star's autograph.

The Sand Trap Inn—with the picture of a B.C. cartoon character swinging a golf club—whizzed by on his right, and then he was down the hill onto Cannon Beach's Main Street, with shop after shop filled with trinkets and books and art for the coffee table or wall back home. Some wonderful, some that would end up on a garage sale table ten months later.

The town blurred by in thirty seconds. A minute after that, he rode over Ecola Creek, took a right-hand turn, and started up the winding mile-and-a-half road that led to Ecola State Park.

As he leaned into the first corner, his peripheral vision caught something up ahead. Fifty yards in front of him the sun flashed against another bike, and dark chestnut hair swirled against the wind as the rider's head turned for an instant.

Looked like the girl from Osburn's.

Micah squinted and called out, "Hey, Watson!"

She didn't turn.

He put his head down and strained to catch her. But Micah didn't gain an inch as he pushed through the canopy of Sitka spruce trees lining the road.

When the park entrance came into view, he prayed she wouldn't ride another two miles to Indian Beach and was rewarded as she swung left down to Ecola. He coasted down the gradual decline into the parking lot and found her sitting on a picnic table, arms wrapped around her knees, looking out toward Tillamook Rock Lighthouse.

She glanced back as his bike brakes squealed, announcing his arrival, but didn't say anything.

"Hey." Micah approached her with stutter steps, his legs still straddling his bike. "We met the other day at Osburn's."

"Mr. Pralines, if I remember right." She spun to face him and flashed a smile.

"Good seeing you again, Watson."

It seemed funny before it came out of his mouth. But it fell flat when she simply said, "Thanks."

"You ride up here often?"

"Mostly during the off-season. Too many summer seekers driving this road during this time of the year, and it's a narrow road."

"I noticed."

"So, are you staying right in town?"

"No, a little bit south," Micah said.

"I'm Sarah Sabin."

"Micah Taylor."

Sarah nodded.

They looked at each other a moment past awkward. Micah got off his bike, leaned it against the picnic table, and shifted his weight from one leg to the other.

"Want to walk down to where the trail washed out?" she asked, breaking the silence.

"Sure."

From the look of Sarah's long, muscular legs and her gait, he guessed her athleticism wasn't limited to biking.

When they stopped, Haystack Rock, three miles south, filled their view. Below them a beach stretched a quarter mile before it stopped at a small cape jutting out into the ocean. Four otters ducked in and out of the swells one hundred feet down.

"Crescent Beach," Sarah offered. "You used to be able to walk down there from here. Not anymore. A winter mud slide washed out the trail back in '94, and they never rebuilt it."

Bits of the old wooden railing leading down to the beach were still visible. They walked in silence until they found a flat spot of grass to sit on with a perfect view of Haystack Rock and Cannon Beach in the distance.

Sarah rubbed her left knee, and when she took her hand away, it revealed three small scars, two on either side of her kneecap and one in the middle.

Micah nodded at her knee. "That's from?"

"ACL surgery."

"How'd the injury happen?"

She took so long to answer Micah wondered if she'd heard him. When she did, it was in a whisper. "Olympic trials in '02."

"Winter Olympics. Skiing?"

"Yeah."

"Wait a minute. You're *that* Sarah Sabin? Cover of *Sports Illustrated*, supposed to win more gold than any other American female in history?"

She turned to him with a small smile and nodded. "After two surgeries and three years of trying to come back, I decided it was time to start another life, so five years ago I came here." She ripped up tufts of grass, threw them up, and let them float toward the ocean in the light breeze. "Got away from the sport, the pressure, and the guilt people loaded me down with for ruining their dream."

"Shouldn't it have been your dream?"

She laughed. "It was, but others wanted to jump on board and do that whole live-vicariously-through-me thing."

"Your dad, right?"

"With him, just the opposite. He was one of the few who truly didn't care how I did on the slopes. He taught me to ski, was my coach for most of my career. He believed in me, was my champion but never once pushed me to be something I didn't want to be. Dad loved me fiercely." Sarah turned her head away. "I miss him so much."

Loved fiercely by your dad? He had no clue what that would feel like. Miss him? His dad had slaughtered any chance of having that emotion when Micah was a kid. Still, he blinked three times before he spoke.

"How'd he die?"

"Cancer. Four years ago."

"I'm sorry about your dad. Sorry about the injury, too."

"Don't be. Sometimes I can't help but wonder what might have been, but I don't have the slightest regret."

"How can you not have regrets?"

"God works all for good." She looked out over the ocean. "If not for the accident and my dad's death, I think I'd be in a radically different world. Not a good one. One without God in it."

Micah shifted his gaze to three sea lions basking on the rocks below them.

He knew the radically different world she would have lived in. It was the one he lived in now. Maybe it wasn't such a good idea getting to know this girl. He didn't need someone else needling him about the God-stuff.

"So that's my dad; tell me about yours."

"No."

Sarah laughed. "No? Just no? You have a dad, don't you?" She leaned back on her elbows and looked up at him.

"Yep. Still alive."

"And . . . ?"

"Kind of an off-limits subject."

"Got it."

Great. First the God-stuff, now questions about his dad. Julie never tried to make him go deep like this.

He fished a twig out of grass and tossed it toward the ocean. "If you've been here five years, you must know everyone."

"The locals still say I'm new in town, but they're friendly, and yeah, I know most of them." She pulled on the silver loop in her ear and smiled.

"Maybe you could introduce me around. Love to find out about the land my house is built on. Its history."

"House?"

"I inherited a home just south of Arcadia Beach State Park."

"There are six or seven homes along that stretch. Could you add some vagueness to your description?" She winked.

"It's on the ocean. Does that help?"

"Oh, that one. Of course!" Sarah laughed.

"It's kinda hard to miss. About nine thousand square feet."

"Wow, that's big. I'm not sure I know it."

He couldn't tell if she was teasing or not. She was bright and would know if a nine-thousand-square-foot home was built in a small town like Cannon Beach.

"You've got to be kidding." Micah chuckled. "It's probably the biggest home from Astoria to Tillamook. And I mean right on the beach."

"Does that make it tough when the tide comes in?"

"Are you always that literal?"

A grin broke out on Sarah's face, and Micah matched it with one of his own.

"So how'd it wind up with you?"

She didn't say this with envy or curiosity or even judgment. He suspected the answer wouldn't matter to her either way. He liked that. "Long story."

"I'd like to hear it sometime."

It wasn't a come-on. He knew it and she knew he knew it. Another friend in Cannon Beach. Hmm. Could be a good thing. As long as the conversations avoided God and dads.

"How 'bout dinner on Tuesday? No charge for a tour of the house or the story."

"Tuesday nights I have a standing date with twenty-three men and women who aren't as mobile as they once were."

"Old folks home?"

"Mature folks home. I read to them, laugh with them." She paused. "Sometimes cry. It's cliché to say, I know, but I get more out of it than they do."

Micah wondered if he should ask for another night, but Sarah saved him the trouble.

"Thursday night is open, if your invitation is still on the table."

Her dark chocolate-colored eyes twinkled at him, and he assured her it was.

As he rode home, he thought about Julie. Was there any hope for them? Did she care anymore? Did he?

And what about this Sarah girl? He wasn't ready for another relationship. Micah shifted his bike into a higher gear and bore down on the pedals.

What was he worried about? It was just one dinner.

CHAPTER 13

Thursday Micah woke early. He wanted the dinner to be perfect and gave himself the whole day to prepare. By the time the sun started its descent toward the sea, he was ready to entertain the mysterious Sarah Sabin.

At 5:57 p.m. the doorbell echoed through the house like a wind chime. Micah glanced in the mirror, smoothed his hair with both hands, clipped toward the door, and opened it.

"Hi, Micah." Sarah smiled.

Wow. Beautiful. Remember, pal, you're not 100 percent sure things between you and Julie are over. Just friends with Sarah, okay? The hint of her perfume made him repeat the thought.

"Hi, Sarah." He tried not to stare. Radiant.

"Can I come in?"

"Oh, sorry."

After Sarah stepped inside, she drifted toward the picture windows. "Wow. That's an amazing view." She gazed slowly around the great room. "I love this place already. You inherited it from your uncle?"

"Great-uncle."

He took her coat and went back to the entryway closet to hang it up. He'd never opened it. The pegs by the front door had worked fine. His eyes narrowed. A stack of letters sat on the shelf, up against the right edge of the closet wall. He pulled them down. They were tied together with twine, and the edges of the envelopes went from yellow at the top to slightly faded on the bottom. The return name and address on the top envelope were Archie's, but the letter was mailed to a Christopher Hale. In smaller print at the bottom was "Attention: Micah Taylor."

His head spun. He riffled through the first five or six envelopes. Same mailing address, same return address. He drew in a sharp, shallow breath. Would these letters answer the house questions ricocheting through his head? They had to. Finally!

"Micah?"

Sarah's voice broke through the world he'd fallen into, and he pulled away from the door.

"I'm sorry, it's just that I found, well . . ." he trailed off, not knowing what or how much he wanted to say.

She graciously moved away from him, toward his picture windows. "You never knew him?"

"Who?" Micah was still returning to the present. He set the letters back on the shelf, then closed the door.

"This great-uncle of yours."

"No. Even my dad doesn't know much about him." Micah paused. "Or won't say."

Sarah meandered over to the built-in shelves packed with hundreds of books on history, photography, art, fiction, and biographies, and tilted her head, probably to read the titles.

"You a book lover?" Micah asked.

She gave a slight nod. "If you gave me five thousand dollars to spend in any store, I'd head straight for Barnes & Noble."

"Are you asking for my checkbook?"

Sarah glanced at him and laughed, then looked back at the books.

Micah moved into the kitchen, noticed a coffee stain on the counter, and licked his thumb. Sarah came over as he got the last of it off the granite.

"Nice clean-up method."

"You don't miss much, do you?" Micah looked up, his face warm.

"Sorry. I could be a little more tactful." She sat on a maple stool next to the counter.

"Not a problem. Most women—"

"—are catty and smile at your face, then stab you in the back. It's one reason why I've never had a lot of girlfriends. I had more friends in high school who were guys."

"So you don't believe in the WHMS Rule?" He moved over to the refrigerator and grabbed two Diet Cokes.

"You lost me."

"The *When Harry Met Sally* Rule. That guys and girls can't be friends. Never saw the movie?"

"Yes, I saw it. I never wanted to believe it, but I will confess most times it's true."

"You know this from personal experience?"

"All through high school and college, I'd ask the guy if we were just friends, he'd say 'oh yes, friends only,' and in the end he'd reluctantly confess he'd been secretly in love with me the whole time."

"It's the way guys are made," Micah confessed. "They promise they want to be buds only, but they tend to be attracted to the girl from the beginning."

"So where does that leave us?"

Micah fell back against the pantry doors as if shot and laughed. "I see what you mean about the tact thing."

"You mean the direct thing?"

"Yeah, that's what I meant." He walked over to her, poured their Cokes, and sat on the bar stool next to her.

"So where does that leave us?" The laughter in her eyes disappeared.

"Simple. We're not friends."

"*Really.* Then please provide the definition of our relationship."

Micah pretended to take out a calculator and punch imaginary numbers into it. After a few seconds he looked up from under his eyebrows. "This is our third meeting so we're good acquaintances. I have a girlfriend back home. If a man has a girlfriend and the person of the opposite sex is informed of it within the first four meetings, he's allowed to develop a strictly platonic relationship. Since I let you know this in only our third meeting, we're ahead of schedule and off to an extremely good start."

Did he have a girlfriend back home? No. Julie had made it pretty clear they were finished. He might as well admit it. But not out loud.

"Cheers then. To a fruitful acquaintanceship." She winked and raised her glass.

"Is that a word?"

"As of now, yes."

They smacked their glasses together just hard enough for a smattering of pop to spill over the sides.

Micah suggested they go out on the deck. Walking beside Sarah across the tan carpet, he easily fell into her rhythm and it stirred something inside he couldn't put a name to. It wasn't infatuation or a crush. He wouldn't even call it romantic. *Natural* was the best word to describe it.

"How 'bout you? Have a boyfriend?"

"No."

She looked at him without elaboration, so he asked the obvious follow-up question. "How long have you been broken up?"

"Why do you think it was recent?" She poked him in the side.

"A girl as beautiful and smart as you is simply not allowed to be single for more than six months. Eight months max. The rules won't allow it."

"Really?" Sarah folded her arms across her chest. "And what do the rules say about telling an acquaintance she is beautiful when the said prevaricator of the line has a girlfriend named Julie?"

"The judges allow it providing three things: It has to be true, it has to be said without any romantic atmosphere or intent clouding the issue, and finally, *beautiful* has to be said within the context of explaining a mystery, like why you aren't with anyone right now. Not just said on its own for the sake of saying it," Micah said.

"Ah. Thanks for the clarification. At least we met two of the requirements."

"No prospects on the horizon?"

"I've sworn off guys." She pulled her hair behind her ears. "I'm done with boyfriends for a long, long time. Finished. Over." A defiant look filled her eyes, and she didn't smile.

Micah tried to laugh, but it died on his lips as Sarah turned away. He didn't expect such a vehement statement from her. Why send him the message with such force?

Silence stretched to an awkward twenty seconds.

"Uh, is that a subject you'd like to elaborate on?"

"Not even the hint of a chance." Sarah walked over to the far end of the deck and leaned against the railing.

Micah waited a few seconds before easing over to her. "Listen, dinner won't be done for another fifteen minutes, how 'bout a tour of the house?"

She faced him, smiled, and the somber feeling lingering in the air vanished. "I'd love to, but what if we took a little walk on he beach instead?"

"Sure, tide's out, great time for a short walk."

||||||

The aroma of Cornish game hen and garlic mashed potatoes greeted them as they walked back inside ten minutes later. Pear and walnuts over greens was first, followed by artichokes with melted butter for dipping, angel hair pasta, and the hen. They topped the meal off with banana bread.

"Impressive," Sarah said with the hint of a tease.

"Hey, c'mon now. Maybe I didn't make the banana bread. Or the pasta. Or the salad. But I melted the butter and got the hen right."

"It was a compliment. Seriously. Most guys our age wouldn't have a clue about putting on a meal like this."

"Well, thanks, but really I just got lucky. I haven't done a lot of cooking, but I've been practicing. One of those 'I'll do it someday' things. Being down here is someday, I guess."

"And how long are you staying 'down here'?"

"That is indeed the $64 million-dollar question."

They walked into the great room toward the fireplace. He motioned to the couch, but she chose the floor in front of the river rock so he did the same and built a fire while they talked.

"I'm working from down here for a while. Seattle is my permanent home, so I go back every couple of weeks to make sure things are running smoothly."

Their conversation turned to high school, college, sports they'd played, and favorite movies. They talked for an hour before Micah realized he'd been doing most of the telling.

"You're good." He laid his arm across his chest and bowed his head a little.

"At what?"

"Asking questions."

Sarah smiled but didn't comment.

"I've been talking. You have not been talking."

"Is that bad?" she said.

"No, I'd just like to know more about your history. I already know my own."

"But then how mysterious would I be?" She grinned.

Micah watched the flames of the fire shift and dance as he thought about the woman sitting beside him. She was smart and beautiful. Playful. And she *was* mysterious. Sure of herself but not in a cocky way. She knew who she was with no pretension. During most first dates—yes, he admitted it was a date—he watched women play a role, presenting as perfect a package as possible. He'd done the same.

Even Julie and he still jockeyed and positioned themselves. For power. For protection. Not this time. Sarah had somehow disarmed him, and he'd told more about himself than he wanted to. She'd told almost nothing about herself. Why the swearing off guys? What happened to her?

The glow of the fire streaked her walnut hair with lines of gold, and he let himself go to merely enjoy the moment.

After dessert they walked out onto the deck, and a rare coastal treat greeted them: the stars. Not all. Just a few breaks in the clouds. But enough diamonds on black canvas to be captivating.

Sarah glanced back to the house. "I can see why he gave you the home. It reminds me of you."

"What?"

She gave him a light smile, as if it were obvious.

"I'll admit whoever decorated this place found my style."

"It's more than style. It feels like you."

His heart agreed, but his mind wouldn't accept it. This wasn't his place. "I don't know. Maybe. But like I said, this stuff isn't mine."

"You don't have to own something for it to be you. Haven't you ever gone into a gallery and seen a painting and said 'that's me'? Or had a piece of music capture something deep down you didn't even know was there? You realize it's always been part of you; you've just never heard it before."

Micah stared at her. She had just unearthed a place in his heart that said "you're home." Maybe he'd known it all along. Maybe that was the reason he hadn't gotten around to selling the house.

He turned away. "Yeah, I know the feeling." He didn't add he was having the feeling right then. "Midnight beach walk?" It was late, but the words slipped out of his mouth before he could stop them. He saw conflict in her eyes.

Sarah shook her head. "Next time."

At her car Micah thanked her for coming. She returned the sentiment with her eyes. He stared at the road long after the bright red of her taillights disappeared down Highway 101.

She made him feel like he was ripping through the water on a slalom water ski on a Seattle summer morning, when the shade was cool but the sun would warm him in minutes; when the lightest of breezes darted through the air like sparrows playing tag; when the smell of western red cedar made him want to climb Mount Rainier or soak in a sunset over the Olympic Mountains.

Not exactly platonic emotions.

As he ambled back to his house, kicking a small round stone like it was a soccer ball, he tried to guess why she'd turned her back on romance. A broken heart? Too many Prince Dudleys?

And how was she able to see how well the house fit him? He hadn't even seen it himself to the extent she had. But she was right.

Sarah seemed to have more answers than he did. He'd listen to any insight she had about the house since ol' Archie hadn't seen fit to leave him any hints.

Wait.

Archie.

The letters!

He jogged toward the house.

Finally he'd get some answers. The letters were sure to give him at least a few clues he didn't have to be Hercule Poirot to figure out.

CHAPTER 14

Micah stepped inside and strode over to the coat closet door. He yanked it open and pulled the stack down from the closet shelf. Yes! Answers. Right here. Right now.

A faded business card stuck out from under the first envelope—Archie's. He pulled it out. A handwritten note was on the back.

> *Dear Micah,*
>
> *Congratulations on finding the letters. Of course if Chris followed my instructions, it shouldn't have been too difficult. There is only one guideline. Read them in order and only read one letter per week. Only one.*
>
> *Your great-uncle,*
> *Archie*

Micah shook his head and smiled. The guy never failed to fascinate. The envelopes were numbered from 1 to 19 in the lower

right-hand corner, almost too small to read. He trotted over to his
overstuffed chair that faced the picture windows, settled in, and
opened the first letter.

> *October 20, 1990*
> *Dear Micah,*
>
> *Our first letter together in the house has filled me with
> joy and anticipation. Some of my correspondence will be
> lengthy; at other times the letters will be much shorter.
> I dare hope all will contain encouragement for your journey
> now begun.*
>
> *As I mentioned in my introductory letter, you will
> have to make a choice to face your past or not. And facing
> your past means more than just dealing with the memory
> of your mother's passing. There is more to deal with
> surrounding her death. Much more.*

More? No, he wouldn't go there again. Ever. Hadn't he finished
that? But he couldn't stop shards of the memory from bursting into
his mind—his dad standing over him, screaming over and over,
"*What have you done to her, Micah? What have you done?*"

Micah slammed the memory back into its dark corner. *Get a
grip!* He pounded his leg with his fist. "C'mon, Archie I need something with a little more hope than that."

> *I expect by this point you have begun to understand what
> the home is. If not, then I am afraid I will be spilling a bit
> of the proverbial beans.*
>
> *The structure is far more than a home and will make
> a significant impact on your future if you allow it to. The
> home is a part of you, and you are part of it to a greater*

degree than you can imagine. I designed it this way with help from a close friend. His singular ability and assistance makes this home extraordinary.

Along with the healing of your heart and the trials that will entail, I pray you find rest as well. The Cannon Beach section of the Oregon Coast has always been a place of peace. I trust it still is. I counsel you to soak in the music of the ocean and the accents of the seagulls crying, and the hope of finding a sand dollar still whole.

Your great-uncle,

Archie

P.S. Remember, Micah, one letter per week. I look forward to being together again in seven days.

Micah set the letter on the armrest, tilted his head back, and let out a small groan. Answers? Archie raised more questions than he'd answered. The house is part of him? What's that supposed to mean? Face more than just reliving his mom's death? What, the memory room wasn't enough?

Maybe the second letter would help. He smacked its edge into the palm of his hand three times in a quick cadence. One a week? Sorry. He wasn't waiting another seven days for the next cryptic letter about the mansion and its secrets.

He slipped his forefinger under the top flap of the second envelope and stopped. Instantly he was seven years old again, sneaking out and opening his presents on Christmas Eve while the rest of his family was snug in bed. Shrugging off the feeling of guilt, he ripped open the envelope. He wasn't a kid anymore.

He sucked in a quick breath, held it, and yanked out the letter. The paper scraping free sounded like firecrackers. He looked around the room and assured himself it was okay.

October 24, 1990
Micah,

I am in a bit of a quandary with regard to how I should start this next letter or what type of forewarning I should attempt to impress upon you before you read the following words. For no matter how complete my effort may be, you will likely be a mite traumatized at the message it contains.

Before I reach the portion of the letter I believe will elicit this reaction, let me assure you I am just an ordinary man; by the time you read these letters, I will likely have been with my Lord Jesus for many years.

Micah put down the letter. He wasn't in the mood to be shocked. He'd had enough surprises since coming to Cannon Beach to last a year. But how could he stop reading?

I know you are reading this letter before I've intended you to. Please do not do this. Stay true to the schedule I instructed of one letter per week. I realize this might be difficult to adhere to. You will want to race ahead and receive answers to your questions right now. It is a strength God has given to you—to strive forward strongly in all that you do—but in this case, it is a weakness and a hindrance to truth.

Please allow the process of being in this home to take the time it needs, that you need.
Archie

Micah's heart jackhammered. He thought little could surprise him after what he'd been through already, but this was over the top. How could a man back in 1990 know he would disregard his request and open the second letter early? There was no logical explanation. A chill swept through the room, and the ticking of the grandfather clock at the top of the spiral staircase sounded like gunshots.

He looked down at envelope number three. It mocked him— dared him—to open it.

It slid out smoothly till a corner of the envelope caught on the twine that held the bundle of letters together. He wrenched it free and ripped it open.

> *October 25, 1990*
> *Dear Micah,*
> *Stick with the order.*
> *Archie*

Heat flooded Micah's body. He picked up letter number four and tore at it in sheer defiance. But his hands trembled, and it took thirty seconds before he read it. When his eyes dropped to the page his fear was confirmed.

> *October 26, 1990*
> *Dear Micah,*
> *One per week. Trust me.*
> *Archie*

Micah closed his eyes and took deep breaths. In. Out. This was beyond strange. First the shrine room, then the painting room, then the memory room, now this. How? The man's been dead for twelve years!

Sweat squiggled down his forehead. He glanced at his watch. One in the morning. Too late to call Rick.

He was out of control again.

Once more Archie showed his penchant for the strange twist—
not only with the house but now with the letters.

He rubbed his temples hard. What was the point of living in
one of Rod Serling's nightmares? Archie's letters were the straw, he
was the camel, and he didn't need any crushed vertebrae. He should
sell the place and get back to reality.

||||||

A week later Micah strode toward his deck with letter number five
grasped in his left hand. His right held his cedar letter opener like
a sword, and his heart pounded.

He wanted to read the letter outside. For all he knew, reading it
would suck him into another psychotic room. This way he could at
least process the letter before facing any new, unwanted expedition.
He knew God could not be put into the tidy box Micah had tried
to squeeze Him into these past six or seven years. And this house
certainly seemed to be the field of battle where that truth would be
played out. So it was with expectation of the extraordinary that he
opened the letter.

He was disappointed.

> December 3, 1990
> Dear Micah,
>
> I pick up my pen again. It is indeed a strange sensation
> knowing if and when you read these letters it will be a
> long time into the future. Forgive me. I am rambling and
> promised myself I would avoid that.
>
> Your heart is a sacred and magical thing, Micah. From it
> flows the wellspring of life. It's why the wisest man who ever
> lived said we must guard it above all else. You won't reach it
> by your intellect. The pathway to the heart is always by the
> Spirit, and the pathway to the Spirit is by the heart.

Are you wealthy, Micah? To acquire a significant amount of money at a young age, elements of life must be neglected. Often the heart. This is what I meant in my introductory letter when I said if you are not yet thirty-five, your heart has not been suitably guarded.

No matter your current age, I imagine you have already experienced a number of extraordinary things in this home—some potentially frightening—and yet if you're reading this letter, you've made the choice to press onward in your journey. This indicates your heart is coming alive again.

Now I finally arrive at the lesson of this letter. It is impossible for man to serve both mammon and God.

With great affection,

Archie

Micah set down the letter and shook his head. Some lesson. He'd heard it since he first became a Christian. The love of money is the root of all evil and all that stuff. What did it have to do with him? So he'd made some money. That meant he was serving it? No way. He'd made it too young? In Archie's day he doubted IPOs could make a young company owner a multi-multimillionaire overnight the way it could today.

He sighed and walked back inside. Might as well pack for the trip back to Seattle even though he didn't have to leave till the next afternoon. It had been fifteen days since he'd started working from the beach, and he was scheduled to show up for a day full of meetings on Friday.

Traffic on I-5 was light on Thursday evening, and he clipped off the miles back to Seattle at seventy miles per hour without having to change lanes. By the time he reached Tacoma, the music on his CDs had grown stale, and he was tired of the late-night radio talk-show hosts who all droned on about the same tired political issues.

His thoughts turned to Archie's letter.

Guarding his heart? What did that mean? Against what? Ninety-nine percent of the world wanted the fame and fortune he had, so he must already be guarding his heart on a Secret Service level.

"The pathway to the heart is always by the Spirit, and the pathway to the Spirit is by the heart." Archie's line sounded like something Rick would say.

Micah rolled his eyes, pushed a button on his steering wheel, and let the sounds of classic rock drown out the questions that played big-time wrestling in his mind.

"God? I'm open to learning what I'm supposed to learn here. Wouldn't want to give me some answers, would You?"

A thought lit up his mind like a flash of lightning.

Get ready.

CHAPTER 15

W ell, well, well, Mr. Taylor, welcome to RimSoft," Shannon said to Micah as he walked past her antique Georgian walnut desk on Friday morning. "So nice to have you come visit our little company during the month of June."

"Hah." Micah stopped and sat in the burgundy leather chair next to Shannon's desk and fumbled for the right words. If God had really talked to him and made the "Get ready" comment, it had to be about RimSoft. And if anyone knew about strange events inside the company, it would be Shannon.

"Anything unusual been going on around here? Rumors I should know about?"

"No, why?"

Micah shrugged. "No reason."

Shannon turned back to her computer and squinted at the screen. But her right ear slowly rose a quarter inch, telling Micah she wasn't seeing anything.

"You want to know the reason."

"Only if you want to tell me, boss."

"This place down in Cannon Beach is making changes in me. Maybe good ones." Micah shifted in his seat and smoothed out his pants. "But I can't lose any control of my world up here. And, uh, I think . . . I mean I had a feeling there might be some different things going on. Just need to make sure we're smooth up here. Understand?"

Shannon tapped the watch on Micah's wrist. "A Corum doesn't run any smoother."

"Thanks." Micah stood and winked at her before heading into his office.

⅋

At noon Micah's laptop chimed twice. Time to check and see if RimSoft was playing nice with all the other kids on the NASDAQ. He pushed the Federal Trade Commission papers needing his signature to the side. Get big and a company gets targeted whether anything illegal was done or not. Maybe RimSoft had skirted the edge of ethical but not so badly they deserved this current hassle.

Micah checked RimSoft's stock price three times a day—at eight in the morning, noon, and at the market close. He told himself it was just a game, that it didn't matter if he was up or down, and at first it had been true.

When RimSoft first went public, he checked twice a week—once on Tuesdays and at the close on Friday. But after the stock streaked heavenward faster than a bottle rocket—and his net worth went along for the ride—he started checking daily.

It became an obsession.

Micah punched up the stock on his computer. *What?*

He felt the blood drain from his face. He shook his head, as if he'd just woken from a dream. Or a nightmare. He slammed a button on his phone.

"Yes?"

"What is going on with the stock, Roger!"

"Hi, Micah. I heard you're back for a few—"

"What in the name of all that is holy is going on with my stock!" Micah stood and paced behind his desk but didn't take his eyes off the speakerphone.

"I'm not sure what you mean. We're up a full point over last week and the volume's been good. And long-term options on the stock indicate a—"

"Up a point from where? Thursday afternoon we closed at 83¼ and this morning we're at 62¼? Did someone not tell me about a three-for-one split?"

Roger sighed on the other end of the line.

"Do I get an answer?"

"I don't know what you're after here, but—"

"What am I after?" Micah snatched the phone out of its cradle and growled into the phone. "I want to know why my net worth just dropped by almost fifteen million dollars! I want to know how it's possible for the stock to drop 20 points between Thursday at 1:30 p.m. and Friday at 11:45 a.m. I want answers from my CFO on why millions of dollars have just covered themselves with magical invisibility powder and—*poof!*—disappeared!"

"I'm going to act for a moment like you're serious."

"O...kay..." Micah drew the word out as his knuckles turned white from his grip on the phone. "Humor me."

"The stock has never traded for more than 74¼. Ever. Heck, we're only off our three-year high by five points. And it looks—"

Micah hung up and clicked his mouse. A graph popped up on his screen showing him RimSoft's three-year high was 72⅜; the low was 14.

He grabbed his temples and pressed hard. He tried taking three deep breaths but didn't succeed. He buzzed Shannon. "I need the hard copies of our monthly statements on the stock price for the past six months. I'd appreciate if you could do it quickly."

"They're all in the compu—"

"The hard copies, Shannon. Right now!" He slammed the phone into its cradle. Fifteen million dollars. Gone.

Something smacked onto Micah's desk thirty seconds later. By the time he looked up, Shannon had turned and was walking back to her desk without comment.

He dug through the reports knowing what he'd find. But he ripped through them anyway and finished by sweeping the pile off the edge of his desk. Terror hammered at his mind as they fluttered to the floor.

Micah picked up the phone. It slipped from his fingers and rattled on his desk. He picked it up again and hit six on his speed dial.

"Hello to you. Rick's Gas & Garage."

"Devin, it's Micah. I have to talk to Rick."

"Hey, Micah, good to hear from ya. What's going on? How are—?"

"I gotta talk to him *now*, Devin!"

"Oh, sorry, he ran up to Seaside to pick up parts we need right away, you know, so, well, you're gonna have to wait or talk to me, I guess."

"Have him call me on my cell the instant he gets back, okay?"

"Sure."

Micah rubbed his hands back and forth on his thighs as he stared at the ticker symbols that streamed across the bottom of his computer screen. Normal volume. Nothing unusual about the Dow or the S&P. RimSoft's stock was steady, riding little waves up and down.

Micah pulled two Wall Street analysts' predictions for the stock. All said RimSoft's stock was a good bet even though it traded near its all-time high. Nothing indicated it ever traded as high as 83.

What was happening? He begged God to talk to him.

A bead of sweat meandered down his right temple. He wiped it away and stared at the moisture on his fingertips. After the third trickle of perspiration, he tried Rick again to no avail.

Micah grabbed his coat and walked out the door. "Shannon, I gotta go. I'm going back down to the beach."

"You're leaving? You just got here. What about this afternoon's meetings?"

He was four steps toward the elevator when her question registered in his fog-filled mind. "What?" He turned and took a half step to the side to keep from stumbling.

"Are you okay, Micah?"

He swallowed and resisted the panic that pressed in. "No. I mean, yes, I'm fine."

She pursed her lips as though she were about to whistle and squinted at him.

"I'm okay, really. I'll be back up in a week, and we'll do the meetings then. I'll give you a buzz Monday. I just need to deal with something right now." There had to be a reason for the stock drop. He would find it.

"The answer to your panic is at the beach?"

"It was after I read something down there that things got weird."

Shannon frowned. "What's been getting weird?"

"I'll talk to you Monday." He jogged toward the elevator, then reached for the button. He didn't push it. Instead he walked back to Shannon. "Sorry for yelling when I asked for the stock reports. I'm . . . it's just that . . ." Micah stopped his gaze from flitting around her desk and settled on her. "No excuses. I was a jerk. And I'm really, really sorry."

He walked out of his building and looked to the left, then the right. Where should he go? Who could he talk to? Julie? No way. Not with the current tension between them. Besides, what if her response was the same as Roger's? She'd accuse the beach of sucking away his sanity and want to get the board involved.

Talk to his dad? Uh, yeah, right. His dad would be convinced Archie's house was making him dance on the tightrope of psychosis, and since he might be right, Micah didn't want to hand his father additional ammo to knock him off the wire.

Other friends came to mind, but there were none he could truly open up to. How could he tell his basketball buddies he just lost more than fifteen million dollars with no tangible evidence to back it up?

He fired up his car and screeched out of RimSoft's parking lot. As his BMW eased onto I-5, he reflected on how depressing it was that the only person he trusted was a man he'd met just eight weeks earlier.

When a person's on top of the world, he doesn't need anyone. But now Micah was sliding down the mountain and running out of rope.

Rick's number lit up the caller ID on Micah's cell phone just before he reached Longview. He threw his Bluetooth over his ear. "Finally! We gotta talk."

"What's going on?"

"I'm heading down I-5 back to Cannon Beach and down the path of lunacy at the same time. Wishing I wasn't taking the trip solo," Micah said.

"Tell me."

"When I checked our stock price yesterday, it was 83¼. This morning it's at 62¾. And everyone at RimSoft thinks that's perfectly normal."

"No chance you're wrong about yesterday?"

"No way." Micah pulled into the left lane and kicked his BMW up to seventy-five.

"Hard copies?"

"They changed."

"Changed? How could they change?"

"Exactly. I have no clue." Micah veered right to pass a sluggish RV hogging the left-hand lane. "But I *know* the stock was in the low 80s yesterday and today it isn't. I've lost almost fifteen million dollars in less than twenty-four hours."

"That's some serious coin."

Something in Rick's tone caught Micah's ear. "You know what's going on, don't you?"

Rick stayed silent so Micah asked again.

Silence.

"C'mon, Rick! If you know something, talk to me. What is going on? I'm not crazy. But this isn't the first—" Micah paused and squeezed the bridge of his nose.

"The first what?"

"Weird things have been happening, quirky things."

"Like?"

"Like my car gaining an instant sixteen thousand miles, which you say we'll talk about someday. Like a couple months back my racquetball partner completely forgets a match we played—claims it never happened. Like calling a guy I met at a party to talk business and he forgets meeting me. We talked for fifteen minutes at that party. I'm not that forgettable."

"No, you're not." Rick chuckled.

"Two different guys forgetting being with me is odd. My car gaining mystery miles is bizarre. But seeing my company's stock drop twenty points in one day and no one knows it but me is not odd. It's *The Twilight Zone* and *The X-Files* in a double pack, up front in living color."

"Here's what I know for certain," Rick said. "God is sovereign. That's an intellectual way of saying He's in control and knows what He's doing."

"Not the answer I'm looking for."

"I know. You're used to having complete control and all the answers to your life in an instant. This time the answers will flit just beyond your fingertips. It will take time to catch them."

"That's it? I need more than that, Rick."

"One more thing that's pretty obvious. The Lord is a better choice to talk to than me."

"Yeah."

Their talk helped. Not near enough, but enough. The rest of the drive he alternated between trying to pray and keeping a lid on his imagination. On one hand he believed God was in control. On another, if his net worth changed that quickly, what else could be turned on its side over a weekend? And would God be the cause of it, or just allow it?

He had to get control of this. Had to keep eyes of an eagle on that stock. The coming week would be a monotonous marathon of tension.

CHAPTER 16

Forty-five million reasons woke Micah early on Monday morning.

When the market opened at six-thirty, Micah walked in from his deck, the smell of his self-made espresso in his hand still filling his senses. He grabbed his laptop, pulled up the Internet, and locked his gaze on a chart showing RimSoft's stock price. He'd set his laptop to refresh once every fifteen seconds so he'd know almost instantly if there was an abnormal drop in the price.

An hour passed before he moved and then only to grab a bowl of Banana Nut Crunch. He brought it over to his desk and slurped it down while he watched his monitor. Another hour with no change. When the market closed at one-thirty, he slumped backward and closed his bloodshot eyes.

Exhausting.

Tuesday the stock was down two, Wednesday up three, Thursday down a half, and Friday up a quarter. When the market closed Friday afternoon, Micah snapped his laptop shut and sighed. A headache throbbed in his temples and radiated down his neck. Finally over!

It was more than the money. It was his company's clout in the computer world. With the stock in the low 60s, RimSoft wouldn't be as influential, making key alliances harder to secure.

But it was more than even that. He'd invested his life in the company. Blood, tears, and gallons of sweat had been poured into it. Even a sliver of it slipping away ripped at his heart. RimSoft gave him identity, a reference point for his entire life. He was RimSoft; RimSoft was him. Sure, maybe Cannon Beach was changing him, drawing him to a deeper identity and things eternal, but it didn't squelch the sinking feeling inside of losing his world in Seattle.

Saturday morning he guzzled a cup of Seattle's Best Coffee, wandered out onto the deck, and watched the seagulls canter back and forth on the wind. He worried. Not about his sanity. Not really. He knew he wasn't losing his mind. It was the daunting images that darted through his mind of other things that might change in an instant.

Time for a run.

On his way to change clothes, the painting room popped into his mind. Yes. Just the thing to take his mind off the madness. After he opened the door, he didn't know whether to feel fear or joy. Significant changes again. He felt light-headed and teetered on his Nikes.

Lush Douglas fir trees now covered the hills, emerald carpet at their feet. The sky was a brilliant sapphire blue, with cotton candy clouds peppered sparsely through the heavens. The artist had started the ocean, but it was too early to tell if the waves would play or rage.

He studied the painting for half an hour. Where the artist

would take it next fluttered at the edges of his heart like a riveting dream that fades upon waking. The artist could put people in the painting, a sand castle, kites . . .

When he finally left, he walked toward his bedroom to get ready for his run. The plan was abandoned a moment later when he spotted another door down the hall he'd never seen. It was framed by ornate carvings of trees interwoven with otters, wolves, and eagles.

This, he would have remembered.

The door was cracked open, the inside tar black. He peeked through the narrow opening. Light from the hall spilled onto the first few feet of carpet in the room and stopped abruptly. Odd. Micah eased the door open halfway.

There was no furniture in the few feet of the room he could see—nothing but carpet washed into the darkness. There was no sound, although it felt like there should be. The room was too still. Too silent. Images of the memory room filled his mind.

A faint rustle came from the back of the room.

"Hello?" Micah called out.

"Hi, Micah," came a voice out of the stillness.

Micah's heartbeat jumped from 65 to 180 in an instant. He staggered back across the hall and smacked into the wall behind him. But he stayed there and didn't run. Something about the voice riveted him to the floor.

"Who are you?"

"Come in," the soft voice soothed.

"*Who are you?*" Micah shouted.

"Hey, get in here." The voice laughed easily. "Come in." The tone was light and welcoming. "Don't freak out on me."

The voice was familiar, as if he'd heard it many times before. He hesitated. There was no reason to go in. That wasn't true. There was every reason to step inside. Everything in this house was somehow related to his spiritual condition. Archie had virtually told him that in his first letter.

But this was different. It was the first time an audible voice had spoken to him without being part of a contained scene or a dream. And instead of being a scene from his past, this was in the present and in the house. This wasn't a changed painting or a room of memorabilia; it was a real, live voice.

He shuddered, once, twice, then moved forward. He inched his foot over the threshold and set his foot down like a dandelion spore settling on the grass in spring. His other foot remained in the hallway.

Laughter again. Warm. Comforting. "Come in, Micah. All the way. I promise, I am a friend. More of a friend than you can imagine."

He eased into the room another step and then stopped. The room felt familiar. Even more than the rest of the house. It was like hearing a phone number and realizing it was attached to someone he knew but not remembering if the person was from the present or a past long forgotten.

"Now that your heart rate has returned to normal, why not come in a little farther so we can talk? There's a chair to your right as comfortable as a big cotton ball."

Micah took slow steps to his right, and his thigh bumped up against the chair. The darkness kept him from seeing even its outline but he felt supple leather. "That's okay; I'll stand."

"I understand," the voice said. "I knew it'd be quite a shock the first time we actually talked to each other."

"Who are you?" Micah squinted into the inky darkness.

"A friend who has been with you since the day you were born."

"Why have I never heard you before?"

"You're kidding, right?" A smile sounded in the voice. "All your life I've been speaking to you. You know my voice."

It was true. He did. More than familiar, it felt like a part of him. But just when he thought he had placed it, the memory raced into a corner of his mind where he couldn't follow. Micah spoke just above a whisper. "Yes, I'll say there is something about your voice I recognize. But I don't know you."

"Yes, you do. You know me intimately. Just as I know you."

"Then who are you?"

"Let your imagination go for a moment. Archie built a truly astonishing house. A home where things that only happen in dreams happen every day. A house so deeply spiritual, miracles happen in every moment." The voice paused. "You know who I am."

Micah knew. But part of him couldn't believe it, and another part didn't want it to be true. It was too strange, too unnerving. And yet a third part desperately wanted this impossibility to be possible for him. Finally he answered.

"You're me."

"Yes."

Micah held his breath. Then he sipped in a swallow of air and spoke. "You're my own thoughts, my own voice, my own impressions." Micah paused, realizing the significance and utter strangeness of what he was about to say. "I'm talking . . . to myself."

The voice chuckled. "Strange yet wonderful, isn't it?"

Of course. It made so much sense. This was why the voice was so familiar. He had been hearing it all his life. "Why the dark?"

"You got me. Guess it makes it easier to talk to each other. It blocks out the distractions. Like when we're praying. It's the same way here. Rather than focus on anything visual, you can—or maybe I should say we can—focus on the words we speak to each other instead of the weirdness of staring into each other's faces."

"How can I hear you audibly here but not outside this house? All my life I've heard you through thoughts and impressions and ideas but never like this. It doesn't make any sense."

"It makes perfect sense. In this house you're becoming more attuned to the spiritual realm around you. That alone would make me easier to hear. And you're hearing the voice of God again, so why shouldn't you hear more clearly the voice of yourself?"

"Last time I heard God's voice, He said 'get ready' and I lost fifteen million dollars."

The voice didn't respond.

"I gotta think this through." Micah turned to leave.

"Great finally talking to you like this," the voice said.

Micah made sure the door was shut tight.

That night he stood on the deck outside his room at the Ocean Lodge, campfire smoke drifting up from the beach. He couldn't believe he was so scared of his own voice he wouldn't go to sleep in his house.

But c'mon. How often did a voice come out of a dark room claiming to be his own? Then again, maybe it was a gift beyond imagination he needed to accept. Yes. An incredible gift. He would simply accept it and the next night sleep back in the house.

Someone down on the beach waved a tiny fireball through the air. Probably a marshmallow that got too close to the campfire. He wished his biggest mystery in life was how to evenly brown a marshmallow.

Rick. He'd talk to Rick about the voice. Tomorrow night.

CHAPTER 17

But Micah didn't tell Rick about the voice. He went with him to his church the next evening, and afterward the mechanic suggested they grab a late dinner at the Lumberyard. Micah avoided the question. He was still thinking about church.

Every time during the service Micah had thought about describing the voice to Rick, dread washed over him. Twice when he turned to tell his friend, a palpable tension shot through his back, leaving the instant he decided not to tell. How much clearer could it get? It wasn't the right timing. No question. And Micah didn't feel like making small talk.

The rooms, the weird things disappearing in Seattle, even the stock dropping was strange, but talking to yourself? He needed to call it what it was. He was hearing voices.

Maybe he was losing it. Archie could have been schizo and somehow rigged the house to trigger the same thing in Micah. Maybe it was time to sell the place and get back to reality.

But there was Sarah. And maybe God *was* in control. As long as Micah could avoid facing whatever was more painful than the memory of his mom's death, he'd stay.

"So you going to join me?" Rick said.

"Nah, early day tomorrow."

"Getting up with the market, eh?"

"Does anything get past you?" Micah shook his head and smiled. "I just want to keep an eye on the stock tomorrow."

"Last week wasn't enough?" Rick threw his arm around Micah's shoulders as they walked through the syrupy fog toward their cars. "I'm just teasing. I'd feel the same way in your shoes."

But Rick wasn't in his moccasins. And Micah didn't like the idea of going through his life barefoot.

||||||||

Monday, Tuesday, and Wednesday all followed the same pattern. Stress about the stock price. Check it incessantly. Check the charts one more time to confirm it never traded as high as 83. Stress some more.

On Wednesday his computer chimed three times with a reminder message. TASK: READ ARCHIE'S NEXT LETTER

Yes! Time for his weekly blast from the past. Micah flopped down on the couch in front of his fireplace and opened the cherry-red shoe box in which he'd placed all Archie's letters. He lifted the next envelope off the top of the stack and tore it open. February 10, 1991. He was ten years old when Archie wrote it. Still too weird.

> *Dear Micah,*
>
> *I hope you are liking the house. Perhaps that is not the correct word. More accurately, I pray the house is making you face yourself and that you are on the path toward*

restoration. I pray you are allowing this to occur. The home will challenge, encourage, and stretch you to your limits. In all probability this comes as no surprise to you; however, if you think you have encountered a number of strange and unexplainable incidents up until this point, it would be less than fair if I did not alert you that stranger things are still forthcoming.

Great. Bizarro home gets even stranger. He could hardly wait.

With that admonition in the forefront of your mind, let me also assure you once again that God is sovereign and in control and I have prayed for and about this home for many years. However, this does not mean there are no dangerous places within the house. There are. This simply illustrates the truth that from time to time we have to be placed in precarious places to learn the lesson God is teaching.
Your great-uncle and fervent supporter,
Archie

He put down the letter. Why couldn't Archie write a letter simply saying, "God is good, the past is over, the future is bright, and it's going to be a fun week"? Micah's nerves were ready to snap from watching the stock bounce up and down all week. He didn't need another lesson right now. He needed to relax.

That night Micah sat on his deck trying to take his mind off the house, the stock, where his life was headed, and lingering thoughts of Julie. He had to talk to her.

She answered on the second ring. "Hi."

"What are you doing?"

"Why are you calling, Micah?"

"I want to know where we're at."

"Shouldn't that be my question?"

He leaned his head back and clacked the front of his teeth together.

"I hate it when you do that."

"Sorry." Micah stared out at the ocean. "I can't imagine a business partner who would be better for me. Your intuitive business sense makes mine look like a first grader. You don't let relationship get in the way of our making money, you—"

"Shut up, Micah. Why don't you just say it?"

"That we're over? You're the one who said good-bye."

"I still had a tiny bit of hope. Now you're going to snuff that out, aren't you?"

"No."

"Yes, you are."

"I am not." Micah ground his knuckles into the deck's railing.

"Fine, so you tell me where you want us to be."

"I don't know. But that doesn't mean we're over." Micah closed his eyes. "We're on hold."

"On hold? Still? Maybe you're on pause, but I'm not."

"I just need—"

"Listen. I'm done with us. For good. Since you don't seem to have the spine for it, let me do the honors. It's over."

The line went dead.

Perfect. That would make life more fun. Micah stared at the waves trying to figure out if what had just happened was good, bad, or somewhere in between.

Micah headed for the media room. He needed something to get his brain off everything. He clicked through his cable choices and settled on an R-rated movie so full of violence and gore that it probably should have been rated NC-17. Yes, it was garbage. But he didn't care. The escape from his anxiety was worth it.

He went to bed the moment the movie finished and lay rubbing the back of his neck till his fingers ached. Maybe not worth it.

His legs twitched, and the blankets pressed down on him like thin sheets of concrete. All night he wrestled with troubling dreams.

Friday morning a light flicked on in his head as he realized how to remove his worry over the stock. Stop orders.

He would put a stop order on all his shares at 10 percent less than their current trading price. If the unexplainable happened again, the stop order would execute and instantly he'd have all his shares in cash—with a drop in value, but a 10 percent drop wins over a 25 percent loss, or who knows how much more, every time.

By 11:00 a.m. he finished entering the stop orders. Good timing. At 11:15 his computer's reminder alarm chimed. Bike ride with Sarah. His heart rate picked up. And that was before he got on his bike.

||||||

They met in front of Osburn's and headed north. They'd decided to ride up past Ecola to Indian Beach to watch the surfers navigate the North Pacific swells. By the time they got to the *T* in the road that would take them farther up to Indian Beach, Micah was sucking in deep gulps of air. Not Sarah. If she'd lost any of her Olympic-athlete conditioning, he couldn't see it.

After they arrived and picked a spot on the windswept bluff overlooking the waves, Sarah said, "What are your plans once you're done down here?"

"I don't know when I'll be done." Micah plucked some of the long grass around them and threw them like darts.

"That's not what I asked."

"Yes, I know." Micah smiled but she didn't return it.

To buy time, he got up, walked back to his bike, and grabbed his water bottle. He took a deep draw of water and squinted at the sun playing hide-and-seek with the clouds. Just before he sat next to Sarah, the sun jumped out, as bright as it had been so far that day.

"Want to walk to the beach?" Micah asked.

"Sure."

They wound their way down to the little beach, full of boulders the size of Volkswagen Beetles. The tide was out, but even so, there was little room to maneuver around them.

"Ever done a long bike ride?" Sarah asked.

"Define long."

"More than one hundred miles in a day."

"No."

"We should do the STP together."

Micah raised both eyebrows as he stepped over a cluster of small rocks.

"The Seattle-to-Portland bike race. One day, two hundred miles. 'Course a lot of people split it into two," Sarah said.

"And we'd do it in one or two?"

Sarah waved her index finger in front of her face.

"Oh, wow. You mean I'll have to get in shape?"

They padded farther down the beach. "Sorry for avoiding the question earlier," Micah said. "I don't have a clue what my plans will be once I'm done down here. I suppose I'll go back to Seattle and come down here three or four times a year for vacation. Relax. Get perspective. You have any better ideas?" He said it with a light-hearted spin, hoping to bring a bit of playfulness to the conversation. It didn't work.

"You wouldn't like my suggestion."

"I'd love it."

"No, you wouldn't."

"Try me." He wiggled the fingers of both hands, inviting her to ask the question.

"You're sure?"

Micah nodded, even though he wasn't sure, a queasy feeling growing in his stomach.

"I think you should start a plan right now."

"To?"

"Get things right with your dad."

Oh, boy. Here it comes. "How is that supposed to work? I have no relationship with my dad. I don't want one. He doesn't want one. Done. Over. End of plan."

Sarah put on her sunglasses. "You don't need a relationship with him to take care of what you need to take care of."

"Oh, really? So tell me, Watson, what this mysterious thing is I need to fix."

Sarah gazed up at him. "Forgive him, for whatever it is he's done."

Micah rolled his eyes. He ought to write a book: *Cannon Beach Conspiracy*. How an ordinary software businessman was ambushed into dredging up his dead-and-buried past.

The problem? It was still very much alive.

Micah sidestepped a wave the incoming tide sent farther up the beach than its cousins.

"I'm sorry, I said too much." Sarah pivoted and shuffled down the beach.

Bull's-eye. Way too much. But he'd asked for it.

She stood twenty yards away, the wind ruffling her hair, obscuring her face, then blowing it free a second later. As he approached her, Sarah turned toward the sun, and tears trickled out from under her sunglasses.

Micah didn't speak till seven waves had rushed up the sand, then retreated back into the surf. "You okay?"

She didn't respond.

"Want to talk about it?"

She sniffed and laughed at the same time. He reached into his shorts pocket, found the softness of a light blue tissue, and pulled it out.

She took it from him. "Why am I crying, right?"

The question wasn't directed at him. But the answer was. She glanced at Micah before turning back toward the white-flecked waves that pounded the sand. "Because I've been praying for you and your choices for many years." She walked back toward their bikes.

As they ambled down the sand together, the rays of the late-afternoon sun danced on her hair, turning it golden. He knew she meant months, so he waited for her to correct herself. But she didn't.

"Months," he said softly, "you meant many months."

Her face flushed. She stopped, looked at him for a moment, then hiked away. "No," she called without turning around, "I meant years."

CHAPTER 18

Micah tried to resist, but Saturday afternoon he called Sarah to ask about the "praying for years" comment. He'd asked her about it on Friday as they rode back into Cannon Beach, but she deflected the question. If she was home now, she wasn't answering, and by midday on Monday, she still hadn't returned his call. He needed someone to talk to.

An idea flashed into his mind. A way to get answers to the two questions bouncing around his brain. After checking in with Shannon to make sure everything was running silky smooth at RimSoft, he closed his laptop and headed into town to find a hardware store.

By one o'clock he tromped through his house lugging a massive Black & Decker light-up-the-universe flashlight under his arm. He'd talked with the voice three more times since his first encounter, but Micah still wasn't convinced it was himself. He wanted to do more than hear the voice, especially if he was going to talk about sensitive subjects. He wanted to see it. It wasn't a *Wizard of Oz* voice that echoed throughout the room; it came from the center, fifteen or twenty feet back.

The voice said it had to be dark, that seeing each other would make it too difficult to focus on talking. Even if it were true, it didn't explain why the room was pitch black.

He lugged the flashlight up to the room, hid it behind his back, and grabbed the door handle. He eased it open.

"Nice flashlight, Micah."

Micah could tell the voice was smiling. "How can you know that?"

"We've been over this. I am you. You are me." The voice laughed. "You can stop doubting anytime, you know."

"So you know I'm going to shine this into the room in about two seconds?"

"Yeah. But do it anyway."

Micah shot the beam straight into the heart of the room. Nothing. The light stopped two feet into the room, as if hitting an opaque pane of glass. The light reflected back at Micah, and he saw a muddied version of himself holding the flashlight. He walked up to the reflection and lifted his hand, expecting to touch the surface of something. But his hand went through the point of reflection, as if it was dense fog, and it disappeared.

"Fascinating, isn't it?" the voice asked.

Micah didn't answer and flashed the beam to his right and left. Same result.

"Here's something you probably didn't realize or expect," the voice said. "I can't see you, either."

"You're kidding."

"Nope. It works both ways. As weird as it would be for you to see me, it'd be that weird for me to see you."

"Then explain how you know things I don't. If I'm you, I should know them, too."

"I can see how you'd think that," the voice said. "But it doesn't play out that way. The whole point and gift of us being able to talk to each other is we get to vocalize and discuss things we do know deep down but haven't voiced even to ourselves."

"So you're a deeper version of me?"

"I don't know exactly, possibly, I suppose. But you're just as deep in different ways. Think of me as the feeling, has time-to-mull-things-over, emotional Micah. A Micah outside the constraints of time." The voice cleared his throat. "Here's another way to think of me. I'm more the right brain and you're more the left. Science tells us the right brain is incapable of putting feelings, thoughts, and intuition into words, but for the here and now, in *this* situation at least, I can. The right brain—me—talking to the left brain—you."

For the first time, it made sense, and Micah realized why it was such a gift from God. Micah had allowed the left side of his brain to dominate his life for so long that the right side of his brain—the creative, feeling, intuitive side—had gone into semihibernation. Now, thanks to the power of the house, it had emerged and spoken to him in a way more influential than ever.

"Makes sense, doesn't it?"

"Yeah. Absolutely." Micah sat in the chair in the room for the first time. "I just wish I could take you around with me everywhere."

"Are you kidding?" The voice laughed. "I *am* with you all the time. You just need to clean out your ears so you can hear me better. In here I speak in words, out there in impressions and feelings."

"All right, I have my ears on now; I'm tuned in."

"We're locked and loaded," the voice said.

Micah laughed and stood. "Just let me know if you figure out what this home is all about."

"Don't worry; that mystery is at the forefront of my brain as well."

"Oh, can we talk about Sarah?" Micah said. "About the 'praying for years' comment?"

"Oh yes. At some point we will most definitely talk about Sarah. In detail. But not quite yet. Not quite yet."

||||||

Micah woke up Wednesday morning with one thought on his mind: Archie day. After grabbing a cup of coffee full of crème brûlée creamer and two slices of multigrain toast smeared with boysenberry jam, he settled down on his deck. He saluted the kite surfer slicing through the waves in front of his house, then pulled out letter number seven and was lost to the world.

> *May 31, 1991*
> *Dear Micah,*
>
> In Psalm 37 David says: "Delight yourself in the LORD; And He will give you the desires of your heart." King Solomon says: "What the wicked fears will come upon him, but the desire of the righteous will be granted." Isaiah says it this way: "And the LORD will continually guide you, and satisfy your desire in scorched places." In the second century Saint Irenaeus wrote this sentiment: "The glory of God is man fully alive."
>
> I could go on, but that will suffice. Our heavenly Father is the Creator and Giver of every perfect gift; gifts that could be described as the talents, attributes, and personality traits unique to each of His children. He delights in observing our growth in these talents. Not for the attainment of fame or fortune, as that focus gives opportunity for the dark areas of our souls to be fed, but for sheer pleasure of taking a gift

bestowed on us by God and returning it to Him. This He delights in.

What father would not love to see his son or his daughter attain a gold medal in the Olympics? I believe it is the same with our heavenly Father. He desires us to reach glory with His gifts so we can share in it together with Him.

The thief of our souls is vehemently opposed to this. He will distract or convince us that seeking excellence is bringing glory to ourselves or, most insidious of all, lead us to counterfeits, occupations, or activities that seem to fill us with life but in reality only distract from the genuine gifts our heavenly Father has placed within us.

In an effort to be clear, let me address the issue in a more practical manner. Is there anything you used to deeply love but have not undertaken in a significant period of time?

Take it up again. A number of interests probably fit that description, but I suggest you start with the one that came to mind first. It is likely the one that needs releasing in greatest measure.

Yours always,

Archie

Micah threw his head back, looked up at the sky, and laughed. This one he didn't have to think about; the answer popped into his mind like neon. *Get in the car. Head for Seaside or Astoria. Buy a guitar.*

Back in junior high and high school, he'd practiced two to three hours a day. He'd been in countless bands, none of which amounted to much, but it never diminished his love for the instrument and his drive to get better. But during college he drifted away from his music, and by the time Julie and he started RimSoft, he'd packed his guitars away for good.

But now he had the time and money to indulge, and the idea certainly fit Archie's criteria.

He grabbed his keys and looked in the entryway mirror to make sure he didn't need a quick shave. He stopped cold. A reflection behind him was out of place. He spun on his heel. A new door.

Rick said God was in his home. He believed it, but it didn't mean he was excited about checking out the new room.

He walked toward the door on his toes, drawing short sips of air as if a deep breath would alert whatever was in the room to his presence. Micah's temples throbbed; adrenaline surged through his body as he turned the knob and pushed open the door.

His heart leaped. Twelve acoustic guitars lined the back wall: Martins, Taylors, and Ovations. Among the nine electrics along the side wall were a 1959 Les Paul Sunburst and a 1969 Stratocaster. Along the back wall was enough recording equipment to produce any sound a heart could desire.

Micah wandered over to a Martin D12-20 twelve string, picked it up, threw the strap around his neck, and let the guitar settle down on him. He looped his left hand around the neck and soaked in that old familiar squeak of fingers sliding on strings. As he strummed the first chord, he closed his eyes and let that deep, rich Martin sound resonate through the air.

After playing his version of the Beatle's "Blackbird," he set the Martin aside, picked up the Les Paul, plugged into an amp, and cranked the volume.

The riding-a-bike principle applied. It had been at least four years since he'd picked up any guitar, let alone his own, but this felt like it were yesterday. The Crate amp pumped out a warm stream of sound with just a hint of distortion, and it was high school rock 'n' roll all over again. He lost himself in it, closed his eyes as the music washed over him, and remembered all those licks he'd learned through endless repetition. When he finally stopped, his eyes lasered in on the recording equipment. Why not?

He roamed around the mixing board and played with the digital editing software, trying everything. Amazing. The learning curve was phenomenal. Not how hard it was but how easy. It was instinctual, as if the room itself guided him along on two separate waves of intellect and inspiration.

By seven o'clock he'd made a CD of four instrumental pieces, with bass, drums, and a piano section to accompany his guitars. He took the CD with him to the kitchen and listened to it as he mashed up avocados for guacamole.

Was he hearing the music for the first time? His head knew he wasn't, but his emotions didn't. The soaring guitar solos ripped open his heart, and he wept. He fell back and caught himself on the kitchen counter. A thought filled his mind.

Songs from the deepest part of you: your heart. So many good things are trapped there. So much of My glory. Your good heart cries for that glory. Remember, Micah. Remember who you are.

He went for a long walk on the beach that night. The talk with God was even longer.

|||||||

The next morning he stopped for gas, and Rick stepped up to the pump.

"Wow, out among your adoring public this morning, huh?" Micah said.

"Yeah, gotta press the flesh every now and then. And give the paparazzi their weekly chance for a photo op." Rick winked. "Still got the Washington State plates, I see."

"I'm not down here permanently. Plus I've only been around for three months."

"Really? Seems like more, ya know?"

"Actually I'd have no way of knowing that since I'm not you," Micah replied, with what he hoped was a crooked smile on his face.

Rick pulled back his grease-smeared Rams cap and squinted at him through the morning sun darts. "But you've been here long enough for me to know I wouldn't get an acerbic comment like that from you unless something, or someone, poured oil all over your Wheaties this morning."

"I need to talk."

"In my office?"

"My midsection says the Fireside." Micah patted his stomach.

"Mine agrees. Meet you there in twenty."

Micah walked toward Morris's Fireside and debated how much to tell Rick. He still wasn't ready to talk about the voice.

||||||||

"How do you stay so clean working on cars all day?" Micah said as Rick slid into the seat across the table.

"I'm an angel. We stay clean automatically."

They both laughed.

"So talk to me. What's going on?" Rick said.

"I think I'm losing it. Hold it. Make that past tense. I've lost it."

"The insanity hasn't reached your face quite yet."

"Good sign, huh?"

Rick stared at Micah, his arms resting on the table, head tilted slightly to the side. Micah decided to start with a shocking statement.

"I think my house is alive. And getting bigger."

Rick didn't give him a strange look or pretend he didn't hear right. "Tell me about it."

After the waitress took their order, Micah told him about

the new room—the music room—and reminded Rick about the
memory room and the shrine room.

"Why do you say the house is growing?"

"The shrine room *might* have been there before I saw it, but the
memory room and the music rooms definitely weren't."

Rick's eyes widened. "Weren't there?"

"Exactly."

Rick glanced around the restaurant and leaned forward.
"You're saying the rooms weren't there one day and the next day
they were?"

"I went through the whole house the first time I came. They
were not there. They are now. I wouldn't have missed them."

"Whew. You've got my attention."

"And get this. The music room isn't the only new room. Now
there's a painting studio in the house. It wasn't there the first
walk-through, either. On top of that, every time I come back from
Seattle, there's more done to this painting."

"You're saying—"

"Someone has to come and work on the thing when I'm gone, or
the thing paints itself. I'm not that easily intimidated, but that is more
than strange. I don't care if you say God is in it, I lock my bedroom
door at night." Micah paused. "As if it would do me any good."

Rick looked more intrigued than surprised. "So why don't you
just throw away the key and have the thing boarded up? Or sell it?"

Micah's eyes snapped up from his coffee. "No way." He surprised himself with how forceful he answered.

"Why not?"

He stared at Rick. He didn't know why. Why *was* he subjecting
himself to a modern version of *The Twilight Zone?* He didn't have to
stay here. He could walk away right now and never come back. Or sell
it like he'd been saying all along and buy another home somewhere
farther down the coast wherever he wanted. Or give it to Rick.

Also, the longer he flirted with the spiritual hinterlands in Cannon Beach, the more it seemed to seep into his life in Seattle. Not in a good way. He could make it all stop—the strange lapses in Seattle; dealing with the past; and the intense scrutiny of his spiritual life from God, or Archie, or whatever force was behind the whole thing.

But as strange as the past three months had been, it stirred something inside he wasn't ready to give up.

"Because I'm on the edge." Micah leaned in on his elbows pushing his silverware to the side. "More alive than I've felt in years."

Rick's right ear raised, and he gave the slightest of nods.

"It's like being in the deepest parts of my own soul in those rooms," Micah continued. "Buried in ripping pain or drenched in joy and freedom. The pain is hell, but the joy is like nothing I've ever experienced. Stuff that happens only in dreams. I'm getting close to God again, and it seems so real. . . . But I don't know if it is real or if I'm going insane. Seriously, I think I might be slipping off the—"

"Insane? No. And you don't need me to tell you it's real. You know. Have you told anyone else about this?"

"No."

"Not even Julie?"

"I haven't seen her for more than seven weeks."

"Not what I asked."

"I told her we're on hold, and she broke it off for good."

"Hmm." Rick stopped with his fork halfway to his mouth and looked straight into Micah's eyes. He didn't need to tell Micah what he was thinking. Micah knew.

"You're right. I need to talk to her. Do the closure thing. Soon."

CHAPTER 19

Micah met Julie early Saturday evening in Chehalis midpoint between Seattle and Cannon Beach. Neutral ground. This wouldn't be easy.

He got out of his BMW and scanned the windows of the Halfway Café. She was already sitting at a table toward the back, next to the window.

The Halfway Café was old but clean—except for one table full of plates with half-eaten cheeseburgers still on them. A few coffee stains had made permanent residence on the dull maroon carpet, but the windows looked recently washed, and Micah guessed at one time it was a hot spot for casual dinners.

Julie had to hate the place.

"Are You Lonesome Tonight" played on an ancient-looking jukebox. The 78s were lined up like kids on the bench in Little League waiting to get into the big game. Still just twenty-five cents to spin a dream.

What record would be appropriate for him to play as he stared at Julie? Elvis was in fine form but didn't stir any emotion in Micah, happy or sad. Maybe that was the key. Just keep emotion out of it.

As he walked over, Julie looked up right on cue. The hazel eyes were just as beautiful; the long blonde hair just as golden.

"Hi." Micah slid into the booth.

"Hey. Nice place," she said with a smirk. "Couldn't find anything less formal?"

"Yeah, they almost made me put on a tie when I came in."

A waitress with a pile of big hair straight out of 1986 sauntered up to the table. "Can I getcha something hot to drink?" She talked like she had gum in her mouth.

"Diet Coke, please," Micah said.

"Classic Coke okay, sweetheart?"

"Sure." Micah smiled.

Julie ordered the same.

"I'll getcha your drinks and be right back atcha." The waitress winked at Micah.

"Haven't lost your touch, have you, Micah?" Julie opened her menu and studied it.

"What touch?" He tried not to laugh.

Julie dabbed her napkin in her water and wiped off her side of the table. "You've never been one to just hang out somewhere since I've known you."

"True."

"Let alone hang out in a place as laid back as the beach. It's been more than three months with no end in sight. What's going on? You act like you want this work-from-the-ocean charade to go on forever."

"It's growing on me."

"What's her name?" Julie spun her knife on the table and watched it twirl.

"There's no name."

"What is her name?"

"It's not a her." He looked out the window at a gray '66 Mustang and folded his arms. Maybe there was a her. But he wasn't ready to think of Sarah in that vein, and it wasn't why he was drawn to Cannon Beach. Maybe a partial reason but certainly not the main one.

The waitress returned with their drinks and took their order. Micah was grateful for a break in the conversation. But it was a short respite from Julie's cross-examination. Up till then, she'd asked questions with a smoldering burn. Now flames leaped from her eyes as she leaned in and spoke in a jagged whisper.

"If it's not a her, then what is it? Our lives were on track. We've pegged off every goal we set for the business, and we finally took our relationship to the next level!" Julie fell back in her chair. "Now you're hanging out at the beach and telling me our relationship is 'on hold.' You wanted to figure things out. You said, 'Six, maybe seven weeks tops, Jules!'"

She pushed her silverware to the side and leaned back in. "Explain to me what is so captivating about a home on the beach that convinces you to spend 90 percent of your life there?"

"You haven't been to the place."

"I don't want to go to the place." She took a sip of her Coke, then smacked it back down on the table.

Micah grabbed a handful of Sweet'N Low packets and built a little wall. A moment later their food came. Both picked at their meals.

Micah felt Julie's eyes on him, studying him as if they were in a deep negotiation.

"You've changed."

She was poking him, trying to provoke him and hear him defend himself with cries of "Not true." But it *was* true. "Yeah, I have."

It stopped her.

"Come see the house, Jules."

"Come back to your life. Our life."

"It's not over yet."

"What's not over? The house is helping you 'rediscover yourself'? Figure out 'who you are'? Are you kidding? I played along when you first said it, but now that three months have skated by, it's a wrinkled, old excuse." Julie waved her hands in the air. "Find yourself. Find yourself!"

"I'm not the same person."

"Whatever you think you're becoming isn't the real you. The real Micah is conquering the world, on his way to becoming one of the youngest *billion*aires in the world. Trips to the Alps. To Saint-Tropez. Parties in Hollywood every other weekend. Hardware companies begging to ally themselves with RimSoft."

Something stirred in Micah. Something saying with deep conviction Julie was right.

"The real Micah is confident, knows where he's going, and is in love with me. You can't keep living in both worlds. You're going to have to choose one way or the other. Not next week. Not tomorrow. Now."

The two worlds flashed into his mind at the same time. The world of the house, Rick, and Sarah, and the world of Seattle, RimSoft, and Julie. For an instant both worlds lingered. Then something snapped.

Business jaunts off to Italy, to Australia, and to New Zealand, being invited onto movie sets whenever he wanted, suites in Las Vegas thrown at him, multimillion-dollar software deals, the magazine covers and TV profiles—he missed it. How could he stay in Cannon Beach? Too small. Too confining. What had he been thinking? For a weekend. Yes. For a life? Impossible.

He was at a decision point. A crossroads.

He looked up at Julie. Gorgeous. Sharp. A remarkable business partner. She'd been on edge lately, but that was his fault. He was the one who had withdrawn to Cannon Beach and snuffed out the candle of their romance. Not her.

It was time to go back to Seattle. Cannon Beach could still happen. God was doing things. But it could be done at a jog instead of a sprint. These past three months he'd played at the edges of his company—not truly involved.

And he missed the world's thunderous applause. He missed the kick of meeting his software heroes he'd grown up reading about, getting box seats comped at any sporting event he wanted to attend, the penthouse suite in every hotel in Europe when he traveled overseas. The rush of the kill filled his imagination. He hadn't given it up, but it had certainly been on hold. An urge deep down demanded he dive back in.

"You can't tread water in this business," Julie continued. "It moves like lightning. You know it. Stay where you are, competitors catch up and you're headed backward."

"I'm that important?" He smiled.

Julie didn't smile back. "Micah, this is serious. In another two months the stockholders won't understand this extended working from the beach. The board already questions your new work ethic. Our employees are spreading rumors about your mental health, and your partner and soul mate wonders if there's any future in the relationship."

It wasn't a threat. She had every reason to make the statement. Plus, she was right. He had to choose.

"You're right." Micah spun his knife counterclockwise. "It's decision time." He rubbed the back of this neck. "Time to get back to life in Seattle."

"Yes!" Julie slapped her hand on the table. "When?"

"A few more days. By next weekend at the latest."

He would throw off this bizarre life he'd been living. And he wouldn't wait till next weekend. His spiritual fantasyland had gone far enough. He'd stride out of the café, leave his car in the parking lot, jump in Julie's, and be back in Seattle tonight. The kingdom there pulled at him. And he *wanted* to be pulled back into that intoxicating world. It was a drug and he wanted—*needed*—a fix.

Micah grabbed Julie's hands, pulled them up to his face, kissed them, and told her he'd go back with her that night.

But the moment he promised his return, his body went cold. It was a lie. Seattle wouldn't last. A verse Sarah had quoted the week before surfaced in his mind like a dolphin breaking free from the water.

"If any man builds on the foundation with gold, silver, precious stones, wood, hay, straw, each man's work will become evident; for the day will show it because it is to be revealed with fire, and the fire itself will test the quality of each man's work. If any man's work which he has built on it remains, he will receive a reward. If any man's work is burned up, he will suffer loss; but he himself will be saved, yet so as through fire."

Was RimSoft gold and silver or wood, hay, and straw? If he was taken through the fire right now, what would remain? If the here and now did echo in eternity . . . what echoes had he created?

The rest of their meal was filled with talk about new products and what part of Europe they'd explore during their next vacation. Micah played along, a sick sensation growing in his stomach. By the time he paid the bill and they stepped outside the restaurant, he felt ready to vomit.

"I'll set up dinner for us at Toro's to celebrate your coming home." Julie bounced on her right leg. "Saturday night work for you?"

"Perfect," Micah replied with as much emotion as he could fake convincingly.

They walked to their cars. The crunch of the crushed red rock under their feet screamed at him to tell Julie the truth. That he wouldn't be back Saturday night. Or the next. Or the next.

Micah stopped and watched Julie take four more steps before she turned.

"What is it?"

He stared at her, looked away, then looked back. A part of him would always be with her. "I'm probably not coming back to us for a long time, if ever."

She closed her eyes and let her head fall back. "I know." Then the tears came. He watched her cry for what seemed like hours. When she looked at him again, her eyes were sad. Tender.

Suddenly Julie kicked the gravel at her feet. "I saw it coming. Religion rears up and roars." She paced in front of her car. After the third pass she stopped. "That's it, isn't it? You've bought into the whole Jesus-thing again, lock, stock, and Bible."

Micah walked over to her car and leaned against it. "What about you?"

"Don't even try. I have nothing against God. I'm sure he's great for kids and little old ladies who like to make quilts but not for people like us." She kicked the gravel again. "Why are you doing this to us? Come back to Seattle!"

"He's real."

"I don't care!"

Micah pleaded with his eyes, but she was shutting down. He had no clue what to say. "Julie, if you would just—"

"No. Let it go." She stood with arms folded, shoulders tensed, and foot digging a hole in the tiny stones at her feet. A sigh. Her shoulders sagged and her arms untangled. She eased over to him.

"Don't try. It's okay." She stepped closer and kissed him on the cheek. "Remember me." She walked to her car without looking back.

He'd lost another part of Seattle, this time by his own choice.

|||||||

A thick fog hugged the coast as Micah arrived back in Cannon Beach, the fog even thicker surrounding his house. Midnight. Too late, too late to talk to anyone but himself.

"How do you think it went?" the voice asked.

"Running the company together is going to be awkward."

"Not really. It's been years since you really ran it together. You do your thing; she does hers. And if you want hard, cold reality, Julie could disappear at this point. While it would create a momentary buzz on the radar screen, RimSoft would survive just fine."

"True. Probably could survive without me too, based on the question she raised."

"Which is?"

"That I need to choose that world or this one. Think she's right?"

"No. I think we can do, should do, both," the voice said.

"Really?"

"Absolutely. We should start brainstorming how we can use our software talents to advance the Kingdom of God."

"Love it. Let's start storming our brains."

"First, I want to talk about the music room and what we created there."

"Not bad was it?" Micah smiled.

"Incredible."

"And what about the thoughts that popped into my head? My Rip van Winkle heart is waking up."

"I think the thoughts were from God, but they definitely didn't come from your heart," the voice said. "We must be so careful when something powerful comes from God that we don't listen to the voice of the enemy alongside it."

"Whoa, whoa, whoa. You lost me. What part of that experience was from the enemy?"

"A small part, Micah. But much truth mixed with a small lie makes the lie so much easier to swallow."

"What part?" Micah folded his arms and leaned against the back wall of the room.

"Jeremiah tells us the heart is deceitful beyond all wickedness."

"Okay."

"And God forgives. But to entertain the idea that our heart is good and there are more good things to come out of it? No. Sorry. The Word is clear on that. Why does the psalmist sing 'Create in me a clean heart' unless it's unclean? Don't misunderstand; the Bible says our sins are washed white as snow. But to describe our hearts as good and holy? No. That's where the subtle lie slipped in."

"Interesting." Micah nodded.

"God gives us a moral code we must follow," continued the voice. "We have the choice to follow it or not. When we choose not to follow it, we sin and He forgives. But to live by the heart is a dangerous thing. We were given the Word so we will not be taken in by the deceptions of the heart."

"I'm not sure you and Archie would see eye to eye on that."

"Man can be deceived, Micah. The Word can't. This is why we need to operate from the mind and not the heart. Now if we could come up with a piece of software that could help us do that 100 percent of the time . . ."

The room went silent. Micah stood. "Wow. That is something to give serious consideration to. Let's figure it out."

"More tomorrow. It's late and I'm wiped."

"Me, too. Talk to you soon."

"All right, pal," the voice said. "Sleep well."

Before sleep buried him, Micah had worked out the basics for the software. He had to tell Rick about it.

CHAPTER 20

Software that would change the Kingdom of God. Rick would love the idea.

On Sunday afternoon Micah walked north on Main Street toward Rick's gas station full of inspiration. Before he reached the garage, he spotted Rick's Rams hat as it bobbed above the crowd half a block ahead.

When Micah caught up to him, Rick said, "I was hoping to bump into you today."

"Really? That was going to be my line."

"Why, you gotta another house story?"

"No, I've got an idea that will revolutionize people's relationship with God."

"Really. Gotta hear about this." Rick motioned them toward the beach, and they turned left at the next corner. Three minutes later Haystack Rock towered in front of them.

"I want to hear your idea," Rick said as they headed south. "But first tell me about your talk with Julie."

"Tough. Glad it's over." Micah paused. "For a few minutes I seriously considered going back to Seattle for good."

"The pull of two different worlds, huh?"

"Exactly, which is what gave me the inspiration for a new piece of software."

"That's what gave you the idea?"

Micah imagined Rick was staring at him but didn't turn to find out if he was right.

"That and a few other things . . . but let me describe it." Micah kept staring straight ahead, concentrating on the gray sand stretching out in front of them.

"If we're constantly pulled in two different directions, if we're constantly trying to figure out the right path, why not give people the answers to every situation they ever come up against? I'm going to develop an intricate set of biblical principles to live by based on Scripture. A set of guidelines that will be the heart of the software. You have a problem? A situation where you don't know what action to take? Plug it into the program, and it'll give you the right thing to do. Even show you a verse that backs up the answer."

"You're serious."

"Yeah, I'm serious. God has given me talent in the world of software. Maybe I'm supposed to use that ability for His good. It would sell."

"I'll bet." Rick's face looked like he'd swallowed a slug.

"It would help people."

"Maybe you're right. Sounds absolutely wonderful. Stellar. Stunning. Magnificent."

Micah frowned. "You're mocking me."

"No, I love it. With a program like that, who needs their heart? For that matter, who needs a relationship with God?" Rick picked up a piece of driftwood and hurled it into the churning surf.

"I'm not saying do away with God. I'm just saying why not use the wisdom in the Bible and modern technology to systematically point people in the right direction?"

"What about deeper relationship with God? Intimacy with Him? His heart knowing ours. Ours knowing His. Hearing His voice and following it?"

Micah watched two kite surfers launch themselves high enough into the air to become silhouettes against the late-afternoon sun. "God gives us a moral code we must follow. To live by the heart is a dangerous thing. We were given the Word so we will not be taken in by the deceptions of the heart."

"Who's been telling you that?" Rick's voice took on a sharp edge.

A wave of heat passed over Micah's face. "No one. Just talking to myself about it."

"Really." Rick stepped in front of Micah and looked him in the eye. "Just yourself?"

"Yeah."

Rick nodded, turned, and trudged down the beach. "So we live only by the Word?"

"Man can be deceived. The Word can't," Micah said as he caught up to Rick. "We need to follow its guidelines."

"So what do the Christians all across the world today do who don't have Bibles? Are they living in less truth than you and I?"

Micah was silent.

"The Word is our foundation. It's what we test everything against. But during the first fifteen hundred years of the church, there were no Bibles in the homes of the people. Not until Gutenberg invented the printing press. Who led them? How did they know truth?"

"You're saying we don't set up principles to live by?" Micah asked.

"I'm saying Jesus is our example and He was never led by rules or set formulas. He was led by the Holy Spirit. Period. And the Spirit rarely did things the same way twice. You can't plug things into some formula and get the answer. Man would like to reduce walking with God to some rule book of pat answers. But that's not Christianity. Man has turned Christianity back into Mosaic Law. Don't drink, don't smoke, don't swear, and don't go to R-rated movies. Bingo. You're a Christian. Most churches use those four unwritten rules to judge whether someone is saved or not. But I don't think any of those things have a lick to do with true relationship with God. Do you?"

"I'd think more than twice about a guy who smokes, swears like a trucker, drinks like a whale, watches NC-17 movies, and then tells me he's a follower of Jesus."

"Me, too." Rick leaned down to pick up half a sand dollar and slipped it into his pocket.

"You're just going to let that little contradiction hang in the air?" Micah asked.

"The Pharisees were the ultimate followers of principles and rules. Jesus called them whitewashed tombs. Look the right way. Say the right things. Do this; don't do that! Jesus blew their minds. He said the wrong things, hung out with the wrong kind of people: prostitutes and tax collectors. Ate the wrong kind of food, healed on the wrong day, sat down to dine too many times with the wrong kind of people." Rick grabbed another half sand dollar off the beach.

"So they branded Him a drunkard and a glutton. A friend of sinners. But He only cared about one thing—setting something free that you abandoned and buried a long time ago." Rick stared into Micah's eyes. "The treasure of the Kingdom."

"And this treasure is?"

Rick leaned in and smiled. "Your heart."

"Jeremiah says the heart is deceitful beyond all wickedness."

"Really?"

"You know this, Rick! God forgives us and washes us from sin. But our heart is good? Sorry. Why would David say, 'Create in me a clean heart' unless it's unclean? To describe our hearts as good and pure and holy? It's just not biblical."

A wave of anger and concern passed over Rick's face so quickly Micah wasn't sure he'd actually seen it.

"You can't change a man from the outside in. And to transform a son of Adam from the inside out, Jesus must go deep into the core and change the heart. Then the outside will change. It's called the new covenant. All things, even your heart, become new."

Micah's head felt like it was full of molasses. Rick was as convincing as the voice had been the night before. "Let's say you're right. How do I change my heart?"

"Allow it to surface. Then invite Him in to do some fixing." Rick turned to Micah, grabbed him by both shoulders, and smiled. "And guard it with everything in you." Then he strode back the direction they'd come.

Micah stood watching the kite surfers free themselves from gravity for an hour before he headed back to town.

Pulling into his driveway, he thanked God that Wednesday—Archie day—was only three days away. Rick. The voice. Confusion. Maybe Micah would get some clear direction from Archie's next letter. He needed it.

CHAPTER 21

Archie time would come early on Wednesday. Micah would make sure of it.

Tuesday night, before crashing into bed and crawling under his navy blue comforter, Micah set his cell phone alarm to go off at 12:01 a.m. Archie wanted him to wait a week before opening each letter? No problem. 12:01 Wednesday morning would qualify as a week. And Micah needed answers.

He'd avoided the voice room the past few days and Rick as well. Too much conflicting advice. He hoped Archie's next letter could slice through some of the fog filling his brain.

> *July 13, 1991*
> *Dear Micah,*
> *As children we were told of the Big Bad Wolf and were introduced to the Wicked Witch of the West in* The Wizard of Oz. *In* The Lord of the Rings *Frodo faces the evil Lord*

*Sauron. Luke Skywalker must face his father Darth Vader
in Star Wars.*

*In every comic book there is a deadly foe the hero must
vanquish.*

*Why does every story contain a villain? Because within
yours one will most certainly be present as well.*

*Satan and his emissaries war against God and His
angels, and if we are followers of the Savior, this war is
directed toward us as well. While on Earth, villains are
set in our path to distract us from the destiny that God has
written for us from before the foundation of the world.*

*Unfortunately I cannot tell you who your villain is. But
I can say his goal will be to kill, steal, and destroy.*

*The target of the assault will always be our heart. And
clarity on where the truth lies will be elusive.*

Wonderful. Micah tightened the blanket wrapped around him
as he sat downstairs in his overstuffed chair in the great room. The
low hum of the ocean sneaked through the walls of the house, but
it still felt silent in the room. The view out the picture windows was
black, the clouds not letting the moon or stars make even the hint
of an appearance over the sea.

He put down the letter and let out a sigh. When he talked to
the voice, it seemed to be truth. When he talked to Rick, his words
rang true. When he read Archie's letters, *they* seemed full of truth.
So where was the sliver of a lie coming from?

Then again, maybe he was Luke Skywalker and his villain was
the obvious choice: his dad. Micah continued reading.

*At this point, five weeks have transpired in our journey
together so my guess is you've already met this foe.*

Wait. The letter seemed to imply he'd meet his villain during his time in Cannon Beach, not before. Did that rule out his dad?

Micah set the letter down again and stared at the dark-paneled ceiling. It was a strange thought. He'd jumped ahead of Archie already and assumed that this foe would of course look like an angel of light and not like a villain at all. It would be one of the people he least expected. Sarah? Hardly. Archie? Yeah, right. Rick? Impossible.

But then Micah's talk with Rick on the beach returned to him and he wondered. He toyed with the idea for an instant, then pushed it to the back of his mind. No way. He knew Rick too well. Didn't he? But if not Archie or Rick or Sarah or his dad, then who? He read on.

> I am speculating, but I surmise you will be predisposed to trust this villain almost automatically, that he will find a way into your heart that you would not expect and therefore have not built a guard against.
>
> And of course this person will not look evil, instead appearing as an ally. But, Micah, no matter how he appears or how smooth his tongue, if his counsel does not line up with the Word of God and the wisdom of the Holy Spirit, you must not let him into your heart.
>
> Be wary, be cautious. Test the spirits.
>
> Nothing can separate us from the love of God through Christ Jesus.
>
> Archie

Micah glanced at the clock on his coffee table. 12:20 a.m. He was wide awake now. Getting back to sleep would be a jousting match with his mind acting as the lance. A cold shiver raced down his spine. The letter pushed the idea of talking to Rick or the voice further down the list of options. Next step?

Sarah. She never confused him. That's who he should talk to. What would she be doing when the sun rose in five hours?

CHAPTER 22

Sarah strode across the sand at a brisk clip. It was her alone time, her God time. She wore two T-shirts and a hooded sweatshirt. Being hungry she could tolerate. Tired? Doable. But cold? No.

The tide chart said a sliver of gold light would peek over the eastern foothills at 5:48. Sarah looked at her watch. Four more minutes.

Her eyes opened and closed every four or five seconds in rhythm to the light melody sneaking out of her mouth. It was a time to sing, to think, to pray, to listen. It startled her when a voice slightly louder than the waves called out from behind her.

"I don't see many people out here this early."

She turned to see Rick twenty yards behind her. Sarah smiled. "That's why I come this time of the day. No one to disturb the quiet. It's a good time to connect with God. And you?"

"For the same reason." He took half-a-dozen long, loping strides to join her.

The slightest hint of wind swirled, as if it couldn't decide which direction to blow. Sarah turned her face to where in seconds the sun would crest the horizon and cast gold on the beach. She glanced at Rick. They went to the same church and talked, often at length, when she filled up her Subaru or when they bumped into each other in town. Yet the way Micah talked about Rick gave her a deeper, richer perspective on the mechanic, and she had enjoyed their little conversations more and more over the summer.

As they strolled down the beach, a wave broke free from the others and sprinted toward their shoes. They stepped back in unison, then watched the water recede into the sea.

"Can I ask you something a bit personal?" Rick said.

"Sure."

"I was hoping we might have a conversation about our mutual friend." Rick pulled off his Rams hat and rubbed his graying head.

"Micah?" Sarah's face warmed, and she replied without looking at Rick.

"You thought I might be talking about someone else?" Rick laughed.

"No."

"I care for him, Sarah. I've seen a lot like him over the years. But not a lot like him."

"Care to explain?"

"Not really. You probably know what I mean."

She knew exactly what he meant.

They walked out among three lone rocks the outgoing tide had left naked. Sarah bent down and touched the back of a burgundy-toned starfish that hid under an outcrop of rock.

"I see amazing gifts in him." Sarah watched the sun sparkle on the waves. "I also see a man in chains of his own making, and he doesn't even know he's bound by them. Someone who deep down wants freedom. Who doesn't know who he is. I see the man he could be. Most of all I see"—she looked up at Rick before finishing—"myself."

"Before your injury."

"Yes."

The wind picked up and Rick zipped up his bottle green Windbreaker in protest.

"What do you see in him?" Sarah said.

"The same. So I'm praying for him. Being a friend. Jesus invited me into his life so I answered."

They eased farther down the sand alone, only spotting an occasional early morning jogger.

"Can you trust me?" Rick asked softly.

She said nothing.

"You *can* trust me."

"And if I do?"

"You're asking yourself, 'Could I fall in love with Micah?' And you're scared of getting hurt because of things you know."

She turned away and begged the wind to dry her tears quickly. Love? How could he know that? Was it that obvious?

"You have to be strong, Sarah. Be true to what God has spoken to you about Micah. Don't push it, but don't hold back, either."

Rick stopped walking. Sarah didn't. How could Rick know what God told her? He probably wanted an indication that she'd heard him. She swallowed and put her head into the wind. She had heard. She had definitely heard.

‖‖‖‖

As she flipped through a mystery in the Cannon Beach Book Company late that afternoon, a muted voice behind her said,

"While we don't mind a small amount of browsing, we have a strictly enforced time limit on how long someone can look at the books without actually buying one."

Sarah didn't turn and said in mock whisper, "Then arrest me, and throw away the key."

She turned to face Micah and tried to keep her heart from leaping ahead of her mind. It had been almost two weeks since they'd seen each other, and she admitted it—she missed him. Badly. She hadn't returned his phone calls about the "praying for you for years" comment. What would she say? She couldn't tell him. But she'd hoped to run into him every day since.

Sarah gazed into his baby-blue eyes and admitted Rick was right. Her feelings went deeper than missing. She was falling in love. A shopper next to them dropped her book, and Micah stooped to pick it up. It was a welcome distraction, giving Sarah a few more seconds to collect her thoughts.

God was drawing Micah, leading him. But he still had to make the choice to follow or not, and it frightened her, because she could tell he was resisting God's pull. Micah had even told her he was. So much of his heart was still wrapped up in Seattle. What if his final choice was not her and Cannon Beach?

"Hey, you, how's life?" Micah stood and brushed a strand of her brown hair back from her face.

"Always fascinating. And you?"

"Same." His warm eyes invited her, drew her in.

"Beach walk?"

"Sure."

After reaching the beach, they headed north toward Ecola Creek. A mild wind tickled their faces as the sand squeaked under their feet, but the breeze had only a hint of coolness. The coastline was nearly empty. Three kites struggled to rise in the soft wind, and in the distance two young families poked in the tide pools at the base of Haystack Rock.

They ambled down the beach and talked about nothing. The waves lulled them into silence until Micah brought up the subject she didn't know how to respond to.

"I need to ask you something. It's not a big deal." Micah kicked the sand. "Actually it is, but it's a weird question, and I don't know where to start."

Here it comes. Sarah clenched her hands. She'd suspected he wouldn't drop the question till he got an answer. "The beginning always lends clarity," she finally answered, glancing at him from the corner of her eye.

"When you came over for dinner, I said you were beautiful. Your answer flew by me at first, but the next day it smacked me like a wave in the face."

She stared at the gray sand, her heart pounding. It wasn't the question she expected. It was worse. Sarah knew exactly what he was about to ask. That night at dinner she'd let it slip. She thought she'd gotten away with it. Obviously not.

"Okay," she whispered.

"It was your response to me saying 'you're beautiful.' You remember?" Micah stopped walking.

She stopped as well, dropped her head, and pushed up a little mound of sand between her feet and Micah's. "Let's say I don't."

"You asked about Julie and me."

Sarah nodded, watching the sand at her feet.

"I hadn't told you her name."

Sarah started walking again.

"How did you know her name was Julie?"

A tinge of warmth blossomed in her face. She felt Micah following her. A flock of gulls soared overhead and squawked at her—as if on cue—demanding she speak. But Micah broke the silence first.

"And the day we rode up to Indian Beach together? The 'praying for me for years' comment still has me curious, too."

Great. A double shot of as-awkward-as-they-come questions. Sarah kept walking as she looked out over the gray waves toward Tillamook Rock Lighthouse sitting a mile offshore. To be that isolated right now would be heaven. She stopped but didn't turn when she spoke. If there was any hope of a future with Micah, she had to tell him, but she didn't have to watch his reaction to her outlandish reasons.

"Five years ago, right after I came to Cannon Beach, I stood alone at Hug Point and watched the sun drop into the ocean. This indescribable peace settled around me, and in that moment I felt like God told me something. Something I've believed at times with everything in me and other times thought I made up inside my own head."

She hesitated. Should she drop it or plunge in all the way? She plunged. "He said one day I would fall in love with a man I barely knew down here in Cannon Beach. He'd be on a journey back to God and I'd be part of it. Then, clear as a flash of lightning against a black sky, I saw the name *Julie* in my mind. It didn't take much to realize there would be a Julie somehow connected to this guy. So I've prayed for years . . ." She trailed off. What more could she say? Silence surrounded her as she steeled for Micah's reaction. Had she said too much?

Since that dinner at his house, Sarah had known it was Micah. She was drawn in, without logic or explanation. Oh, the man he could be if he would choose life!

He was bright, funny, handsome. But what drew her was more. Deeper. It had God's fingerprints on it. Rick said not to push it and not to hold back. Which one had she done by answering Micah's question? She feared the former.

Tears pooled in her eyes as she stopped walking and fixed her gaze on the horizon where the ocean and the sky met. The waves were too loud to tell if Micah was still behind her or if he had walked silently away.

The next moment his arms slid around the sides of her waist from behind and pulled her back gently into his chest. He nuzzled her hair away from her cheek and kissed her there like the first ray of morning sun.

She turned, and this time his kiss was on her lips. Warm. Tender. Lingering. A long embrace followed that wrapped around her like a waterfall of comfort, drowning out the sound of the ocean, the wind, and everything else in her world. She was home.

A moment later her tears spilled onto her cheeks. If only it could last.

CHAPTER 23

Over the next week Micah took Sarah on two mountain bike rides and out to dinner three times. They watched *Singin' in the Rain*, *Casablanca*, and *Pride & Prejudice* in his media room, followed each time by a walk on the beach and kisses that probably would have made anyone watching blush. He talked with her for hours about the house, not everything but enough to clear his head and hear her always-wise insights.

They talked more about their plan to do the STP bike race together next summer and maybe a triathlon as well. They definitely would hit the slopes as soon as Mount Bachelor opened their full set of chairlifts.

"You'll make me look so bad on the snow," Micah said as they strolled through the soft sand.

"Yep, I sure will." Sarah laughed, grabbed him around the waist, and pulled him to the ground. "I'm kidding, it's only July.

There's five months for me to teach you the secrets of skiing before we hit the snow."

Was he in love? Not sure. But he was definitely in heavy, heavy like.

Although Sarah seemed to feel the same, there were times he spotted sadness in her eyes. Or fear. He couldn't tell which. Maybe both. When he asked about it, she said it was nothing. He knew it wasn't. And it felt like the sadness was directed at him.

But overall, by the time next Wednesday rolled off the calendar, he felt at peace. Nothing strange had happened in the house, and Shannon assured him daily that RimSoft was under control.

Maybe his life had stopped to catch its breath. Even Archie's letter was positive and intriguing, in a good way.

> *July 22, 1991*
> *Dear Micah,*
>
> *I feel compelled, at this point in our journey together, to give notice of a particular room within your home. It is priceless and beyond the confines and restrictions of imagination. It is a room truly too wonderful for me to attempt description.*
>
> *There is no need to try in any case, as I believe after reading this letter, you will find it soon. Remember the purpose of man: To know God intimately and enjoy Him forever.*
>
> *In awe of the King,*
> *Archie*
> *P.S. Psalm 16:11: "You will make known to me the path of life; In Your presence is fullness of joy; In Your right hand there are pleasures forever."*

Micah found the room just after seven o'clock that evening. The smell that came from under the door intoxicated him—a potent mixture of roses and apple trees in full bloom. Light streamed out from under the door and made the hallway dim by comparison.

There was no knob, so he reached out to push open the door. But before his hand touched the wood, he stopped. Heat or coolness—he couldn't tell which—radiated off the door. He touched his finger to the wood and yanked it away. Was the door scorching or refreshingly cool?

He touched it again. Longer this time. It was cool, like an alpine lake on the hottest day of summer. Micah put his entire hand on the door, but he forgot to push as an overwhelming sensation engulfed him.

It felt like a waterfall bursting open in the middle of his soul, then racing to see which end of his body it would reach first. Neither won, as they tied in drenching him in a thundering wave of joy. He fell back from the door breathing hard.

Whatever was behind there could kill him. But he wasn't sure he cared.

He eased forward, closed his eyes, placed his palm on the door again, and pushed. Once more wonder swept through him as the door moved inward, achingly slow. Then it stopped. He backed up and stared at where his hand had been. Where he'd pushed was a perfect imprint of his hand, an inch deep into the surface of the door. He could make out his fingerprints. As he stared, the imprint of his hand moved back into place.

Unreal.

His eyes dropped to the brilliant light that streamed out from under the door—almost liquid. He stepped backward, bumped into the wall behind him, and slid slowly down it. He watched the light till sleep stole over him. When he woke, the light was gone, and he tried pushing on the door again. Unyielding, ordinary wood. And it still wouldn't open.

||||||

On Saturday Sarah and Micah drove south to Heceta Head Lighthouse, took pictures, toured the Sea Lion Caves, and munched on fish 'n' chips at Mo's chowder house. Sunday was a bike ride down to Oswald West State Park, dinner and laughter that night at the Fireside with Rick, where for dessert the three of them demolished a chocolate torte in less than two minutes.

That night Micah sat on his deck and watched the stars vanish behind a shroud of clouds rolling in off the ocean. He closed his eyes and smiled. Heavy like was over. He'd fallen in love with more than just Cannon Beach. Sarah had taken up residence deep in his heart.

RimSoft's stock had risen two points over the past two weeks, and e-mails between Julie and him—while not exactly warm—were polite.

But an e-mail arrived Sunday night that promised all in Seattle was not well.

CHAPTER 24

Micah slammed the snooze button on his alarm Monday morning and groaned. Still nighttime! The e-mail from the night meant getting up at 4:30 so he could get to RimSoft in time for a 10:00 firing.

He showered with his eyes shut but was wide awake by the time he reached his office and growled at Shannon. "I should still be in Cannon Beach. Why do I do this to myself?"

"Good question, boss. They would have taken care of it for you."

Micah shook his head. "With Federal Trade Commission on the attack? No, I need to do this. Make sure there are no mistakes."

"He'll be in your office in ten minutes."

Micah made a half turn to walk toward his office, then spun back. "It's the only solution, don't you think?"

Shannon didn't answer. Her expression said more clearly than words could that he was about to do something wrong.

"I need to make a quick phone call. Soon as I'm done you can send him in." He walked into his office.

"Have fun letting him go," Shannon said.

At 10:15 Micah walked out of his office behind the man he'd just fired. He stared at Shannon as he tried to push down the guilt that churned inside.

"How'd it go?" Shannon asked as soon as the man walked beyond earshot.

"Fine." But Micah's conscience screamed for attention. He kept telling himself it was just business, but his heart wouldn't let him believe it. On his way to his condo that evening after work, he called Sarah.

"How's Seattle?"

"Empty without you. I'm ready to come back." Micah lowered his windows and let the soft coolness of a Seattle summer evening fill his car.

"And that will be?"

"Tomorrow afternoon. I've got two more meetings to slog through. Just thought I'd call and say hi."

"Hi."

They laughed softly.

"So anyone fascinating drop by today for a Double Fudge Rocky Road?"

"Actually a couple of movie stars came by."

"Seriously?"

"No."

"You are funny," Micah said.

"I try not to bore you. Like your meetings. So any major moves in the world of software today?"

The firing flashed into his mind. "Well, not really, but since I've got you on the phone, let me run a hypothetical situation past you. To test your business acumen."

"Ready."

"You might have to fire a guy to solve some problems unrelated to him. Has to be done quick. It's the only answer. But he does a pretty good job." Micah pulled onto Denny Way and headed west.

"Pretty good?"

"Yeah, not great, not horrible. Let's call him a B worker."

"Is he dishonest? Reliable? Is his effort a B or his work a B?"

"No to your first question, yes to the second. Work is a B, effort an A."

"So he's honest, reliable, and hardworking." Sarah snorted. "You're kidding about firing him, right?"

"No. Why?" Micah switched his Bluetooth to the other ear.

"Because it's obvious."

"No question, you'd keep this guy?"

"In this hypothetical situation, what makes him worthy of getting fired?"

Micah went silent.

"You're playing with someone's life."

"Before you condemn me, get a few more details. We had to do it to get the government off our back. FTC claimed we violated a bunch of monopoly rules, all garbage. This appeases them, problem solved. And believe me, this guy will be taken care of. We'll give him a huge severance package, plus I've already called a friend who has promised he'll hire him. He'll make more money than he did here."

"So you make him feel like a loser, but since he gets another job and makes more, it's okay?"

Micah took a right and drove up toward the entrance to Seattle Center. "There's a bigger picture to look at. The reasoning is right."

"I don't care if the reason is perfect, Micah. It's wrong."

"The reason *is* perfect, Sarah. We fire this guy, and a significant legal and PR problem goes away. And the guy gets more than taken care of financially." He pulled into a parking lot near the Children's Museum, threw his car into park, and yanked the key out of the ignition.

"Ninety-nine percent truth mixed with 1 percent lie is still 100 percent lie. Always."

"So you won't let me explain why it won't upset the guy in the least?"

"Doesn't matter. You're not dealing in truth. Every choice we make takes us farther down one of two paths. Both paths lead to a kingdom, Micah. You have to decide once and for all which kingdom you want to live in. Because eventually one of the kingdoms has to—and will—disappear. You're still living with a foot in each world. God gives only two choices: hot and cold. Living in the world of lukewarm gets you spit out."

Micah bit into his lower lip. "I know your vast experience in the business world gives you the right to judge me. So while we're at it, do you have any other great moral teachings? Like a holier way to brush my teeth?"

"This isn't like you," she replied just above a whisper. "I don't need your sarcasm right now, and you don't need to give it. I'm not teaching morality here and you know it. I'm talking about the heart. Yours. What is the Holy Spirit that lives in that heart telling you? Did you ask Him?" She sighed. "I'll see you when you get back down here."

"Sarah!"

The line was dead.

Micah ripped off his Bluetooth and hurled it onto the passenger seat of his BMW. What a wi—! He stopped himself, shocked at the anger that wrestled to get out.

He was not an angry person. Wit, humor, maneuvering situations with the power of persuasion were his weapons in controlling his business and his life. But anger? It never advanced anything. He'd buried his anger and his pain a long time ago. Micah rubbed the scar on his left hand. This wasn't about his father and what he'd done to Micah after his mom died. He wouldn't let it be.

A moment later he got out of his car and walked toward the fountains in the middle of Seattle Center. As they shot water fifty feet in the air, kids played in the spray raining down, dodging, ducking, laughing. He slumped onto a bench and took Sarah's advice.

"God, I want the truth. What's the right move with this firing? There has to be . . ." He didn't finish. No need to. He sighed, jammed his hand into his pocket, and grabbed his cell phone.

"Yes?" his senior VP answered.

"It's Micah. When are you doing the exit interview?"

"Ten tomorrow morning."

"Cancel it."

"What?"

"We're not letting him go. Call him. If he wants to stay, tell him we want him back. We'll figure another way out of this."

"That is a surprising decision. You do realize you're running the risk of losing a significant portion of what we've gained over the past two years?"

Micah tapped the bench he sat on with his car keys. "Get the team together tomorrow morning at 9:00 so we can put together a strategy."

He hung up and stared at the wooden bench, faded almost white from years of being doused in Seattle's winter rains, then baked with July and August sunshine. He watched two seagulls scream at each other as they fought over an abandoned bag of popcorn and a tourist—probably from the Midwest—take pictures of them.

As he alternated between watching the people and the almost cloudless sky, peace settled over him. A few minutes later a couple rode by with crimson helmets that matched their bikes. Micah pushed a button on his cell phone.

"Hello?"

"Me again."

"Hey," Sarah said.

"I think we're due for some mountain biking."

"Mad still?"

"I'm sorry." Micah clamped his lips together for a moment. "Thanks for having the guts to speak truth."

"You're welcome."

"So you want to ride?"

"How 'bout Friday?" Sarah said.

"Perfect." He lowered his voice. "I miss you. Love you."

"Me, too."

He walked back to his car, planning to go straight back to his condo. But by the time he started the engine, he decided to find a distraction. No doubt he'd made the right decision about his employee; however, it didn't make the frustration—and necessary strategizing that went along with the problem—any easier to deal with. Maybe a movie—no, he didn't need to ingest another helping of his usual high-octane violence or blue comedy flicks. *You are what you eat.* Maybe he'd just find a restaurant with a game on.

Like he used to do with . . . Julie.

That morning Shannon had said she was doing fine. He hoped it was true. He should at least tell her what's going on with the firing, or nonfiring. Besides, it would be good to touch base, see if she'd talk to him through more than just e-mail.

He raced down Mercer, then pulled onto I-5 and headed north. It had been more than two weeks since he'd met Julie at the Halfway Café. Time to break the face-to-face ice.

Six miles up the concrete river, he took the 85th Street exit and headed west toward Green Lake. A world he'd pushed out of his mind rushed back: Julie; her neighborhood; her house; the mountain of hours they'd spent planning RimSoft; the good, the bad, and the wonderful. Micah looked at his watch: 6:50. Probably should have called first, but he was already here.

He rang the doorbell and waited. The door swung open and revealed Julie's familiar face—the striking looks, intelligent eyes, the softness of her blonde hair. Romance might be gone, but he didn't want to lose the relationship. They'd been through too much together, accomplished too much, held too much of each other's history in their heads and hearts to let it all slip away. If she was willing, he wanted friendship.

"May I help you?"

"Jules, listen, sorry to pop in without calling first, but it's been a couple of weeks. I was close by and thought we should touch base."

"Who—?"

"I meant it about being friends. And we own a company together. We should talk every now and then."

She frowned and finished the sentence she'd started five seconds earlier. "Who are you?"

"All right, point taken." Micah smiled. "I know I've been completely incommunicado the last three weeks other than e-mail, so I deserve that. But I want to start fresh and—"

"Listen, pal, if one of my friends set you up to do this, the humor part isn't coming through." She started to close the door, but he blocked it with his foot.

"What are you doing?"

"That's it. If you don't vanish off my porch instantly, I'm dialing 911."

Micah removed his foot and his stomach jumped, as if on a roller coaster at full throttle. She wasn't kidding. Julie pushed the door hard, but he threw his hands out and stopped it before it slammed shut. "Why are you doing this?"

"Jake! I need you here." She turned her head. "Now!"

Micah didn't know whether to shout or turn and run. He probably couldn't have done either, even if he'd wanted to. The shock of what was unfolding froze him in place. Three seconds later Jake and his Popeye-sized forearms stood at the door. He didn't look like a light joke would loosen him up.

"You got a problem, buddy? Need some help?" Jake's tone of voice made it obvious he wasn't about to help anyone.

"No, I'm fine thanks." Micah steeled himself and turned to Julie. "Really sorry. Got the wrong house. But it's weird how much you look like my old . . . an old friend of mine. You could be twins."

Micah turned and left. The only sound behind him was Julie's door slamming shut and Jake swearing at him from behind it.

He staggered down the steps and nearly crumbled face-first onto the sidewalk. As he dug his keys out of his pocket, he steadied himself with one arm on the roof of his car. Once inside he let his head smack against the steering wheel. He gripped the wheel to keep his hands from shaking.

There had to be an explanation.

After a few minutes he glanced up at Julie's house again. Jake stood in the window with his finger pointing down the street. Micah pulled away from the curb.

||||||||

Heading back to his condo, it took three tries before he succeeded in dialing the right number on his cell phone.

"Hello?"

"Rick, it's Micah." He swallowed hard. "We gotta talk."

"What's going on?"

"She's gone!" He slammed his fist into the steering wheel. "Julie is gone."

"You mean she moved? She's leaving the company?"

"I went to her house to touch base, and she acted like we've never met."

"Was she joking?"

"No way." Micah rubbed his face hard as he took the Mercer Street exit off I-5 and screeched up to a stoplight.

"How do you feel?"

"Feel? Are you kidding? She was an intricate part of my life for six years. We built an empire together. Talking to you right now is the only thing convincing me I'm not going insane."

A horn behind Micah blared. He glanced at the green light and crunched the accelerator.

"God is in this."

"I'm on the edge, Rick. I'm right on the edge here. During the past four months I've accepted a lot of weird scenes, but this one takes the cake and swallows it whole."

"God is in this," Rick repeated.

"In what? Systematically stripping me of my entire life?"

"You can make it stop."

"How?"

"You know how."

"I don't need cryptic clues right now. I need hard-core answers."

"Then choose which world you want to live in."

"What?"

"You're living two lives, Micah. God is showing you what is and what could be. Not in your imagination but in real life. Your choices in every moment affect both worlds. You can't step into freedom in Cannon Beach without it affecting the world of slavery back in Seattle."

"Slavery? What are you talking about? Seattle represents more freedom than most people will ever imagine."

"So why not stay there?"

Seattle Center blurred by, and Micah glanced at his speedometer. Twenty-five over the limit. He stomped on the brakes. A conversation with a cop wouldn't be good right now.

"Both worlds can't survive," Rick continued. "At some point you'll have to fully embrace one or the other."

"Why can't I have both?"

"When will you be back down here?"

"I have to meet with my senior VPs tomorrow morning," Micah muttered. "So tomorrow, late afternoon,"

"Fine. Take the evening to settle back in, and we'll meet first thing Wednesday morning."

Micah hung up and tried to smother the turmoil that pinballed around his stomach. His mind spun—not only from the terror of what had just happened but also with chaotic scenarios of what else he might lose. Sure, he'd secured his stock with the stop order, but if he'd lost Julie, why couldn't he lose his entire company? Could God simply wipe RimSoft out of existence?

Of course. Micah snorted. With God all things are possible.

His meeting in the morning to address the Federal Trade Commission quandary shouldn't take more than an hour. The instant it was finished he'd head for Cannon Beach. No matter how evasive Rick was, Micah would get answers.

CHAPTER 25

The instant Rick sat down Wednesday morning at the Fireside, Micah fired his first question. "What is God doing to me? I'm trying to follow Him, trying to change, and then yesterday I lose my temper like I've *never* done in front of my entire team of VPs."

"You did?"

"At one point I took off my shoe and hurled it against the window."

"Wow."

"Yeah, I was over the edge and halfway down the cliff."

"What about getting some food?" Rick took a long sniff. "I love the smell of bacon in the morning."

Micah waved his hand. "I've already ordered for both of us. Should be here by now."

"You're not going to comment on my subtle *Apocalypse Now* reference?"

"Sorry. Not in the mood. And it wasn't subtle."

"So what happened?" Rick dumped two packets of sugar into his empty coffee cup. A few seconds later their regular waitress scuttled by with their order and coffee for Rick.

"What happened?" Micah said. "I honestly don't know. All of a sudden this volcano explodes out of me. I was a certified platinum jerk. I chewed out the entire team because—get this—they wanted to protect me from the FTC. And I cannot figure it out."

"Figure what out?"

"I never get angry. Not that kind of angry. The last time I lost my temper, I was in third grade. I might get sarcastic, zing someone with a verbal barb, but I don't get tomato-face angry. But I lost it with Sarah the other day on the phone, and then yesterday it came out of nowhere—again! It was like the TV had been turned on at high volume in an instant and I couldn't pull the plug. The scene played out like an episode of *How-to-Be-a-Class-A-Pinhead*, and I couldn't do a thing to stop it."

"Like a running back reacting without thinking to avoid a tackle?"

"Exactly, only after it started I *was* thinking. Part of me shouted, 'What are you doing, get yourself under control,' and part of me had cruise control set at 120 miles an hour, hitting everything on the road. And *liking* it." Micah added more coffee to his cream. "So I repeat, what is God doing to me?"

"He's going deeper after your heart," Rick mumbled through a bite of his ham-and-cheese omelet.

"By making a temper tantrum worthy of a five-year-old come out of nowhere?"

"That kind of anger doesn't come out of nowhere." Rick took a slurp of his coffee.

"What's that mean?"

"It means over the years you've become extremely proficient at keeping your anger buried—through sarcasm, witty banter, or dry, cutting remarks—while all the time, deep down, you're seething."

"Seething about what?"

"I don't know. But the Holy Spirit, who does, is causing these things to surface." Rick drained half his orange juice and started in on an English muffin dripping with honey.

"Enlighten me as to why He's doing that."

"Did you ask Him to?"

Micah stared at Rick as he realized the answer. "I didn't think this would be the response."

"Most people don't."

"What comes next?"

"He wants to fix the broken places in your heart."

"Okay, still lost. Need the fog lights here, not real clear what you're saying."

"To heal a wound the Lord needs to bring it to the surface. I'd say He showed you a symptom today. He'll show you the cause if you're willing."

"Willing to what?"

"Well, something inside caused that outburst. As you said, a part of you couldn't keep from exploding. So you have to be willing to go deep into your heart with the Counselor and uncover the cause."

"I have no idea what that means."

"You don't have to." Rick smiled.

"This is about my mom dying, isn't it? About what my dad did afterward."

"I don't know. Maybe. I'm not God."

||||||

When he got home from breakfast, Micah grabbed a fruit punch Powerade, flopped onto an Adirondack chair on his deck, and thanked God it was Wednesday. Archie letter day. He needed answers.

August 11, 1991

Dear Micah,

Have you considered what the strongholds are Paul talks about in his epistles? A friend recently presented me with this explanation: A stronghold is anything that keeps us from the freedom of being in Christ Jesus.

The Gospel of John tells us if we know the Son we shall be free indeed. The apostle Paul says it was for freedom's sake that Christ set us free. He didn't set us free for duty or obligation but for freedom itself. This is indeed a staggering and amazing thought. With that in mind, we must ask what the strongholds are that Jesus wants to set us free from.

The answer is not overly complex. They are anything we've given room to in our lives in an attempt to cover up our wounds from the past; be they from friends, family, coaches, or teachers.

Or parents.

Great, Micah thought. Here we go.

If we do not face the wound, we will fabricate a variety of salves to dull the pain and thus bury it. The relentless pursuit of money, the quest for fame, the approval of men, drug abuse, illicit sexual relations, movies of a degrading nature, even an addiction to food. The list is long, but the reason is always the same.

We try to forgive those who wound us, but this only deals with the symptoms. The wound remains like a field of dandelions with their tips cut off. No, we must always go after the root of the tree and remove it completely so there is no opportunity for the stronghold to return. Only then can we truly forgive.

So he had to forgive? Easy. He would. And he didn't need to go into some wound to forgive someone. As long as someone didn't include his father.

> *I pray you have the strength to go to the root.*
> *Across time,*
> *Archie*
> *P.S. Psalm 51:6: "Behold, You desire truth in the innermost being, And in the hidden part You will make me know wisdom."*

Micah sighed. He felt it. The Counselor wanted to uncover some causes.

He tossed the letter aside. No thanks. Rick always said he had a choice. This time he would choose no.

||||||

That evening he sat in the chair facing his picture windows and numbed his mind with a mystery novel in an attempt to distract himself from the loss of Julie, his outburst at RimSoft, and whatever Archie meant by "going to the root." His escape was interrupted after seven pages when he stretched and a flash of color to his right caught his attention.

Up on the bookshelves surrounding the fireplace sat a picture he'd never noticed. A Little League team looked down on a Seattle Mariners game, all of them in uniform. The backs of their heads were to the camera. He turned it over to look for clues. "Wildcats '91" was scrawled across the back. That was the name of his team when he was a kid.

He slipped the photo into the back pocket of his 501s, sank back into his chair-and-a-half, and eased back into his novel. He refused to focus on any unsolved mysteries for at least a few hours.

Micah didn't think about the picture again till he stripped off his clothes for bed. He pulled out the rumpled photo and stared at it. It could be a picture of any Little League team in the Puget Sound area, out to see the big boys play. Twelve kids, some too big, some too little for the uniforms that united them for a spring of dreams. But something about the picture tickled the back of his mind. He propped the picture up against his nightstand lamp, buried himself in his comforter, and disappeared into sleep without another thought.

Until the dream started.

He stood in a hallway. His house? Micah wasn't sure. Dim light floated in through the windows telling him the last black shaving of night was about to give over to the rush of dawn. He walked down the hallway slowly, feet padding without noise on the thick tan carpet.

Light spilled into the hallway from the first door on his right. A muffled sound came from behind it. Micah pressed his ear against the six-panel door. Yes. Someone inside the room was crying.

He touched the door and the crying stopped, like the mute button being pushed on a TV remote. Micah pushed open the door and stepped inside. Daylight splashed all around him, and he threw his hands up till his eyes could adjust. The smell of overcooked hot dogs swirled around him along with shouts of, "C'mon, need a hit now!"

Sitting. He was sitting somewhere. He lowered his hands and looked around. Third base was right in front of him, stale popcorn at his feet, a crowd of more than fifty filled the faded bleachers.

Little League baseball. He gazed at the scoreboard. Bottom of the ninth with two outs, the team at the plate down by one run, the count two and two with one man on second.

Classic. The glory every kid dreams of.

The terror every kid dreams of.

The kid at the plate was average size. Eight, maybe nine years old. His back was to Micah, dark hair jutting out from under the kid's helmet. He gripped and regripped the bat, as if he could strangle it into getting him a hit.

"You gotta knock this one out!" the third-base coach screamed. "There is no choice. Now is the time. *Now!*"

The pitcher dragged the toe of his cleat across the rubber on the mound, set, wound up, left leg kicking high, and threw a lightning fastball.

The kid lunged toward the ball but didn't swing.

"Ball!" the umpire shouted, and the pitcher feigned disbelief.

Three and two. The next pitch would tell the story.

Another windup. Another pitch. Fastball again.

Another lunge.

The pitch smacked into the catcher's glove like a firecracker and sent a tiny dust cloud into the air.

"Sttteeeeeeeerike three!" the umpire yelled. "Yer out! This game is over!"

But not for the kid at the plate. He dropped his bat to the ground and turned to face the third-base coach. The man strode toward him, shouting through his teeth.

Micah gasped. His throat felt like it was in a vise grip, and the blood drained from his face. He should have seen it coming, but it had been buried so long. This was the day it happened. Six weeks after his mom died.

"You idiot! For the love of Babe Ruth, what were you thinking? You didn't even swing! Do you have any idea what's inside that skull of yours! Do you? Well, I do! I know exactly what's in there. So I'm gonna tell you. Absolutely nothing. Zero. Zucchini. Nada! Just like you!"

The coach took off his hat and spiked it to the ground. "Where's your heart? I'll tell you—you don't have one! You could've at least stuck your bat out there. What a waste. What a complete waste."

The coach reached for the kid and grabbed his jersey at the

collarbone. It tore as the coach yanked at it, sending the kid to his knees.

"I'm sorry—"

"I can't believe you're my son. Unbelievable."

The kid's face was ashen. He again tried to say he was sorry, but the coach told him to shut up. A third apology, a second shut up. When the kid started to say he was sorry the fourth time, the coach swung his clipboard and whacked him over the head with it. The clipboard snapped in two with a sickening crunch. The boy crumpled forward onto his knees and elbows and gasped for air.

"You killed this game. You single-handedly killed it." The boy's dad spun on his foot, took two steps away, then turned and pointed at the boy. "Just like you killed your mom."

An instant later it all vanished: the coach, the people in the stands, bats and balls, the popcorn, everything. Even daylight.

A full moon of silver lit up the infield, lit up the grass, lit up the boy sitting in center field fifty feet from where Micah braced himself against the bleachers.

Micah eased off his seat and walked toward the boy. This was just a dream. Not real. Couldn't be real.

The boy sat just beyond second base, where the grass met the dirt infield, his back to Micah. The torn jersey lay to the boy's left, his glove resting on top. If he heard Micah approach, he didn't show it.

Micah slumped to a squatting position next to the kid and took a deep breath. He knew he was about to look into the eyes of someone he knew intimately.

"Hey. My name is Micah. What's yours?"

The boy turned.

Wake up! He did not want to go through this.

"My nickname is Flash. I guess 'cause I run fast." The kid stared at the grass as Micah sat next to him.

"It's a good name."

They sat together not speaking, just sitting on grass so short and smooth it looked like a fairway.

"I saw the game."

"Yeah," Flash said. "I didn't even swing."

Micah felt a presence inside him speak. *I am here.*

"Why did You bring me?" Micah asked.

You know.

"To bring healing?"

Yes. To bind up a broken heart and set a captive free. Do you want to be free?

"Yes." Micah watched Flash loosen the thin brown laces on his glove, then retighten them. "I'm sorry about what happened today."

When Flash spoke, Micah strained to hear. "I don't really want to live anymore." Flash picked at his shoe.

As the words rang in his ears, the dream faded, as if something was pulling him awake. Part of him wanted to give in, get free of the pain. *Just wake up.*

"I'm so all by myself. Have been since Mom went away during Memorial Day weekend."

Wake up!

No. He had to face it, finish it.

In that instant every infinitesimal detail of the day erupted out of the deepest vault of his heart. Not the day he was seeing now, the day the horror started.

The baseball diamond vanished, and he stood on the beach watching his nine-year-old self beg his mom to save his beach ball.

"Mom! Wind's got it! It's going into the ocean!"

"I'll get it."

"But those waves are big monster waves—"

"They're much bigger to you than they are to me."

"But what if—?"

His mom stopped and smiled. "I'll be fine, Micah. Really."

They ran up to the edge of the water as the wind shoved the ball farther out into the ocean.

Micah tried to smile.

"Don't worry, honey, it's just a few strokes away." His mom jogged into the water, and the waves were soon up to her waist. "Stay there; I'll be with you again in two shakes of Peter Rabbit's fluffy tail."

But she didn't come back. Ever.

"No," Micah whimpered as his mom struggled against the riptide that dragged her out faster than he could believe. "Mom, where are you going? Mommy, come back!"

Once more Micah watched himself scream up and down the beach, "Help her! Help my mom!" He took two halting steps toward the houses behind him. A step north. One south. Then he froze, not knowing which way to go. What to do. He stood on the beach shaking, moaning.

Time seemed to slow as his dad appeared over the crest of the tiny dune his brother, Mick, and he had parked behind. A moment later his dad dropped the bag of groceries and sprinted down the sand, past Micah, out into the surf.

Micah bounced on his toes, trying to keep the sound of his whimpers inside his throat.

Faster! Why couldn't his dad get to her faster? She'd be okay. She'd be fine. She'd promised.

Twenty-five minutes later paramedics carried his mom's lifeless body off the beach toward the ambulance parked next to his dad's car, the gray blanket they'd placed over her fluttering in the breeze.

His dad turned to him, his face white and full of disbelief. "What happened?"

"I don't know."

"Tell me!"

"Mom and I were playing and . . . my beach ball . . . it went into . . ." Micah looked at the sky, the sand, back to the sky. "And . . . and . . . and I asked Mom if she could get it, and she said . . . so she went into the ocean . . . and—"

"Why didn't you—?"

"I didn't know what to—"

"Why didn't you go for help?"

"I tried to, Daddy, I tried, but . . . I was scared."

"You should have found someone!"

"I wanted to . . . but I couldn't move . . ."

"What have you done?" His dad took Micah's shoulders and shook him hard. "*What have you done?*"

Tears rushed up, filled his eyes, and ran in little rivulets down Micah's cheeks.

A few moments later his father turned and walked away.

"Daddy?" Micah stumbled after him. "Daddy!"

"Leave me alone." His father didn't look back; the only sound was a slight swish of his feet through the sand.

Micah ran; it didn't matter where, tears blinding his vision.

His foot caught on a twisted piece of driftwood just below the surface of the sand, sending him hurtling through the air. A lone cluster of jagged rocks stuck up a few inches out of the sand.

He threw out his hands to break the fall and was silent as the sharp point of one of the rocks sliced into his left palm.

The scream came an instant later as pain surged into his hand and blood oozed into the miniature canyon that started at the base of his forefinger and ran down his palm to the start of his wrist.

He found his father ten minutes later, sitting with his back to the front tire of the family van, his eyes vacant.

"I hurt myself, Daddy."

His father looked at Micah's hand for a long time. Thirty seconds, maybe a full minute, then out toward the ocean. "Sorry, but you'll have to figure it out yourself." He stood and opened the van door. "I'm going to the hospital."

Micah sat and watched his dad and brother drive off, the blood on his hand drying, along with the tears that covered his cheeks.

In that moment his heart changed.

Six weeks later on that baseball diamond, it had shattered. *"Just like you killed your mom."*

"I'm so sorry, Flash."

The boy didn't speak.

At nine years old he was alone in the world. No one would love him, no one would guide him. From then on he'd taken control of his life: the good, the bad, and the hideous parts.

"You think there's no one who loves you," Micah said.

"There isn't."

"You feel abandoned, totally alone."

Flash nodded. "I am." The words were a whisper.

Tears flowed from the boy and turned into racking sobs. Micah grabbed Flash and pulled him close, and they cried together.

The tears eventually slowed, and a strand of hope weaved its way into the pain till it overshadowed the sorrow. Healing.

"It's better," said the young Micah. "But I probably won't forget."

Micah hadn't forgotten. How could he ever? As hard as he'd tried, that day at the beach had caused this day on the baseball field and so many other memories like it as he grew up under his father's loathing.

Are you ready? the Voice inside said.

"Yes."

Let's bring the broken part back to where it belongs.

"Flash?" Micah said. "Jesus is going to talk to you now."

"Okay."

I will never leave you, Flash. Ever. You are not alone. I'm here now. I've always been here, and nothing can separate us. Nothing. Do you know that?

Flash nodded.

And I love you with a love that nothing can stop. Do you believe this?

Flash nodded again. Huge tears dropped from the boy's eyes as he crawled up on Micah's lap and wrapped his thin arms around Micah's neck. He held his younger self for ages.

Your turn now, Micah.

"What? Mine? I can't forgive my dad."

I'm not asking you to. That will come. You must first forgive another that will bring great healing.

"Who?"

Yourself.

"For what?"

You did not kill her. It is a lie you have believed for too long. There is nothing you could have done to save her. We must break the lie now.

"I know I didn't kill her; I was nine when I believed that."

Your mind knows the truth, but your heart still believes the lie. In this area of your life, you are still nine. We must heal that part of your heart. Are you willing?

In the dream Micah began speaking.

||||||||

The next morning at 6:30, Micah woke with only a slight recollection of the dream. But the dream didn't slowly fade from consciousness as most did. It went the opposite direction. After two minutes every nuance of the encounter with the younger Micah was etched into his mind.

The healing he'd experienced in the dream went to his core. But was it real?

He mulled it over as he walked toward his weight room. He was up. Might as well get in a workout.

On the way there he stopped by the library to pick up a book on kayaking. Perfect way to stave off boredom in between sets. He stepped toward the bookshelf but stopped cold. Something was definitely out of place. One door was all the library ever had. But now, in the far wall, was a new door.

He inched toward it as his heart pounded. No doubt. It was the door from his dream. He didn't hesitate. He had to know. The door opened without a sound.

There was no baseball field, no grass. Just a small room with a single spotlight shining on a Wildcats baseball jersey. Number 11. His.

His fingers barely touched the jersey as he slid them slowly down its surface. The tear down the middle was gone. No evidence it had ever been torn.

As Micah sank to the floor, a peace he'd never known swept over him. It billowed around him like a space heater pumping out warm currents. He opened his left palm and pulled his finger across it like he was touching a newborn's cheek. He gasped and a puff of laughter escaped his lips.

For the first time in twenty years, it didn't hurt to touch the scar.

He looked at the clock on the wall: 6:45. At 6:48 he was speeding down Highway 101 toward Rick's garage.

CHAPTER 26

Micah was convinced Rick was an iceberg, that he knew far more about the home than he'd ever revealed. It was time to throw on some scuba gear and get to Rick's hidden knowledge, especially about the Wildcat room.

At 7:05 a.m. Micah watched Rick's truck pull into the gas station, Carrie Underwood blaring out the windows. Micah chuckled. Country? Was he kidding?

"You're late," Micah called out to Rick as he eased out of his truck.

"For what?"

"Breakfast. Can you?"

"If we keep hanging out together, I'm going to need a new belt," Rick said.

Their usual waitress stood ready with pad and pen moments after they sat down.

"French toast scramble please. Link sausage and—"

"—over medium on the eggs. Got 'er, Rick. Micah?"

"Eggs Benedict. Thanks." Micah smiled. "There are things on the menu other than the French toast scramble."

"What menu?" Rick raised his coffee cup and looked over the top of it. "How's Sarah?"

Micah couldn't keep a grin from rising to the surface. "Having lots of dinners together. Movies. Walks on the beach. Running together. We're going to do a triathlon. Spending a ton of time hanging out. Plus lots of phone time."

"Have you mentioned the L-word yet?"

"Yeah, most definitely." Micah laughed.

"And the latest on Chateau Taylor?"

When Micah finished telling him about the Wildcat room, all Rick said was, "Sounds good," and stirred his coffee.

"Sounds good?" Micah snorted. "Don't you mean sounds bizarre?"

"How so?"

"Are you kidding? Anyone else would think I'm ready for a white-coat fitting. When's the last time you heard about someone having an encounter with themselves from childhood?"

"Does that make it bizarre?" Rick cocked his head. "Or just rare?"

"Both, maybe. I don't know. I had things happening to me that would never happen in real life. Time to tell me what's going on, Rick. I know you know more than you're telling me."

"How do you know it wasn't real life?"

"I was dreaming."

"So was Joseph when an angel appeared and told him not to divorce Mary. And what about the repaired jersey?"

Micah just shook his head and took a bite of his sourdough toast.

Rick continued. "As you're wrapping your mind around this latest room and trying to decide if it's good or bad, be sure to remember the fruit test."

"Fruit?"

"Jesus says you'll know them by their fruit. What is the fruit that's come out of this? Are you more free?"

"I'll give you that at least."

"When Jesus said He came to heal the brokenhearted, He meant it literally. We talk about people with broken minds wandering around our streets pushing shopping carts full of aluminum cans or sitting in institutions counting ceiling tiles. Their minds are literally broken. So when we say, 'It broke my heart,' we need to realize our hearts are truly broken."

"So that explains why parts of me—"

"—have been broken off and never fixed."

Rick doused his French toast in maple syrup, careful not to let it touch his sausages. "You wondered why you lost it in front of your VPs? Now you know. You wouldn't ask an NBA basketball pro to dunk on a broken leg that had never healed right. All humans have buried wounds that need mending." Rick paused to take a swig of coffee. "Explains a lot, doesn't it?"

"Let's say you're right—and I'm not saying you are. What other parts of me need fixing or healing or whatever?"

"How would I know?" Rick laughed. "The Counselor does the counseling."

As Micah drove home he threw a prayer up, only half serious. "All right, Lord. You want to do more work on my heart? Have at it."

||||||||

The next morning Micah walked down the hallway to his bedroom and noticed a new door just past the linen closet.

Another room. He was almost getting used to it.

Micah was positive it hadn't been there before, yet it was so small there was the ever-so-slight possibility he'd overlooked it. Yeah, right. As if telling himself that would make him feel better.

It was hardly a door, about two-and-a-half-feet tall by two-feet wide, curved at the top with no trim and no doorknob. But still a door. There was nothing to pull, so he dropped to his knees and pushed it open. He ducked his head inside but saw nothing. After a few seconds a sound like a giant lawn mower straining to get up a steep hill roared toward him. Then came voices, men by the sound of it, shouting to be heard over the din.

"Hello!" he hollered into the shadows. No response.

He crawled forward. The instant Micah's head popped through the door, he found himself staring at the interior of a small plane with no seats. A large, dark-haired man, who looked to be in his early sixties, bellowed at him over the roar of the screaming plane engine. "Ready?"

The man had a massive grin and amber eyes that bored into Micah's head. A harness dug into his shoulders, and he reached up to feel goggles on his head.

Skydiving.

Micah glanced around at the other faces staring at him. No question. They expected him to jump. He scooted backward into the hallway of his house, but his heel smacked into something hard. He turned and stared at the cold gray steel kissing his Nikes. The door he'd come through had vanished.

"What're you looking at, mate?" the big man roared, his Australian accent thick.

"The door where I came in! Where is it?"

The Aussie laughed and pointed to the open door across from them. "That's the door we all came in, and that's the door we're all going out!"

Micah pressed himself into the steel of the plane, and his body went numb. Heights and he refused to dance. He'd fallen out of a tree at eleven and been in the hospital for five weeks. To imagine jumping out of this airplane was to contemplate the impossible.

"No way. Indulge your lunacy if you want to. I'm staying here."

"Suit yourself, mate. But paying $325, then backing out at the last second, that's what I call crazy."

A crystal blue sky framed Mount Rainier shimmering in the distance. Ten thousand feet below cars moved like ants in slow motion along pencil-thin roads. No way. If he jumped, there would be no control, no influence on whether the chute opened or not. But a protest started deep down inside.

Do it.

"Well, mate? Ya coming?"

This wasn't happening. He was still in his house in Cannon Beach. But his head lost out to his heart, which screamed it was most assuredly real. The plane, the sky, the danger, the fear—all sickeningly genuine. Then another impression fluttered up from his heart.

Let's do it. Risk it.

His legs ached above his knees, and he looked down. His fingers were white where they dug into his thighs like iron claws.

The big man watched him intently. "Hey, get some blood back into those hands of yours and give your legs a break. No pun intended; you'll need them when we land." The Aussie looked at him with a kind, knowing expression.

Micah loosened his grip as he watched the other obvious first-timer get ready to jump. The man turned to Micah. "Why are you jumping?"

"I have no idea."

"Exactly!" The other jumper laughed. "Seriously, I just think it's something I gotta do. My heart's pounding like a jackhammer, but it's one of those life things. Big risk, big reward, you know?"

Micah knew.

The man and his tandem-jump instructor scraped along the bottom of the Cessna, then eased up to the edge of the door.

"Ready?" his tandem partner said.

The man nodded, a wild look in his eyes. "Tell me it's going to be okay!"

"It's going to be okay."

"No! Tell me over and over again!"

His tandem instructor laughed. An instant later they plummeted toward Earth. Despite his fear, Micah's morbid fascination compelled him to look, and he watched the pair shrink from life size to a small dot, like an old TV being shut off, faster than he'd thought possible.

"All right, mate, we've rumbled up to the crossroads. Gotta jump within the next fifteen seconds or it's too late. We going?"

Micah closed his eyes and pressed himself for a decision. Every fiber shrieked no. Why risk something that wasn't even real? What would he prove? He would tell the man no, hope that ended this nightmare, and be out of this "room" and be back in the more normal places of the house.

"Ten seconds. We going?"

He turned to say no but the words stuck. And his head nodded yes.

"You're gonna love it." The big man slapped him on the back.

Micah eased over to the door. "Whether it's real or not, Lord, keep me from dying."

"Good prayer, mate!" the Australian yelled, all his teeth showing. "All right, I'm going to count to three and on three we jump. I want you to push off with everything you have. Then arms out, legs out, and we fly like a gonzo eagle shot out of a cannon."

Micah nodded. He imagined hearing his heart over the roar of the engines, pounding out a beat in triple time.

"One. Two. Three. Go!"

He pushed off hard. In that instant his heart changed. Control vanished. Only faith remained; faith that the rivets securing him to the Aussie would hold, that the parachute would open. That jumping was the right choice.

The world turned upside down like being on a monstrous roller coaster somersaulting through the sky. The wind tore into his face and clothes, and his stomach surged with a double shot of adrenaline as the ultimate thrill ride started.

Fear vanished. There was no room for it. The speed intoxicated him, and the rush of nothing above or below for thousands of feet grabbed him, shook him, then released him only to grab him again seconds later harder than before.

"Whoooohoooo!" He let the scream out with abandon. Micah flew 120 miles per hour straight down.

The chute snapped open, and he floated down with nothing but three thousand feet of empty air between the soles of his Nikes and the lush green carpet of spring wheat below. He gazed at Mount Rainier lying before him like a gigantic, white mud pie.

He had done it.

The quietness surprised him—the noise of the airplane, the rush of the wind now gone.

"Well?" His instructor clapped him on the shoulder.

"Never felt more alive."

"Chuting will do that for you. What else makes you come alive, risk it all?"

Coming to Cannon Beach made him feel alive. Starting RimSoft had made him come alive. That had been a huge risk. Actually it wasn't true. He'd been young with nothing to lose. Now? He had everything to lose. And he had little desire to risk what he'd gained.

"You're not taking anything with you, so you might as well store up some treasures in heaven," the Australian said. "Gotta risk your life to save it."

A parachuting preacher, Micah mused.

"Enough theology, Micah. The ground is coming up quick to say hello, so let's get prepped."

After landing they joined the other jumper for a group picture, then walked toward Micah's car. The Aussie threw his arm around Micah's shoulder and squeezed hard. "I'm proud of you. You did well . . ."

During the last three words the Australian's accent faded, and Micah turned to face the man. He was gone. The only thing around his shoulders was a heavy blanket as he sat in his leather chair in front of the Mariners game that played softly on the big-screen TV in his bedroom.

He threw the blanket aside and raced back to the little door. It opened on silk hinges. There was no plane, no roar, nothing but a small closet with a cloth wrapped around something rectangular. Pictures wrapped with a rubber band. He gasped at the first one. A group of men stood in front of a plane holding a sign that said: WE FLEW LIKE EAGLES! September 2, 1996. Micah was one of the men.

He looked down at the T-shirt he had on right then and grabbed a handful. It was the same shirt as the one in the picture. A memory flooded his mind. A few months before his sixteenth birthday his three best friends bought him an early present: a skydiving certificate. But when the day came, his fear of heights emerged victorious and he'd stayed home. He'd always regretted it.

Now, somehow, the house had made the day happen.

This room brought a different kind of healing, a wound of lament healed through the idiotic act of jumping out of an airplane. But it wasn't idiotic. It was the physical form of a long-buried desire.

It was time for another jump.

He walked into the mahogany-rich den that served as his office in Cannon Beach and called Shannon at home. He asked her to put together a meeting with the board as soon as possible.

Micah was about to jump out of another plane.

CHAPTER 27

Four days later, on Tuesday morning at 10:00, Micah cleared his throat and looked around RimSoft's conference room at the members of his board. This could get rough.

"Friends, even though Julie isn't here yet, I want to get started. You'll have questions and I don't want to go past noon. So let's—"

"Who's Julie?" Shannon said.

Micah's stomach felt like it had spent three hours on Disneyland's teacup ride. For the past few weeks whenever Julie had popped into his mind, he'd strangled the thought into silence. And now via Freudian slip, he'd set the problem front and center, making him face the loss in front of his board of directors.

Julie had been a friend and confidant since college. They'd built a company together, had shared years of laughter, sorrow, and success. She would always have a piece of his heart. But he wasn't even the smallest piece of hers anymore. Another part of his Seattle world sliced off and melted away.

"Who's Julie?" Shannon repeated.

Micah's face warmed, and his mind raced for an answer.

His oldest employee rescued him. "I think he's joking. His original partner in the company was named Julie. She hung on for about two years before she bailed. I started a few weeks before she left." He turned to Micah. "I'm probably one of the few who even remembers she exists, don't you think?"

"Yeah, just you and me." Micah coughed and pushed out a weak laugh.

His head swirled. So Julie had been part of his life for a time and part of RimSoft. So why didn't she remember him when he went to her house?

"Micah?" Shannon said.

"Yeah, sorry, mind is wandering." He paused and rested his hands on the conference room table. "That's one of the reasons for this meeting. I've been creating, driving, and sustaining RimSoft for six years now. I've taken a total of three weeks of true vacation during those six years. By my choice I admit, but that's not enough. I need a break where vendors or partners are not along for the ride. A long break."

He took a long swig of coffee.

"Working from Cannon Beach these past two months has helped me find out what I really value. Now I want to take this exercise a step further. In the end it will make me a better leader and make RimSoft stronger than ever before."

For the next hour Micah answered questions about his sabbatical.

"How long?" asked one board member.

"Do you realize how this could impact the stock?" another said.

"Software moves too fast for you to take a sabbatical," protested a third.

"This is not a good move. Shannon, talk to him," chimed in one of his VPs.

In the end he quelled the board's concerns and established the parameters of his time away. His two senior vice presidents and Shannon would handle the day-to-day operations. Once a month the three of them and Micah would have a conference call to discuss any major decisions needing his input. Other than that, he would be absent from any and all operations of RimSoft. No phone calls, no e-mail, no communication except through Shannon, and then only if the emergency was significant.

He crossed into Oregon at 5:30 that evening and stopped off at Fort Stevens State Park to walk the beach and think before arriving back in Cannon Beach. It had been years since he'd seen the wreck of the *Peter Iredale*. Had the ship sunk any further into the sands of the North Pacific shoreline?

Not much as it turned out. He found a secluded spot to watch the sun seep into the ocean and ask God for desperately needed guidance.

He'd told the board he would be taking a break, but he wondered if God would let him. Micah had been running an emotional marathon in both Cannon Beach and Seattle, and he was exhausted. Weren't the miles up yet? Couldn't he give his mind and heart the chance to snooze, even for a day?

After praying for ten minutes, he gave up. God was on mute.

When he opened his eyes, a glossy piece of paper caught his attention. It stuck out of the sand to the right of the log he sat on. It was a magazine cover: *Coast Life*. The weather had beaten it up, but it was the July-August issue from a year ago.

He started to toss it aside when a name in the lower-left corner caught his eye. Taylor. He looked more closely. The first name was smeared, but he could still make it out. Micah. Underneath, even more clearly, he saw the sell line: Talent rising. An Exclusive Interview.

Micah knew every magazine he'd ever been interviewed by, and *Coast Life* was definitely not one of them. He jogged back to his car, got in, and headed for the Seaside library.

His life in bizarroland had added another chapter.

‖‖‖‖‖

"Good magazine," the Seaside librarian offered when Micah asked about the publication. "Just not enough readers. Went belly up nine months ago."

"Do you have any back issues?"

"Maybe." The librarian chuckled. "Problem is, a lot of people don't realize when you check a magazine out of a library, you're supposed to bring it back." He stamped the inside of a book with almost enough gusto to break the spine, and Micah gave him a courtesy smile. The librarian stepped away from the counter. "Let me do a quick check."

When he returned, Micah knew the answer before he spoke. "None right?"

"Sorry, good magazine, you know."

Too many questions. Not enough answers.

The marathon continued. At a sprinter's pace.

He needed explanations, not a slew of more questions.

As he drove back toward 101, he pulled up Astoria movie theaters on his cell phone. Bingo. Time to catch a flick and get his mind off the insanity.

‖‖‖‖‖

After the film was over, Micah took one step outside the Astoria Cineplex and yanked his Seattle Mariners baseball hat down over his face. He rubbed his hands on his shorts and glanced up and down the street twice before jogging across the lot to where he'd parked.

He scrambled into his car and hunched down in the seat. What was wrong with him? For crying in the ocean, was it a crime to go to a movie?

He turned the key and his car purred to life. As he pulled into the street, Micah tried to loosen his grip on the wheel. Boatloads of Christians were going to movies like this one. So it was a little raunchy, the humor a deep shade of blue, and they showed a little skin, but so what? All comedies these days were rated R. He was living for God again; it didn't mean giving up everything.

How else was he supposed to get a moment's escape?

Still, he couldn't shake the feeling that he'd just stolen something and couldn't return it. When he got home, he went to talk to himself about it.

"How are you?" the voice said as Micah stepped into the darkness.

"Saw a movie tonight."

"Yeah."

Silence.

"We blew it again," the voice said.

"Bad choice." Micah slumped against the wall next to the door. "I knew it and did it anyway."

"Will we ever stop?"

"God keeps forgiving, right?"

"Hebrews worries me."

"What?"

"Chapter 10 says if we go on sinning after receiving the knowledge of the truth, then there no longer remains a sacrifice for sins."

Micah leaned forward. "What does that mean?"

"Maybe just what it says. We *know* it's a movie we shouldn't see, but so many times we go anyway. So maybe for those times we're not covered. I don't know. It just worries me."

Anxiety rose in Micah. The promises he'd made not to touch another movie he wouldn't be proud to bring God to roared through him. Promises he kept breaking.

"I'm scared He'll finally leave us forever." The voice breathed hard. "I'm an idiot."

"You're right. You are. We are. A follower of Jesus? Sure. The straight and narrow? I'm on the highway to hell."

A deep sigh floated out of the darkness. "We're not overcoming anything down here. Seattle's not perfect, but parts are pretty awesome. I think it's time to go home."

"You're right." Micah nodded. It felt good to say it. Less failure. Less pressure to be good. Less facing all the painful issues from his past. A world where his relationship with God didn't pour so much guilt on his head.

He walked out and pulled the door hard behind him. No matter how many times he talked to himself, it was still a little strange having his own voice come out of the heart of a tar black room.

Tomorrow morning he would find a way to get control and fix this vice forever.

CHAPTER 28

The next morning a ray of August sunshine woke him at 6:30. The movie from last night splashed into his mind, and he groaned. Guilt peppered his heart as he threw on his sweats, laced up his shoes, and shuffled out the door to make himself pay.

He ran north toward Haystack Rock and pushed himself. Hard. He gasped for air within a few minutes but refused his body's plea for relief. It was a self-inflicted penance he often performed after one of his "movie nights." But it was a sponge in his ocean of guilt.

After a shower and breakfast, he started a biography of C. S. Lewis. No help. He picked up his Bible and through sheer willpower stayed with it for more than an hour. It was hot sand through his brain.

"You're blowing it" pounded through his mind, and he knew it was true. Prayers sent skyward just bounced off the ceiling like racquetballs. He needed to give himself a break. All this guilt was a little over the top.

It was just a movie.

He walked out on the deck, down the stairs to the beach, and followed the tiny stream to his left that carved its way to the sea.

But still, why couldn't he get control over this thing?

Micah drove down 101 all the way to Newport and spent the day poking through kite shops and art studios, looking for something and nothing, anything to divert his mind.

By the time he got home, it was late and he headed straight for his bedroom. That's when he discovered the new hallway. It was short, maybe five feet long. A thick mahogany door stood at the end with detailed carvings on it, almost a language.

He started toward it, then hesitated. Although by now he fully believed God was in control, it still unnerved Micah every time he found a new room.

Fascinating.

Frightening.

Just because God was in it didn't mean it was safe.

He inched toward the door and guessed the language was Hebrew. There was no doorknob. He pushed the door. It was like rock. "Lord, if You hear me, do You want me to get in?"

Nothing.

When he fell into bed a few minutes later, he tried reading, but the book slithered out of his fingers almost immediately, and sleep buried him.

When the dream came, he stood in front of the new door wondering how to get in. Then his surroundings went Dalí, and the door, carpet, and walls melted into each other. When the swirling stopped, he stood in a dimly lit room staring at the back of a door.

He instantly knew where he was—on the other side of the door, now inside the room. A small TV threw off a greenish tint, enough light to see the room was crammed with piles of something. As he groped for a light switch, a soft light streamed under the door from the hallway, enough to show him what the piles were made of.

DVDs, from floor to ceiling. All labeled, all in alphabetical order. Movies and TV shows from as far back as twenty years ago, right up to the movie he'd seen the night before. Every questionable show he had ever allowed to sink into his soul.

The ceiling of the room looked as if thousands of cigarettes had been puffed in it, a dull haze hanging in the air, as if the smoke had never fully dissipated.

A knock at the door stopped his heart. With the sound the brightness along the bottom of the door increased like a dimmer switch being turned up to its highest setting.

"Who is it?" Micah eked out.

"One who would help." The light under the door grew even brighter.

A wild fragrance seeped in, full of oak and the smell of a surging river in the heart of summer.

Micah's pulse raced. "You don't want to come in here." He used both his hands to push against the door.

"Why not?"

Silence.

"If you are from God, you know why."

"If I know, why not let me in?"

"Because this is a room of . . . that I've . . ."

"I know what is in the room. It has been forgiven."

Micah's hands shook. Only One could forgive.

He whirled back toward the DVDs. Shame flooded through him. He loathed the idea of opening the door. It didn't matter that the Lord knew about this room. It didn't matter that he was forgiven. But there was nowhere else to turn.

"All right!" He pulled his hands off the door, as if they were smeared with rubber cement.

"The door doesn't open from this side. You must let Me in."

Micah reached for the door and froze. Images of the anger about to lash out at him flooded his mind, the disgust and disdain that would be hurled his way. The crushing disappointment in His eyes. Micah dreaded the discipline he knew must come. The thoughts bounced around like a pinball as he steeled himself, closed his eyes, and wrenched open the door.

The Lord burst into the room and strode for the back wall without even looking at Micah. Before reaching it, He drew a sword that radiated light like the mirrors of a thousand lighthouses. He brought it down on the stack of DVDs along the back wall so fast Micah couldn't follow the arc. Light exploded as the sword struck and the DVDs vanished, revealing a door. It was shackled with thick iron chains, each link dense and rough. Six ancient-looking bars across the door guarded it from entry.

The Lord's eyes sparked as He turned and winked at Micah. He raised His sword and brought it down like a flash of lightning. The iron bars, the chains, the locks, all shuddered. As the second blow fell, faint lines formed in the bars and the chains. At the third strike of the sword, another flash of light exploded, and the iron bars and chains shattered. A pungent odor accompanied their destruction, but it faded, and the fragrance of pine needles filled the room.

"Ready?" The Lord motioned toward the open door.

Micah dropped his head. "I am so ashamed . . . the shows . . . I'm so sorry. I just . . ."

"I don't care about the shows, Micah. I care about your heart."

He stared in bewilderment. "But those shows—"

"Are garbage."

Micah waited for the rebuke to come. But it didn't.

"They are full of death," the Lord said. "To your heart, your soul, your mind. But do you need Me to tell you that? The critical issue is why you watched them, not what they contain."

"I don't understand."

"I desire truth in your innermost being, Micah. There are broken places to fix. Because there is lack of truth there and a choice you must make."

"Yes, but—"

"We must go in." The Lord motioned again to the open door.

Fear surged out of the room. "What's in there?" Micah took a step backward.

"Come and see."

"I can't." He stared at the opening. He was certain facing it meant massive pain.

"You can."

Only a dream. This was only a dream.

Micah stepped through the dim opening, the Lord beside him. They stood in a hallway at least fifty-feet long. A movie screen covered the far end. As they walked toward it, the screen flickered to life.

A young woman lay in a hospital bed, her ivory arms wrapped around a newborn. "Isn't he beautiful?"

"Perfect," the man said.

The woman laughed as she looked down at the pink face buried in the blue cotton blanket. "You'll be more in love with him than me before the week is over."

"I'll love this Micah kid crazy fierce, but I'll never love him more than I love you. Not a chance." The man ran his forefinger over the woman's cheek. "Never more than you."

"So what should we have next?" the woman said. "Another boy, or should we have a girl this time?"

"Do we get to choose?"

"Sure." The woman handed the baby to the man who rocked it gently.

The scene faded as another one filled the screen.

A little boy tried to climb a Douglas fir tree in a backyard drenched in sunshine. His father sat in a white-and-green striped chair, strawberry lemonade in one hand, the day's newspaper in the other.

"Daddy, Daddy!"

"Hmm?" came from behind the paper.

"Do you think I can do it?"

The paper snapped down. "Do what?"

"Climb it! Climb the tree!"

The father folded the paper and tossed it to the ground. "Not only do I know you can do it; I know you *will* do it. But we need something first." His dad picked up the camera sitting next to the chair. "We need to document this moment, don't you think?" His dad winked and held the camera up to his eye. "Ready!"

The boy strained for a branch just out of reach until the twig underneath his foot snapped, and he spilled onto the concrete patio. Hard. Tiny streaks of scarlet sprang out of both knees.

"Micah!" His dad leaped toward him and yanked a paper towel from his pocket. "Here, let's take care of that." He rubbed the boy's back. "You okay?"

The boy nodded as his dad wiped the blood off his knees.

The scene faded but the screen didn't go black.

Sounds of hammering rang out before a scene of a boy building a tree house came into focus. The floor was done and one of the walls was in place. A twelve-year-old Micah jumped down from the eight-foot-high floor and walked over to a second wall lying on the grass.

The sun glinted off his father's pitching wedge as he chipped foam golf balls at a bucket ten yards in front of him.

Micah hoisted the wall and strained to shove it up the side of the tree into his brother's wanting hands.

As it wobbled, Micah said, "Dad, some help here maybe?"

His father kept chipping as he said, "You get hurt, son, and you'll have to find your own way to the emergency room. Stupid idea, building that thing. Once again you've proven you need a microscope to find anything going on inside that brain of yours."

As the scene faded to black, Micah's face went cold. His long-buried pain rushed to the surface as more memories like the one he'd just relived filled his mind. The screen shifted again.

A 1985 Toyota Celica screeched around a corner and sent autumn leaves swirling into the air. The car pulled into the driveway of a modest house too fast, but the man standing with his arms folded didn't budge as the driver screeched to a halt, then popped out of the car.

"Hey, Dad, I got it. Whaddya think?"

"How much did you pay, son?"

"Seventeen hundred. He asked for $1,950 so I think I got a pretty good deal. And, man, does this thing move!"

"No, son, $1,575, maybe even $1,625 would have been a fine price. But $1,700 for this car is overpriced. I studied the blue book value and local ads and that is the truth."

"But it's my first—"

"Son, you made a stupid mistake. Again. But not much harm done. You'll have other chances."

The scene faded and lit up with a new scene for the fifth time.

On-screen rain blanketed a stadium filled with blue and red umbrellas. Athletes huddled in small bunches around the track, white towels over their heads. Small numbers pulled sweat suits off or on, getting ready for their race or having just finished.

Around the far corner of the track came nine runners: the three in front synchronized stride for stride, the rest scattered in behind.

Two of the leaders started their kick at the same time. The third waited an instant longer. Micah knew who would win: the one who started his kick last. It was himself, at the Washington state high school track finals, in the eight hundred meters. The finish would be excruciatingly close. They went to the photo in the end to be sure. But he had won. State title in the eight hundred meters.

Dread hit him like a sledgehammer. He knew what came next. The scene shifted, and he watched himself walk into his childhood home, Mick bouncing out from the kitchen with a big grin on his face. "Hey, bro. Not bad. You smoked 'em all."

After giving Mick a high-five, Micah turned to his father.

His dad sat in his twenty-five-year-old beige Barcalounger with no shred of emotion on his face.

"I had it today, didn't I, Dad?"

"It was good, yes. However since the state record remains unbroken, it is apparent that you did not have quite enough. Might even describe that as losing."

Part of him regretted what happened next. Part didn't. His eyes watered as he gave his dad the finger and stormed into his bedroom. It was the day he vowed to leave home as soon as possible and never look back.

Micah collapsed to his knees. The dam burst and pain poured out of him.

The Lord knelt beside him, strong arms pulling him in tight. "Let it out, all of it."

Wracking sobs spilled over as the grief hit Micah full force.

"What have you longed to hear since the day your mom died, Micah?"

"I don't know."

"Yes, you know. I've had you live the wounds again for a reason."

"He took care of us after mom died. We always had a roof over our heads and food on the table, and he even bought me things I didn't need."

"What did you need to hear?"

"He was always home from work by 5:30; he bought me decent clothes; he—"

"What did you need to hear?"

As Micah tried forming the words, a surprising emotion arose: anger. Unbidden. Unexpected. And unstoppable. "I hate him! He destroyed me. He abandoned me! Why was it so impossible for my dad to love me after she died? Even for a moment? Couldn't he care about me at all? Would it have killed him to say 'nice car'? I won state in the eight hundred meters! I beat *everybody*. But it wasn't good enough. Listening to him you'd think I'd been tearing the livers out of neighborhood dogs." His voice dropped to a whisper. "Why couldn't he have loved me just a little?"

"Your success will never answer the question."

"I just wanted him to say, 'I'm proud.' That I have what it takes to be a man."

"You've numbed the pain with TV shows and movies that scintillate and tease, but they're cotton candy. You've hidden your shattered heart behind money and fame."

The tears kept coming.

"Your heart broke again and again, and you tried to fix the pieces with the salves of the world. But they can only dull the pain; they cannot heal. You have been chained. You've hidden your heart in the dark places. But I came to heal the brokenhearted and set the captives free."

"I'm not worthy of You."

"That's a lie from the enemy of your soul." The Lord smiled. "You are more than a conqueror, and you are worthy because I am inside you. It is time to believe it. I am proud of you, Micah. I am proud."

The words sank into his heart and grew like seeds shown in time-lapse photography, growing so fast he wondered if he could contain the emotions pushing to burst out. He was a son of God, adopted into His family, Kingdom, and glory. Loved. And forgiven. For all time, all eternity. Astonishing.

The Lord held him tighter. "The treasure of My Kingdom are the hearts of the ones who are Mine. Let it sink in to the innermost parts. Listen. Your heart is the treasure of My Kingdom. And I have done everything to set it free. And I love you with an unfathomable, unquenchable love."

"Now, it is time to let go of your anger toward your father." The Lord swung around till He knelt in front of Micah and held out His hands.

"I can't."

"You can. You must choose."

"No."

"Time to let go of your anger."

Micah rose to his knees.

"Time to forgive."

Micah reached out and placed his palms in the Lord's and opened his heart to the fire that swept through him.

When it was finished, the Lord said, "Now come."

Micah slowed as they approached the DVD room.

"You have a question?" the Lord said.

"What about the DVDs?"

"Ah yes. Let's take a look, shall we?"

As he stepped through, Micah stared in amazement. All except seven DVDs were gone. The Lord walked over to the shelf and pulled one off, tossing it to Micah. "That's a good one."

Time slowed down and the DVD floated toward him. *Braveheart.* Micah looked up at the Lord, but He was gone. Micah looked at the DVD again, and it dissolved along with the room.

He woke with a start. His eyes flew open and looked out the window. Daybreak. The dream!

He rolled out of bed and caught his foot on the covers. Yanking his leg free, he dashed toward the hallway from last night. The door was still there. Still shut. But it had changed. The Hebrew inscription was translated.

I will go before you and make the rough places smooth;
I will shatter the doors of bronze and cut through their iron bars.
I will give you the treasures of darkness
And hidden wealth of secret places,
So that you may know that it is I,
The LORD, the God of Israel, who calls you by your name.
(Isaiah 45:2–3)

Micah lifted two fingers to the door and pushed. It glided open without sound. He walked straight for the door at the back of the room. It was gone, no evidence the door or the room behind it had ever been. Movie posters covered the walls, depicting epic battles and tender love stories, and the shelves were filled with the movies promoted on the walls and many more.

The tears came again. Of joy. Of freedom.

The bars had been broken, the treasure of the Kingdom released.

He had to talk to himself about the freedom. Micah let out a whoop and raced toward the room that contained his voice.

CHAPTER 29

As Micah opened the door to the room, the voice spoke. "Hey, buddy, I was hoping you'd come to debrief. That was quite a ride."

"Unbelievable."

"From the beginning. All the details."

"But you know all the details. You, we, were there together." Micah laughed. "Why hear it again?"

"Because this way I can just soak it in and not have to think about it. And after it's spoken aloud, we'll both know it and remember it better."

So Micah told the story about the door, the dream, the healing of the wounds, the waking up and discovering it was all real. How mountains of chains had been conquered, demolished in his heart.

After he finished, the voice stayed silent for a long time. When it spoke, it was just above a murmur, the tone tentative. "I have a thought. Something I think we should consider."

Micah was taken off guard. He expected excitement, joy, even laughter as they celebrated together. Instead he sensed discouragement and even a hint of desperation in the voice.

"We must be exceedingly careful with these 'healing-the-wounds' experiences we had in the Wildcat room and the one last night. Who knows when it might happen again," the voice said.

"Why wouldn't we want it to continue till we're set free of every chain?"

"Maybe we should; maybe we shouldn't. We have certainly slipped over into an area graciously described as the unknown. An area of confusion and speculation. And even possible deception."

"What are you talking about? There's no confusion." Micah made tiny, involuntary shakes of his head. "I'm freer and more in love with Jesus than I've ever been."

"There are all kinds of dreams, Micah. Most of the time dreams are the subconscious trying to make sense of the conscious world. It's usually simply the brain processing the events of the day. And sometimes it can even be a dark area where the enemy is trying to deceive us."

"You're saying these experiences are deception? No way. God spoke through dreams and used dreams in the Bible—"

"Yes, absolutely true, and I'm not discounting it. But over the thousands of years in which the Bible was written, how many times did God talk to people in dreams? Eight? Nine times? And each time they were major events. I'm not saying God can't talk to us in dreams. It's possible even in this day and age. But isn't it presumptuous to say He spoke to us in a dream when there's really no proof? Taking dreams at face value without really examining them is inviting a potentially deadly ruse from the enemy."

"Hold on." Micah stepped forward. "The day before, I can't get into the room. Now I can and everything has changed inside. Drastically. You're saying that's not genuine?"

"Do you hear what you just said, Micah? The room changed drastically in the *dream*. You hadn't been inside it *before* the dream. The reality is the room has always been the same. The only difference is that before you weren't able to get in. Now you are. Just because it changed in the dream doesn't mean it changed for real."

"But the change inside *me* is real."

"I'm not saying there's been no change. I think our mind did a wonderful thing for us by telling us a story as we slept. But we have to examine what happened in light of the Bible and not in light of our emotions."

"You're saying my emotions aren't valid?" Micah said. "That they aren't evidence things have changed inside my heart?"

"God is not a God of touchy-feely pop psychology but a God of truth and moral action. We are to be outward focused, not inward focused. This preoccupation with self and self-freedom that has crept into the church is dangerous. The story of life is not about you; it's about God. And any time we focus our energies on anything other than the advancement of the Kingdom, we advance the kingdom of the enemy."

Micah sat stunned. What he had gone through in the movie room was without question the most powerful spiritual experience of his life, and his own inner voice was questioning if it was from God.

"So you're saying freedom is not worth pursuing? That Jesus didn't come to bind up the broken hearts and set the captives free?"

"Freedom is most worthy of pursuing. But we don't attain freedom by turning inward and focusing on fixing ourselves and trying to feel good inside. It comes from reaching outside ourselves to those who do not yet know the Father. When Isaiah says set the captives free, I seriously doubt it means we are to be freed of any and all the tiny hurts from our childhood. We are new creatures;

the old has passed away. That is the truth we must cling to and stand on."

Micah threw back his head as a tiny moan of laughter escaped his lips.

"We must leave those hurts behind and press on to the upward call. Not muddle around in the past. As the Bible says, I am no longer a child so I put away the childish things. Setting the captives free means we can be free of sin and the devil, and we are free from having to spend eternity apart from God. Amen and amen."

"Rick says—"

"We both agree that Rick is kind and often wise. But he is a mere man. He doesn't have all the answers any more than *any* man does. His opinions are interesting and sometimes true. But the real answers are always in the Word of God. Show me in the Bible where we go into our past and heal personal wounds and, my gosh, let's do it more and more. I don't think you'll find it because it's not there."

The voice stopped, and Micah didn't know where to start.

"But the verse on the door—"

"Easily taken out of context and often distorted. Those verses are talking about Israel and God's people taking the land and God subduing the nations. It is not a personal message to those of us who have hit some bumps along the road of life. I'm sorry. I wish it was a message the way you've interpreted it, but it isn't."

Micah's mind spun as confusion poured down on him. It felt as if the air in the room had thinned, the remaining oxygen refusing to enter his lungs. The dream had brought him more freedom, built more faith, and given him greater hope in the love of Jesus than he could have imagined. And it was wrong?

"You're saying we shouldn't feel at all? C'mon."

"No, no, no, of course we should feel." The voice laughed. "All I'm saying is we need to admit feelings are what they are. Just feelings.

Not reliable, solid evidence of God. As it says in the Word, we have
been given a sound mind and must live out of that sound mind. We
take 'every thought captive' with our minds, not our emotions."

Micah sighed and turned to leave.

"You're going so soon?"

"There's a lot for me to think about."

"I love you, Micah."

Micah slammed the door to the room and walked down the
hall.

He was beginning to hate himself.

||||||||

Late that Thursday afternoon Micah took a long run to clear his
head. Turmoil over his conversation with the voice still swirled in
his mind, and he played both sides of the argument back and forth
without resolution.

The evening, however, held a ray of hope. He'd intention-
ally not read Archie's letter the day before. Now he was glad he'd
waited. He needed a good one.

> *August 28, 1991*
> *Dear Micah,*
>
> *Today I must let the Word of God speak for itself so this
> will be a brief correspondence.*
>
> *"Look among the nations! Observe! Be astonished!
> Wonder! Because I am doing something in your days—You
> would not believe if you were told." (Habakkuk 1:5)*
>
> *He is beyond imagination, Micah, and He is drawing
> you to Himself.*
>
> *Trust Him. Seek Him.*
>
> *Archie*

Instantly the confusion from his talk with the voice vanished like fog retreating under a blazing morning sun. Peace rushed in, and an image of what he called the brilliant room—where light seemed to pour out from under the door—filled his mind.

Yes. Time for another try.

He took his spiral staircase two stairs at a time and in seconds stood before the door. He sat on the other side of the hall and closed his eyes. Peace floated off the door like snow slightly heavier than the air around it. It settled on him and eased into his heart.

Images filled his mind—times as a child playing in a park full of lush maple trees with his mom somewhere nearby, allowing him to soar with no cares, no worries except for how high he could swing or how fast the merry-go-round would spin.

Sunshine streamed through those maples, making the emerald leaves of summer a more vivid and striking green than he thought possible. The image shifted and he stood in a cathedral of towering redwoods, a deep cold river sliding in between them, dwarfed by their silent majesty.

Every time he came to the door, the same stunning sensations surrounded him, and every time he'd tried to enter without success.

Micah stood, reached out, and pushed on the door. He jerked back. Astonishing. There was no resistance. After recovering he pushed again and watched as his entire hand eased into the door till the wood surrounded his wrist, as if the door were water. He laughed.

He moved his hand all over the door but couldn't push in any deeper than his wrist. As he moved it, sweet freedom swept through him.

Seconds later the door changed into ordinary wood again, and Micah's head rested against it. He longed to enter. "When, Lord?"

Soon.

⁛

The next evening around 10:00, Micah met Rick at Haystack Rock, and they headed south down the beach, watching the glow of August campfires and breathing in the smell of burnt marshmallows. He desperately wanted to tell Rick about the dream, but it meant telling about the voice as well, which he still wasn't ready to do. Instead Micah asked his friend for his latest theory on what was in the brilliant room.

"In trying to get to the bottom of what the brilliant room—and for that matter, what the entire home—is all about, I think you've overlooked a fundamental question," Rick said.

"Which is?"

"The history of the house."

"What history? The thing is barely six months old."

"I mean, who built it."

"Archie, you know that." Two runners, a guy and a gal, whizzed past them heading north up the beach. Micah needed to go for a run with Sarah. They'd gone for one a few days before, but he felt like he hadn't seen her in months.

"Archie built it? Fascinating. You're saying a man dead for twelve years built a home nine months ago? Now that's what I call strange." Rick winked at him. "Sure, Archie left the money and instructions on how it was to be constructed, but if he wasn't alive, someone carried out his guidelines. And unless that person died in the last six months, it's a pretty safe bet you could track him down."

"Agreed. But the title and escrow records don't give a clue. So how do I find this mystery man?"

"Pretty obvious, isn't it?"

Micah shook his head.

"You said the letters were mailed to a Chris Hale, right?"

"Sure."

"Well, I'm guessing Archie wrote the letters and mailed them to this Chris character so he would dump them in your house when it was finished. So since Archie's gone, I'd sure be looking up ol' Chris Hale to see if he's still alive. If he is, bet he could shed some rays of light on the whole thing."

Micah tilted his head back with what he imagined was a stunned look smeared all over his face. Of course. Why hadn't he thought of that?

The next morning, as soon as the clock crept past eight, Micah would try to get Chris on the phone and find answers to why this home had buried his world in an ocean of chaos.

CHAPTER 30

The phone rang four times on the other end of the line Saturday morning, and Micah readied himself to leave a message on Chris's voice mail. But on the fifth came an answer. "Hello, Chris here." The voice was relaxed, warm, and just a notch above deep.

It put him at ease immediately. "Hi, Mr. Hale. My name is Micah Taylor, and I think we have a mutual friend. My great-uncle was Archie Taylor."

"Hello, Micah. It's wonderful to hear your voice." Chris didn't sound surprised.

"You expected my call?"

"Well, I can't say I was expecting it. But I hoped you would call one day."

"You knew Archie."

"Ah yes, knew him well. And he knew me. One of the best friends I ever had, without a doubt. He died not long before my wife did. Whew, was that a year. By far the toughest one of my life."

"I'm sorry."

"It was more than twelve years ago." Chris chuckled. "And odds are I'll be joining them soon. Some days I still miss Archie terribly. Sarah even more so."

"Your wife's name was Sarah?" Micah choked the words out.

"Yes, is that unusual?"

"No, it's just that I . . . Mr. Hale, could we meet?"

"I'd enjoy that. As long as you can refrain from calling me Mr. Hale."

|||||||

Three days later Micah stood on the porch of Chris's North Seattle colonial home. The chime of the doorbell had long since faded with no answer, and Micah looked at his watch. Four o'clock. Right on time. He reached up to ring again when a voice inside called out, "Thanks for your patience. Almost there now."

Chris greeted him with a broad smile and grabbed Micah with both hands. "Welcome, Micah! Welcome." He looked like Norman Rockwell. He even had a pipe.

"Thanks for having me over, Mr. Hale."

"As much my pleasure as hopefully it will be yours, Mr. Taylor."

"Right." Micah grinned. "Thanks for having me over, Chris."

Chris guided him into the sitting room of a home old enough to have one. The wicker chair Micah sat in was aged but restful, and the black-and-white pictures on the walls and old books that lined the shelves made him comfortable immediately.

Chris excused himself to the kitchen and returned with two glasses of iced tea along with more in a pitcher. After a few minutes of banter, Chris raised his voice a pinch. "Well, I can see you have the personality to make small talk as long as necessary, but why don't we get to it since you're probably bursting with questions about your great-uncle."

"Yeah, I have a few."

"A few?" Chris raised his eyebrow, a mock frown on his face.

"A few dozen. Three or four dozen."

"I'll answer as many as I can, but before that, tell me about your experiences in the house so far."

Although he trusted Chris instinctively, Micah wasn't sure how much to tell. He decided to touch on some of the supernatural aspects of the home without telling too many of the details. When he finished, the sunlight on the old leather couch had moved more than two feet. It made him realize how significantly life had changed since the day Archie's letter showed up.

When he'd finished, Chris merely nodded his thanks.

"So what's the secret of the house . . . my house?"

"Secret?"

"Why is it so supernatural? What's the connection between it and me? Why did Archie have it built for me? Did he know strange things would happen there?"

"First question: God is God. Second question: everything. Third question: because God told him to. Fourth question: yes."

"Touché." Micah laughed. "All right, I'll put the question-six-shooter away." He mimed placing a gun in a holster at his side. "How 'bout starting with how you and Archie met?"

"Fine." Chris patted down the tobacco in his pipe with his pinky finger, lit it, then settled back in his chair. "I met Archie in the navy. He was the most popular aboard ship, even though no one could figure him out. He told jokes with the best of them. When the other guys brought out the jokes with a blue tint to them, Archie didn't laugh, but he didn't condemn those that did.

"He wasn't the best at the physical demands of being on a naval vessel, but no one ever tried harder, and of course most of his shipmates respected him for that. I was pretty shy then, so I was taken aback when he sat next to me one day in the mess hall. He looked me straight in the eye and asked, 'You want more out of life?'"

The smoke from Chris's pipe curled toward the ceiling, and Micah watched Chris relive the memory.

Chris chuckled and gave a little shake of his head. "I stared at Archie. It was pretty forward, and I wanted to laugh but was too self-conscious. There was no, 'Hello, how are you doing, my name is Archie.' The first thing out of his mouth was, 'You want more out of life?' A lot of answers popped into my mind, but I decided on the simple truth. 'Yes, I do,' I told him.

"So right there in the middle of a mess hall full of guys, he starts telling me Jesus came to Earth to bring me back to God and to set me free. 'Course I'm staring at him like he's just come out of the loony bin, but I can't help asking the follow-up question, 'Free from what?' And you know how he answered? He didn't. He just smiled at me. Archie probably knew I already had the answer. There were so many things I needed to get free of I didn't know where to start. My chains had chains."

Chris paused and looked right at Micah. "You know what I mean, don't you? Archie worked on me, and I guess I helped him a bit, too. During the four years we served together, we became best friends. More than best friends. Brothers."

Chris's eyes moistened a little. "But I have monumental doubts you came to watch me get sentimental." He patted the arm of his chair. "Archie carved out a solid career in architecture. Did very well. They still use a couple of his designs at the University of Washington to show students how to infuse a sense of freedom in the structures they design."

"Everything about Archie pointed toward freedom, didn't it?"

"If you're going to focus on one thing, it's a pretty good choice, don't you think?" Chris leaned forward and clasped his hands. "And he loved to show people how to live for something bigger than the next ball game or vacation. Help them find their destiny and glory."

"I wish I'd known him." Micah let the regret settle. "So, if it wasn't Archie, who oversaw the construction of the house?"

Chris smiled and realization washed over Micah. Why hadn't he figured it out sooner? He shook his head. "You did an awesome job."

"You like it?"

"Feels like it's part of me. I've never felt so at home anywhere."

"Ah, I'm glad. Archie would be so pleased. These days, Hale & Sons Construction is 99 percent Sons, but I got pretty involved with your home."

"It's perfect for me."

"Good, good, good." Chris gazed at Micah for ten seconds before continuing. "Archie never had kids of his own, as you probably know. Just didn't work out that way, although I know he wanted a wife and children. But this life isn't perfect, is it? So when your dad married and had you, Archie prayed in earnest. Couldn't talk about much more than you most of the time."

Chris repacked his pipe and lit it again. "Don't exactly know why, but God built quite a love inside Archie for you."

Micah shifted in his chair. "It doesn't make sense. If Archie had this great love for me, why didn't I ever meet him?"

"You did. Only once though, shortly before he died."

"What?" Micah lurched forward in his chair.

"Regretfully, the time you met, he didn't tell you who he was as he wanted to see you again. He feared you might tell your dad about it without thinking. And you know how your dad feels about followers of Jesus, and especially about Archie."

"I asked my dad once what he had against Christians. Last time I made that mistake."

Chris pulled off his glasses and rubbed them on his pants.

"After your mom's accident, some religious acquaintances of your dad invited him to an evening Bible study. Out of respect for your mom's beliefs, he went. At first it was okay. They let him talk through the pain, but soon they started asking him for money to support their church. He said no, but they argued with him, telling your dad if he gave a certain amount, he'd meet God and it's what Jesus would want him to do, what your mom would want him to do. Not exactly true Christian behavior." Chris sighed.

"That incident soured him on Christians. Then it got worse." Chris held up his glasses and squinted through them. "Yep, clean. You want to hear this, Micah?"

"I need to."

"Shortly after that, Archie made a trip back from Europe—where he was living at the time—to see if he could do anything for you, your dad, and your brother. Well, he came to one of your baseball games—"

"Not *that* game?"

"Yep, one and the same. The next day Archie confronted your dad about how he treated you. About the choices he was making. Then they talked about the Lord, your dad saying God had stolen your mom and Archie trying to explain that that wasn't God's heart, along with a lot of other things. Suffice it to say, it didn't go well. Your dad hated Archie for speaking the truth and has despised all Christians ever since."

Micah sat squeezing his knees, trying to assimilate the revelations Chris had just given. It explained so much. And Archie had tried to rescue him from his dad.

"You knew my dad?"

"No, no. Only through what Archie told me. Now you know why anyone who walks with God is on Daniel's do-not-disturb list." Chris leaned over and refilled Micah's glass of iced tea.

"The puzzle pieces are falling into place."

"That's why your dad never let Archie near you once he moved back to the States. Shame. Shame." Chris sighed. "If he had found out Archie was spending time with you, your dad would have made sure it didn't happen more than once."

"But you said Archie did meet me one time."

Chris sat up and nodded. "One day Archie said, 'I'm going to do something crazy and try to meet Micah.' I said, 'How?' and he didn't really answer. Just said God would help him with it."

"How old was I?"

"Oh, you must have been around sixteen or seventeen. Archie came back and said he knew you had it in you, whatever *it* was. He was proud of you for taking the risk. Said you talked about laying up treasures in heaven."

Micah's heart pounded as a question sputtered out of his mouth. "What did Archie do in the navy?"

"Oh, he was in communications so he worked the radio and helped with letters and memos; he was a pretty good writer."

"Did he do anything else?"

"Not for the navy." Chris looked at the ceiling. "Only other activity of note during those years was his jumping out of all those airplanes, doing that parachuting thing with his buddy in the army. He loved it, got pretty good."

"Did Archie ever speak with an Australian accent?" Micah felt like his heart must be hammering away at two hundred beats a minute.

Chris's face lit up. "Now, Micah, tell me, how in creation did you know that?"

Micah's mind reeled. So what really happened in that room in Cannon Beach? Was the skydiving real? If so, when did it happen? Did he go back in time when he went into that room, or did it all happen in the Spirit and Archie had experienced it outside of time as well? Certainly God is outside of time, but . . . Just when Micah thought nothing else could shock him about this journey he was on, something did.

Chris's voice brought him back to the moment and forced Micah to squelch the questions sprinting through his mind. "You know, I am truly sorry to say this, but I think I'll have to call it a day."

Micah reluctantly agreed. "I've got more questions than when we started, but I appreciate the time so much."

"You're welcome, Micah. And we'll do it again sometime. I know Archie would be immensely proud of you. It sounds like you're going down the narrow path few choose."

"I think it's the only path without a dead end."

"Yes, yes it is." Chris grabbed both of Micah's hands and smiled widely. "Thank you for coming by."

Micah approached the front door, then turned and gazed at Chris's sitting room once more. A series of black-and-white photos lined the back wall. One of Archie on a fishing boat—looking younger than he had on the plane—grabbed his eye. Chris stood next to him along with another man. It couldn't be. The haircut was different, and he had on wire-rimmed glasses, but the man looked almost identical to . . .

"Who is that next to Archie?" Micah sputtered. "It looks like the twin of—"

"Let it go, Micah." Chris took his arm and led him to the door. "Someday all the questions of this life will be answered. But not yet. If they were all answered right now, we'd forget how to be curious. And how much fun would that be?"

Driving away from Chris's house, Micah mused on their conversation. Now he understood Archie's motivation for building the home, even though it didn't explain how he anticipated Micah's every choice or how the supernatural aspect of the house worked.

Micah eased onto I-5 and merged into the flow of cars. Part of him wanted to head farther south, but the more practical side of him won out, and twenty minutes later he reluctantly took Seattle's Union Street exit and headed toward his condo.

The familiar buzz greeted him as he swiped his key and walked into the lobby. Right choice, he thought as he trudged over to the mail slots. He was wiped. Head for the top floor and crash.

Micah had purchased the penthouse suite as they were building the condo so they'd offered him the choice of where his mail slot would be. Normally it would be in alphabetical order, but since they asked, he told them far right. That way he could get his mail even in a blackout.

It had become so automatic over the years he hardly looked anymore. Key in. Open slot. Take mail. Close slot. Except this time, it didn't work.

Micah sighed, tried again, looking intently at the keyhole this time. No problem. The key went in like velvet. It just wouldn't turn. All he could get the mailbox to do was rattle. He bent forward to read the name on the mailbox. Where it should have read *Mr. Micah Taylor*, it clearly read *Mr. & Mrs. C. Murphey.*

Tendrils of panic crept into his mind and heart, and perspiration dotted his forehead.

There had to be a logical reason for this.

But he knew there wasn't.

He snatched his cell phone and dialed the building's super. Five rings. Six. *C'mon.*

"Hallo."

"Phil!"

"Yes. You have reached me."

"Micah Taylor."

"Mr. Micah. Always good to hear you! What can I do for you on a Tuesday night?"

"You can tell me what's going on with my condo!"

"What is wrong, Mr. Micah?"

"The name on the mailbox for the penthouse suite." Micah closed his eyes and rubbed his forehead.

"Yes?"

"It's not mine."

"Yes?"

"Doesn't that seem a little strange to you, Phil?"

"No, but what are you saying, Mr. Taylor? You want that you should move up?"

"Move up? What are you talking about? Move up where? How do you get higher than the twenty-first floor when the building only has twenty-one floors?"

"So you want up to the penthouse, eh? Well, when Mr. Murphey bought the whole twenty-first floor; he say he will never sell. I know you are much rich now with your company and big dollars are with running software, but I do not know, you know? I believe that Mr. Murphey has pleasure with owning the whole floor, yes?"

Micah tried to stop from hyperventilating.

"But, Mr. Micah, there is nothing wrong with the nineteenth floor. View from there is fine too and it is available. I call Ronie for you, and she will see if you can move there. The nineteenth floor, right away you know, if you want. Two thousand square feet, just like you have now. You think that would work for you? In the morning I will call her and—"

"Where do I live now, Phil?"

"I do not understand."

"Please. Just tell me where I live."

"In your condo, Mr. Micah, of course."

"Which floor?"

"Eighth floor like you always have. You feel okay?"

"Fine. Thanks." Micah snapped the phone shut and ran his finger down the mail slots. Saxxon, Swenson . . . Taylor.

He opened the slot and yanked out the contents. Three pieces of mail scattered to the floor, but it didn't matter. He looked at four different envelopes in rapid succession. It was the same on each of them: Micah Taylor, 4210 2nd Street, 8th Floor, Seattle, WA 98717.

He slid down the wall like syrup on a cold day. When he reached the floor, he took his head in his hands and held it for a long time. When he finally rose, he got in the elevator and punched the button for the eighth floor. He had to sleep somewhere.

Entering the condo he took a slow look around. Bizarre. Nothing had changed. Absolutely nothing except for the fact he now resided on the eighth floor instead of the twenty-first. Same furniture. Pictures. Books. Same coffeepot with the tiny chip in the glass on the right-hand side.

Sleep came slowly and ended early. He looked at his bedroom clock: 5:43. Too early to call and repeat the same conversation with Rick he'd had multiple times. At least it was Wednesday. Archie day.

He took his coffee out onto his veranda along with the envelope containing letter number twelve. He could see the shimmering waters of Puget Sound. When he sat, the building directly across the street blocked his view.

"C'mon, Archie." He needed something solid, some light for his future from the archives of Archie's past. He gritted his teeth and opened the letter.

September 2, 1991

Dear Micah,

As you are aware, Jesus says we must make the decision to give up our lives. However, as you are no doubt discovering, this is easier to execute in theory than in reality, is it not?

Your old life is crumbling out from underneath you, and there is no hope or promise of anything else to fill its place.

I am sorry. I wish I could tell you this journey you're on will come out perfectly in the end. But it usually does not. This is most often due to the propensity inside each of us to imagine different definitions of perfect than the Father defines for us.

Also, bear in mind this is a process. A process you have the ability to slow down or speed up by your choices.

I am praying you choose wisely,

Archie

Micah sighed and closed his eyes. When he opened them, he stared at a billboard below advertising a new exhibit at Seattle's Art Museum.

Archie's letter slid from his hand and fluttered to the floor. That was it! That was the connection. It had been in front of him the whole time.

Twenty minutes later his BMW was chewing up the miles back to Cannon Beach.

The painting in his house at Cannon Beach was the key.

CHAPTER 31

The gravel groaned as Micah pulled into his driveway Wednesday afternoon and stomped on the brakes. He didn't bother to shut the car door as he marched toward the house, and he ignored the stinging rain pelting his face. His mind was fixed on one thing: get to the painting.

When he flung open the door to the painting room and strode in, he saw the changes immediately. The small cliff was now fully developed, and the home sitting on it was starting to take shape. The gold and russet hues of the beach were now flawlessly intertwined with each other, and the last touches on the sun were finished.

As Micah took it in, he realized his revelation that morning was right. How simple. How obvious. When a piece of Seattle falls apart, the painting gets closer to completion. Two worlds. Like a scale adding weight on one side making the other side go down.

Micah desperately wanted to see the finished painting. He was more than drawn to it; he felt like part of him was contained in the painting. But how much did he have to lose of Seattle before this vision was complete?

|||||||

"You there?" Micah said as he strode into the voice room.

"I'm always here," the voice said.

"What is going on? Any clue? I gotta get some perspective on this."

"I think we should talk to Rick."

"Why? Would he say anything different from what he's said before? 'Stick it out. Stay strong. God is in this.'"

"God *is* in this, Micah."

"I know. All I'm saying is Rick will just spout some line about God being in control and He knows what He's doing. I'd like some concrete, hard-core answers."

"But then where does hope and faith enter into the equation? Romans says if we see what we're hoping for it's not hope. But if we eagerly await it—"

"The problem is not that I went from the penthouse to the eighth floor," shouted Micah.

"Really? What is the problem?"

"That I have no idea where it's going to stop."

"What's the worst that could happen?"

"I don't know." Micah took two steps left, spun 180 degrees, then took two steps right.

"Then we need to start using logic," the voice said.

"Like?"

"It's obvious that if something significant happens here, then something significant happens back in Seattle. We gain something here; we lose something there."

Micah nodded and kept pacing.

"So if we want to stop the happenings back home, we have to stop what's going on in Cannon Beach."

"All right, Einstein, how do we do that?"

"You know," the voice said.

"I go back to Seattle and stay."

"Yes."

Micah stopped pacing and looked straight into the darkness. "And let the journey down here end?"

"No. Who says you have to stop coming here altogether? No one. Why can't we just come down here every now and then? Once every five or six weeks?"

"But what if that slows down the discoveries, the changes in my heart, the completion of the painting?"

"So things go a little slower. So what? Progress will still be made on the painting. We've accomplished the important part already. We've come back to God and are with Him again. Does it matter if the rest of the journey comes a little less rapidly?"

Micah rubbed the back of his neck with both hands.

"Let's get our life in Seattle going again," the voice said.

"I don't know. What if God is saying stay here?"

"Staying here while our world in Seattle falls apart? For how long? Till everything we've worked for is gone? How does that glorify God? We need to go after God's will, but it's rather difficult steering a parked car."

"But what if God is saying park for a while?" Micah turned and walked to the door. "Thanks for the confusion."

As he walked out, the voice sighed.

Welcome to my world, Micah thought.

|||||||

The next morning Micah called Shannon to check in.

"Hey, stranger. How's the surf?"

"White, how are you?"

"Things are fine," Shannon said. "It's nice to hear your voice, but you're not due to touch base for another week and a half. Are you missing us already?"

"Missing you?" Micah paused. "Yeah, actually I am. You're a good friend, Shannon."

As the words escaped Micah's mouth, it surprised him. Surprised he'd said them and surprised it had taken him this long to say it. She *was* a good friend. Like an older sister and a mom wrapped up together. "But not missing much else. I like it here. Good changes going on."

"I'm glad for you. You sound well."

After a few routine questions about the company, Shannon assured him business continued even smoother than expected, and everyone would be ready to talk with him during their scheduled conference call on Thursday next week. As Micah hung up the phone, he let out a sigh. Maybe Seattle had stabilized.

Relief swirled through him.

As he laced up his running shoes, he thought back to his talk with the voice. He might be right. Why not drop in every five or six weeks? Or even once a month? God could still work in him. This wasn't a race.

If choices and actions in Cannon Beach affected Seattle, why not spend more time there and make sure those changes weren't out of his control? Sarah could come up and spend a few days in Seattle in between his visits to Cannon Beach. Yet at the same time, Shannon said things were fine. So did he have to go back right now?

He walked onto the beach and glanced at the sky. Rain threatened, but he didn't mind running in the rain, even if it did let loose. Would keep others off the beach and leave him alone with his thoughts.

He considered the other side of the coin. This was the first time he'd had any real break from the company since its inception. As long as the board had given him the time off, Micah might as well take it. What was the worst that could happen? He might wind up on the ground floor of his condo, but he'd still have a minimum of $45 million dollars of stock ready to be exercised almost instantly.

He'd stay in Cannon Beach a few more weeks, announce to the board during the conference call what he was doing, and try to relax and enjoy his time at the ocean.

After making the decision to stay, a dull ache shot through his left ankle. Dull but still severe enough that he stumbled and wound up in a heap on the sand.

He sat up and rubbed the ankle with both hands. He rotated it clockwise, then counterclockwise. It wasn't excruciating, but his run for the day was finished.

He favored his right leg on the way home. Old age would take at least another twelve years to settle in; this had to be something else. After icing it for just under an hour, Micah wrapped the ankle in an ACE bandage and rested it the remainder of the day.

He went to bed early that night. The ankle would be fine by morning. It was. The problem came when he tried running Friday afternoon, and the ankle flared up again, much worse than before.

This time it wasn't better the next morning. Or the next. Sunday night Sarah and he were heading back to his car after dinner and a movie when she said, "Want to tell me about it?"

"What?"

"The limp you've been trying to hide all night."

"I took a run on the beach the other day, and wham, it just hit me."

"You twisted it?"

"No, it came out of nowhere."

"Well, I know this will fly in the face of macho-acting males everywhere, but why don't you see my doctor about it? I promise he'll only poke and prod a little."

"Thanks for looking out for me, Sarah."

"Always."

He pulled her close for a long soft kiss. As she lingered in his arms, he frowned and tried to ignore the feeling his visit to the doctor wouldn't be as comforting.

CHAPTER 32

Monday morning at just past eleven, a doctor walked into the waiting room of Cannon Beach Medical Clinic that looked like Foghorn Leghorn in human form. He smacked his clipboard against his hand with a sharp pop as he grinned at Micah.

"Howdy! Chart here tells me you're Micah Taylor, friend of Sarah's. Nice to meet you and all that stuff."

Micah smiled. Sarah hadn't mentioned her doctor's robust personality. "Hi, Dr. McConnell."

"Why don't you ease on back to my office, Micah, and we'll do the ol' look-see."

When they were both seated, the doctor asked for "the lowdown."

"I started a run a few days ago when this dull ache in my left ankle came out of nowhere. No big deal; I gave it a few days, figured it'd get back to normal."

"And it didn't." Doctor Foghorn nodded and looked at his clipboard. "When were ya born?"

"1980."

"Almost thirty and old age is already kicking in." The doctor laughed. "Ever felt anything like this before?"

"Never."

"You didn't smack your foot into anything lately, fall down, twist it, something like that?"

"No."

"All right, partner. We'll fire some X-rays through those bones of yours and see what turns up." The doctor walked to the door, then spun on his heel toward Micah. "Give us about an hour, and we'll have some fine shots of that ol' right wheel of yours."

"You mean my left whe—ankle."

"You're sharp, partner." The doctor pointed at Micah and laughed again. "I see why she likes you."

As he waited for the X-rays to develop, Micah walked gingerly up and down Main Street twice, stopping in two art studios, Geppetto's Toy Shoppe, and the Cannon Beach Bakery without seeing anything inside them. He returned to the doctor's office, and ten minutes later the doc stepped into the waiting room.

"Well, no great mystery here. But let me ask a quick question first to make sure I've hopscotched to the right conclusion about that ankle."

Micah nodded.

"You been working the wheels pretty consistently, haven't you?"

"Four or five times a week down on the beach."

"There you go. Mystery solved, case closed. Elvis, you can now leave the building." The doctor smiled, as if he'd been bestowed a fellowship at Scotland Yard.

"So are you going to let me in on the details of the case?"

"Good one!" The doctor slapped Micah on the back too hard and laughed. "The X-rays say you tore up your ankle pretty good a while back, broke it in two places, might've torn a ligament down there, too, from the looks of those two little metal screws there. See 'em right there?" The doctor tapped the X-ray with a mechanical pencil. "Can't really tell for sure with only an X-ray. You'd need an MRI to be 100 percent sure, but if I were a betting man, I'd lean that direction."

As the doctor pointed out where the screws were on the X-ray, heat filled Micah's body, and he felt ready to faint.

"Whoever worked on ya did a good job, FYI. So anyway, you're just getting a little aching from working the ol' ankle more often than normal down here where the moist air works its way in there and stiffins ya up a bit."

As the doctor talked, the heat continued rising into Micah's face. He'd never had an injury to that ankle in his life—ever—let alone had surgery on it. But he stared at an X-ray clearly showing the break and the two screws in his foot. Either this wasn't his ankle, or something extremely strange was going on.

Again.

"You're sure that's my ankle?"

"Pretty sure!" The doctor chuckled.

"Is there any way to find out when the surgery was? And where?"

"You okay, boy?" Dr. Foghorn's perpetual smile vanished. "You seriously don't remember this?"

"No."

The doctor started to say something else but stopped. Micah watched him study his notes but knew the doctor wasn't reading anything. The perspiration under Micah's arms trickled down the sides of his torso, and a drop splashed onto his stomach.

The doctor sat in front of Micah, his hands crossed and his

elbows on his knees. His jovial delivery disappeared. "Look, Micah, you seem like a bright, articulate kid, but to entirely forget this part of your life is pretty unusual."

Micah blew out a long breath. "I've never had amnesia; I've never had any kind of memory loss. And I swear to you, I've never had surgery on this ankle, let alone any kind of injury on either foot."

The doctor stared at Micah for ten seconds without speaking. Finally he stood and clasped his hands behind his back and returned to his buoyant disposition.

"Okay then. Now, if you want to poke around at the bottom of the well on this one, let's jump on the Internet and pull up buckets of info."

The doctor led Micah down a short hall into an office dominated by pictures of the doctor, his wife, and two college-age girls. He directed Micah to the leather couch along the opposite wall.

For all of the doc's down-home country persona, it was obvious he knew his way around a computer. After asking Micah for his Social Security number and middle name, his fingers flew, and the mouse clicked like popcorn popping. Within five minutes he'd found exactly what they were looking for.

"All right, here we go. Everything you want to know about the health, wealth, and stealth of Micah Taylor, except for the wealth and stealth parts."

The doctor's eyes shrank into a slight squint as he studied the screen, then leaned back and let out a whistle. "Woowee, I can't say I blame you for trying to forget this one. That break was a whopper, plus you ripped a ligament for good measure. Ouch on steroids."

The doctor turned to Micah. "You know, the PTs would've been working you over every few days for at least three or four months. You still telling me you remember zilch about that?"

"Nothing." But then a wave of nausea hit him. In that instant Micah did remember. At least a part of him did. Small streaks of memory circled the edges of his mind. He knew but he didn't know, as if it were someone else's life he'd heard vague, scattered details about.

"Where was the surgery?" Micah said.

A second later he knew the answer. Before the doctor could tell him, he said, "Portland, wasn't it?"

"Starting to come back to you, eh?"

"I never lived in Portland. Why would I go there for surgery?"

"But you remember it?"

"Yes. No." Micah held his temples. "I don't know."

"None of my business, partner, but I'm wondering if you need a little help with the ol' cranium to go along with your ankle. I know some good docs in that department."

Micah tried to smile and shook the doctor's hand. "If I go that direction, you'll be the first to know. Thanks for all the help on my ankle."

||||||||

When Micah got home, he headed for the voice room. "All right, tell me, do you remember us tearing up our ankle?"

"No and yes. I remember bits and pieces just like you. Nothing more."

"We have to figure this thing out."

"Meaning?" the voice said.

"Meaning if we're both getting flashbacks of something happening to our ankle, then maybe something really did happen to our ankle."

"Well, certainly the physical evidence is there." The voice chuckled.

Micah paced just inside the door; three steps to the right, turn, then three steps back. "But whose life is it? Not ours. Not when the operation happened in Portland and we never lived there."

"But when we feel our ankle—?"

"—we know something tangible happened at some point in our life that produced evidence on the X-rays and caused this pain."

"Exactly," the voice said.

"So where is that other life coming from? If it's just in my head, then I'm crazy and we have our answer. But the physical evidence keeps piling up."

"Like the magazine cover."

Micah stopped pacing, closed his eyes, and sat down, back against the wall. "I'm sitting in his office with no memories of an ankle injury. Then right before leaving, I start seeing little fragments, like half a second of physical therapy, then a flash of a pickup football game where I think it happened. But I can't tell you where or when. Then I get an image of maple wood crutches in my hands but only for an instant. Then it's all gone, and I can't tell if I'm remembering real memories, or if I've made it up inside my head to keep myself sane. You know, we have to consider the very real possibility we're losing it."

"We're not."

"Really? Are you saying people who go insane are fully aware when it's happening to them?"

"Trust me, Micah. We're not going insane."

"So what's the solution?" Micah sighed.

"Simple, as I've said before. We land on the side of wisdom and make sure things are okay up in Seattle. We go up there and stay put for a while."

"The Lord is becoming the most important thing in my entire life. I'm just supposed to leave that in a closet down here? And what about Sarah? We're a little more than casual friends at this point."

"Let me repeat what I've said too many times before. I'm not saying stop coming down entirely. I'm saying we take a break. Who cares if the board gave us this time? It's killing us. Let's go home, get things under control, make sure this parallel life stops sticking its head in where it doesn't belong, and get settled."

"And come back when?"

"When we're ready. Maybe it's a month, maybe two; we won't know how long till we know."

Micah shook his head and sneered. "It's easier for you."

"Really?"

"You haven't bought into the whole heal-the-brokenhearted, set-the-captives-free thing like I have. You're not feeling what I am. It's easier for you to leave all this."

"And maybe it's easier for you to see our world in Seattle slowly disappear than it is for me," the voice said.

"Neither place would be easy to give up at this point."

"We don't give up either one. We come down here every other weekend. Or every third weekend."

Micah stared into the darkness. The voice clearly contradicted itself, and Micah didn't know why. Maybe it was due to the bizarre fact the voice was himself, so his uncertainty was bound to make the conversation a bit schizophrenic. Whatever the reason, Micah was tired, and his ankle still ached.

"You know," Micah called over his shoulder as he walked out the door, "sometimes the way you think pushes me to the brink of sanity."

No answer.

Maybe he should stop listening to himself. Maybe he'd do what he wanted to. Maybe he'd stay in Cannon Beach forever.

Impossible. He couldn't give up what he'd created in Seattle.

To stay. To go.

He needed a sign.

CHAPTER 33

When Micah stepped out on his front porch the next morning, he found a box wrapped in white paper with a bleached white sand dollar on top. He opened the small card attached to one side and smiled.

>Micah,
>For you.
>Love,
>Sarah

He took the box out onto his deck, the roar of the ocean providing background music as he opened it. Inside he found a dolphin carved out of teakwood. Micah smiled. Perfect. He carried it with him as he picked up the phone and dialed.

"Hello?"

"Can I come over?" Micah asked.

"You got it, hmm?"

"You're amazing, Sarah."

"Thanks, so are you. And yes, come over."

They spent the day talking, laughing, strolling on the beach, then stopped at Morris's Fireside for a quick dinner that lasted three-and-a-half hours. After that another walk along the beach at the edge of the water, counting the campfires; little orange markers for families making memories.

"I have two serious cravings," Micah said as they walked hand in hand toward Haystack Rock.

"For?"

"S'mores and s'more of you."

"Bad pun, bad, Micah. Really, really bad." Sarah snuggled her head into his shoulder. "That doesn't mean I don't agree."

Twenty minutes later they sat on the bluff in front of Micah's house burning marshmallows and sticking them in between graham crackers and squares of chocolate.

"S'mores are better with dark chocolate," Sarah said.

"Not a chance." Micah stuffed the last of his third s'more into his mouth.

"So, if you get married someday, will you let your kids make their own choices? Whether to put milk or dark chocolate into their s'mores?"

Micah put another marshmallow on his homemade roasting stick and held it close to where the coals burned red. "How many kids do you want?"

Sarah stared into the fire and swallowed. "Who says I want any?"

"No one. But if you did?"

Sarah pulled off the shell of a burnt marshmallow revealing the pure-white sugar ball underneath. "Three. One boy, one girl, and one for chance to decide."

"Sounds perfect." Micah sat in the beautiful awkwardness of what they had just said to each other without really saying it and smiled. He wondered what Sarah was thinking. But not really. He knew. At least he hoped he did.

After he finished his fourth s'more, he pulled her close and gave her a kiss that lingered on his lips long after he pulled away. "Life would be utterly incomplete without you."

"I agree." She buried her head in his chest and held him tight.

|||||||

Micah went to bed that night feeling better than he had in days. Being around Sarah always settled him. He'd said life would be incomplete without her, but a more accurate description was she completed his life like no woman ever had. The next time he was in Seattle, he'd have to stop by E.E. Robbins. Just to see what kind of engagement rings were out there.

Sarah, his relationship with the Lord, his friendship with Rick, the beauty of Cannon Beach—RimSoft could wait. Couldn't it? The problem was, there was no way to know for sure. Parts of his world up there could vanish without him knowing it till he got there. A sliver of fear worked its way into his mind.

He needed Archie's next letter to be a good one.

|||||||

September 13, 1991
Dear Micah,

Again I give you just one verse from Scripture today as the whole content of this letter. But it is a verse full of power and desire.

> *"God Almighty will be your treasure, more wealth than*
> *you can imagine." (Job 22:25* The Message)
>
> *After you allow this piece of Scripture to sink down into*
> *your heart, I trust you will know which room you are to go*
> *to. Inside that room is the treasure of the Kingdom. Let me*
> *repeat myself: The treasure of God's Kingdom is contained*
> *in that room.*
>
> *Joining in His relentless love toward you,*
> *Archie*

Micah sat on his deck for a long time, meditating on the verse. He wanted to leap up and rush to the brilliant room, but he restrained himself, knowing the verse Archie had given him was not to be simply read but digested and savored before being acted on.

After an hour he rose from his chair, walked inside and upstairs to the door he longed to enter. The room had captured his mind, emotions, and deep parts of his heart. He had little doubt answers were inside.

Since his entry partway into the door two weeks ago, there had been no progress. He hadn't even been able to get that far again, and the door remained ordinary wood. But now, with Archie's letter and the verse as support, he held on to the hope that this time he would enter completely.

Reaching the top of the stairs, he saw movement on the surface of the door. Colors swirled like a slow-spinning galaxy of gold and silver. He pressed forward as if his feet were in honey. The instant the index finger of his left hand touched the door, he was caught up in a whirlpool of warmth, and his eyes closed involuntarily.

Peace consumed him. There were no cares, no worries, only an overwhelming sense of rightness and love—as if infinite joy surrounded him, reaching deeper into his body every moment. He moved forward, one step, two steps, three steps, as if the door were liquid. But he still wasn't inside.

And he wasn't in the hall.

As impossible as it seemed, he stood contained inside the door. The sensation was like being underwater, with the temperature a perfect balance between warm and cool. The door seemed to move around him, and although his eyes were closed, he sensed the light grow brighter with each step forward. There was no sensation of breathing, although he must have been, somehow.

He opened his fingers wide and waved them. Yes, the atmosphere was like water. He pressed forward again, but this time Micah couldn't go any farther. Seconds later an ever-so-slight pressure built in front of him and nudged him backward out into the hallway, like a mother laying a sleeping child into its crib after holding it close.

He opened his eyes. The door was normal again, with no indication of what had just happened. An impression shot into his mind. Soon he would fully enter the room.

As Micah walked out onto the beach, he made a decision. Cannon Beach was where he must stay. His voice was wrong. No matter what might be happening in Seattle, it was not worth leaving what God was doing inside him. Yes, he would go back to Seattle to check in on things soon, but this would be his base of operations for the foreseeable future.

That night Micah ate seafood fettuccine with smoked salmon while he told Rick in detail about the brilliant room.

"You know what's inside there, don't you?" Micah said.

"I think I might. But it would be a breach of our friendship to tell you." Rick smiled. "It's a discovery you need to make for yourself. Plus I could be wrong."

Rick's confidence was encouraging, but it frustrated Micah not being able to speed up the process. God was not someone you rushed. Got that. But how long would he have to wait? A week? A month? He wanted discovery now.

Driving home he tried to tell himself his world was perfect, but the fear needling the corners of his mind wouldn't let him. Micah sensed something was coming. And it wouldn't be anywhere near perfection.

CHAPTER 34

Micah was convinced Rick knew exactly what was inside the brilliant room. But how could he get Rick to tell him?

Thursday afternoon Micah shuffled down Main Street, brainstorming an answer when a voice sliced through his mind like a knife, spinning his thoughts in an entirely new direction.

"Micah?"

He knew that voice. Micah turned. Ten feet away a woman wearing khaki shorts and a blue tank top scuttled toward him. She pushed a stroller; the features of the child inside made it obvious she was the mother.

"It is you, Micah. I can't believe it. Really, truly can't believe it! I always wondered if we'd bump into each other again. I mean you said you'd probably settle somewhere up on the northern coast, but we never get up here, till now of course. And well, I thought if we ever did, wouldn't it be a kick if I ran into you? But I never expected it to actually happen and now—"

The woman threw her head back and laughed, then threw both arms around him and squeezed. "I'm sorry, listen to me going on like a jukebox packed with quarters. Tell me about you. My gosh, how long has it been? Too long, of course. Wow."

Micah stepped back, hoping the woman couldn't tell the grin on his face was pure plastic. Did he know her? He knew the voice, but her? Wait. Maybe. As he stared into her eyes, shards of memories slipped into his mind like scenes from different childhood TV shows all out of context with each other.

The woman waved her hand in front of his face. "Are you okay?"

"No, I mean yes. Good." He forced out a laugh. "It's just a shock to see you."

"Yeah, yeah, I know. After all this time, right? We promised we'd definitely stay in touch, didn't we?" The woman held up her fist with her thumb and pinkie finger sticking out as if it were a telephone. "But nah, neither one of us. Well, that's life. Wow, you look good. Catch me up! What have you been doing with your life? Where'd you go when we headed for different ends of the earth?"

More memories surfaced. Late-night walks with her somewhere, along narrow beaches? The ocean? Yes. How long ago? Seven, eight years ago? More? Less? "I live in Seattle. I started a software company."

"You're kidding. Software? Really? That tweaks my mind, I gotta tell you. Didn't think you'd ever go that direction, not with the passion you had for your—"

"Wahhh!" The woman's baby split the air with piercing cries in rhythm with the tapping feet of a man standing behind her.

One glance at the perfectly pressed maroon polo shirt, spotless tan slacks, and a frown line to match told Micah this guy was the jealous type and didn't appreciate the enthusiasm this woman was pouring out.

"Uh, honey, more than two people here," the man said.

A slight grimace ran across the woman's face before she turned toward the man. "Right, right, right. Honey, this is Micah Taylor. We dated for a while years and years ago; I probably told you about him one time or another. Micah, this is my husband, and this is my little prince." She lifted the baby out of his stroller and set him on her hip.

"Passion for what?" Micah said.

"What?"

"Passion for what?" he repeated.

"I'm sorry you lost me. What passion for what? You mean, what am I passionate about?"

"No, you said something about being surprised I started a software company because of my passion for . . ."

"Oh, right. Yes, yes, yes." She laughed as she set the baby back down in the stroller and wrapped a dark blue blanket around him. "Don't tell me you've abandoned it. I never saw you giving up your dream."

The woman's husband cleared his throat without much subtlety, and she whipped around to face him. "Honey, don't get your knickers twisted into bunches. We'll go in just a second. I just want to get Micah's info so we don't lose touch for another six years."

They exchanged e-mail addresses as he tried to put the puzzle pieces together. He wouldn't be able to question her in detail, not with Igor standing over them like a Puritan chaperone at a high school dance.

"Gottta run, Micah. Great seeing you. Don't give up the dream."

"What *was* the dream?"

"As if you didn't know!" She laughed and clipped away.

Was it impossible for anyone to give him a clear answer? If not software, what was the dream?

||||||||

When Micah got home, he walked through the house not going anywhere in particular, looking for—hoping for—inspiration and answers. He wound up looking down the hallway that led to the painting room.

Good idea. Time to see if anything's changed.

He eased open the door and the painting came into view. Definite changes; subtle, but significant. The outline of two people had been added at the left edge of the painting, and near the water it looked like a little boy would build a sand castle.

"Take me into that panorama, Lord."

The next thought followed quickly. What had he lost in Seattle?

Micah called Shannon and made up a paper-thin excuse for checking in. Once again she told him things were fine at RimSoft. Maybe he was wrong. Maybe perfection had landed on him like a butterfly and would stay forever. He hung up somewhat reassured but still uneasy. No matter what he told himself, he couldn't shake the feeling of disaster rumbling inside.

After dinner Micah sank back in his overstuffed chair in the great room and tried to drift off. He was tired of thinking, tired of praying, tired of trying to figure out what God was doing to his life.

To his lives, plural.

He'd almost slid over the edge into sleep when the phone rang. "Yeah?"

"Hey, you," Sarah said.

"Hey back. I was just thinking about you."

"Good thoughts?"

"Great thoughts." Micah smiled, his eyes half closed. He stood and wandered over to his couch in front of the fireplace, letting himself freefall backward into the overstuffed cushions strewn on top.

"Wanna have some fun?" Sarah asked.

"Rhetorical question, right?"

"Yes."

"The idea?"

"Nehalem's Art Festival. How 'bout we go down and take a look this weekend?"

"You said fun, not shopping."

"So that promise you made about seeing locally made crafts with me at least twice this summer . . ."

"Yeeeeees!" Micah stood and launched into his radio voice. "And that promise is about to come true! Ladies and gentlemen, boys and girls, can you think of a better way to spend your Saturday? No? Me neither! The Nehalem's Art Festival. Yeehaw!"

"You think that's amusing, don't you?"

"Mildly."

"How's tomorrow, as long as you're not previously engaged."

"And if I am?" Micah wandered toward his kitchen.

"Tell her you're utterly intrigued by another woman."

"You're funny—"

"Thank you."

"—sometimes," finished Micah. "Pick you up at eleven?"

"Perfect."

Micah hung up the phone and smiled. Definitely in love. The wanna-spend-the-rest-of-my-life-with-you type of love.

|||||||

The Nehalem's Art Festival boasted more than thirty booths, some stuffed to overflowing, others with just the right amount of merchandise, the artists manning them having figured out the fine line between having too much and too little space to display their treasures.

They wandered past dried-flower arrangements, handcrafted cribbage boards, and strawberry-scented candles before they stopped at a booth featuring paintings. The artist sat on a tall pine stool, her back to them. She was engrossed in the beginning stages of a new painting, a dried-out riverbed in the high mountains.

"You like these?" Sarah motioned to the finished pieces.

"Yeah, I do. And you?"

"Not really my style."

"So what is your style?"

"I'll let you know when I see it," Sarah said.

Micah watched her move off, then turn back after realizing he hadn't moved. He continued to study the paintings. Sarah eased back alongside him. "Why do you like them so much?"

"They make me think—create impressions in my mind. Her technique intrigues me."

"You have thought for my painting, yes?" The artist spoke without turning as Sarah and Micah smiled at each other and mouthed in unison, "Good ears."

"Yeah, I have a thought," Micah said.

"You will share it with me, yes?"

"Your paintings remind me of LaQue's work with your use of shadows and of Thomas Glover's use of detail."

"Good! Very good. I studied the work of both extensively. You are collector or studied art in college?"

"No, but I . . . I do like your paintings."

The lady turned and looked at Micah with a quizzical expression. The right side of her mouth turned up in a tiny smile. "You are serious? You are not student of art? An artist then, maybe? You must be painter yourself." She set down her brush, got off her pine stool, and walked over to them.

"No, not an art student. And no, I don't paint." Micah looked down. "Actually, I don't even know where that comment came from. It came out of nowhere."

"Thoughts must come from somewhere, yes? Among laypeople those two artists are known little. Their styles are far from each other. So your pickup on their influence is unusual. Your insight and appreciation of painting is deep, no?"

"Um, thank you. Best of success to you."

They walked away, and Sarah poked Micah in his side. He jumped a foot and a half sideways.

"Hey! Do you have to keep doing that to me?"

"So do I need to add art critic to your list of accomplishments?" She laughed, threw her arms around his neck, and kissed him.

"No."

"What do you mean no? That lady was genuinely surprised. And impressed. Obviously you know quite a bit about art to name her influences."

Micah rubbed his forehead and kept walking.

"Micah?"

"I don't know where that came from." He turned and rubbed his face with both hands. "Seriously. For some reason I just knew the names and saw their styles in her painting. But it's gone now. I can't even remember a word I said."

"What?"

"One second I'm just staring at the painting like everyone else; the next this lightbulb goes off in my head and—bam!—I know who influenced her style and their names. As clear as I know software. A window opens and I see another world." Micah snapped his fingers. "Then just as quick, the memory is gone, the window slams shut, and I'm back to being me."

"And this has been going on—?"

"For three months." Micah stopped and looked Sarah in the eye. "And it's accelerating."

"Accelerating?"

"It's happening more often." Micah walked toward the beach.

"Want to talk about it?"

Micah shook his head and stopped again. "Yes. I'm going to take a huge risk here and tell you in detail the things that have been happening, okay?"

Sarah nodded.

"Remember the other night when you asked me what was going on with my spiritual journey? How I was doing? Well, if your ears are still standing by, I'm ready to give you *War and Peace*."

"Why a huge risk?"

"Because when I'm done, you'll either think God is at work in a rather strange, beautiful, and incredible way, or I'm long overdue for a visit to the funniest of farms."

Sarah touched his forearm. "I already know God is constantly working in strange and incredible ways, so you'll have to make your story really weird to make me think you're going insane."

"This one might do it. You realize you've officially abdicated your right to come back to me when I'm finished and tell me I'm crazy."

"Agreed. Now please begin, Weaver of Fantastic Tales."

When they reached the beach, they sat on a mound of sand, and Micah told Sarah everything: from the day Archie's letter arrived at RimSoft to the present. He described the memory room, shrine room, skydiving room, the painting, the movie room, the Wildcat room, even the brilliant room he couldn't enter.

He told her about the *Inc.* cover vanishing, about *not* playing racquetball with Brad, and about *not* meeting a man named Rafi at a party. About how Julie vanished from his history, about finding the *Coast Life* magazine cover with his name on it, and how his ankle went from perfect to injured in an instant.

He talked about running into an old girlfriend, the fall of his company's stock, going from owning his condo's penthouse to living on the eighth floor, and how his car had gained a year of miles in a day.

When he finished, Micah kicked sand toward the ocean. "Do you think I'm insane?"

"I think God is in all of it. But I wonder if you feel the same."

"Of course I think He's in it. Why?"

"I know you believe it intellectually. But do you believe it in your heart?"

Micah didn't answer.

"Surrendering to the Lord is winner take all. Ninety-nine percent isn't enough. It's all or nothing."

"Your point?"

"That when I hear you talk about the things you've lost, like the stock, your condo, your car gaining sixteen thousand miles overnight, you talk like you've lost your best friend."

"Well, of course I don't like it." Micah snorted and ran his hands through the sand. "Tell me one person who would. My life is a tornado, and I'm nowhere near the eye of the storm. I'm in the heart of two-hundred-mile-per-hour winds. I've lost specific events in my life I know have happened and gained others I know didn't happen."

"But those things did happen, Micah."

"What do you mean?"

"How can you deny the physical existence of something like your ankle? Or the magazine cover?"

"I can't."

"So is it real? This other life?"

"I don't know." Micah rubbed his eyes and sighed.

"I'm going to really weird you out now." Sarah sat forward and took his hands in hers. "But it might help you accept that this other life you're getting bits and pieces of is real."

"All right."

"I remember you talking about it."

"About what?"

"Your ankle. The original injury. How it happened."

"Where was I during this supposed conversation?" Micah stared at her.

"We talked about it a month ago. You told me you messed up your ankle by landing hard on another guy's foot playing touch football about six years ago. That's why I noticed the slight limp and wasn't surprised when you asked for the name of a good doctor in town."

Micah smacked the sand with the back of his hand. "This is *exactly* what I'm talking about. As bizarre as my life has been the past four and a half months, don't you think a sprinkle of terror is warranted?"

"I'll admit it's unusual."

Micah stared at her in disbelief.

"All right, more than unusual, but God has done some amazing things in your life since you came down here."

"Agreed."

"So, do you trust Him fully or not? Are these bizarre changes part of His plan or not? Do you believe no matter what happens, you don't have to control it because He's in control?"

Again, he didn't answer.

"I think the reason it's so hard for you, Micah, is because you're still hanging on."

"To what?"

"Your life." Sarah stood, brushed off the back of her 501s, and reached down to pull him up.

Micah stared at her. "I know you're good for me, even though you drive me crazy sometimes."

"I'll take that as a compliment." Sarah smiled.

The car was silent most of the way back to Cannon Beach. Sarah was unusually silent. Perceptive as always. He needed time to process their conversation, and she was giving it to him. It might have been better if she had talked. In the quiet he had to face her words. As usual she was right. A wave of frustration swept over him.

He was getting tired of her pushing him, forcing him to wrestle with . . . Maybe he'd be better off without her. What? He blinked at how powerful the thought was. Dump Sarah? No way. Crazy thinking. He shook his head, as if to toss the idea from his mind.

As they drove through Arch Cape Tunnel, Micah held his breath, a habit left over from childhood. A perfect snapshot of his life. Feeling lost in darkness and holding his breath to see what would happen next.

Tomorrow he'd do something to take his mind off his dual existence. Something so engrossing he wouldn't have time to think.

Something probably a little bit stupid.

CHAPTER 35

Micah woke Sunday morning still determined to take his mind off his two intertwined lives. Sea kayaking would be the perfect distraction. He'd read a book on the sport and decided it was the ideal day to forage the waves of the Oregon Coast. So he'd never done it. Big deal. Maybe it was a bit risky, but how hard could it be?

Ten minutes later he stood in Cleanline Surf Shop perusing kayaks. He'd need a wet suit, too. Even though it was early September, the water temperature wouldn't be more than fifty-four degrees, and Micah had no desire to freeze out among the foam.

"You done this before?" the clerk said as he rang up the sale.

"Yeah." Micah thought back to the time he'd paddled around the glassy surface of Lake Union up in Seattle during high school. "Sure. Why?"

"It can get a bit intense out there. I just don't want people to be caught off guard."

"I'll be fine." He wished he felt as confident as he sounded.

||||||||

He would put in at Oswald West State Park, a fifteen-minute drive down the coast from Cannon Beach. He'd heard it was optimum for sea kayaking. Indian Beach just north of Ecola State Park was closer, but the bay here was wider, had fewer rocks to negotiate, and hopefully fewer people would be there to watch his freshman attempt.

A fine, steady rain fell as he pulled into the Oswald parking lot. By the time he had his kayak off the car, the wind had kicked up to fifteen miles per hour.

The walk down to the beach was longer than he would have liked, but its beauty eased the fatigue the hike brought on. Massive Douglas fir trees almost completely blocked the rain, and the stillness of the forest brought a feeling of peace. The only noise was a river he crossed twice with the help of rough-hewn wooden bridges.

Just before he reached the bay, he stopped in front of a sign that said, "Unusually high sneaker waves, deep water, and strong outgoing currents. Use extreme caution." Micah glanced at the bay, then back at the sign. No problem. He'd be careful.

By the time he reached the sand, the winds had picked up even more, but the rain was dying into a fine mist that swirled, then settled softly on his face.

He waited a few minutes to catch his second wind and watch the chaotic pattern of the roaring waves in Smuggler's Cove. He smiled. He felt alive. And alone. Surprisingly there had been no other cars in the parking lot, and he'd seen no one on the hike down except for a squirrel that screamed at him when he sat on a log to rest.

Securing his hood, Micah watched a mixture of sand, water, and foam swirl around his ankles. The waves moved slightly north to south, so he planned to paddle out to the north end of the bay and work his way back in, letting the waves push him to the center of the cove.

Nice plan.

He sliced through the first attack of surf as if it was whipped cream, and a rhythm built in his arms and paddle, but Micah struggled with the second set of waves. They were stronger and fought to push his craft sideways. But he pushed through as his breaths deepened and his eyes went steely.

The rain picked up again, and the winds were in concert. The soft kiss of the earlier mist became stinging needles on his face and forearms. But he was caught now in a web of determination, and he ignored the distractions.

The final set of breakers loomed, and the salesperson's words blistered his mind. *"Just don't want people to be caught off guard."*

Part of Micah wanted to make the intelligent decision, but a louder voice drew him deeper into the sea. He ached to recapture a life of living on the edge, with high risk and high reward. Like when he'd started RimSoft. He'd tasted it in the skydiving room, yes. But this wasn't an alternate reality God had taken him into. This was here, now, in vivid living color. He wanted it. Needed it. It flicked at the edges of his heart and stirred something inside larger than himself.

A wave raced down. Above him. On top of him. Not one of the benign four-foot swells he had imagined, but the eight-foot wall he'd seen from shore but ignored. Micah strained to turn his kayak directly into it but was a few precious degrees off. Just a fraction, but it was enough, and the full weight of the water crashed down on him.

He sucked in a breath just before the ocean surged against his nose and mouth, pushing for a way in. Then a kaleidoscope of tumbling, shoving, and pulling as the wave ripped him from his kayak and shoved him to the bottom of the ocean.

Five seconds felt like fifty. He searched for sunlight—his only clue as to which way was up. The most powerful part of the wave moved over the top of him, and Micah fought to surface.

He was running out of air.

He broke the water ceiling and gasped.

Another wave broke, and he was plunged under the torrent again, somersaulting to the bottom where his foot ripped across a jagged rock. The thought of sharks leaped into his mind, then instantly took a backseat to simply surviving long enough to take another breath.

He surfaced again and swam hard toward shore. His hope was to keep breathing long enough to reach the smaller waves and bodysurf them to the beach.

Micah went under again but with less intensity. Hope rose.

He was going to make it.

Except for the rocks.

A jagged cliff lined the south side of the bay, and the wave pattern pushed him toward it, much faster than he'd anticipated from shore.

The beach was only fifty yards ahead, but the rocky crest was only ten yards away, the waves still five-foot swells—quite capable of depositing him wherever they liked. He'd been caught in an unrelenting progression that would end in bone quickly meeting rock.

Panic grabbed his gut, the mental battle now as fierce as the physical one. If he panicked, he'd have little chance of surviving. A voice screamed, *Give up!*

"No!" he raged back. "Lord, hel—!" Micah cried out, but the words were smothered as another wave shoved him under and closer to the rocks.

Suddenly the miraculous struck. The next wave drove him north instead of south. On his right a slick, jagged, black rock slipped by his face, inches away. It didn't make sense. Then another wave pushed him north, away from the cliff and into shore. Peace washed over Micah more powerful than any of the waves that had vowed to take his life. From deep inside a different Voice said, *Look up.*

At the back edge of the beach, just in front of the tree line, stood a figure in an olive raincoat. Micah couldn't make out the face within the shadows of its hood. He couldn't even tell if it was a man or a woman. The moment he looked, the person turned and strode into the trees. Micah's view was swallowed by another black wall of water, and he was once more pushed toward shore.

After that he remembered nothing.

Micah's eyes opened to the trees at the edge of the beach out-lining the dark gray sky. Small eddies of seawater swirled around the side of his hood, but the waves were a world away now. The question of who was on the beach spun through his mind as he pushed up to his hands and knees, waited a moment, then sat back on his heels.

He knew there was a connection between the person he'd seen and his rescue. Without the hooded figure, he had little doubt his life would have ended on the bottom of the ocean floor.

He struggled to one knee, then stood and eased over to the spot where the person had been, hoping to make out a shoe print in the sand, a clue to the identity of the spectral observer of his near death. The sand was soft from the rain, and a clear impression of a boot or tennis shoe should have been easy to spot. But there wasn't even the hint of a footprint.

|||||||

Less than a mile north of Ecola Creek a cape jutted into the ocean blocking the way to Crescent Beach except at extremely low tide, so the route wasn't heavily traveled.

But Micah and Rick rose early enough on Tuesday to get around the point with only half an inch of water swimming up to kiss their running shoes. It had been almost a week since they'd talked, which was unusual, so a combination run and conversation was an excellent way to start the day.

The deep scrape on his foot Micah had gotten during his kayaking ordeal still stung but not enough to keep him from this run. It was good to be with the mechanic.

Micah glanced at Rick as they fell into an easy rhythm beside each other. He still didn't know how to describe the man. A little too young to be a father figure; a little too old to be the wise big brother. Maybe he was simply a mentor.

Micah had had business mentors before, who had helped further his and their own careers as RimSoft grew. But his relationship with Rick was different. The taste of ulterior motive never flitted around the edges of their friendship. Rick never seemed to want anything from Micah, yet Rick pushed him, drove him, forced him to look at his life in ways he'd never considered.

He couldn't see what Rick got out of the relationship and didn't think about it too deeply. Micah didn't want the illusion to be shattered that, for the first time in his life, someone knew about his money and success but couldn't care less how either might benefit him.

They jogged around the point, and Crescent Beach opened up in front of them. It looked as if no one had stepped on it in months. With the old trail from Ecola Park above washed out, the only other way to access the beach was a much steeper and longer path from the parking lot above, which many people didn't realize existed. So their indentations in the sand were possibly the first of early fall.

Micah challenged Rick with a smile, and they broke into a dead sprint across the sand. Even with the difference in ages, Rick wouldn't give up without a fight.

Seventy yards down the beach, Micah glanced back. Rick pounded down the beach just three paces back. After about 150 yards Micah's lungs won out over his mind, and he staggered to a stop. He bent over, hands on knees to catch his breath. Rick did the same not far behind him, both of them laughing between gasps for more air.

After their heart rates returned to normal, they found a log, long battered by the wind and waves into a functional seat, and sat down.

"You think about death?" Micah said after a few minutes of watching two otters joust in the water.

"Yep."

"Yes? That's it?"

"Yeah."

Micah knew he was teasing and waited for the mirth to burst out of Rick's mouth.

"What do you want to know?" Rick said after his laughter subsided.

"I went kayaking a couple days ago." Micah paused as the emotion of the event swelled inside. "Nearly drowned. I was stupid. Thought I knew what I was doing. Wrong."

Rick eyes drilled into Micah's, but he didn't comment. Micah thought he didn't understand.

"I'm not saying I got in a little trouble out there. I'm saying I truly came within a breath of dying."

"What were you thinking as you were about to be smashed against the rocks?"

"I felt like an alarm went off and I was finally awake after years of sleep. I haven't felt that alive in years. As crazy as this sounds, even though a big part of me was scared out of my mind, another part of me loved it."

"On the edge of life."

"Exactly." Micah picked up a handful of sand and let it slide over his fingers. "Ready for the weird part?"

"Sure. After you tell me about the *normal* parts of almost dying."

The comment lightened the moment just enough.

"At the point I knew I was going to bite it, the waves tossed me *against* the current. Makes no sense. Then I look up and someone's standing on the beach. Two seconds later? Gone." Micah glanced at Rick before continuing. His face showed no expression.

"The thought riveted itself in my mind that this person standing on the beach and the waves saving me were connected. But after I get to shore, when I look for tracks, nothing's there. So was the person a ghost? A hallucination?"

"Was the sand too hard to take a footprint?"

"It took mine. In the same spot I saw the person standing." Micah pulled a long sliver of wood off the log he and Rick sat on and pushed it into the sand at his feet.

"Your conclusion?"

"He wasn't there physically."

"You mean it was all in your mind?" Rick said.

"No, and that's where it gets strange. I saw someone. No question. But maybe what I saw was a vision. Maybe whoever it was, he doesn't exist on a physical plane."

"Or he didn't think you'd see him. Forgot to leave footprints."

"You lost me."

"Could have been an angel." Rick stood and stretched his hamstrings.

Micah chuckled but Rick didn't join him. He glanced at his friend to see if he was joking. He wasn't.

"You're serious," Micah said.

"Get sappy, pop-culture angels out of your mind. I'm talking about the fierce warriors you find in the Bible."

"Warriors?" Micah stood and joined Rick in stretching his legs.

"Read Daniel 10 or 2 Chronicles 32. Angels are intense creatures with battle on their minds. God gave them incredible powers, and they continually wield that power on Earth." Rick began stretching his back. "The Bible tells of angels taking on human form and people not knowing it. So I think it's possible what you saw on that beach was an angel, sent the instant you called out to God. Was it God, a weird current, or an angel? Don't know, but it's worth considering all possibilities."

Micah stared at the sand crystals at his feet and thought back to the times over the past four and a half months he had called out to God and how the answers had come. Could Rick be right? Angels? Micah couldn't get his mind around it.

"So let's pretend for a moment it was an angel," Micah said. "Why did it only come after I called out to God? Why not act before?"

"Ah, you presume to know more than you do."

"What does that mean?"

"You're only looking through the eyes of your own experience. Your mind couldn't contain all the times God or His angels have acted on your behalf when you had no clue He was doing it and you didn't call out."

"You got an example?"

"I don't need to come up with one, just point out a few you know yourself." Rick laughed. "Wake up, boy!"

"Fine." Micah glared at Rick. "How 'bout telling me what I already know."

Rick's smile faded. "Has life changed since coming to Cannon Beach? Do you have more freedom? Are you closer to Jesus? Had any powerful experiences? Who got you here in the first place? Did you just up and one day decide, 'Hey! I think I'll take a little road trip to Cannon Beach?'" Rick finished stretching and jogged lightly in place.

Micah's relationship with God, the healings in his soul, the painting, Sarah, all flashed into his mind. And yes, he was freer than he'd ever imagined possible.

"Micah," Rick said softly as he stopped warming up and stood still. "Who guided Archie to write the letters and have the house built? Who set up our friendship or led you to meet a girl in an ice cream shop?"

Rick sat back down on the log, and they sat for five minutes saying nothing as guys are able to do. Micah was grateful for the time to reflect. The man he'd been when he first set foot in Cannon Beach was gone. He was more alive now than he'd ever been. Yet in some ways it was so far from the world he'd come from, he still felt the foreigner. Not exactly true. Here felt like home, but at the same time the days in Cannon Beach often came at him like an out-of-control freight train, and he couldn't figure out how to get off the tracks.

Rick broke the silence with words that went to the heart of Micah's condition. "The King calls us to a life of risk, adventure, and a continual journey into the unknown. The Bible says the Word is a lamp unto our feet. Not a lamp unto our head or a set of running lights where we can land our aircraft. So take one step at a time. Right now you're desperately trying to figure out how your journey ends. But you must have faith enough to let it go and let Him unveil it in His timing."

"So what do I do while I'm waiting?"

"Know Him. Grow in intimacy. Follow His voice, and in every decision make the conscious choice to take the narrow path." Rick got up and walked to the edge of the surf. "Want to do a little wading? We'd better head south unless we want the tide to wash our kneecaps."

They made it around the south point of Crescent Beach with only minutes to spare—their feet only slightly moist as they jogged back toward Haystack Rock.

As they parted, Rick looked back and gave Micah a cryptic smile. "If I were betting, I'd lay pretty good odds your kayaking beach buddy was indeed an angel."

"What makes you so sure?"

"In time I have no doubt you'll figure it out for yourself."

Rick jogged off, his back to Micah. But Micah could still feel the smile on Rick's face.

||||||

The next morning Micah chuckled as he read Archie's letter because the whole thing was redundant.

> *October 13, 1991*
>
> *Dear Micah,*
>
> *I have prayed for six days over this letter. I am still not convinced it is the time to explain how I have known so much about your present from my vantage point, which from your perspective is the past. However, I will sally forth nonetheless.*
>
> *Five years ago I met a genuine angel of heaven.*
>
> *He revealed to me that someday you would lead many to freedom through the abilities the Father had bestowed on you, and I was to have a role in making certain those abilities were used for God's glory and not buried.*
>
> *Over the course of a year, this angel revealed to me specifics about your life and instructed me to write them down. I was to then write a series of letters, which of course you now have, and convey to you the things he revealed.*

Whether you believe in angels or not, hopefully you have found wisdom in these letters and can see they are written with the hand of the Father on them.

My greatest prayer is wherever you are in your journey, you will continue to trust that God has designed this rather odd relationship between you and me and His plans are never wrong.

Across time,

Archie

For the first time in months, Micah went to bed feeling like a mystery had been solved. Finally! An explanation of how Archie knew the things he did. Micah still wasn't sure he believed angels were popping up in Cannon Beach and other parts of the world to buddy up with Earth's mortals, but Rick had made a pretty decent case for their existence. It was the best reason he'd found so far to explain Archie's letters.

Angels? If they were real, he'd need them in the morning. Something told him his conference call with Shannon and his RimSoft VPs would be just as rough as his kayak adventure had been.

CHAPTER 36

Micah woke Thursday morning with a severe case of RimSoft on the brain. He couldn't shake the feeling something was wrong. Probably nothing. Just feeling a bit rusty due to lack of day-to-day interaction with the company.

He made himself steroid-strength coffee and pounded down two cups in six minutes. Being wide awake was essential. His sabbatical had been in effect for three weeks, and today was the day for a phone conference with his VPs to plow through everything needing his immediate decisions. He needed the call to go smoothly. He needed assurance RimSoft was still booting up without bugs. He needed a few days of normal life, please.

Shannon answered before the second ring. "This is Shannon—"

"Hey, it's me. Everyone ready?"

"Who is this?"

"In other words, no one's ready?" Micah chuckled.

"Who . . is . . . this?" she snapped.

"What are you doing? It's Micah."

"Micah Taylor?"

"Yeah. Hello. Remember me?"

"Well, hi, Micah. Good to hear from you. How's the long vacation going?"

"It's called a sabbatical."

She cleared her throat. "Well, when the president of the company calls your time away a vacation, it's a vacation."

"Exactly. And since I'm not calling it a vacation, it's not a vacation."

No answer. Micah started to ask if she was still there when Shannon responded with cool professionalism.

"I like that. Ambition is an excellent quality. And if you are the president of your own company someday, you can call it whatever you like. But for now we'll call it a vacation."

Micah sighed and poured a little more coffee to go with his French vanilla cream. "Listen, Shannon. I'm not in the mood for a lot of humor this morning. I just want to get this conference call done and get on with the rest of my day, okay? So let's get to it."

Her tone changed from polite professional to ice. "Listen very, very closely. I appreciate the hard work you've given this company. I also appreciate that you're one of its rising stars, but you keep acting like you own the place, and I'll rip the remaining rungs on this corporate ladder out of your hands and put them in the shredder. Got it?"

Micah's whole body was instantly hot. She was dead serious. There'd been another shift, and this time it was major.

"Who's the president of RimSoft?"

"You mean RimWare."

Micah's head sank to the oak coffee table.

Not even the same name! RimWare? Didn't Rick call it that a couple of times? "And my position with the company?"

"Now or before this conversation started?"

"Before."

"When it started, I had you slated for vice president in a few years. Maybe less. But this display you just put on is not winning you any elections. I don't have time for these games and neither do you."

"Listen, I'm really sorry about this." Micah swallowed hard and dug his knuckles into his forehead. "Just testing out some new ideas I read about on social, uh, trying out ways to influence people and—"

"You're a strong asset to this company, Micah. But you keep trying that kind of nonsense, and you'll have more time to relax than you want. Understand?"

"Yeah."

"Fine. No harm done, but lay off the Carnegie crap and enjoy your vacation, okay?"

"Sure. Of course."

"You're back when?" She didn't wait for an answer. Micah heard keys being punched through the phone. "Looks like next Tuesday. Have a different attitude when I see you next."

Micah's head reeled. "Can I take one more minute?"

"One."

"I was just curious about RimSof—uh, RimWare's stock options."

"Who have you talked to?"

"No one."

"Then how do you know I'm taking the company public?" He heard her tapping a pen or pencil with a rapid beat.

He slid to the floor. "I have no stock," he whispered to the waves outside his window.

"No one has stock. Yet. But if the Wall Street rumors are true, the IPO could rocket out of the gate. The board could easily vote up to five thousand shares for employees of your level, which means based on conservative early estimates, on paper you could be worth as much as $550,000 instantly. You probably wouldn't vest for a year or two, but that's relatively quick."

Micah had a hard time breathing and said nothing.

"Are you there?"

"Um-hmm." He didn't trust his voice.

"Are you all right?"

"Yeah."

"Good. I have to go. See you next Tuesday."

The phone went dead. Setting it back in its cradle was like putting an octagon peg into a square hole. He finally got it in place and just stared out over the ocean. But didn't see anything.

||||||

"Am I losing my mind, Rick?"

"No."

Rick worked on a breakfast fit for a ranch hand, even though it was past 1:00 p.m. Micah only had coffee, which he hadn't touched.

"Then what is going on? Some kind of twisted cosmic joke God is playing on me to entertain the angelic host? The ultimate *Candid Camera?*"

Rick shoved the last of his eggs smothered in Tabasco sauce into his mouth.

"Are you listening to me?" Micah said.

"Yep." Rick went to work on his sourdough toast.

"Do you hear what I'm saying? Two weeks ago everything at RimSoft ran like a Swiss watch. As of today I've gone from seriously rich to having virtually nothing. Not only am I no longer president; I don't own a single share of stock. What'll I lose next? My life?"

"Uh, maybe, I don't know," Rick said as if Micah mentioned it might rain.

"Are you hearing what I'm saying?" Micah popped his hand down on the table hard enough to rattle all the silverware. A few surprised looks came their way, and the waitress who was about to fill their water glasses did a 180 on her heel and skittered back toward the kitchen.

"Knock it off." Rick looked up, his eyes dark and intense. "You know exactly what is going on here. And you've made the choice to make it happen every step of the way."

"What? I'm living in *The Twilight Zone*, and you're saying it's obvious what's going on? What choices have I made? Enlighten me."

Rick stood, took wrinkled ten- and five-dollar bills out of his wallet, dropped them next to his plate, and looked down at Micah. "If you need it spelled out for you, it's in Matthew in black and white. Chapter 13, verses 44 through 46. For you it's jumped off the page and turned into real life. An amazing gift. But you have to make a final decision on whether it's worth the price."

When he got home, Micah slammed the door and screamed at the top of his lungs, "Lord, where are You? Why are You doing this to me?" He hurled his keys at the kitchen counter and watched them crash into the coffeepot, shattering the glass.

He knew he should pray but was exhausted. Tired of no concrete answers. Tired of trying to figure out which life was real and which one he wanted. Most of all tired of seeing his life disappear out from under him.

He glanced at his coffee table in front of his picture windows. Archie's remaining envelopes sat there, mocking him. He glanced at the calendar on his refrigerator. Six days early. He didn't care. Micah snatched up letter number fifteen and ripped open the envelope. With the fourteen previous letters, he'd shot up at least a quick prayer for wisdom and understanding. Not this time.

> *November 4, 1991*
> *Dear Micah,*
>
> *I have prayed before each letter written in an attempt to write only the words the Lord God would have me write through His guidance and the guidance of the angel I told you about in my last letter. However, in the end I am just a man, and it is only in Him and in His strength I can approach perfection.*
>
> *That is a lengthy introduction to say I have most assuredly made mistakes in the letters you have read so far, and for that I offer my apologies and ask for your forgiveness. My prayer is that you are taking every scene, decision, and circumstance these letters stir up in you to deep prayer, that my mistakes might be filtered out, and the only remnant that remains would be pure truth.*
>
> *In the end only one voice matters. Only one.*

Micah set down the letter. Of course. In the end only one voice mattered. His own. And he hadn't been listening.

> *The end of your journey is coming soon.*
> *Seek Him.*
> *For eternity's sake,*
> *Archie*

Micah folded the letter, then slid it back into its envelope. A sliver of hesitation and apprehension had grown toward the voice, but he pushed through the emotion and strode down the hall. Archie was right. One voice mattered.

Micah pushed open the door and eased inside. "Hey, you awake?"

"If you're awake, I'm awake." The voice laughed.

"Yeah, okay. You're me. I'm you, etcetera."

Micah sat with the voice in silence.

"My life has disintegrated. Our life. But I'm going to figure this thing out. I refuse to let it beat me. I think the way—"

"The time for thinking and talking is over," the voice said. "We have to act. Now. You know it. Look what's happened since we hesitated."

Micah ran his teeth over his bottom lip and paced.

"Talk to me, Micah."

"What do you want me to say? Okay. I admit it. I was wrong. I should have listened to you. Archie's letter spelled it out in black and white. There is only one voice I can trust. Myself."

"Yes."

"But if I'm really supposed to go back to Seattle like you say, two things make no sense."

"What?"

"Those verses in Matthew. You'd have to be spiritually blind not to know what Rick was driving at."

"What is that?" the voice said.

"Oh, c'mon. I'll assume that question is rhetorical."

"Let's talk it out to be sure."

"Hello? The pearl of great price? I have to give it all up. All of it. Everything I had, and have, in Seattle for the relationship I have with the Lord down here. That is the choice."

"Do you want to give it all up?" the voice whispered.

Micah was silent.

"We must be careful not to take any verse out of context. The Christian life is a journey. We're not instantly at the point of perfection the moment we start out—are we?"

Micah didn't respond.

"I don't think that's what Archie was driving at or what those verses show us."

"Your theory?" Micah said.

"Don't misunderstand." Light laughter floated out of the darkness. "I'm not saying we don't need to be willing to give everything up and that we shouldn't be working toward that attitude. We do, but we certainly don't have to literally give up everything."

"Maybe I do. This life or Seattle. Not both."

"Look to the Scriptures, Micah. Zacchaeus, for example. He gave up half, not all, *half* of what he owned, and salvation came to his household. The question was whether he'd given up everything in his heart, not the amount of physical wealth he turned over.

"We cannot just sit back and let God's blessings come to us. We must take part. We must take action. That is how to show we truly believe. Without action how can we pretend we have faith?"

"And going back to Seattle is a step of faith." Micah coughed and settled to the carpet, his back against the wall next to the door.

"Yes. We don't know what we're going to find there. To leave all that is going on here, to see if what we've lost in Seattle can be salvaged, with no promise of any of it coming back? Yes, that is a step of faith."

"Rick would say the step of faith would be to let all of Seattle go and trust God is in it."

"Rick is an excellent friend. Wonderful and wise. But with all he is, Rick isn't you, isn't us. Don't you realize how difficult it is to give someone advice when your opinion is skewed by your own life experiences and attitudes? Rick's experiences taint his advice. It's why we need each other more than ever. We have the same experiences, the same joys, the same hurts. We know what is right for us because we're one and the same. What a gift to be able to plan the best course together."

"And the best course?"

"Don't you think those in Seattle need to see this new Micah as much as the people down here? The Micah deeply committed to his God again, who can now be an example to all at RimSoft? It just isn't true that we have to choose one world or the other. I believe with every ounce of who I am that we can have both."

"Stay involved in both worlds."

"Cannon Beach is our spiritual escape, a place for renewal and relationship with Rick and Sarah and others. Seattle is for career, fulfillment of your dreams, and the godly influence you can have on so many more people than you can down here."

Micah's head felt like it was stuffed full of cotton candy. It sounded so right.

"We need to take action before—"

"Shut up and let me think." Micah threw his head back and closed his eyes. "I can't give up what I've found here," he finally said.

"Neither can I. But we don't have to. You've been given so many talents that can only be used in Seattle. Do not discard the gifts of God lightly. You've been given the best of two worlds, and to reject either one is to reject a great gift given from God's own hand."

"But Rick says—"

"Let it go, Micah. Stop fighting. Your striving won't change things, make them happen faster or slower."

"You're saying I shouldn't strive for freedom? And the changes God has made in my heart?"

"No, not at all. To want that is so good. But stop pushing so hard. Do you have God's peace right now? No. Relax and let the changes take their natural course."

"Rick would say we are in a battle and it won't happen naturally."

"Exactly. There is a battle going on in Seattle right now. We have lost almost everything we've created, and Rick is absolutely right. To sit here and wish for the things we used to have to return is futile. We must act now. The window of opportunity to get our old life back is closing. This is the moment to make your choice— the truth or a lie. There is a battle in this instant for your destiny, and you must decide who to believe. Now is the time to reverse this."

Micah got up and paced for a full minute. Then he turned and spoke in complete confidence. "All right. We'll go. Just give me a day to tell Sarah."

"Even a day might be too late, Micah. We must hurry."

||||||

By 8:00 that night he'd called Sarah four times. He needed to talk to her. With a decision this monumental he couldn't leave a message on her voice mail. Where was she? She always answered her cell if it was him, even at Osburn's. Maybe he should drive down there. No. Being with her would shatter his resolve to head back to Seattle. It would draw the conversation out for hours. He needed to leave immediately.

As he paced on his deck, he watched a somber sky turn dark from gray clouds bunching up on the horizon like sheep forced up against the shearing pen.

He sat on his Adirondack chair, shook his head, and laughed. What was wrong with him? This was not a big deal. He'd be back down all the time. It wouldn't change his relationship with Sarah a nanobyte.

As he picked up his phone to call her again, his hands began to sweat.

CHAPTER 37

Osburn's was shutting down for the night, and the Saturday evening crowd had thinned down to two customers who meandered out the door. The ice cream machines were rinsed and cleaned out, but Sarah still needed to clean the tables, mop the floor, and wash the windows. Heading home for the night seemed years away.

"You okay?" asked the gal helping Sarah close up the store.

Sarah's rag grew cold in her hand, but she continued using it to wipe up the tables stained with Chocolate Chip Mint, Oreo Cookie Crunch, and fourteen other flavors that had slid down customer's throats that day.

"Yeah, good. And you?" Sarah answered without looking up.

"You sure?"

"I'm sure." But she wasn't.

It had been two days since Sarah had heard from Micah. It wasn't normal. Eight hours without at least a phone call was unusual. Something was wrong. Twinges in her stomach said more than wrong.

She tried to ignore the feeling as she finished her cleaning and flicked off the store lights, sending Osburn's into shadows for the night.

Ten minutes later the gravel moaned under her Subaru as Sarah pulled slowly into the driveway of her one-bedroom apartment. She threw the gear shift into park, turned off the car, but didn't get out. She sat and replayed the conversation she'd had with Micah two days ago. It had just felt . . . off.

Finally she pushed open her car door and stepped outside. A brisk wind brought her the smoky aroma of a beach fire, and she wondered who sat around it. It should be Micah, waiting for her to join him.

As she opened her front door, her eyes jumped to her answering machine. Yes. The red light blinked. A beacon of hope? Or an emergency siren?

She walked toward the machine in slow motion, closed her eyes, then opened them to peek at the digital readout of the last call. Micah's cell phone number. She reached out to hit play, and her arm froze. Part of her desperately wanted to play the message. Another part screamed, "Don't!"

She released a tiny moan, walked to the refrigerator, swung open the door, and stared at the Crab Louie from last night. Her right leg twitched. Nerves were fraying and dread crept in for a visit.

In a daze she grabbed a quart of orange juice, poured a glass, then took a sip. She carried it to the kitchen table, wondering why it had no taste. Rubbing her eyes, Sarah stood, sighed, walked over to the machine, and pushed the button.

"You have one new message. Message sent today at 9:17 p.m."

"We have to talk, Sarah." Micah's voice paused, and she sucked in a quick breath in concert with the one he drew on the other end

of the phone. *"I can't expect you to understand this."* Another pause. *"I don't understand it myself. But my time here is done, at least for a while, so I need to go back to Seattle. I'm supposed to go back."*

She heard him pause once more, and seagulls out over the ocean filled the silence as if from a universe away. *"There are some things I need to recapture. I wanted so badly to do this in person. I called your cell phone four times, but either you weren't answering or you didn't have it with you, and I didn't want to leave a message on it, in case—"*

Sarah looked at her cell phone, which had sat cradled in its charger for the past two days.

"—you weren't going to get it for a while. I'm not leaving us. I'll be back down again in four or five weeks at the most, and we'll talk on the phone every day while I'm up there. Call me as soon as you get this."

She should have been relieved. Micah wasn't ending it—just taking some time up north to work through all the life changes he'd been through during the past four-plus months. He'd been through so much; of course he needed time. But her stomach still churned. This was not the right thing for Micah. For her. For them.

She pushed aside the orange juice, dropped her head to the table, and cried till no more tears would come. After the silence got too loud, she picked up the phone.

He answered on the first ring.

"Micah . . ." She hesitated. "With everything in me, I know this isn't right."

"It is."

"Don't go."

"I need to do this. For me. For us. Please don't try to stop this and make it harder."

She closed her eyes. "It's burned onto my heart like a branding iron that you should not go."

"You're acting like I'm moving to Siberia." Micah gave a weak laugh. "We'll see each other all the time. I'll be back down in six weeks tops. Next time you get two days off in a row, you can come up. And by going back to Seattle, I'll recover what I've lost. I believe I can get it all back. Believe with me it can happen."

For fifteen seconds the only noise was the hum of the connection.

"Sarah?"

Silence.

"Are you there?"

"Yes."

"Listen, they've got this great new invention that keeps people connected when they're apart. In fact we're using it right now. It's called the telephone.

She didn't laugh. "It's not about us being two hundred miles apart. It's not about how often we'll be talking. And it's not about me coming up to see you. It's about you going."

"Then give me a reason."

"It's wrong." Sarah sat slumped back, kneading the knots in her right shoulder.

"That's not a reason."

"Everything inside me tells me it's wrong, that the enemy is in this, trying to make you take a path the complete opposite of the way you should go."

He sighed. "You know I listen when God tells you something. What you feel matters deeply." He paused, then whispered, "But this time, it's not enough to keep me from going."

Tears spilled onto her cheeks and collected on her chin.

"Sarah?"

"Don't go, Micah. I don't want to lose you. I don't want to lose us."

"You won't lose me. Ever. I promise. I'll call you every day."

Sarah didn't respond for a long time. "I gotta go."

"I love you, Sarah."

"Me, too, Micah. All of me."

|||||||

The next morning just before sunrise, Sarah stood alone on the beach and watched little bubbles burst on top of the sand, indicating clams digging away from her probing shoes.

She wanted to believe Micah's going back to Seattle was good. Why couldn't it be? He could recover some of the life he'd lost and figure out the connection between that world and this one. But her heart was breaking because she knew the choice was wrong. She tried to convince herself she wasn't living by faith, that she needed to trust God was in control. But the thoughts were hollow and slipped through the fingers of her mind like wind through the trees.

She staggered toward the waves and stepped into them till the water lapped around her shoes.

The first time Sarah had met Micah, her heart surged. She knew he was the answer to what God had spoken years ago. But the battle of how much of her heart to give him started the moment she handed him his Pralines & Cream ice cream cone four months earlier. Because she'd also known last night's conversation would come.

She pulled out her cell phone and dialed Micah's house. She had to try one more time. No answer. He was already gone. Must have left last night.

Sarah watched her hand drop to her side as if it were someone else's. Her cell phone spun loose and dropped to the sand. Waves raced up and smothered the phone, and the icy September water found its way through her shoes and bit into her feet.

From the beginning she had feared he would choose the life without her. Despite their love, he would listen to voices other than the Holy Spirit's, and it would take him away forever. She'd tried to steel her heart for the moment when he left and even believed she could change his mind, but none of her practiced anticipation prepared her for this kind of pain.

She slipped to her knees and dug her hands into the saturated sand, trying to hold on to the grains. But the water swirled around her and washed away her hold. And she continued to add her tears to the ocean.

Then she heard a voice. Soft. Strong. "Sarah?"

Hope against hope she turned and looked up. But it wasn't Micah.

Rick stood ten yards down the beach at the edge of the waves. She stared at him, deciding whether to answer or get up and walk away. "Micah's gone. Back to Seattle," she sputtered.

"Yes, I know."

"You're not going to quote some verse about this being for the best for me, are you?"

"No, nothing like that."

"Then what?"

Rick walked to her and pulled her up and into his chest like a dad. She shuddered as she fell into him and held on with everything inside. Again the tears came.

"Let's get you into some dry clothes and grab some coffee. There's some things we need to talk about."

"Like?"

"Where you go from here."

Sarah nodded and trudged alongside Rick, leaning into him, needing him to be a rock because she couldn't be. Rick would try to speak words of comfort, would try to tell her it would be okay. But it wouldn't. It just wouldn't.

Because Micah was heading into a world where she didn't exist.

"Let's get you into some dry clothes, get you a new cell phone, and grab some coffee. There's some things we need to talk about."

CHAPTER 38

Micah stutter-stepped toward Shannon's office on Monday morning and strained to keep a scream from bursting out. Calm. Composure. He was positive ripping the Andy Warhol pictures off the walls wouldn't set the right tone for his return. But RimSoft was his opus. Was. Now he'd be proposing a plan to a woman who two and a half weeks ago had been his secretary.

That was a cheap shot. She'd always been far more than a secretary. If anyone was worthy of running the company in this parallel universe, it was Shannon. But that didn't abate the strangeness of this role reversal, or his fear she would wrap an anchor around him and his proposal and drop-kick them into the Pacific.

He approached the woman who sat in the exact desk Shannon used to sit in. "I'm here for a 9:00 with Shannon."

"Hi, Micah." She flipped her red hair off her shoulders. "She's running a few minutes behind. I hope your trip was a good one."

Trip? He stared at her. Did he know her? Early twenties, slightly heavy, dark blue eyes. He would have remembered those eyes.

Before leaving Cannon Beach, he and the voice had formed their proposal. Although the players had changed, they reasoned that the basic direction of the company probably hadn't. Micah would use this inside knowledge to impress Shannon and present the reasons he should get a shot at a vice presidency.

"Micah!" Shannon walked up and grasped both his hands. "Great to have you back. Let's catch up."

He walked into what used to be his office and tried not to cringe. It definitely had been given a woman's touch. He sat in a taupe-colored leather chair in front of a coffee table that displayed two ornate miniature fountains. They circulated water over tiny river rocks in a never-ending cycle.

"All right!" Shannon clapped her hands three times. "We'll talk business in a minute, but first you've got to tell me. Europe was wonderful, wasn't it? You loved Spain, I know you did. I hope you went to Gaudi's Cathedral. You promised you would. By the way, I applaud you for not calling in for the entire three weeks. I bet my husband you'd call. You cost me five hundred dollars." She laughed.

As she talked, anxiety grabbed Micah's stomach. Europe? Three weeks? He started to protest when shards of memories streaked through his mind. He saw himself standing in front of Gaudi's Cathedral, then on the shores of Saint-Tropez, and after that Ibiza. The Eiffel Tower blazed into his mind and then a small village, where he sipped wine with a man and woman he didn't recognize.

"I've been on vacation in Europe for the past three weeks." Micah stared at her, his lips slightly parted.

"Well, I sure hope so."

"No, I remember. I mean, yes. It was a great time. Really."

"Dealing with a little jet lag?" Shannon frowned.

"Probably."

"Well, I didn't even expect you today. Flying in last night and setting up a time to see me? No one can say you don't feel the need to succeed."

"I think there's more I can offer this company."

"Really? More than you've already done?" Shannon leaned forward and folded her hands across her knees. "I'm all ears."

Micah clipped through his proposal. Not so fast she would miss any of the nuances, but not so slowly her mind could wander.

When he finished, Shannon unfolded her hands and leaned even further forward. "Excellent."

"If you give me the freedom to implement these ideas and they work—"

"Knowing you, I have little doubt they will."

"Thanks. I'd just like to put a little carrot out there for myself."

"Carrot?"

"An incentive plan. When these projects succeed, I want a promotion to vice president and be vested in fifty thousand shares of stock immediately."

She stared at him, giving no clue whether he'd pushed too hard. A wisp of what Micah interpreted as concern passed over her face as she brought steepled hands to her lips.

"This is European humor, right?"

He'd gone too far. "No, I just think—"

"Micah." She glanced at the walls, as if she was worried they might hear. "You've been a vice president at RimSoft for a year and a half. You're vested in more shares than anyone but me. On the last report I saw, you have acquired at least three hundred and eighty thousand shares. But if another fifty thousand will make you happier, I'll get them for you. Certainly."

Three hundred and eighty thousand shares? And Rim*Soft*? Not Rim*Ware*. Yes! He swallowed and tried to keep the rush of victory from taking over his face.

"But I have to say at this stage of the game, I didn't think it was about the money for you. More the thrill of the kill, you know?" Shannon got up and walked over to her desk, her back to him. "You've got a little over $36 million in your portfolio. You want to explain why you think another $4 million will dot the i's and cross the t's in your life?"

She turned, arms folded tightly across her chest. "You and I have always played it straight. Look me in the eye and tell me you didn't go to Europe and somehow decide drugs is your new thrill-park playground."

Drops of perspiration beaded on his forehead. He couldn't lose it now. Stay calm. Hold it together.

"No. I'm fine. Really. I don't know what I was thinking." He ran cold fingers through his hair. "But now I'm realizing I should have taken one more day. To get back on Seattle time."

Shannon nodded. He hadn't convinced her. "The real Micah will be back tomorrow?"

"Guaranteed."

He'd done it. He was back. He felt the voice inside him cry, "Yes!"

‖‖‖‖‖

The next morning confirmed his Seattle life was snapping back into place. After ten minutes on his feet making breakfast, his ankle still felt fine. More than fine. It was the first time in two weeks standing in one place for over a minute didn't cause a dull ache. He bounced up and down on his left foot twice. No pain. He knew a new X-ray would show there had never been a break.

Unbelievable.

Thank You, God.

When he got to the office just after 8:00, Shannon stood on the lobby stairs, hands clasped behind her back, watching the employees file in as he used to do. She saw him, raised her eyes in acknowledgment, and motioned him over.

He took the stairs two at a time.

"Feeling better this morning?" she asked.

"Fantastic."

"Good to hear it, partner. This week will be intense."

"What did you say?" Micah spun toward her.

"Intense week coming. That's a surprise? You thought you'd continue your vacation? Sorry."

"No, the part before that."

"Good to hear you're feeling better?"

If she had said *partner* in more than a conversational way, then his life in Seattle had snapped back into place so completely it was unreal.

"You called me partner."

Shannon stared at him for a full five seconds.

"What is it with you? Does your brain have permanent jet lag? Would you rather I say, 'Good to hear it, fellow majority shareholder, cofounder, and owner in the corporation known as RimSoft?'"

Micah repressed a smile struggling to burst onto his face. "No, that certainly is a rousing bit of phrasing, but 'partner' will be fine." He couldn't suppress the massive smile any longer.

She glared at him. "Tell me you're okay. We need to sit down and catch up. But I need you sane."

"Two o'clock, your office?"

"Fine."

Amazing. Micah strutted toward the elevator, flipped open his cell phone, and dialed.

"Phil, Micah Taylor. What floor do I live on?"

"What, Mr. Micah?"

"My condo. What floor is it on?" The silver elevator doors slid open; Micah stepped in and pressed the round button for the eighteenth floor.

"The same floor it has always been. You are on the twenty-first floor."

"The penthouse."

"Yes, Mr. Micah. Why do you ask this question?"

"I want to make sure all aspects of my life have shifted back into alignment."

"I am not understand."

"That makes two of us. But it's all good, Phil. All good. Thanks."

How could he start to thank God for this? Why hadn't he listened to his own voice earlier?

The elevator doors opened, and he stepped onto the eighteenth floor. He walked toward where his old office used to be, which is exactly where it was now. A young man he didn't recognize sat at the desk outside his door. "How are you?"

"Good, Mr. Taylor. Thank you."

The young man stood and offered his hand. Damp. Micah shook it and tried not to grimace.

"I'm from Smart Temps," said the young man. "I'm filling in while your regular executive assistant is on vacation."

Micah turned and wiped his hand on his right hip.

"She'll be back tomorrow," the temp said.

Once inside his office he pulled a picture of Sarah out of his briefcase. So beautiful. Sarah sat on a small grassy dune in her black biking shorts and a dark blue Windbreaker, Haystack Rock looming in the background. Her windblown hair partially obscured the right side of her face. He stared at the picture, then kissed it.

He wanted to spend the rest of his life with her.

Picking up the phone, his hand danced over the buttons. After four rings her exquisite voice came on the line. *"Hi, this is Sarah. You leave the message; I'd love to call you back. Bye."*

"Hey, beautiful. Me. Just checking in. I know you're at work, but hearing your voice is better than nothing. Some fascinating developments up here. So cool. Way beyond what I could have imagined. Sorry to say it, but you were wrong. It was right to come back. Call me."

Micah hung up and walked toward the awards that covered his walls. He touched the frame of the Innovative Software of the Year award. Part of him loved the software business, the financial freedom, the challenges, and impact his products had on the world. But more than all of it, he loved Sarah. And more than Sarah, he loved the Lord. All of the glory of his Seattle world was nothing compared to the healing and freedom he'd found in Cannon Beach.

It made sense. To gain Seattle back, he had to lose it first. His voice was right.

Now he had it all.

Micah booted up his computer and found four hundred-plus e-mail messages sitting like little penguins all in a row, insisting on a moment of his time. He smiled. It was nice being in demand again.

Before he dove in, he called his CFO to confirm the return of one final piece of his life. His CFO said he owned 725,345 shares in RimSoft. He punched up the share price and did the math. He felt the voice deep inside smile. Just over $60 million dollars. All was right with the world again. He wanted to tell Sarah immediately. Well, if he couldn't share it with her, he could try Rick.

"Rick's Gas and Garage."

"Hey, Devin, it's Micah."

"Micah?"

"Micah Taylor."

"Um."

"From Seattle?"

"Oh, yeah, that's right. How are ya?"

"How many other Micahs do you know?"

Devin didn't answer so Micah asked for Rick.

"Out till Friday. Had some family business back east I think, not exactly sure where. Want me to give him a message?"

"Yeah, tell him to buy a cell phone."

Micah hung up the phone and pored back and forth between e-mail and snail mail. Nothing unusual till two-thirds of the way down the stack. A letter from Chris Hale.

> Hello, Micah.
>
> I hope you are well as you read this.
>
> Enclosed please find another letter from Archie. I must apologize. This letter was intended to be in the pile I left in the house, but I obviously misplaced it somehow and didn't notice it missing from the original stack.
>
> Please forgive my oversight. I've made copies of the letter and sent one to your Cannon Beach address and one to your work address.
>
> I would have sent a third to your Seattle residence, but I don't have that address.
>
> Let's connect again soon.
>
> Chris

Micah opened Archie's letter and sat down. It took all of three seconds to read.

June 23, 1992
Dear Micah,
Matthew 16:25–26.
With my great affection,
Archie

Micah looked at his bookshelves although he didn't need to. If he was back in his old office, there was no Bible on them. He Googled the verses, and two seconds later they were on his screen:

> *For whoever wishes to save his life will lose it; but whoever loses his life for My sake will find it. For what will it profit a man if he gains the whole world and forfeits his soul? Or what will a man give in exchange for his soul? (Matthew 16:25–26)*

Micah fell back in his chair. Chris loses the letter, finds it, then sends it. And he ends up reading it on this specific day. Coincidence? No way.

But so what? Yes, he'd gained some of the world—his world—back. It didn't mean he'd forfeited his soul. He was closer to the Lord than he'd ever been. Ever. Yes, he had some treasure here on Earth again. Big deal. It's not where his heart was. At least not the majority of his heart. So why read something into the timing of this letter when there was nothing to read into it? But all of Micah's mental machinations didn't quench a gnawing feeling in his stomach that something was askew.

An impression formed in his mind. It was the voice.

Relax. As good as it's been, the last two days have been pretty stressful. Don't let your imagination take you somewhere we shouldn't go.

That night Micah celebrated his return to the top with a longtime basketball buddy. They dined at Palisades in Seattle on porterhouse steaks accompanied by crab legs, Caesar salads, and a double portion of tiramisu. They watched the million-dollar yachts bob in Puget Sound and talked sports, business, and movies. To simply sit with an old friend and enjoy a fine dinner refreshed him. And helped Micah avoid feeling the tiny snag at the center of his heart.

As they ate, Micah spied a young man across the aisle chatting with a brunette. The man punctuated his story with light laughter, and she joined in each time. She leaned in, relaxed, with a smile that never faded. The man kept pulling his palm away in order to demonstrate his story, only to return it to her waiting embrace a moment later.

Micah's gaze shifted to two men, one older, one younger at another table close by. Father and son? Looked like it. They interrupted each other, recalling a fishing trip up to Alaska where everything went wrong. But to hear them tell it amid their laughter, it had obviously turned out to be a trip they treasured.

It could have been Sarah and him at the one table, Rick and him at the other. His life before them, before Cannon Beach, only dabbled at the edges of God. It was a life devoid of freedom and healing, a life without true life.

Now he had it all. Riches. Recognition. And the deepest things: Sarah, Rick, and an intimate relationship with the Creator of the universe.

"Hello? Micah?"

"Yeah?" Micah dropped his steak knife on the table, and it rattled against his water glass.

"Hey, bud, where'd you go?"

"Sorry, took a little trip in my mind back down to Cannon Beach." He lifted his glass to his friend and made a toast. "To Sarah, to Rick, and to my King, Jesus. May His freedom advance in my life and the lives around me."

"Wow. Nice preaching. Sounds like you had quite a time down there." His friend clinked his glass against Micah's.

"You have no idea."

As the last bite of tiramisu slid down his throat, Micah decided the time to head back down to Cannon Beach was not in a few weeks but in a few days. His voice had said take five or six weeks to get things settled. But things weren't settling in Seattle; they *were* settled. Going back down every weekend would be much better timing. Without Rick and Sarah, Seattle was hollow.

After saying good-bye to his friend, Micah walked out on the dock in front of the restaurant and stared at the yachts and sailboats tucked into their slips like the fingers of an elegant woman inside a white glove. Two thoughts swirled like yin and yang through his mind. First, he always meant to buy one of those boats. Second, the desire had faded to a shadow of its former self.

He stared at the stars. Why had he been given the best of both worlds?

He closed his eyes as it once again felt like God had gone mute. He chalked it up to the intensity of the past few days and headed home.

Sarah! He grabbed his cell.

Again no answer on her cell phone. "Hey, it's me. Missing Rick, missing Cannon Beach, mostly missing you."

The next morning he got up at 5:00 to spend some time praying and reading the Bible to try to push through the distance he felt toward God. After an hour he gave up in frustration. It was so dry it was brittle. The only voice he heard was his own, and any semblance of peace had flown.

Where was God?

Heading into work, he pondered what he missed most about Cannon Beach. It wasn't the house, the ocean, Rick, or even Sarah. God was in Cannon Beach. Micah had been set free of chains he didn't even know existed. But up here God seemed to be on vacation.

He popped his steering wheel with his palm. His pipeline to the Lord had dried up like a valve being shut. As he pulled into his parking spot, he admitted it had closed the moment he'd stepped through the doors at RimSoft two days earlier. He'd just been too elated and busy to acknowledge it.

As he ambled out of the elevator a few minutes past eight, he remembered his regular assistant should be back. Sure enough, a woman with blonde hair sat with her back to him in the chair Perspiration Boy had occupied the day before. Would he know her? Micah started to say hello when she turned and pranced around her desk with tiny high-heeled steps. He was too stunned to move.

"Welcome home, stranger." She threw her arms around his neck. "I had an awesome time on my vacay. Hope you did, too." She pulled herself up to his ear and whispered, "I know we've only been going out for a month, so fire me if this is too forward, but I think we should take our next vacation together, don't you?" She gave him a quick kiss, then flounced back to her chair.

Micah tried to find words. Only one came. "Julie?"

She laughed, cocked her head, and pointed a crimson fingernail at him. "Micah."

"You're not my partner."

"No, not yet. You offering? All right, I accept."

His mind spun on a merry-go-round far over a safe speed. "Why . . . uh, wha . . . Why are you . . . ?" He stopped and stumbled into the chair next to Julie's desk. No question would make sense so it was impossible to finish the sentence.

"You okay?"

"Yeah, good. I just . . ." Just what? Just realized his world was still shifting wildly and he wasn't in control of any of it? He gripped the arms of the chair and tried to stop the spinning sensation.

No, it wasn't surprising Julie would be back in his life if the other things were back, but as his assistant? Why? He forced the thoughts pounding through his brain to stop, and he looked up at her. "Listen, it's great to see you, great to be back, so let's catch up as soon as I can get unburied from three weeks of work."

"You're thinking dinner tonight?"

"Yes. Love it. Perfect." Micah smiled, hoping it looked real, stood, and turned toward his office door.

He staggered into his office and slammed the door. Not out of anger. Out of fear. He flung his coat and briefcase onto the chair next to his desk. The coat slid down the side of the chair and crumpled to the floor. Micah didn't bother to pick it up. He was staring at the picture of Sarah he'd put up the day before.

She wasn't in it.

CHAPTER 39

Micah weaved through Seattle's late-morning traffic like Speed Racer as he sped toward the University of Washington's arboretum. It had been his place of solace since high school. His spot to be alone. To think.

He had to calm down. Get a handle on the insanity that pulsed through his entire body. He felt his neck with his forefinger. Heart rate? Probably 140. Clothes? Soaked with sweat.

He looked down at the picture clutched in his hand. Haystack Rock in the background in the late afternoon sun gave everything a golden hue. But where Sarah had sat was now only sand. He'd called Rick four times over the past hour, as if logging multiple calls would bring his friend back from his trip faster. During the fourth call, Devin almost hung up on him.

Micah stood on a secluded bulkhead overlooking Lake Washington, trying to pray, but the prayers seemed to vanish into the charcoal skies. As he started back to his car, his cell phone rang. He fumbled in his pocket for it, fingers numb. Caller ID said Unknown.

Please be her!

"Hello?"

"Micah? It's Sarah Sabin."

"Finally." A monsoon of relief landed on him. "I have missed you unbelievably."

"Are you the person who's been leaving messages on my cell phone?"

"Am I the *person?*" He laughed. "Yeah, what other Micahs do you know?"

As the words came out of his mouth, two questions struck like ice water. Why did she give her last name? And why ask if he'd left the messages? She knew his voice as well as anyone's.

"You're the only Micah I know, but I have to say your messages were a little weird."

"Weird?"

"I enjoyed bumping into you up at Ecola and enjoyed our talk. And I was looking forward to dinner at your place next week, spend a little time together, get to know each other. But your messages made me think that's not such a good idea."

Micah's legs went weak, and he crumpled onto the rough wooden planks beneath him. He couldn't speak, couldn't breathe.

"Are you there?"

"I'm in Seattle," he sputtered. "And it's all back. I've got it all back."

"Okaaay." Sarah drew out the word. "Got all what back?"

He tried to think of an answer to stop this nightmare. A sense of low, smug laughter coursed through him. The phone slipped from his grasp and dropped over the bulkhead wall, crashing onto the smooth rocks twenty feet below. It bounced twice and then splashed into the dark green waters of the lake.

"Everything."

||||||

Sleep, and the dream, didn't come till 2:00 a.m. Micah stood in the middle of a wheat field. Rolling hills swept out from him in all directions, the late afternoon sun turning the wheat into waving strands of gold. He did a full turn, squinting as he looked into the sunlight. Nothing but fields of gold . . . wait! A silhouette on the horizon. As Micah stared at the figure, he began floating toward it.

The man stood on a three-foot, splintered platform straight out of the late 1800s. Just like the man. He was tall, with white hair swept back till it touched the collar of his light brown, turn-of-the-century suit. A wide circle of lush, jade green grass surrounded the platform.

The instant Micah entered the circle, the man's words rang out crisp and powerful. If the man noticed Micah arrive, he didn't respond. The man fixed his gaze on the field, the heads of wheat like a vast audience hanging on every word. Perspiration trickled down his forehead into his eyes, but his focus was absolute, nothing distracting his fierce countenance.

"The fields are ripe for harvest! Beseech therefore the Lord of the harvest to send workers into the field to gather the wheat from the tares!" The preacher glanced down at the ragged Bible in his hands. "Now heed the words from the Revelation of John from chapter 3, verses 15 and 16." His voice dropped to half its former volume as he read from the old Bible. "'I know thy works, that thou art neither cold nor hot: I would thou wert cold or hot. So then because thou art lukewarm, and neither cold nor hot, I will spue thee out of my mouth.'"

The preacher looked up slowly and fixed his eyes on Micah and repeated the last sentence. "So then because thou art lukewarm, and neither cold nor hot, I will spue thee out of my mouth."

As he repeated it a third time, the preacher's face changed. All but his eyes, which only increased in intensity. This time the words were a whisper, and when he'd finished, the transformation was complete.

It was Jesus.

A moment later Micah woke, soaking wet. He looked at his watch. Already twenty minutes past noon.

After a quick shower Micah stepped onto the veranda of his condo to collect his thoughts before doing the obvious and heading for Cannon Beach. There was still hope. If the dream was only a warning, there was time to fix the mistake of returning to Seattle, and time to restore things with Sarah.

If coming to Seattle caused his life in Cannon Beach to vanish like a vapor, returning to the beach would restore it.

It had to.

As he packed, he considered calling his office to let them know he was leaving. But for what? By the time he reached Cannon Beach, his role with the company could be significantly different. A phone call now might not even exist by the time he got back to the beach.

He took one last look around his condo. Would he ever see the twenty-first floor again? What would he miss the most? His eyes swept over the awards and pictures lining the walls. Pictures of him standing next to the pretty and powerful. Trips around the world. Could he take the photos with him? Or would they just disappear on the way down to Cannon Beach, leaving empty frames crowding his backseat?

So what if he ended up as one of the up-and-coming computer programmers at RimSoft or RimWare or whatever it would end up being called by the time he got back up to Seattle. So what if his salary was only a quarter of what it had been and there was no stock?

He didn't care. Nothing here mattered. Not anymore. He would still have gold: Sarah, Rick, and God.

Time to go home.

When he crossed the border between Washington and Oregon, a subtle pain brought overwhelming relief. His ankle started to ache.

At 7:50 that evening he parked on Main Street and headed for Osburn's. Adrenaline pumped through him. He'd stood in front of some of the most influential men and women in the world of business, his neck tight and mouth dry. But as he stood on Main Street looking up at the Osburn's sign, Micah admitted that butterflies had never attacked his stomach with this much force. His breathing was shallow as he watched the last few customers stroll out of the store. He glanced at his watch. Almost closing time.

Best-case scenario, Sarah and he would be right back to where they were before he'd left for Seattle a few days ago.

Worst case, they would have lost a few weeks, maybe even a month, of their relationship. But he didn't want to lose even an hour. During the past four weeks their relationship had burst from deep friendship into full-blown love. He'd told her everything that had gone on inside the house during that time. Told her about living parts of two lives. And she'd all but said she wanted to spend her life with him.

He shook his head and ran both hands through his hair. Why hadn't he listened? She'd been so adamant about him not going. She had been right. Now he would fix it.

He glanced inside. No one left but Sarah.

Micah stepped through the front door. The bells announcing his arrival sounded like the warnings of a five-alarm fire, and his heart pounded like the bass drum at a rock concert.

"Hi," Sarah said without turning from her cleaning. "Five minutes to closing, I hope you're not wanting a triple-decker four-fudge float."

"Sarah."

She looked up. "Hey. How are you? This is a nice surprise." She smiled and tilted her head to the side.

His mind froze. He didn't know what he'd anticipated, but it wasn't this. He'd expected to know with one look what her heart did or didn't hold for him. But he didn't. As he studied her face, he saw recognition, but what kind? Anger from the cell phone calls? Concern? Was everything back to normal and she simply waited for him to make the first move, to admit returning to Seattle was a mistake? She obviously knew him, but how well? There were no answers, and he had no idea where to go with the conversation.

"I'm good. Hey, uh, first I just wanted to apologize for the weird messages I left on your cell phone." He hesitated. If everything was back to normal, then maybe the calls wouldn't have even happened in Sarah's world.

"You left me a weird message? More than one?"

Yes! The calls no longer existed.

"Yeah, well, I . . . Yeah, I did and—"

"When?"

"A day or two ago."

"Really? I must not have gotten them. Strange. Want to give them to me now?" She smiled but it didn't reassure him.

Oh no. He saw it in her eyes. Uncertainty. Then an obvious clue he should have picked up on the moment he'd called her name. She still stood behind the counter instead of rushing over to him. Not a good sign.

"Instead of giving you the weird message, how 'bout I ask you a weird question?" He shifted his weight and tried to smile.

Sarah put down her towel, walked around the counter, folded her arms, and put a mock skeptical look on her face. "Ready."

Micah inhaled slowly, then sighed.

Sarah winked at him. "Wow, this is going to be good."

"When was the last time we saw each other?"

"What?"

"When's the last time we talked?"

"Wow! I'm that forgettable?" She raised her eyebrows. "Three days is all it takes, eh?"

"No, not at all, I just—"

"Just what?"

"I've—"

"You're serious."

"Yeah." Micah shrugged.

"I must be a pretty boring dinner guest."

"Dinner? Which one?"

Sarah backed up and leaned against the ice cream display case. "Are you okay? Since we've only had one, it's that one."

This could not be happening.

He slumped into an oak chair against the wall.

"You're spooking me a little here, Micah. You cooked for me at your house. We talked until 11:00 p.m. I think we both had a good time. You have to remember *some* of that conversation."

"I remember all of it. It's just . . ." Micah felt the blood rush out of his face.

"All right then, I feel better now. I think." Sarah laughed. Micah could tell it was forced.

Sarah turned and walked back around the counter. "I hope you don't mind my cleaning up while we talk."

He swallowed hard. "If you're kidding about this to say, 'I told you so,' now would be a great time to stop."

"What are you talking about?"

Panic surged inside. She wasn't kidding. There was no "I told you so" coming. The past four months with Sarah had disappeared.

He grabbed the sides of his jeans and squeezed so hard his fingers hurt. In that moment he lost control and blurted out, "You have to remember us."

"Us?"

"You and I are in love. Three days ago the last thing you said to me was, 'Don't go back to Seattle' because you knew in your gut it was wrong. Tell me you remember!"

Mistake.

Big.

A sliver of fear flitted in Sarah's eyes, but he couldn't stop.

"You said don't go, that it would be a horrible mistake. I said it would be okay and obviously it wasn't, but I won't let that take away what we had. We've built so much—"

"Okay, you know what, Micah?" Sarah glanced at the people passing by Osburn's windows. "I'm thinking we should postpone our bike ride out to Indian Beach next week, and if we're ever supposed to do anything together again, we'll let Providence handle the details."

Micah held up his hands in protest. "I know it sounds bizarre, but listen! We've been seeing each other very seriously for almost five weeks. I went back to Seattle to . . . and . . . things changed down here because of it, but now I've left Seattle to get my relationship with God back. Get you back."

Sarah stared at him, her eyes full of fire.

"But it didn't get back to the way it was down here. I don't understand why. But I know I love you. I know we're destined to be together."

Sarah let out a low whistle and shuffled backward till she reached the back wall. "This is a small town. So avoiding each other completely is probably impossible. But when you see me, you'll cross to the other side of the street. If you're out to eat, you'll check the tables to see if I'm there. If I am, you'll turn around and come back in an hour and a half. If you're on the beach and you see me, you'll pretend you forgot to turn off your espresso machine and head back home. Do we understand each other?"

"Don't do this, Sarah. I can talk you through it, help you remember."

"You need medical help."

"No, I need you. And you need me." He pursed his lips together and closed his eyes. "Think back to that person you went on the bike ride with. That's me. And we fell in love. I can't pretend it didn't happen."

"And I'm supposed to pretend it did because you're delusional? Maybe this fantasy stuff works in your world, but in mine two people actually have to get to know each other without acting like they came from Jupiter before they can fall in love. Get out. Now!"

Micah stood still as perspiration wound its way down his back while he pleaded with his eyes for her to believe him.

She walked to the windows. "There are plenty of people right outside who could make your life uncomfortable if you insist on making more of a scene than you already have. Unless you get out right now, I'll shout loud enough to break the glass."

Micah swallowed and left without a word.

The jingle of the bells on the door as he stepped onto the sidewalk seemed to come from a distance. He stumbled south down Main Street and turned right at the end of the block headed for the beach. Micah held it together till he reached the edge of the water, where he emptied his stomach onto the damp sand.

He'd given up Seattle, all of it, and returned to what?

He stood and staggered toward Haystack Rock. Enough twilight remained for it to stand out as a looming shadow against the sky.

"Where are You, God?" Micah yelled.

The roar of the waves was the only answer. Micah felt more alone than he'd ever been. God was more distant than before he'd first come to Cannon Beach, and Sarah was gone.

He dug in his pocket, wrenched out the new cell phone he'd picked up earlier in the day, and punched in Rick's home phone number.

C'mon, be there!

Little hope remained as he listened to one, two, three rings. Even if Rick was there, how much of *their* relationship had been wiped out? Two months? Three? The whole thing? The fourth ring turned into Rick's recorded voice.

"Hi, this is Rick, sorry I'm not here. But we'll talk soon if you care to leave a message."

"It's Micah Taylor. Call me, please. The number is—"

"Hello."

"Rick?"

"Yes?"

"Micah Taylor."

"I think I know your voice by now." Rick chuckled.

"So you haven't forgotten me?"

"No."

"None of it?"

"Nope."

Relief showered him. To be sure, he asked when they'd talked last.

"The Fireside restaurant just a few days ago, and we talked about choice. You chose Seattle."

"Sarah doesn't remember any of it. Her last memory of us was our first dinner at my house!"

"You made a choice, Micah. You sowed, and now you're reaping."

"English. I need it in English."

"No you don't. As strange as the past five-plus months have been, deep down you know what has happened, what the King has been doing with the two lives you've been living. He has shown you the paths your choices will take you. The Seattle path and the Cannon Beach path."

"I have chosen! I came back."

"Now you face the final choice between the two worlds and the consequences of your final choice."

"It's not that simple. I need you to explain how I've been living the events of two separate lives. I remember parts of a life I never lived as clearly as the one I did live. I need you to explain how huge chunks of Seattle can be wiped out, then return, then disappear, then return in a mutated form! I need—"

"No," Rick interrupted, his voice sharp. "You need to seek the King with all your heart. All your mind. All your soul. All your strength. He is sovereign, and He is most certainly in control."

"That's it? That's what you're leaving me with? You're the only one who seems to understand both lives."

"Seek the King."

"I need more than that—"

"Seek the King, Micah."

"That's not enough!"

"Seek Him."

Micah snapped his cell phone shut and filled the night with a guttural moan. He had never been so empty. Seek the King? He'd tried! No sense of God, no peace, only his shredded life for an answer.

When he got home, night had fallen. He hadn't left any lights on, and the house felt like an ominous mountain he was about to tunnel into.

After flipping on lights all over the ground floor, he poured a Diet Coke, stepped out onto the deck, and replayed every moment from the past week as he stared at the stars. The voice told him he could have both Seattle and Cannon Beach, that he should go back to Seattle.

The voice.

His voice.

The bottom of Micah's glass dented the redwood railing as he slammed his drink down. He strode toward the dark room, his heart pounding.

CHAPTER 40

Micah ripped open the door and leaped into the dark room. "I want answers!"

"Hey, buddy, how are you?" the voice said.

"Swell."

"It is a time of turmoil."

"Nice understatement," Micah muttered. "You were so wrong."

"No, Micah, you were. You made the wrong choice."

"No kidding, Einstein. And you pushed me into it."

"No, I didn't. You're talking about the choice to go to Seattle. I'm talking about the choice to return to Cannon Beach."

"What?" Micah cocked his head. "Are you insane?"

"I said go to Seattle, get our life back, and stay there for at least *six weeks!* Not come back after three days."

"Don't use that against me. My relationship with Sarah vanished. My relationship with the Lord vanished—the two most important things in my life. And you're telling me I should have stayed?"

"Yes."

"This ought to be stellar." Micah folded his arms.

"First, Sarah. You want to spend your life with her. Is that your plan or His? The Word says we must forsake mother, father, brother, sister. If Sarah is more important to you than following God, then you are not worthy to put your hand to the plow. We need to let her go."

"Sorry, I don't buy it. The Lord brought us together. Sarah even said the Holy Spirit told her about it years ago."

"I believe Sarah was called into our life. But for a season. To give us the chance to choose God over her in the end. We are called to obey. Not to question. Remember, Micah, I'm you, so this is as painful to me as it is to you."

"Where's your pain?" Micah slumped against the wall and slid down to the carpet.

"I am you, but a different part. I more easily separate logic from emotion so we can see clearly."

"I don't see clearly?"

"When you allow fear to creep in, no. Like right now. The loss of Sarah is blinding you to the fact that God is in this. That He has another out there for you. Fear and faith cannot exist together. The questions and doubts always come down to faith in the end. And what good is our faith with sacrifice? And this is a sacrifice God has asked us to make in order to be fully His."

"Sacrifice?" Micah slammed his fist into the wall behind him and stood. "I've given up my company, my career, my awards, my condo, my money, my fame, and you say that's not enough? I have to sacrifice Sarah, the one thing left on this earth that means anything to me? And I have to sacrifice my relationship with God?"

Micah turned to walk out, then stopped. "The moment

I crossed the city limits back into Seattle, God vanished. Since then my prayers have slammed into a ceiling an inch above my head. Yeah, sure, that makes perfect sense. The Lord is asking me to sacrifice my relationship with Him for Him!"

When Micah finished, sobs seeped toward him out of the darkness. "I know it's hard, so hard. Feeling so distant from God. But we cannot rely on feelings, only on truth. He is taking us through a dry time now to see if we will still choose Him, still choose the hard path even when we can't sense His presence nearby. This is our desert time, and we must not turn back to the pretend comfort of a mirage but keep walking the straight-and-narrow path through the wasteland to the true oasis God has designed for us."

"You know, I'm finished with your ornate oratory. Just say what comes next."

"Start over."

"What does that mean?" Micah again sank down the wall into the thick carpet.

"Go back to Seattle. Stay this time, even if RimSoft is completely gone. Build another company, this time for the right reasons. Not your outcome but one with eternal impact."

"Impossible. I'm done with that life."

"With God all things are possible." The voice paused and cleared his throat. "Besides, there is a small part of you that isn't done with that life. That still wants it. We can fan that ember into a flame again."

It was true. Images of the European and tropical trips filled his mind. The restaurants in Spain, the beaches in French Polynesia, the awards, the interviews on national TV, the money to buy anything he wanted.

"The world needs you to start that new company. Think of the lives you could touch with the message of truth."

"This is where I want to be."

"We are to deny ourselves and pick up our cross daily."

"You exhaust me and offer nothing but confusion. I need clarity." Micah stood and walked out, slamming the door with enough force to knock a picture in the hallway off the wall. He didn't bother to pick it up.

⁜

The next morning Micah ran down to Hug Point and back to clear the confusion swirling around him.

No help.

After he finished his run, he showered, then pushed through the first two chapters of Galatians in his Bible.

Dust.

As he finished cleaning up his breakfast dishes, he glanced at the cordless phone in the kitchen. What if the voice was right about RimSoft being completely gone? He had no delusions it would bring good news, but he couldn't stop himself from dialing that familiar number.

The third ring had just started when the receptionist chirped, "RimWare, what can I do to make your day better right now?"

Micah rolled his eyes. He never would have let anyone answer the phone with something so trite. "Human Resources, please."

"Of course. One moment, please."

He started pacing after ten seconds. At a minute and a half a male voice squeaked, "May I help you?"

"Hi, my name is Allen Vorreiter from Norwest Medical, and I need to verify the employment status of one of your workers."

"Norwest Medical? Yeah, okay. Who?"

"Micah Taylor. Just need to know what department he works in."

"That's it?"

"That's it."

"Uh, yeah, hang on."

After an intolerably long forty-five seconds, Human Resources Guy coughed out, "You don't happen to know what department he works in, do you?"

"That's what I was hoping to find out from you." Micah gritted his teeth.

"That's right!" The guy snorted. "Sorry. Be back in a sec."

Micah wandered into the living room and watched the waves thunder onto the beach as he waited for an answer. Two minutes later he had it.

"Sorry, I went through everything in the database, and then I even flipparooed through the hard copies. You sure he works here?"

Micah's eyes closed as his head slumped onto his chest.

"Hey, are you there? Is that all you wanted to know?"

"That's it."

He dialed another number, then another. Seven minutes of calls confirmed there wasn't a shred left of his Seattle life. He called his bank, his CPA, his insurance agent, his condo association. None of them had ever heard of Micah Taylor. Nothing was left. No home, no company, no money.

What remained? A gorgeous mansion on the ocean with huge yearly taxes and no way to pay for it. He had no income. No Sarah. No career. No direction. No relationship with the Lord. Nothing. Utterly and completely nothing.

Is this what God wanted?

Now what? If Seattle no longer existed, what life was he living? He slumped onto his couch in front of the fireplace and dialed one more number.

"Taylor residence. Daniel speaking."

"Hey, Dad."

"Well, hello, son."

"I have to ask some questions about the past six years that might seem a little strange."

"Since, in my opinion, many of your choices since college have been a bit off, I don't think any question you pose will surprise me."

Micah got up and walked over to his picture windows, head in hand. "What have I been doing since college?"

"I'm not sure I understand the question." His dad sighed. "Aren't you still trying to figure out a way to make a decent income?"

"I'm not in software?"

"Always thought that's where you'd end up. And"—his dad cleared his throat—"and I, uh . . . when you didn't, I . . . I just want to say . . . Well, I probably could've handled things a little better over the past six years."

Micah slumped to the carpet. Was his dad saying he was sorry? Was it possible?

"Yeah, well I could have—"

"So were there any other questions?"

It was obvious from his dad's tone that his landing on the tarmac of apology was only for an instant.

"I just want to get a handle on what I've been doing with my life and figure out what I'm going to do with this mansion down here and—"

"Mansion? Did someone buy you a winning lotto ticket?"

"I told you about this house six months ago."

"Six months, eh? Let me consult my journal."

As he listened to his dad turning pages, Micah's fingers grew white due to the stranglehold he was giving the phone.

"No, son. If you'd inherited a home down on the coast, I would have made some notes about it."

"C'mon, Dad. Your uncle Archie had it built for me."

"Archie? Nuttier than a fruitcake."

"We've been over that."

"Is that all you wanted?"

"Where have I lived for the past six years?" Micah stood and walked out onto his deck and let the wind pummel his hair.

"You don't remember where you've lived?"

Micah closed his eyes and lied. "I know where I've lived. I just want to hear you say it."

"Strange question. I have to ask why."

Micah stepped out on a plank he'd never been on before. "No, Dad, you don't. You *want* to ask why because you have to have all the details of everything in the entire universe at your fingertips at every moment of your existence and under your control. This time I'm asking you to humor me and tell me where I've lived since college with no explanation of why I'm asking." Micah swallowed. "Please."

The only sound was the slight hum in the phone line and the swish of the wind racing through the trees.

"You're right; I'm . . . I shouldn't always . . . I've . . ." His dad clucked his tongue three times. "You lived with me for two months right after college. Then in Bandon, Oregon, for a year and a half. Then Newport, Oregon, almost four and a half years. Now Cannon Beach for just over a year." He cleared his throat three times before going silent. "And, uh . . . I'm . . . What I mean is, I'm sorry for butting in and for . . . sorry."

Micah's body went limp. "Dad?"

"Yes?"

"Thanks. Really, I mean it. Thanks."

Silence.

"You're welcome, Micah."

He hung up and plopped onto a deck chair, stunned. His dad had said the words. It wasn't his imagination. He'd said it: *"I'm *sorry.*" A miracle. Maybe not on the level of the loaves and fishes, but for him it was close. And he'd called him Micah. Not son. Micah.

A flicker of hope toward his dad darted through his heart, almost too ethereal to accept. He pushed the thought aside and wondered what he'd been doing in Bandon and Newport for the past six years.

His focus turned to the surf smattering around two towering rocks that sat a hundred yards offshore, a haven for seagulls and sea lions in repose. It reminded him of something. The painting!

He sprinted to the room, heart pounding.

When Micah reached the door, he hesitated. What if it hadn't changed? And even if it had, it wouldn't explain the madness blowing through his life. He'd prayed multiple times, asking to know the meaning of the painting and how it tied into his two realities. There were no answers.

But still, it drew him like a magnet, and he continued to believe it was the key to unlocking the ambiguity his life had become.

Micah stole a quick breath, stepped into the room, and gasped. He saw the change instantly: the home was just a few brush strokes from being finished.

It was his home, standing on his bluff, overlooking his stretch of beach.

Why hadn't he seen it till this moment?

As the painting had developed, there had been enough similarities between it and his own stretch of beach to make him wonder, but not enough to be sure. Somehow the painter had used a perspective of his beach that didn't make it obvious. Now he understood why. The image was reversed, a mirror of his house and the beach in front of it.

The edge of the bluff stood slightly higher and narrower in the painting, but it was his bluff. The mountains in the background were higher and held fewer trees, but they were his. The waves were thicker, richer, more powerful, but it was the surf he'd grown to cherish.

But there were no subtle differences about his home. The closer he looked, the more detail he saw. Even the way the light played on the windows was intricate and exactly the way it looked when he came back from his early morning runs.

He'd taken photos of the house from the beach, even enhancing the colors with Photoshop to make the picture more vibrant. But those photos didn't touch the richness here.

Why had he been chosen as the one person to see this masterpiece?

An hour, maybe two, and it would be finished. When?

He longed to know the artist, be immersed in the knowledge of how waves could be made so lifelike, mountains so majestic, the home so lifelike.

For more than an hour Micah sat and soaked in the painting, until a melancholy feeling settled over him. The changes were exhilarating, but they revealed nothing as to why his life had disintegrated.

After dinner he sat in his favorite overstuffed leather chair, Archie's next letter resting on his 501s. Micah had avoided reading the letter earlier in the week as the last few had been portents of devastating circumstances. But where else could he turn? Rick had all but abandoned him; Sarah and Micah didn't exist in this current reality; and the voice? He sighed. The voice was batting below .100.

He held the envelope up to the golden light that came from the lamp next to his chair. "Lord, if You're anywhere near Cannon Beach, have Archie give me some hope."

CHAPTER 41

November 24, 1992

Dear Micah,

Soon it will be time for you to confront your greatest foe—your villain—face-to-face. It will be just you and him, confronting one another in a fierce battle for truth and freedom. Ah, but Micah, the good news is, it will not be just you and him. For as the Scriptures tell us, greater is He who is in you, than he who is in the world. In the strength you possess alone, there is no hope of victory. But with Him, as the apostle Paul says, we are more than conquerors.

The King of the universe is inside of you. You are in Him. As it says in the epistle to the Romans, if God is for you, who can be against you? Put on the full armor of a saint of God and swing the sword of the Spirit with all your might.

I am proud of you, Micah. Fight the good fight, and may the Spirit of the living God protect you on the right and on the left, as you come and as you go.

Courage,

Archie

P.S. If you have been counting, you must realize that at this point in our journey together, only two letters remain for you to read. Instead of waiting two more weeks to finish them, please open the next one the day after tomorrow and the last one four days after that. I will see you then.

Micah set down the letter. Was Rick the villain? C'mon. Still, he couldn't shake the feeling it was the mechanic.

And he had to fight? He shook his head and stared at the ocean. So much thunderous power in the waves, yet untapped. So much power in the Lord, yet untapped. But it didn't give him any hope. He didn't know how to fight this kind of battle.

||||||

Micah woke at 5:30 the next morning and headed for Cape Lookout, a headland fifty miles south of Cannon Beach. There he would rip the emotions from his heart and lay them all out. He'd wrestle with the question of what to do with his life, away from the house, away from the voice, away from Rick—away from everything.

He'd heard the cape was spectacular. It jutted a mile and a half straight out into the ocean, five hundred feet above the waves. Apparently it gave dazzling views. Miles to the north, impressive Tillamook Head was visible. Looking south, the sand dunes of Cape Kiwanda could be seen on cloudless days. The Internet said massive spruce and hemlock trees hovered above an emerald green understory of salal, sword ferns, and salmonberry bushes.

He pulled into the parking lot a bit past 6:45. Not surprisingly his was the only car, and his shoulders relaxed. He didn't want to meet anyone on the trail, and an early start would give him a sizable chunk of time alone, even if others started the hike after him.

A light mist drifted down on his windshield as he stepped out of his car and grabbed his day pack. When he reached the trailhead thirty seconds later, the rain came down in sheets. Micah smiled. Excellent. It would probably stop others from making the hike.

Fifty yards down the trail, the tree cover blocked out most of the rain, and his Mariners baseball hat handled the rest. The trail morphed from hard pack into black mud in spots but overall it was firm, and he clipped along at a fast pace.

He didn't know why getting to the end of the cape in rapid fashion held such importance. But it did. So he plowed into the two-and-a-half-mile hike and only stopped once, to look at a memorial plaque commemorating the crew of a B-17 plane that crashed into the cape in 1943.

Three-quarters of the way into his trek, the clouds parted and the sun broke through with such strength Micah took off both his jacket and his sweatshirt. The sun shone through the raindrops hanging off the leaves, creating diamonds everywhere he looked. The steam rising off the fallen logs looked like tendrils of smoke and made it seem as if an unseen fire burned somewhere on the forest floor.

The beauty on the outside softened the turmoil inside, if only slightly.

Finally the thick Sitka spruce parted, and he stood five hundred feet above the Pacific Ocean. The coastline from where he'd come still sat in a shroud of fog right up to where the surf and the beach met.

It was as if Cape Lookout were singled out to receive the sun's blessing while the rest of the coast was regulated to sit in the grayness of an encompassing cloud. It should have been a perfect setting to figure out where his life would go from here. But it wasn't, because unbelievably, someone crashed down the trail behind him.

He didn't expect to know them, let alone know them well.

Rick.

Loathing swept through Micah, and a thought slammed into his mind as clear as any he'd ever had.

Enemy.

Rick stopped twenty yards away and didn't speak. His usual smile had flown, no hint of the typical laughter in his eyes. His being here was wrong.

Villain.

He glared at Rick, disgust joining Micah's anger. There was no rationale for the feelings. Rick was the one person in the world who could help him work through the devastation his life had become. But logic had vanished. He could only react to emotions pumping through him.

Micah's lips parted slightly, his teeth ground together, his eyes never leaving Rick's.

Rick returned the defiant stare with an intensity Micah had never seen. And Rick's body seemed different; taller, broader. The way the sun bounced off his clothes made it look like light came from inside him.

Micah couldn't hold Rick's gaze and dropped his eyes.

Rick took three strides forward and spoke with an authority that startled Micah. "Freedom is waiting to burst forth in you, Micah. You must not quench it."

Anger surged like flashes of lightning inside him, and he had no idea how to rein it in. But he didn't want to. It felt good. Very good.

"What gives you the right to tell me anything?" He hurled his pack to the ground. "You've done nothing but assist in destroying my life!"

"You've been listening to lies." Rick took another step forward.

"Lies? Really? Your lies maybe?"

"You know what lies."

"What are you talking about?" He turned his back and glared at the ocean.

"The voice."

Micah whirled back. "I've never told you about—"

"The voice in your house? No, you haven't." Rick took another two strides forward. A large rock shattered into dust as his foot came down on it.

"You've been spying on me?"

"Why haven't you told me?" Rick's eyes flashed like steel.

"What gives you the right to demand that of me?"

"Why haven't you told me?" Rick took another step forward.

"So that's what our relationship is about? Me describing every intricate detail of my entire life? And what has it gotten me? Since I met you, my life has been destroyed. I've lost *everything!*"

Rick took another two steps forward, and the ground seemed to shake. "Ask yourself, why didn't you tell me? So many times you've wanted to." His voice thundered. "What held you back?"

"You know what's going on with my life but won't tell me. Now you show up here without warning and start attacking with some feeble courtroom cross-examination about what I have or haven't told you."

As Micah spoke, an invisible chasm split the ground between Rick and him. He couldn't see it, but it was as real as the cape they stood on. Physically they weren't more than five yards apart. In all other ways it was miles.

"You feel it right now, don't you?" Rick said. "We can't see it, but it is definitely there. Pushing us away from each other. Dividing us. Stirring up rage in you. You know in your heart I'm your intimate ally, but something is speaking to you right now, fanning the flame of evil emotion, telling you not to trust me. And you're listening." One more step toward him.

"You are the villain!"

"Now is the moment where you must make your choice. Right

now. The truth or lies." Rick took three more steps. His eyes never left Micah. Rick was now just six feet away. "There is a battle for your destiny in this moment, and you must decide whom to believe."

"The same exact words my voice said to me!" Micah spat out.

"Yes, the exact words. Freedom is fighting for you, but you must make the choice. He cannot make it for you."

"Why don't *you* make it for me? The man with all the answers. The man with the truth."

"Fight it, Micah. This is not you. It is the sin that dwells within you talking. Seek the truth!"

Micah heaved a tree branch over the edge of the cape and watched it float down toward the waves. It would be so easy to follow the branch down to the ocean.

"Don't listen. The Lord is a sword and shield. Call on Him," Rick said.

"I'm tired of it. Archie, Sarah, you, the voice—everyone has a different angle, a different spin for my life."

"In the Truth there is no spin."

"Whose truth? Tell me, O Enlightened One!" Micah spewed. "Which voice is the final voice? Which one is the authority over all the others, huh? I'm ready."

If his attempt to goad Rick had any effect, it didn't show.

"In the end only one Voice matters."

"What a surprise. Exactly what Archie's letter said. But wake up. When I listen to my voice, it contradicts everything you and Archie say. It sends me back to Seattle where I lose Sarah and even lose God. But a minute ago you slammed my voice and slammed me for not telling you about him. Now I'm supposed to listen to it? Makes perfect sense."

"As bright as you are in your natural mind, the enemy has greatly dulled your wisdom in your spirit."

"What's that supposed to mean?"

"The voice in your house is not the one you must listen to."

"What?" He stared at Rick.

"It is not a part of you in any way."

Rage and fear had mixed inside, anger the more dominant emotion. But now fear grew exponentially as his anger seeped away like a retreating wave. In desperation he tried to recapture the fury that had fueled his battle with Rick.

"And where is the truth, O Great and Holy Rick? Where is this voice I should listen to?"

"In you."

"Oh, really?" Micah locked his arms across his chest and kicked a rock over the side of the cape. "Inside sinful Micah, huh?"

"Don't put words in my mouth, son. Sin dwells in you, yes. If a man says he does not sin, the truth is not in him. But you forget, man is also the dwelling place of God. The heart is the temple of the Holy Spirit, the living God."

Rick's eyes bored into Micah's. "You don't have to go outside yourself to find the answer. You don't have to listen to me, or Archie, or Sarah. And you don't have to ask a voice living in utter darkness inside your house. You need to listen to the Spirit of God that makes His home inside you. That is the one true Voice. Go there now and ask the question. Now."

Micah wanted to lash out at Rick with the last of his fading anger. A thought screamed through his mind: *Push Rick over the side!*

"You lie. *My* voice has been with me every step of this journey and has again and again given me perspective and insight I would never have seen without him."

"He has deceived you. Time and again."

Instantly the voice filled Micah's mind: *Everything with Rick ends in pain. He's trying to control you, destroy you. Resist him!*

Rick stepped forward. "The Word says, 'Take every thought

captive to the obedience of Christ.' You have to fight the thought attacking you right now."

Micah didn't want to fight. Despair hammered him to his knees, and he pulled in ragged breaths.

Why fight this? He could just get out of here and clear his head. That's what he came to do, not debate this clown.

The thoughts peppered his mind like machine-gun fire.

Get away from him! He is the villain. You know that!

He shook his head, rubbed his eyes, and whispered, "Lord, if You're here, I need help."

Immediately the thoughts stabbing at him like a knife vanished. He leaned against a boulder and buried his head in his hands.

"It is time," Rick said.

"For?"

"Surrender. Complete surrender."

"I have."

"No. Not all. You've never fully surrendered all that you are to Jesus. You must give Him everything. Nothing less is enough."

"Tell me how," Micah whispered.

"Seek Him now, in this moment, with all your heart, all your mind, all your soul, all your strength. Die to everything you've ever dreamed, ever wanted, ever hoped for. I'll be warring for you in prayer as you seek the truth." Rick walked fifteen yards back toward the trail and disappeared behind a grove of spruce trees.

The last bubbles of anger inside Micah popped as Rick's footsteps faded. Micah was done fighting. But who was right? The answers were nowhere and everywhere.

What had Rick said? The answer was in his own heart because God's Spirit was there. If only it were that simple. He sighed. Where else could he turn?

"Jesus, all of it. You can have all of it. I surrender everything I am or ever hope to be. My hopes, dreams, Seattle, Cannon Beach, Sarah . . . everything. Talk to me."

Waves of peace filled him instantly. All doubt vanished, and he knew without hesitation, without reservation, that above all else God loved him with a passion he couldn't comprehend. How long Micah sat in this tornado of love he didn't know.

It stopped when a verse sprang into his mind like a lighthouse out of the blackest night. *"The word of God is living and active. Sharper than any double-edged sword, it penetrates even to dividing soul and spirit."*

Exactly what was happening to him right now. His soul, mind, will, and emotions knew what was happening while his spirit experienced a depth of union with God he had never encountered. Too deep for words.

"Show me the truth," Micah said.

His body shuddered as the answer flashed through his spirit and his mind at the same time with such clarity it made him gasp. *The voice is not you.*

"Then who is it?"

The thief comes to kill, steal, and destroy, but I have come to bring life abundant.

A waterfall of joy pounded up out of Micah with such force he didn't know if he would survive. Infinite power, yet only an infinitesimal amount of God's strength.

I give streams of living water.

And still the waterfall grew in strength, overflowing into his soul, his mind, his body. He fell onto his back, his arms spread wide, immersed in love beyond words and too much to hold in.

"Abba!" Micah screamed. Then more words poured out of his spirit beyond his understanding, and the waterfall became an ocean, and he drowned in the love of the One who loved him. All sense of time vanished as he was buried in sweet freedom.

When he opened his eyes, the shadows told him his deep communion had lasted hours. He stood and wiped the last of the tears from his eyes.

Rick sat, elbows on his knees, on a slab of granite twenty yards away with a smile so wide it drowned out the rest of his face. His eyes burst with delight, and Micah broke into hearty laughter as he ran to meet him. Rick grabbed him in a massive bear hug that Micah returned with all his strength.

"Thank you, Rick. Thank you," was all he could say.

They walked together in silence to the end of the cape and watched the white-flecked surf and the seagulls ride the currents hundreds of feet below. Micah wished he could freeze the moment. He was known by God, and this God—who had created the universe and all it contained, lived inside him.

On the hike back to their cars, Micah said, "I've gotta confront the voice."

"Yeah." Rick nodded. "You do. Now."

CHAPTER 42

Micah touched the door to the dark room with his forefinger; it swung open silently. The same familiarity was there—and something else. A dense, palpable tension. Micah wondered why he'd never felt it before. There had always been a lingering doubt if the voice was truly himself. But never the fluttering sense of dread that poured out of the room now. Fear. Pungent. Dark.

"'Greater is He who is in you than he who is in the world,'" Micah quoted. He stepped through the doorway. The blackness didn't grow darker. It just seemed like it did.

"Hello, Micah."

"Hello, voice."

"You've been listening to lies."

"Yes, you're right. I have."

"Ah, so you've come back to the truth. That is good. So very good."

"I've realized something," Micah said.

"What is that?"

"Many claim to have the truth. But there is only one Truth."

"Go on."

"I have a question."

"Fine. That is why we're here for each other. To ask the questions, find the answers, and press forward together, stronger and freer."

"Do you acknowledge that Jesus Christ has come in the flesh and is from God? And is God?"

The voice didn't answer for a long time. "We are the same, Micah. I am you, and you are me. You know this. Why are you testing yourself? Once and for all put the doubt to rest and let us embrace each other as the brothers we are. Are you not freer now? Have I not guided you and helped you in your journey?"

A small part of Micah believed it. Accepted it. Wanted it to be true. It seemed right, comforting. The voice spoke again, this time only in his mind as it had on the cape.

Rest, Micah. Put doubt and battle behind you. It has only served to weary you. Where is the peace of God in all that? Come away with me. Let us rest together. Rest. Sweet peaceful rest.

He knew this voice. He'd heard it as far back as he could remember.

It continued chattering in his mind, enticing him as it had his entire life. Micah lifted his hands to his head and massaged his temples. "Lord," he whispered, "come into this. I need truth. I can't do this. I need Your strength."

The voice stopped, and a soft coolness washed over Micah.

Then another Voice came, gentle, powerful. Not from the room or inside his mind. From his heart. He gasped at the contrast. The distinction between his own familiar voice and this Voice was like white hot fire next to the coldest ice.

Go. Battle. I am with you.

Micah didn't hesitate. He took two steps directly into the inky darkness and spoke with power. "Say it. Jesus Christ is the Son of God Most High and has come in the flesh. Say it." Another step forward, now shouting into the ocean of darkness. "Jesus Christ is Lord!"

Immediately an intense heat filled the room, the smell of sulfur filled his nose, and a low buzz started directly in front of him. It changed to a guttural snarl almost too faint to hear before it abruptly stopped.

The fear in the room became physical, pounding him, intent on grinding him into the carpet. But it wasn't carpet anymore. He stood on a floor of massive flat stones, ice cold, that reached out with tentacles of pain, piercing, winding their way into the soles of his feet.

Micah's tongue was thick as he spoke again. "Jesus is Lord. His cross is between us. I bind you by His power. His authority. Given to me by Him and His Father, the host of angel armies."

The snarl returned, louder, longer this time before it again snapped off.

A razor-thin beam of light passed in front of Micah like a windshield wiper across a dirty window. In that flash a silhouette materialized like a black panther emerging from the dead of night.

Utter evil.

The light grew.

He saw the outline of a chair, black wrought-iron with ornate carvings on it.

In it sat the demon, a pinprick circle of black in the center of its pure white, unblinking, dead eyes—its ashen gray lips turned up ever so slightly in a sneer of confidence.

Its face was stunning.

Beautiful.

And horrific.

Chiseled cheekbones and thick, pitch-black hair swept straight back from a perfect forehead, above a perfect nose.

Its skin was a pallid gray, lips a shade darker, eyebrows matching the midnight tone of his hair. Its grotesque beauty stirred something inside Micah—drew him.

Revolting.

Captivating.

"Jesus," Micah whispered. As the word came out of his mouth, an intricate series of thin, black scars started at the demon's hairline and spiraled down its cheeks, down over his perfect chin, twisting and circling along his throat till they disappeared into a black, skin-tight long-sleeved gauze shirt.

A second later the scars vanished.

Its rancid eyes flitted around the room as if its gaze could stop the darkness from lifting, then settled back on Micah.

Micah couldn't move. The reality of a demon sitting only ten feet away paralyzed him. His mind froze, and blood pulsed in his head as the demon's thoughts echoed in his head.

Death.

Excruciating pain.

"Lord, help," Micah whispered.

A flicker of peace. Only a flicker.

"I will destroy you for presuming to challenge me, Micah Taylor." The demon drew the words out, then licked his perfect lips with a black tongue. "To throw that name at me like a weapon? No mercy now. No mercy." The demon sat back in its chair, and although its mouth didn't move, a shriek rang in Micah's mind, and his stomach felt like it was being torn by a jagged blade.

Micah cried out in pain.

"That is nothing compared to what is coming." The demon crossed its legs.

"Jesus. I need You here. I need help."

The peace increased, as did the demon's attack.

"I will crush you. Destroy you and everything and everyone you hold dear." The demon spoke each word slowly, quietly with a guttural voice, supremely confident. "Annihilation is your destiny now."

Each word pressed into Micah's chest and tunneled into his heart.

"Your supposed *king* will not, cannot, help you. You have built a fortress for me stone by stone that I will not leave. Ever. You have made agreements giving me the right to your very life. But I will give you one chance for survival. Surrender to me now and live. Give up your pretend religion, and I will show you true might, true power, true dreams."

The demon breathed through its teeth, then silence. When it spoke again, its voice was honey. "Who do you think brought you your fame? Your fortune? The favor of the world? And what do you have now by following this pretend king? You said it yourself, not less than a day ago. Nothing. But surrender now, and I can bring it all back. All of it. You have my word."

Micah's mind flooded with images of the power and money he'd had and of the people who clamored for him. A life part of him longed for again.

"I can feel it. You want those things to return. Why wouldn't you? You've not forgotten your dreams. You've tried to bury them, but they remain. Return to them. The tangible ones. Not some fairy tale, romantic religious fantasy hollow down to the core. And that's not all. Far, far from it." Its voice, so smooth, like water in a summer pond easing down into a stream, drew him in. "I can even bring back Sarah."

Micah gasped.

"Yes. Yes. You'll be with her again. All your times together back in her memory. It can be done in an instant. Just surrender. Sweet surrender."

Could it be true? Could the demon make it happen?

"Yes, Micah. I can make it happen. Instantly. Surrender to me."

He pictured her running up to him, burying herself in his arms. Yes. He needed her. With her back—

"No! You lie. Not even Sarah is worth turning my back on my King. Get out of my head."

"So be it."

Instantly Micah's lungs felt like they were being squeezed in a vise. Tighter. Tighter. He couldn't breathe. Stars swam in his eyes and his throat constricted. Laughter played at the corners of the demon's mouth. In seconds Micah would black out.

"Yes, my dear friend. You are about to die."

"Jesus, help me," he rasped with the last of his air.

Immediately the pressure on his lungs and throat vanished, and the demon's gaze shifted to something behind Micah. Recognition flickered in its eyes, and the quiet, penetrating cadence it had been using changed to a snarl.

"What right do you have to come here now?" the demon spat out.

Micah turned. Rick stood in the doorway, his face unmoving, as if carved from marble. He said nothing in response but stepped forward till he stood beside Micah. Rick stared at the demon and fear flashed across its face.

"Turn now, Micah Taylor, or the destruction promised will fall on you."

"I'm scared, Rick."

"Look at its wrists," Rick answered softly.

Micah looked at the demon's wrists lying on the armrests. Two white cords, thick and rough, cut into its skin. The demon strained against them, but there wasn't the slightest flexibility.

"You know you did that, don't you?" Rick said.

Micah stared at the demon's wrists and then back at Rick. The realization staggered him. He had done it, through his words, through Christ's power in him.

"For our struggle is not against flesh and blood. . . . The weapons of our warfare are powerful, for the pulling down of strongholds, of principalities, and demonic forces in high places," Micah said.

"Yes," Rick said.

Even in the midst of the revelation of what he had done, fear swirled, searching for a crack. For a way into his heart.

"One last chance before you die," seethed the demon.

"How do we get rid of it?"

"Send it to Jesus," Rick said without emotion.

"No. You will not. Not there." The demon tried to steady its quavering voice. "Listen to me, Micah. We can go to heights you've only imagined. Will you throw it away for nothing?" It screamed; its back arched, straining to be free of the chair.

"Don't answer him, just send it."

The demon writhed in the chair, an inky blackness oozing from its eyes and its wrists where it wrenched against the cords.

"Finish it, Micah."

Micah clenched his jaw and stepped forward. "It's over. I will never listen to your lies from the pit again. By His blood and His glory, go. Now!"

Micah shouted the last word with everything in him, and before its echo had died, the demon vanished. A moment later the chair was gone as well. A stench lingered a few seconds more, and then light filled the room along with the scent of wheat fields.

He walked forward to where the demon had sat, puzzled to see the white cords lying on the carpet. He bent down and reached out his forefinger to touch them. They were warm, and a faint white light circled them. He looked back at Rick who nodded slightly.

Micah picked them up and held one in each hand. Heavy. The warmth grew till the heat penetrated his entire body. They felt more solid and more real than anything he'd ever touched. Then they faded. Their color changed from white to the color of his skin before they sank into his palms, slowly at first, then more rapidly till they disappeared completely.

He turned to Rick, and they grabbed each other in a crushing embrace.

⁓

Micah stood on the beach in front of his home and watched the last shards of the sun sink into the ocean. An older couple to his left lit their fire; to his right a young family packed up their plastic buckets and shovels and headed for the path up to the parking lot a quarter mile north of Micah's home.

A hint of smoke from the campfire squiggled up to him; he closed his eyes and inhaled deeply. Yes.

"Thank You." He opened his eyes to gaze at the sky above.

This day would be burned into his memory forever.

As he ambled back to his home, he pondered what the next few days would bring. Great things. He knew it. There was no doubt in his heart. Tomorrow he would rest. Monday he would open the second to last letter from Archie. It would take him to a place unimaginable.

CHAPTER 43

Monday morning Micah rose before the sun, a cup of coffee laden with hazelnut creamer in his right hand, Archie's eighteenth letter in his left. He sat on his couch in front of his massive river-rock fireplace. After switching on the lamp next to the chair, he slipped a table knife under the lip of the light brown envelope and sliced it open.

> November 25, 1992
> Dear Micah,
>   The room has always been ready for you, and now you are ready for the room.
>   You know, of course, the room to which I refer.
>   1 Corinthians 3:16–17.
> For eternity and His glory,
> Archie

Micah stood in front of the door of the brilliant room only a moment before it opened on its own. Light streamed out in a flash flood of power, surrounding him like a tidal wave.

It was too much ecstasy to contain. He stepped into the room and froze. It was glorious and overwhelming. Bliss flooded his heart, spilled over, and didn't stop. His mind said this place was too holy, too right, too pure for him. But his heart didn't agree. Micah fell to the floor, stunned. He knew where he was.

He stood in the presence of God. Surrounded by Him.

And this room was his own heart.

His heart.

His.

The holy of holies. The place where the Spirit of God dwells within the hearts of men.

Rick said it yesterday on the cape. The verse in Archie's letter confirmed it. Yet till that moment it had been words. Just words.

Tears came, a hidden well broken open. Deep, cleansing tears. Freedom. Forgiveness. Peace. Nothing could separate him from this unquenchable love. Nothing he could do would make this Spirit of God love him any less.

Utterly and relentlessly loved beyond all imagination.

He had entered into the holiest place in the universe. It was inside him. Because God was in him and he was in God. And He had been there all along.

After ages passed, Micah rose to his knees. Images flashed across the walls all around him: mountains, oceans, deserts, lakes, all in the most brilliant colors he'd ever seen. The images shifted; now they were of him running, flying, lying in an emerald field hundreds of miles across, his face bathed in elation.

He was a drop of water in the ocean of the universe. Microscopic in the vastness of time, space, and history. Caught up as if the ocean of that universe were pure delight pouring up out of him only to swirl back and bury him again in its intoxicating waves.

A framed parchment on the wall caught his eye:

Utterly engulfed,

And wanting more.

Buried,

Drowned,

Intoxicated,

With the vastness of Love.

Losing myself as the waves wash over me,

Through me,

Surrounding me,

Caught up in a hurricane of overwhelming peace,

I have let go,

And He has found me.

Micah didn't leave the room till evening fell on Cannon Beach nearly nine hours later. He eased out to his deck, down the long set of stairs to the beach, and padded across the sand toward the surf.

Three teenagers laughed as they tossed their oval skimboards into the water at the edge of the ocean, leaped onto them, and floated across the thin water cushion.

The perfect visual.

Micah was floating and never wanted to land.

||||||

A rare cloudless horizon filled his vision as Micah sat on his deck that night with strawberry lemonade in his hand. He sat without thought and without care, his only focus the waves caressing the darkening beach.

His cell phone vibrated, and he looked at the caller ID. His dad. *Take it. Don't take it. Take it.* The choice ping-ponged through his head.

"Hello?"

"Micah, it's Dad."

"Not, it's your 'father'?"

His dad sighed. "I probably deserve that."

"No, you don't. Low blow. Sorry."

Silence.

"How are you, son?"

"Good. Really good. And you?"

"Good."

Again, silence.

"It's good to hear your voice," his dad said.

"Yours, too." A small part of him meant it.

His dad cleared his throat three times.

"Micah . . . I know ever since your mom died I've caused you so much . . . I mean, a lot of . . ."

The line went still.

"What I'm trying to say is, I was just thinking about, you know . . . You see, I checked the Mariners' schedule. We could—I could get us a pair of tickets to a game coming up in the next few weeks. Not that you'd want to drive up—"

Wow. Not what he'd been expecting. Not what he wanted. After all these years, he was supposed to run to his dad with open arms? Pretend everything was okay? Yeah, right. Forgive? Yes, he'd forgiven his father, but . . .

"I don't know, Dad. I don't think that's going to work for me."

"Not a problem. I understand. I didn't think you'd be able to get away." His dad coughed. "Maybe next season."

Suddenly Micah's body flushed with heat, and tears threatened to spill onto his cheeks. Love. Not his. God's. He tried to sweep away the emotion that fluttered through his heart, but it wouldn't leave. "Dad?"

"Yes?"

"Let me check my calendar and get back to you. I'll make it work. I'll be there."

As he went to sleep that night—more at peace, more whole than he'd ever been—Micah still couldn't rid himself of one sliver of pain: Sarah.

There had to be a way back to her, but if there was a path, he couldn't see it.

But it didn't mean he would stop looking.

CHAPTER 44

A breeze dropped in from the north Thursday morning as Sarah and Rick trudged along the beach next to Haystack Rock. With the tide out, the pools around the rock were ringed with people poking at the jade green sea anemones and pointing at the purple-and-orange starfish clinging to the rocks.

Rick said he wanted to talk about something important but wouldn't say any more than that.

"Do you think fathers give good advice?" Rick asked after they'd moved beyond the tide pools.

"Depends on the father."

"Say I'm the father."

Sarah laughed. "Are you saying you're old enough to be my dad?"

"Many times over."

"You look pretty good for being so ancient." Sarah cocked her head toward Rick. "Yes, if you're giving fatherly advice, I'll definitely listen."

Rick nodded. "Micah Taylor."

Two boys raced by on recumbent beach bikes, sand kicking up behind their tires. She didn't answer till they'd shrunk to specks, five hundred yards down the sand. "You'd need a very persuasive argument for me to have any involvement with Micah."

"Want to talk about it?"

Sarah told him about the scene at Osburn's the previous Thursday night, and Rick listened without comment. "I've gone out with guys who tell me they love me after the first date. Ones where the guy says five words to you the whole time and thinks he's poured his heart out. Guys who talk about their conquests on the golf course like they're Jack Nicklaus and ask zero questions about me. But I've never had someone pretend we were madly in love with each other after one dinner. After that dinner I thought it might go somewhere. But he has one too many bulbs burnt out in that house of his."

Rick snagged a wayward Frisbee as it floated down in front of them. He spun it back to the thrower with a perfect toss. "If an intelligent, perceptive man like Micah tried to win your heart, would it make sense for him to pretend you were in love in a parallel life?"

"I'll assume that's a rhetorical question."

"So then you have to consider the fact that his saying those things makes the story more plausible, not less." Rick zipped open his Windbreaker.

"Unless he's crazy."

"Do you really think he's crazy?"

She looked away and sighed. "He walks into my ice cream shop unannounced and proceeds to tell me that I need to fall in love with him because we were together in a parallel universe? That God has ordained it? That's sanity?"

"Well, what if it was true?"

"What part?"

"That you were in love in a parallel life. That God brought you together."

"This is the moment where I ask if you're serious, and you nod your head and tell me absolutely, right?"

Rick nodded and smiled. "So here's the fatherly advice. Give him another chance. Entertain the possibility, ever so slight, that he told you the truth. That there was another life where you fell in love, and the enemy is trying to steal it."

Sarah hugged herself and blew out another long breath. "So I'm just supposed to believe some guy who seemed okay, more than okay at first, really *is* okay? I simply believe he's not psychotic and skip off into the sunset with him?" She bent down and picked up a lone agate.

"Will you give him another chance?"

She didn't answer.

"Sarah?"

She gave what she imagined was an imperceptible nod.

When Rick spoke again, his tone changed. "I need to tell you some things now that will surprise you. And might even change how you look at Micah."

As they walked next to the rumble of the waves, she stared at Rick, eyes wide. When he finished, tears spilled down her face, and she buried herself in his chest.

||||||

Thursday afternoon the phone rang as Micah stuck two pieces of wheat bread into his toaster. He decided not to answer it. Today needed to be a day of reflection. Alone. But a glance at caller ID told him it was Rick. Gotta take that one.

"Hello?"

"It's Rick; we need to talk. In person."

"About?"

"Soon."

"No hints?"

"Best if there's no prelims. Can you do it now?"

"Sure. Where?" Micah's hand went to his stomach and squeezed. Something was wrong.

"How 'bout Oswald West State Park? It's a gorgeous day, and we'll probably be able to find some privacy there. This is a talk to have without an audience or interruption."

"Sounds good." But it didn't sound good. It sounded like an omen. Why no audience? He stared at the phone and thought about the location. Oh, wow. Rick had given him a clue anyway.

He pulled onto the highway and nursed the speedometer up to sixty. As 101 South moved smoothly underneath him, the answer popped into his mind so abruptly he almost expected to hear a *ding*. He knew exactly what Rick would tell him. This would not be fun.

Micah hiked down to the cove trying to stretch time. With everything in him, he didn't want this conversation. When he reached the sand, Rick was already there, sitting on a log about a hundred yards to the north.

For a few moments he watched his friend toss rocks into the surf. Micah's shoes felt heavy as he trudged toward the log. He sat without speaking and continued to watch Rick toss wave-polished stones into the ocean.

"I've got to go now, Micah."

The words hung in the air, and the silence stretched out. His friend's voice had never sounded so serious and full of sorrow. Micah bent down and picked up two dry sticks. As he broke them into smaller and smaller pieces, he looked up. "What do you mean, go?"

But he knew what Rick meant. Somehow asking the question was a way to hold off the pain, if only for an instant longer.

"You know what I mean. I'm sorry." Tears wound their way down both sides of Rick's cheeks. It reflected Micah's own.

"Now is the moment when you tell me who you are."

"Yeah." Rick threw another rock. "But I don't really need to, do I?"

Micah shook his head.

The day at Cape Lookout when Rick had shown a sliver of his glory—the rock disintegrating under his foot, how he seemed to grow larger, light seeming to come off his body—all rushed back at him along with a dozen other clues from the past five and a half months. It all made sense now. Micah picked up a stick lying next to the log they sat on and drew lines in the sand.

"You were the man standing here, at the edge of the beach that day I almost drowned kayaking."

"Yes."

"You were there during my junior year of high school when I'd had enough of life and tried to drive off the edge of that cliff. You're what stopped me."

Rick nodded.

Micah blew out a long breath. "You're in that picture with Archie at Chris Hale's house, aren't you?"

"Yeah."

He knew the answer to the next question but wanted to ask it anyway. To make the moment complete by hearing the answer from Rick's lips. He swirled his stick through the sand, watching the tiny grains part and then gather together again as the wood passed between them. "You've been with me since the day I was born, haven't you?"

"Yes." Rick waited a moment, then added, "I won't stop being with you. It just won't be in the same form."

The reality of Rick's words swirled through his mind, and Micah steadied himself against the log.

Rick, an angel. *His* angel. Archie's angel while he was alive. The wonder of it circled Micah, lifted him, then slammed him down with the reality of Rick's departure.

The last five and a half months spun through his mind like a DVD playing at thirty-two times normal speed. Conversations, runs on the beach, movies together. Coffee taking the edge off early foggy mornings, countless meals at Morris's Fireside. Rick his confidant, mentor, and best friend.

Micah stayed silent, desperately hoping that if he didn't speak, Rick would have to stay. Even if Micah had wanted to say something, what words would he use? He raised his head and stood. Rick was already standing and drew Micah up to his chest and squeezed hard.

"Don't go."

"I have to. It is time. But I'll still be here." He eased Micah away, his hands now on Micah's shoulders, Rick's eyes locked on his. "Who knows, maybe our destiny is to see each other face-to-face again before you step into eternity."

"How can I live this life without you?"

Rick laughed his familiar, dancing laugh. "Walk with God. Listen to the Holy Spirit. You know His voice. You'll come to know it better as you practice listening. And listen to your heart. It knows the truth, for as you know, that is where the temple is and where the King dwells."

"Does Sarah know?"

"Yes."

"When did you tell her? What did she say?"

"That's for her to tell you, not me."

"Does that mean she's going to—?"

"Micah."

"You gotta—"

"Micah," Rick said again, slightly louder. "God is for you and He is sovereign. Trust Him."

Micah watched in wonder as a faint, paper-thin light started to outline Rick's body—the purest light Micah had ever seen.

As the light thickened, Rick turned his palms up and stretched his fingers as far as they could go. "I love you with the love of the Father, the Son, and the Holy Spirit." A grin split his face ear to ear in sharp contrast to the tears that streamed down his face.

Micah stepped back and the transformation quickened. Rick's features changed from the ones Micah knew so well into the most handsome face he'd ever seen. The light around Rick expanded farther, and his body grew with the light till he stood at least ten feet tall and two men wide.

Micah couldn't keep his eyes off Rick's face. Love streaked out of it; tears and joy mixed together in a radiant display of glory. A few seconds more and the brilliance coming off Rick's face became blinding, and Micah shut his eyes.

When he opened them, the beach was empty.

He slumped back onto the log and sobbed. Tears of sorrow for Rick's going and of gratitude for the gift of his friendship. Finally tears of peace. Great pools of peace.

|||||||

The next morning Micah walked onto his deck as dawn fired golden light over the eastern mountains. The fog had retreated fifty yards off the beach and formed a wall of white. The sun lit it up, making it look like a giant movie screen made of cotton. The perfect setting. A blank screen to open Archie's final letter in front of.

Strange to think the journey had ended and Micah wouldn't be listening anymore to this remarkable man from his past who had become such a large part of his future. But in many ways the journey was still starting, and if he knew Archie, this last letter would be a doozie.

He opened the envelope, and a key dropped out: small, brass, and nondescript. He placed it gently on his deck's pine picnic table and pulled the sharply creased letter free of the envelope.

Micah smiled. What a trip it had been. He owed Archie his life. He thanked God for the man yet again, slipped the edge of his thumb underneath a corner of the letter, and eased it open. He smoothed the creases three times before letting himself read the familiar penmanship that would go to his heart one last time.

> *December 23, 1992*
> *Dear Micah,*
>
> *Regretfully this is my last letter to you. Do you harbor that lament as much as I do? During the last few years, it has certainly been a joy putting my pen to paper with you in mind. If all has gone as I have hoped and prayed it would, then a number of extraordinary things have happened, not the least of which is you discovering the Father, Son, and Holy Spirit in ways you never have before.*
>
> *Has your heart surfaced? Are you listening? I know you are. Sobering, is it not? What most of us bury is the treasure we long for all our lives.*
>
> *Was it worth it? You had the world and had almost given up your soul to get it. Now you have sold the world to gain back your soul, heart, and spirit. Was it a fair trade?*

A grin burst onto Micah's face. Fair? No. The trade was heavily leveraged in his direction. He had gained his life, the Kingdom, and a restored heart. All the favor spun his way.

> *Freedom, Micah, the Lord is always about freedom. Where the Spirit of the Lord is, there is liberty. If what you do brings freedom and life, it is most likely Christianity. If it doesn't, it is probably religion, and there is already too much of that in the world.*
>
> *However, you didn't open this letter to hear another one of my sermons. You want to discover where and how your adventure concludes. I must disappoint you. I don't know, only He does.*
>
> *By now Rick has told you who he is, and I imagine he has left. I'm sorry. Everything has its ending.*
>
> *One more surprise before I say farewell. Last week I drove down to Cannon Beach and paid for a safety deposit box at the Bank of Astoria. The key in the envelope will open it. Inside the box is another key, the one to your true heart's desire.*
>
> *Finally, please do not think your adventures into the supernatural are over. Hardly. No, this was just the introduction. I will see you on the other side.*
>
> *Forever your great-uncle,*
>
> *Archie*
>
> *P.S. Some choices are irreversible and some cause irreversible change. Others are not and do not. Regarding Sarah, I have no answers. But we both know His will, and your destiny will not fail to be accomplished.*

How did Archie know about Sarah? Right, what *didn't* Rick tell Archie? Micah sat on his deck and turned the key in his hand over and over again wondering where Sarah was right now. And what time the Bank of Astoria opened. A quick visit to the Web told him 10:00.

He would be standing outside their door tomorrow at 9:59 a.m.

CHAPTER 45

He'd have answers in one minute and thirty-two seconds. Thirty-one. Thirty. At precisely 10:00 Micah pushed open the bank's front door. It squealed like a pig at feeding time.

The Bank of Astoria was small but comfortable. There was a sitting area with cloth chairs to his right, a stand with a large stainless steel coffeepot and packets of Coffee-mate creamer to his left. Caffeine? No way. It would push him off the chart. The adrenaline in his veins had already given him the shakes. The key to his heart's desire? *Bring it on, Archie.*

"Looks like you could use some WD-40 on that door," he said with a smile to an elderly lady behind the counter.

"May I help you?" She glared at him over the top of her tortoiseshell glasses.

"I'm here to look at a safety deposit box, thanks." He pinched his lips together to stifle a laugh. "Here's my key. The number is on it."

"We know how these things work, sonny."

He stayed silent as the Ice Queen shuffled over to a file cabinet and pulled the file on the box in question. When she came back, she had a new personality.

"Well, well, well. You must be Micah Taylor. Yes, yes, yes." She turned to two bankers who sat at their desks ticking away on their computer keyboards. "It's him. Micah Taylor is here. Right here! I told you he would show up, and now you all have to watch me fill my piggy bank."

"You know me?"

The teller pranced toward the back of the bank with a dance step she probably did a good deal better thirty years earlier, too locked in to her jitterbug to answer his question.

A male employee that looked like Santa Claus with a buzz cut wandered over. "You'll have to excuse Madge's unorthodox bank behavior there." He stretched his paisley suspenders, one thumb on each side, and continued. "You see, that safety deposit box has never been opened, and there is one, and only one, name authorized to use it. Of course that's you.

"The box was first rented quite a few moons ago. Yes sirree Jim-Bob, it has gained quite a reputation over the years. We were given explicit instructions to do nothing with the box until you came and opened it, and we've all had a little bet going as to when—and frankly if—you'd ever show up. Madge had only ten more days for you to show before her guess was up, and since the cash prize to the winner has grown to a nice little chunk of change—good conservative bank investing over the course of seventeen years—you sure made her day just now."

"You've had this thing for seventeen years?" Of course they had. Archie first rented the box back in 1992.

"Bank's been bought out three times since the box was first registered, but it was prepaid for twenty-five years so it's stayed put."

Madge waltzed up to Micah with her eyebrows above the rims of her glasses, the smile still on her face, gold showing where she hadn't brushed well enough when she was younger. "I have the box in the back in the private booths. Would you follow me, please?"

Micah was led into a tiny room with two booths. Madge gestured to the one on the left, and he stepped inside and pulled the curtain closed. The box sat in the center of the small desk.

He sat down and held his breath. This was it. Last contact with Archie. The final puzzle piece.

Micah inserted the key Madge had given him into the box and turned it, as if it were a Q-tip in a baby's ear. It wouldn't rotate. With slightly more effort the clasp opened with a light click. Part of him wanted to throw the lid back with abandon; another part didn't want to open it at all. Rick was gone. So was Sarah and Seattle. Now Archie's voice from the past was about to blink out.

He'd given up his world and gained his soul. There was no turning back. But where did it leave him? Cannon Beach without Rick and Sarah was poorly flavored. And there was the nagging question of income. He had little money left, and although the mortgage papers he'd gotten from Chris assured him the house and land were paid for, when tax time rolled around, he would need a hefty sum to cover a nine-thousand-square-foot home on the ocean.

A light tapping on the wall just outside his curtain startled Micah. He jerked upright and cracked his knee on the cubicle desk. "Yes?" He winced.

"Just making sure everything is going a-okay in there, Mr. Taylor."

It was Granny Good-Grin.

"Fine. Thanks."

He rubbed his knee as his eyes settled back on the box.

Might as well.

He opened it. An old manila envelope sat at the bottom. On top of it was a note from Archie. Micah lifted the card as if it were a butterfly's wing.

> *Micah,*
> *I thought you might like to have a reprint.*
> *Archie*

A fine layer of dust covered the envelope. Micah unwound the string sealing it, his palms sweaty. He turned it upside down. A photo and a key taped to a note card slid out. Micah stared at a copy of the picture he'd seen at Chris's house. Chris, Archie, and Rick stood on a fishing boat, their arms around each other, grins splashed on their faces. This he would treasure.

Four lines were written on the note card:

> *A key to open heart's desires,*
> *Yours and those beyond,*
> *Cords are cut and chains are broken,*
> *When we live our calling strong.*

Micah pulled the key off the card and examined it. "A key to open his heart's desire." Archie's last letter had said the same thing. Micah hadn't expected a literal key. One side had deep scratches. He looked closer. They weren't scratches. They were words or numbers. Too small to make out but definitely writing.

He gathered up the treasures, said good-bye to Madge, and dashed down Main Street to find a magnifying glass. After buying one at Trinkets & Treasures, he sprinted to his car, got in, pulled out the key, and shoved it under the glass. The writing leaped out at him.

An address was engraved into the key in a soft, fluid script. He was dumbfounded.

The address was his own.

Then he felt it. A physical sensation this time. His world had shifted once again, even though from where he sat parked everything looked the same. The last vestiges of his Seattle existence had fallen away. He knew it. Only Cannon Beach and the unexplained parallel life remained.

Micah started his car and headed for home. He was so dazed it wasn't till he shifted into third gear that he realized this wasn't the BMW he'd gotten out of half an hour earlier but a Toyota Camry.

He took the corner into his driveway at twenty miles an hour. Adrenaline shot through his veins as his tires threw up a curtain of crushed gravel, and he slid toward the bank in front of his house. He slammed on his brakes and skidded to a halt inches from the end of the driveway.

Streams of light poured through tiny openings in the fog bank above him, as if randomly sprinkled spotlights announced his arrival.

The house looked the same. But Micah knew it wasn't. It couldn't be.

He got out and walked to the front door. The beat of his heart increased with each step forward.

The moment he opened the door and stepped inside, he saw the change. The painting. It hung over the fireplace, three spotlights pouring down on it.

It was finished.

The last bit of sky and clouds had been filled in, and a lone seagull skimmed across the wind, its body in partial silhouette against the brilliance of the sun. The sand castle next to the little boy was finished, and the people along the left edge were complete as well. The figure walking out of the painting to the right was Rick. Of course.

But something else had changed. What? He had studied every intricacy of this painting. He knew every brushstroke, every nuance of color. It was subtle, or he would have seen it immediately. The change toyed with him, played in corners of his mind, dared him to discover what it was.

He paced in front of the painting, glanced away, glanced back, as if he could sneak up on the difference by turning his head fast enough.

Finally it clicked. There! A small black streak in the corner of the painting. He knew instantly it was the artist's signature tucked in among azure and emerald waves. Finally. He would know who painted this masterpiece that had captured his heart. He eased toward the painting as if approaching too quickly might make the name vanish into the surf it rested on.

The signature was so small he had to get within inches of the canvas to see it. Before reading the name, he closed his eyes and laughed. All this buildup for a name he probably wouldn't even recognize. Then he lifted his lids in slow motion. The name wasn't difficult to read. But Micah only saw it for a few seconds before he slumped backward to the carpet, head in his hands. Archie had said his heart's desire.

Astonishment filled him. It couldn't be.

The final piece had fallen into place. The puzzle was complete.

He ran out onto his deck and shouted till his voice grew hoarse. "Yes! *Yes!*"

||||||||

Moments later he remembered everything. Every scene from the last six years of his life melded into place. His old girlfriend Joan, the ankle injury, and every other detail.

For six years he'd starved while he painted ocean scenes all up and down the Oregon Coast—from Bandon to Florence to Newport. Getting better, selling a few paintings, galleries taking an interest, his reputation as an artist growing. And how one year ago he'd received a note down in Newport from his great-uncle Archie telling him he'd inherited a home on the Oregon Coast.

As he bathed in the memories, the scenes and memories of his Seattle life faded. There had been another life, hadn't there?

Yes, Seattle. He had lived there, worked there. Made money there? Yes, a lot. RimSoft. He'd been famous. He was sure all of those things were true. A few moments later he wasn't. There were bits and pieces, scattered memories, puzzle pieces that even if they were all put together wouldn't show him enough of the picture to remember it clearly. It didn't matter.

He walked back inside and glanced down at the coffee table just inside the door. A worn magazine looked up at him: *Coast Life*. He picked it up, smiled, then gently laid it back down. He'd read about himself a little later.

Micah walked around the side of the house toward the top of the bluff. A small circle of ocean-smoothed stones formed a fire pit. He grabbed the kindling sitting next to it, and five minutes later crimson-and-gold flames shot toward the sky. It was an altar to the final disintegration of his old life and a celebration of the one just begun. He didn't go inside till the last embers faded.

||||||

That night sleep evaded him. He tried. Pushed Sarah from his mind thirty times an hour.

But it was futile.

Archie had said some things were irreversible. Others not. So which was Sarah? To give her up, stop loving her was like trying to stop the waves from crashing onto the shore.

His feelings of love for her pummeled him without a break. Relentless. But he didn't want them to stop.

Tomorrow he would find her. He had to try one more time.

CHAPTER 46

Sarah asked herself for the twentieth time why she was going but didn't turn the car around. By the time she reached Micah's driveway, she had resigned herself to the task but was determined to make the visit as short as possible. Say what she had to and then leave forever.

She parked at the end of his drive and sat for ten minutes, her fingers the only part of her moving as she drummed them on her steering wheel. Most of her wanted to drive off and never look back. But a small place inside kept her from heading home. Besides, she had promised Rick.

She walked toward Micah's house and saw him through a window. He sat in front of a painting of the ocean hanging over the fireplace. Gorgeous. A picture as captivating as she'd ever seen. As she studied it, Micah turned. Their eyes locked; neither moved. Then he disappeared from view, and the front door opened a few seconds later.

"Sarah."

"Hi."

Surprise flickered over his face but he didn't speak. She wondered how to start and groped for words that wouldn't give him false hope. "I'm here for one reason."

Micah didn't respond.

"I promised Rick I'd come."

"Because he told you who he is." Micah opened the door wider.

"Yes. And a few other things."

"Come in?"

Sarah didn't answer but stepped over the threshold and into the living room toward the painting. "I love this."

"Thanks." Micah smiled, a look of peace on his face. He closed the front door and motioned her toward the picture windows overlooking the ocean.

She stood in the center of the room, arms folded. "I know God can do amazing things, but I don't believe we had a romance in another life. Wouldn't I sense it or at least have some miniscule feeling it happened?"

Sarah was angry. Angry for being here. Angry that Micah had stolen away any chance at there being something between them with his bizarre behavior. Angry Rick had asked her to give Micah a second chance, knowing she wouldn't refuse.

"You don't have even a little bit of that feeling right now?"

It stopped her cold. The truth? She had felt something the second Micah stepped into Osburn's ten nights ago. Something small but persistent saying they had a deeper connection than just one dinner together. But his weird performance next to the ice cream counter had crushed any hope of it being real. When it had turned bizarre, she forced any thought of a connection to the far reaches of her heart.

"What do you want, Micah?"

His eyes closed and his lips moved silently. Probably praying. After a few seconds he opened his eyes, and with penetrating confidence said, "I want the impossible. I want to take you into my heart."

"Your what?" Sarah squeezed her arms tighter.

"If you knew my heart, you'd believe."

Sarah didn't answer. As strange as the statement was, the maniacal attitude she'd seen at Osburn's was gone. His countenance had changed. A quiet confidence stood in sharp contrast to the image she'd seen the other night. The man in front of her knew who he was.

"I can't convince you with words that we've had more of a history than you remember." He turned to look at the waves. "I can only reveal my heart to you and then let you choose."

"And how are you going to show me your heart?"

"I don't know." He looked up at the painting.

The next words out of Sarah's mouth shocked her. "But God knows."

"What?" Micah turned. A faint smile appeared on his face.

Sarah didn't answer. Her eyes were riveted on something to the left of where he stood. She spoke in a whisper. "When I had dinner with you here, that door was not there."

"What door?"

"There. Right there." She pointed to his left, and Micah turned to look.

It was normal height but twice the width of a standard door. An intoxicating aroma flowed from it. Like roses mixed with apple trees in full bloom. Light streamed from under it. The confused look on Micah's face told her he didn't see it.

"What door?" he repeated.

But in the moment he asked, his eyes danced, and she knew he could see it.

The door to his heart.

She reached for Micah's hand, and together they walked forward. The door opened before they reached it, and she stepped through into what looked like liquid light. It was pure and piercing. Worries, pain, wounds, fear, all slipped off, consumed by the river of radiance.

A moment later they stood in a grove of trees. It was daytime—early morning by the look of it. Dew covered the grass, and the angle of the beams of light that streamed through the trees said the sun had only been up for moments. Beyond the forest swelled an ocean. But not the Pacific. This ocean was too blue, too big, the pounding emerald waves too full and rich, the foam at the top of the waves too white to be one of earth's oceans.

So much passion and power. So much love she felt her heart would burst. The sounds, the light, everything said this was the place she'd been longing for all her life. She was in the presence of God.

"Where are we?"

"You know."

"Your heart."

Micah didn't answer her. He didn't need to.

An instant later a circular curtain of transparent light surrounded them, and Sarah gasped as vibrant images came to life on every inch of the curtain's surface.

She watched herself in Osburn's the day Micah and she met, then saw bike rides together, dinners, their hike up Humbug Mountain and up the Astoria Column. Their trips to Fort Stevens and excursions down to Manzanita, their first kiss, and even a few of their fights. Scene after scene from their months together.

She stared at him in astonishment.

Rick and Micah's first meeting at Hug Point, his breakup with Julie, visiting the doctor about his ankle, almost drowning in his kayak.

She watched herself implore Micah not to go back to Seattle and him say it would be okay.

She remembered. All of it. Every moment they'd spent together. Her head sank into her hands. "I remember." She turned to Micah. "You and me. I remember." She moved toward him, tears in her eyes.

He drew her in tight.

The screen vanished, and they stood in a high mountain meadow; Indian paintbrush and Canterbury bellflowers swarmed through the tall grass. But the beauty paled in comparison to the Presence surrounding them.

Sarah buried her head in Micah's shoulder and rested there, maybe for hours. Maybe years. It was a moment snatched from eternity.

|||||||

Micah had closed his eyes the moment Sarah and he embraced inside his heart. He opened them in bed, staring at his ceiling. He whipped off his covers and bolted upright.

It had to be more than a dream!

He pulled on a T-shirt and some sweatpants and raced for the front door. He yanked it open and sprinted down the driveway, ignoring the gravel cutting into his feet.

"No!"

There were no tire tracks where Sarah's car might have left some. Lunging back into the house, Micah grabbed the phone and called her house, then Osburn's. No answer at her house, and the girls at Osburn's hadn't seen her.

Setting down the phone, he let the sorrow come. He wandered over to the fireplace, sat down in front of it, and closed his eyes. "You are still Lord."

When Micah opened his eyes minutes later, his gaze rose to the painting, and his breath caught. It had changed one final time. A figure had been added—a woman—walking straight toward his home. He leaped to his feet and sprang out onto his deck to search the beach.

Fifty yards away Sarah strolled toward him, hair flowing in the wind like a river, her radiant smile filling his world.

It wasn't a dream.

The dream had just begun.

‖‖‖‖‖

A few days later Sarah and Micah sauntered among the bleached driftwood scattered along the beach, holding hands, neither of them speaking. The sun eased behind the clouds leaving a russet smear across the sky. They rounded the point just north of Micah's home to the sound of pounding hammers.

A small house was coming into shape among a small grove of poplar trees. They squinted to see the name on the sign at the edge of the lot that would tell them the name of the builder. It was Hale & Sons Construction Co.

"Oh, my," Sarah said. "Do you think they're building—?"

"Yes." Micah smiled. "I think they are."

Dear Reader,

Toni Morrison says, "If there's a book you really want to read but it hasn't been written yet, then you must write it."

That's *Rooms*. I didn't write it for readers as much I wrote it because I wanted to read Micah Taylor's story. I *needed* to read his story. A story of freedom. A story of healing.

I long to step into the freedom that Micah discovers, to live more completely in the divine design and destiny God has created for me, to be victorious over the voices that hold me back from living the full life God intended me to live.

I loved writing *Rooms* because it's my story. It's your story. It's the story of anyone who wants to step into greater freedom, step into the glory of how God uniquely made him or her, step into the destiny planned for them from before time began.

He is the Great Healer of wounds. He is the Great Restorer of freedom.

If you'd like to explore more ideas together on how to live with freedom, come visit my Web site and blog at www.jimrubart.com.

For freedom's sake,
James L. Rubart

DISCUSSION QUESTIONS

1. What would you describe as the theme of *Rooms*? Is there more than one?

2. Before coming to Cannon Beach, Micah seemed to have it all—fame, money, influence—but he was still searching because he'd buried his heart. Do you feel like your heart has been buried or lost (Galatians 6:9)? What things caused this? Are you trying to get it back (Luke 19:10)? If so, how?

3. Throughout the novel God takes Micah into specific rooms—to heal his wounds and to set him free (Isaiah 61:1; Luke 4:18). If you could physically walk into the rooms in your own soul, which room do you think God would lead you into first? What other rooms would God take you through?

4. One of the pivotal scenes in *Rooms* is when Jesus enters the movie room within Micah's dream and heals the deep wounds he received from his father (Jeremiah 30:17; Acts 28:27). What are the deep wounds that need healing inside you?

5. Were you surprised that Jesus ignored the movies (the symptoms) and went to the cause (Micah's deep wounds as a kid) instead (Luke 15:11–24)? Why or why not?

6. For much of the book, Micah thinks the voice is himself. Can you relate? Can you look back on your life and think of times where the enemy of your heart has spoken to you through thoughts and impressions you thought were your own but now realize were not? How did he say it? How did it make you feel? What do you do when that voice is speaking to you?

7. The voice at one point convincingly tells Micah that following Jesus means following principles and rules. Eventually Micah discovers it's not about those things but about a relationship with Jesus. He doesn't follow Jesus out of obligation but love. What is the story of your spiritual journey? Have you followed more out of love or obligation or a combination of the two?

8. It's not only the voice that speaks to Micah. God does as well through a distinct impression in his mind and/or heart. Jesus says, "My sheep hear My voice" (John 10:16, 27). What does that mean to you? Do you hear God's voice? If so, what are the ways He speaks to you?

9. One of the recurring themes in *Rooms* is freedom, a foundation of the Christian faith (John 8:2, 36; Galatians 5:1; 2 Corinthians 3:17) yet one that many followers of Jesus don't experience. Are you free? If not, what is the thing you'd like to be free from most? What holds you back from more freedom?

10. In one of Archie's letters, he quotes Saint Irenaeus saying, "The glory of God is man fully alive." What makes you come alive? Are you doing it now? Why? Why not?

11. When Micah skydives, it is a huge risk, but it gives him the courage to risk taking a sabbatical from RimSoft, which ultimately sets him free. Is there anything you need to risk in order to follow God's call on your life (Acts 15:26)?

12. We get hints of Micah's artistic destiny early in *Rooms*. During Julie's meeting, she says, "You're always doodling" when he sketches the house, and early on we learn he painted in high school and college. Later he tells Julie he might paint at the beach. It's always been there, but Micah didn't see it. Whether it's painting or writing or music or hiking or travel or counseling or a hundred other different passions, many people would say, "It's always been inside me." What passion has always been inside you? Are you pursuing it? What steps do you need to take to find it?

13. Micah's choices send him down two very different paths. Are you facing any significant choices right now that could take you down a wonderful or destructive path? How do you know which is the right path to take? What specific steps are you taking down that path?

14. The day Micah got his scar shaped his life. Does one incident from your childhood control or affect your life in a way you wish it hadn't? Explain.

15. Throughout the novel Micah desperately wants to enter the brilliant room. When he finally gets in, he's stunned to discover it is his own heart, where the Holy Spirit lives. First Corinthians 3:16–17 says this is a holy place. If you're a follower of Jesus, do you think of your heart as a holy place? Do you think of it as the place where God lives?

Cannon Beach, Oregon, is beautiful all year long. The following are a few of the many Web sites where you can find out more about the town and the surrounding area, as well as information on some of the places Micah goes in Rooms.

www. cannonbeach.org

www.cannon-beach.net

www.el.com/to/cannonbeach

Arcadia Beach State Park: www.oregonstateparks.org/
    park_187.php

Ecola State Park: www.oregonstateparks.org/
    park_188.php

Hug Point State Park: www.oregonstateparks.org/
    park_191.php.

Oswald West State Park: www.oregonstateparks.org/
    park_195.php.

Cape Lookout State Park: www.oregonstateparks.org/
    park_186.php.

www.morrisfireside.com

www.theoceanlodge.com

www.cannonbeachbooks.com

ACKNOWLEDGMENTS

I thought writing a novel was primarily a solitary endeavor. Wrong answer. Try again. To describe a novel as a solo effort would be like saying the director is the only person involved in a feature-length film. Consequently, passionate thanks go out to:

Ruth, Jennifer, Tanya, and Jeff Scorziell for reading that *long* first draft of *Rooms* and giving great feedback and encouragement.

To Pat, Royce, Laura D., Scott, Kelli, Jill, Debbie A., Barb, and Helen for reading version two and pumping me full of hope. To Taylor, Jimmy Rub, Laura C., Bob C., Ronie, Leonard, Paul, Marcus, Mitch, Dave, Dan, Tina S., Ron, Tina D., Dineen, Robin, Jamie, Jeff, Debbie C., Glen, and my Good Buddy for reading version three and sending your excitement my way.

The greatest gift someone can give me is to read what I've written, so sincere thanks goes out to you, my reading friend, for investing your time in *Rooms*.

To Jennifer Fry for pushing me to take action. To my Band of Brothers: Jeff Stucky, Eric, Mark, Bob L., Jim R., and Peter for prayer, belief, and your constant willingness to listen as I told—on and on and on—of my roller-coaster journey to publication. To the Winklings for encouragement, laughter, critique, and belief.

To Sharon Sabin for continually asking how *Rooms* was coming along and believing from the beginning.

To the Carters: Rick, Evelyn, Todd, and Lindsay for reading *Rooms*, being such incredible encouragers, and for having almost as much passion for the book as I do.

To David Webb for being my champion, Susan May Warren for your outstanding teaching and friendship, and Sharon Hinck for friendship, belief, and that stellar conversation at Mount Hermon.

To Randy Ingermanson for that first huge boost and for being a great friend. To Tim Riter, Bryan Davis, and Jeff Gerke for their early friendship, wisdom, and encouragement. To Mary Beth Chappell, Beth Jusino, Janet Kobobel Grant, and Steve Laube for your excellent counsel and encouragement. To Tricia for wisdom, belief, and dropping everything to help someone you barely knew! To Elaine for early, early belief and intense education.

To Carla, you are my prayer warrior! To Robert Boyd Munger (*My Heart—Christ's Home*) for writing such a powerful piece. To Roy Williams for telling me the truth and helping me believe.

To Bob Lord for dazzling brainstorming as the story formed, challenging critiques as you read, and for continually reminding me, "It's all in the execution!"

To John Eldredge for widening my own path to freedom.

To Diana Lawrence, art director at B&H, for designing a stunning cover.

To my B&H fiction marketing manager, Julie Gwinn. You're incredible!

To Karen Ball, my executive editor, not only a wonderful editor but my dear friend.

To editor Julee Schwarzburg, who took *Rooms* far beyond what I could have made it on my own. Are all editors as brilliant as you?

To Chip MacGregor, who is not only my agent but my friend as well.

To Cec Murphy, mentor, friend, and teacher.

To my critique partner and lifelong friend, Royce Cameron, for dedication to the craft and to me. I hope to be as good a writer as you someday.

To Jim Vaux who spoke it out during that dinner in Woodinville ages ago and wars for me in prayer like no other.

To Miah Silva for brotherhood, supernatural counsel, rabid belief in me, and never letting me forsake my heart and the reason for it all.

To Mom for loving me, believing in me, praying for me, for seeing my destiny, and never, ever, doubting it.

To Dad for giving me the gift of writing and showing me what joy unleashed looks like.

To Taylor and Micah for believing in me and being better sons than I could ever have imagined.

To Jesus for life, freedom, and making my dream come true. It all begins and ends in You.

Finally, to the toughest person to thank, since words are far too frail to convey my overwhelming gratitude—but I must try—my wife, Darci. Without your tireless love, unwavering faith, laser-focused edits, vision for the future, and deep counsel about the things in this life that really matter, this book would not have happened. You are far beyond what I ever dreamed a wife and best friend could be. In you I found my Sarah. In you I am truly blessed.